"Perhaps we can be friends," Lord Ashton began.

Friends? So that was to be his technique, was it? Margaret was pleased that she had finally figured him out. She grasped the handle of her picnic basket and rose to her feet. "That certainly is a unique approach, Lord Ashton, but I'm afraid you are wasting your time."

He stood up, giving her a puzzled look. "Wasting my time?"

"I'm sure there are many heiresses who would fall for such a gambit," she said, "but I am not one of them. So if you are looking to marry a fortune, you will need to look farther afield. I have no interest in marrying you."

"But all I suggested was friendship."

"After the discourteous way you have behaved toward me, how can you expect us to be friends?"

"I like you."

"Indeed? That is a pity, because I don't like you."

His amused laughter followed her as she walked away.

Books by Laura Lee Guhrke

Prelude to Heaven
To Dream Again
Conor's Way
The Seduction

Published by HarperPaperbacks

The Seduction

⊷ LAURA LEE GUHRKE ⊶

HarperPaperbacks
A Division of HarperCollinsPublishers

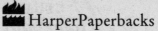 HarperPaperbacks
A Division of HarperCollins*Publishers*
10 East 53rd Street, New York, N.Y. 10022-5299

This is a work of fiction. The characters, incidents, and
dialogues are products of the author's imagination and are not to
be construed as real. Any resemblance to actual events or
persons, living or dead, is entirely coincidental.

ISBN 0-06-108403-4

HarperCollins®, ®, HarperPaperbacks™, and
HarperMonogram® are trademarks of HarperCollins*Publishers*,Inc.

Cover illustration by Vittorio Dangelico

First printing: April 1997

Printed in the United States of America

Visit HarperPaperbacks on the World Wide Web at
http://www.harpercollins.com/paperbacks

❖ 10 9 8 7 6 5 4 3 2 1

For Sandy Oakes and Rachel Gibson, who believed in Trevor's story from the very beginning. This one's for you, with my heartfelt thanks. No one could have more loyal friends.

Prologue

Cairo, 1882

Trevor St. James believed in life's simple pleasures. French cognac, a Turkish cigar, silk sheets, and a passionate woman. Tonight, he had enjoyed them all. He leaned back against the headboard and took a sip of the cognac, his gaze slowly perusing the softly rounded form of the sleeping woman who lay beside him. He paused to appreciate the luscious dent in the small of her back before his gaze continued downward. Lucci really did have excellent taste, he thought, admiring the enticing curve of her buttocks.

She stirred slightly in sleep, reminding Trevor that it was not wise to linger here. He set the drink aside. He'd come for a purpose beyond a romp in the sheets, and he couldn't accomplish it if Isabella awakened.

He rose from the bed. In the dim light of the lamp, he dressed without making a sound. He began to search the room, keeping one eye on the woman as he silently opened the drawers of her dressing table.

In the third drawer, he found her jewel case. It was locked, but he easily opened it. Within, he found a treasure of diamonds and pearls, the evidence of Lucci's passion for his young wife. But diamonds and pearls did not interest Trevor. What he sought was far more valuable. More important, it was *his*, and Trevor never relinquished what belonged to him.

He had removed three trays of jewels from the case before he found the object of his search. He smiled as he removed the ancient necklace of gold and lapis that Lucci had stolen from him. The British Museum would definitely get their money's worth from this piece.

He pulled from his pocket the paste replica he had brought with him and laid it carefully inside the case. Then he put back the other trays of jewels, careful to return them in the proper order. After relocking the case, he set it back in the drawer exactly where he had found it.

The drawer made a grating sound as he closed it. He glanced at Isabella, but she did not awaken. Picking up his jacket from the floor, Trevor tucked his prize into the breast pocket, then laid the jacket across a chair and walked to the bed. He leaned down to kiss that lovely dent in her back, knowing he had to leave and feeling a hint of regret at the prospect. He trailed kisses along her spine and heard a soft murmur of sleepy pleasure from the depths of the pillows.

Isabella turned her head and rose up on her elbows, shaking the dark curtain of hair from her eyes as she looked at him. "So soon?" she asked, her voice still husky with sleep.

He brushed a wisp of hair from her face. "I must go. My ship leaves at dawn."

"Hours away," she whispered, pressing a kiss into his palm.

"Lucci could change his plans, and I don't want him to find me here."

"He won't change his plans. He has gone to Alexandria on business."

Trevor already knew that. But he also knew that Lucci was foolishly besotted by his beautiful wife and might miss her enough to return unexpectedly. He shook his head. "It's too risky. I don't wish to die at the hands of your jealous husband."

Her lips curved into a pout. "You would not be willing to die for me?"

Trevor smiled and caressed her cheek. "No, my sweet. I would not."

"Bastard." The word was soft on her lips, an endearment rather than an epithet.

He laughed as she rolled onto her back and held out her arms. "Stay. Even if he did come and he found you here, Lucci would never be able to defeat you in a fight. He's too fat."

"Somehow, that does not ease my mind." Trevor caught her wrists and pulled her arms wide to place a kiss between her breasts. "And I am his most hated rival."

He released her and sat up, then reached above her head for his cravat, which was draped carelessly over the headboard. He gave her a cynical smile. "But then, I suspect the fact that Lucci and I are rivals in business heightens the pleasure for you, doesn't it, my sweet?"

She stretched like a cat and yawned. "Yes," she confessed. "I've wanted you for a long time, Trevor. When I saw you at the opera tonight, I knew this was the perfect opportunity."

Trevor had known it, too. Isabella thought tonight's pleasures had been her idea, but he'd been planning this ever since Lucci had stolen the necklace from him. He had known all along that his prize would end up in her hands. Lucci always gave the jewels to his wife. He really was a fool. That necklace would bring several thousand pounds on the open market. She sighed, watching as he rose from the bed and walked toward her dressing table. "I wish we had more time together. I don't see why you must go to England anyway."

"I don't have a choice. I am an earl now. That carries certain responsibilities."

"Such as?"

He bent slightly at the knees to see his reflection in the mirror and began to tie his cravat. "According to my mother, they include stepping into my late brother's shoes, marrying a well-bred girl from a respectable—and, it is hoped, wealthy—family, and producing an heir."

"You?" She laughed merrily. "Is that why you're going? To chain yourself to a lifetime of fox hunting and playing the country squire? How dreadfully conventional. A man like you isn't made for a life like that. I don't believe it."

Trevor paused in the act of buttoning his waistcoat and thought suddenly of home, of the green fields and rose-covered cottages of Ashton Park, of roast beef and trifle, of chestnut trees and roaring fires and thick feather mattresses—all the things he'd left behind ten years ago. An unexpected pang of longing hit him, and he made a sudden realization.

"Actually," he said and resumed buttoning his waistcoat, "I'm looking forward to it."

"You're not serious!" She sat up in bed and

frowned at him. "Have you fallen in love with some whey-faced English girl on holiday?" she demanded. "Is that what this is all about?"

He pulled on his jacket and met her gaze in the mirror. "What does love have to do with getting married?"

She laughed and fell back against the pillows. "I see that we are very much alike. I, too, married out of necessity." She paused and gazed at him hungrily. "I will miss you, *mio caro*. But when you grow tired of your English wife and your country house and your dismal English rain, perhaps you will return and we will enjoy each other again."

He remembered the necklace and didn't think his return a very likely possibility. Nor did he care. Both of them had gotten what they wanted, and that was the end of it. He started for the door.

"Take good care, Trevor," she called.

"I always do." He paused in the doorway and looked at her. "You should take care as well. Lucci might find out about this little rendezvous of ours."

She seemed unperturbed by that possibility. "If he does, he will be furious, but he'll forgive me, and he'll believe whatever explanations I give him. He always does. He loves me."

"For now."

His skeptical reply and cynical smile shook her complacent vanity for a moment, and she looked at him with uncertainty. "Don't you believe in love?"

Trevor laughed. "After tonight, darling, how can you ask me that?"

"I am talking about the emotion, not the act."

"They are both the same." He saw her frown, her expression one of pique and wounded feminine pride. "What were you expecting? That I would now be as besotted with you as your husband is? Don't pout, my sweet. I know it is not my love you seek, and I am not like Lucci, to be manipulated and made the fool."

He paused then added, "Don't push him too far, Isabella. Even the most ardent husband's passion will fade."

She rose up on her knees, shaking her dark hair back from her shoulders and displaying for him all the charms he was leaving behind. "Will it?"

He studied her exquisite body for a long moment, then said what was expected of him. "No. Perhaps not."

"Do not forget me, Trevor," she whispered.

"Never," he vowed. "I will remember you and treasure this night all the days of my life."

She sank back against the pillows, her scarlet mouth curved in a smile of satisfaction as Trevor walked out the door. But the moment it closed behind him, he promptly forgot her existence.

1

Italy, 1882

Margaret Van Alden wondered if it was truly possible to die of boredom. If so, she was certain to drop dead at any moment.

The ladies were having tea, a dreaded occasion in Margaret's opinion, and one to be gotten through as quickly as possible. For over an hour now, they had been discussing the scandals brewing back in London, the dire state of everybody's health, and the weather.

The Duchess of Arbuthnot said, "England is so dreary, I'm told. Lady Morton has written to me that the rain is going to drive her mad." She set her teacup back in its saucer and went on, "We are so fortunate to be in Italy just now. It's lovely this time of year. And the countryside is so beautiful."

Margaret glanced longingly out the window at the bright Mediterranean sunshine and wondered why, if it was so lovely, they were sitting in this stuffy drawing room. She racked her brain for an excuse, any excuse, to depart. Perhaps she could suddenly be ill. A headache would do. Or perhaps the shrimp sandwiches. One never knew with shrimp.

"The Italian people are so marvelous," Lady Lytton said. "So charming and unspoiled."

"Quite," the duchess agreed. "Although they are somewhat brazen in their manners."

"More tea, ladies?"

Cornelia gestured toward the tea service, and at the voices of assent, the maid began to pour out. Margaret knew that since this was her father's villa and these were her guests, it was her responsibility to be the hostess, but she felt no guilt at allowing her cousin to play that role. Cornelia was so much better at it than she. Margaret took a chocolate biscuit from a plate and nibbled on it as she weighed the cost to her social status of simply making a mad dash for the door. Or perhaps she could faint.

As she speculated on various ways to escape, she could hear the duchess directing the conversation toward Italian art. "You will find the museums of Italy quite splendid. The Italian masters were so gifted."

Margaret wondered how great a stir would ensue if she opened the window and climbed out.

"Take the sculpture of David, for example. You can appreciate the true talent of Michelangelo when you see it. Such exquisite line and form. So beautiful, so natural—"

"So naked," Margaret put in, unable to stop herself.

The shocked gasps of the ladies answered her. She looked around with wide, innocent eyes and plied her fan with ladylike zeal, but had to bite down hard on her lower lip to keep from laughing at their horrified faces. English ladies were so stuffy, Margaret thought with the staunch patriotism of an American. The Duchess of Arbuthnot's haughty nose quivered with disapproval. Lady Lytton veritably swooned, and her two daughters, Lady Sally and Lady Agnes, stared at Margaret, their rosebud mouths gaping. Although she didn't venture a glance at Cornelia, she knew her cousin was probably sinking through the floor.

Margaret couldn't sum up even the tiniest hint of regret for her outrageous comment, but she did feel a twinge of pity for Cornelia. It was, after all, her cousin's responsibility to launch her in European society, but during the past year, she had not been very successful.

The awkward silence was broken by the arrival of Giuseppe. The butler entered the drawing room and announced, "Lord Hymes."

The ladies stirred, making hasty preparations, and Margaret's faux pas was forgotten. Lord Hymes walked in with all the pompous assurance of the British aristocrat. He greeted the married ladies first, as expected, then moved on to Lady Sally and Lady Agnes, then finally to her.

The gaze that met hers was admiring, making it clear she was the one he had really come to see. But the look in his gray eyes was also coolly assessing, as if she were a painting he was thinking of buying. She might just as well be put on the auction block at Sotheby's and sold to the man with the highest title.

"Miss Van Alden." He bent over her hand in the customary gesture and pressed his lips to her fingers. The kiss was not a long one, as Roger Hastings never stepped beyond the bounds of propriety. Margaret found him incredibly dull.

He released her hand and stepped back. Margaret waited until he sat down, accepted a cup of tea, and replied suitably to the duchess's questions about his health before she gave an exaggerated sigh. "Oh," she moaned, and pressed a hand to her forehead.

Everyone in the room looked over at her with worried expressions. All except Cornelia, whose glance was definitely skeptical. "Oh," she said again and wilted slightly in her chair, praying for the question that would enable her to escape.

Lady Lytton provided it. "Margaret, my dear, are you ill?"

She lifted her head and tried to look convincingly sick. "My head," she murmured. "It's aching so dreadfully." She rose and continued in a weak voice, "I'm so sorry, but I fear I really must lie down. Pardon me."

She cast an apologetic glance at the others, then left the drawing room. Once out of their sight, she raced across the tiled foyer and up the stairs. Safely inside her bedroom suite, she shut the door behind her and let out a heartfelt sigh of relief. Thank goodness that was over.

Lord Hymes was probably disappointed at her hasty departure. Maybe he'd take the hint, return to his estates in Durham, or wherever it was he came from, and stop following her about.

Hymes, she knew, wanted to marry her. He had already spoken to her father on the subject, but she had no intention of considering Lord Hymes as a husband. To Hymes, marriage meant landing a rich wife who would get him out of debt.

Well, Margaret certainly met the requirement. Her father had so much money that it made the stodgy old New York Knickerbocker set back home ill to contemplate it. No wonder she had suitors standing in line.

Fortune hunters. During the year she'd been in London, there had been dozens of them, all vying for the Van Alden millions, none of them vying for her heart. She despised some of them, pitied others, but she hadn't fallen in love with any of them. And she found it hard to believe that any of them had ever been in love with her. Hymes certainly wasn't.

Margaret walked through the French doors, out onto the balcony. The sun fell over her like warm honey, and the breeze caressed her face. Her view faced the countryside of wooded hills and meadows. She stared out over the lush, green landscape with longing, wishing she had time to take one of the horses out, but it was too late in the day for a ride. At home in America, she would have thought nothing of it, but on this side of the Atlantic, going out alone, especially in the late afternoon, was an unpardonable breach of etiquette.

She had been thrust into a world where everything exciting seemed to be a breach of etiquette. She shifted her weight restlessly and, not for the first time, she chafed under the rigid rules of her existence.

A knock sounded on her door. That would be Cornelia. With a resigned sigh, Margaret walked back into the sitting room of her suite and sat down on the sofa. "Come in."

As expected, it was her cousin who entered the room. But, to Margaret's dismay, Cornelia had brought extra ammunition with her. Margaret's father.

Henry Van Alden was a powerfully built man, with piercing gray eyes and a square jaw that clearly showed the determination that had made him one of America's wealthiest men. Just now, he wore a frown that the financiers of Wall Street and Margaret both knew very well. The men of Wall Street would have been intimidated by that frown. Margaret was not.

The pair took chairs facing her. Margaret gathered her defenses and prepared for yet another confrontation about her future. Her gaze moved defiantly from her father to her cousin and back again. "Why don't you give me the lecture and get it over with?"

"Hymes came solely for the purpose of seeing you," Henry said, "and the minute he arrives you plead a headache and leave."

She shot an accusing glance at Cornelia, and her father saw it. "Cornelia didn't tattle on you, miss. The Duchess of Arbuthnot told me, and she expressed great concern over your future."

Margaret found that concern hard to believe and expressed it succinctly. "Hah!" she said in an exact imitation of the cantankerous old lady.

Henry let that pass. "The fact remains that Lord Hymes asked my permission to court you, and I gave it. Hymes would make you a good husband."

"I don't think so."

"What's wrong with him?" Henry demanded, clearly exasperated and puzzled. They'd had many similar discussions during the past year, but Margaret knew he still did not understand her nor the reason she refused one man after another. "He seems a good enough fellow. He's a viscount. Quite a catch, Cornelia tells me."

"Is he? I am informed that he's desperately in need of money."

"So is nearly every other British peer. What of it?"

"He's nothing but a fortune hunter. Doesn't that bother you?"

Her father's frown deepened into a scowl, and Cornelia spoke before the shouting could begin.

"Maggie, you can't expect your father's financial status to go unnoticed. A dowry is always important to a man thinking of marriage. But just because Lord Hymes is a bit short in the pocket doesn't mean his feelings for you aren't genuine. I'm certain he's an honorable man."

"Then why don't you marry him?" Margaret countered gloomily.

Her cousin smiled and moved to sit beside her on the sofa. "I'm already married, remember? I think Hymes really does care for you. I think he wants to marry you for more than your money."

Margaret looked at her cousin with envy. Cornelia had the good fortune to have fallen in love with a man who had more wealth and a higher social position than herself. There was no doubt his feelings for her were genuine. As long as she remained Henry Van Alden's daughter, Margaret would never have that certainty. "Hymes doesn't want a wife. He wants a banker."

"Damnation, Margaret!" Henry's voice exploded like a rifle shot, his patience obviously at an end. "It's important that you marry a gentleman who moves in the right circles, a man who can give you the respect of his name and position. Hymes can do that."

Margaret pressed her fingers to her temples and realized her feigned headache was becoming a reality. Respectability mattered so much to her father because it was the only thing his money could not buy. Though the powerful men of New York willingly dealt with him in business, their wives and daughters had closed ranks against the upstart Van Aldens. Hoping the British were more amenable, Henry had taken her to London and placed her in the hands of her cousin. Cornelia had married a viscount the year before and her excellent social connections made her perfectly suited to the task of finding Margaret a titled husband.

Thus far, the experiment had proved a dismal failure. Her father had received many offers for her hand, but Margaret had no intention of buying her way to respectability by becoming Lady Whatever and had refused every suitor that came her way.

"If I ever decide to marry, it will be for love and no other reason." She glared at her father, setting her jaw in a stubborn line that mirrored Henry's own. "I don't love Hymes," she said through clenched teeth, "and I'm not going to marry him."

"You're twenty-three, and I won't allow you to become an old maid. I intend to see you married before another year goes by. You say Hymes isn't the right man for you? Fine. Then pick another—Edgeware, Montrose, Worthington—I don't care which. They've all offered for you. So choose one, and let's get on with it."

The fact that her father could be so oblivious to her feelings made her angry and reckless. "Perhaps I'll just fall madly in love with some starving artist who'll paint me in the moonlight and whisk me away to a quaint little hovel on a Greek island where we can live in sin."

Her shot hit home. "You'll do no such thing!" Henry roared. Margaret knew she had gone too far. "I've had enough of this foolishness. You'll be properly wed to a respected gentleman. I'm getting old, and I want grandchildren before I die."

His words caused Margaret's anger to fade away. Her father had been talking a great deal about his age lately. "Don't say that."

"I'm fifty-two. No man on my side of the family has lived past fifty-five, and I probably won't either."

"You're not going to die for a long time yet, Papa."

Cornelia gave a delicate little cough. "Perhaps this discussion should be continued another time. It's after six o'clock, and the ball does begin at eight. We must be getting ready."

Margaret shot her cousin a grateful glance.

Henry rose to his feet. "I don't see why women need two hours to dress for a ball," he grumbled. "An hour is more than enough time."

"For men, perhaps," Cornelia replied. "But women require more time to look our best."

Margaret stood up and walked around the table to her father, hoping to make peace. "Don't worry, Papa," she said, linking her arm through his. "I will probably marry someday, if I find the right man. There's plenty of time."

"Time slips away faster than you think, my girl. I want you settled with a husband and children of your own." Henry paused. "You don't believe this, I know," he said heavily, "but love isn't everything, and it really isn't necessary to a successful marriage. I didn't love your mother, and she didn't love me. But we had a good, solid marriage just the same, and we were quite fond of each other."

"Yes, Papa, I know," she said, thinking a lifetime of good and solid and being fond of a man sounded horribly dull. She gave him an affectionate peck on the cheek before she gently ushered him out the door. When he left, she closed the door behind him. "Cornelia, you're an angel," she said, turning to her cousin. "Thank you. I'm so glad that's over. He seemed to take it rather well this time. At least he didn't threaten to disinherit me."

"I do believe he thought you were serious about

the artist. Really, Maggie, sometimes you are so outrageous! A Greek island!"

"I think I shocked him with that one," she agreed, walking over to the sofa. "But sometimes Papa can be so overbearing. He thinks he can bully me into doing whatever he wants. And you're no help. Must you keep pushing Hymes down my throat?"

"If you hadn't already refused Lord Edgeware, Lord Worthington, and Lord Montrose, I wouldn't have to." Cornelia's expression became thoughtful. "I know it's sometimes difficult to believe, Maggie, but your father loves you. He wants you to be happy."

"So I am to be displayed all over the ballrooms and drawing rooms of England and the Continent like wares in a shop window? Am I an item to be traded, along with my substantial inheritance, for the price of a title?" Margaret shook her head as she sat down on the sofa. "No, thank you."

"You've been reading too many suffragette pamphlets. Courtship and marriage aren't like that at all."

"Aren't they? If you marry a man who does not love you, marriage is a prison."

Cornelia lifted her hands in a gesture of surrender. "I understand why your father becomes so exasperated with you, I honestly do! Maggie, I have introduced you to dozens of eligible men, yet you reject them all."

"I know what I want, and I won't settle for less. What's wrong with that?"

"No real man ever lives up to your expectations. You dismiss them all without giving any of them a chance to win your affections. You hardly know Lord Hymes, yet the moment you found out he didn't have money, you convicted him as a fortune hunter. You might get to know him before you make such a harsh judgment."

The clock on the mantel struck half past six, and Cornelia jumped up. "Heavens! We can't continue chatting away. We've got to get ready." She ran for the door. "Think about what I've said," she urged. "I'll see you downstairs."

Her cousin departed in a rush, and Margaret reached for the bell pull to summon her maid. The girl arrived within moments carrying Margaret's gown for the party. After Molly helped her dress, Margaret sent her away. She wanted to be alone.

Her father called her foolish. Cornelia called her unrealistic. Perhaps they were right, she thought, staring at her reflection in the mirror above her dressing table. Not exactly a face and figure that would inspire a man's passion. She saw a round face with brown eyes and a wide mouth, ordinary brown hair without a hint of gold or red to make it interesting, and a plump figure that no corset could mold into the fashionable wasp waist. She saw a taller version of the chubby child she'd once been.

Margaret wrinkled her nose at her reflection and sat down. It didn't really matter what she looked like. She could be a troll with a voice like a corn crake and suitors would still be standing by with their pedantic notions of courtship, treating her with kid gloves for fear of spoiling their chances. She had met many men like Hymes, and she was tired of their hypocrisy.

She thought of her friends—Ann, Eliza, Josephine— girls who had grown up in identical circumstances to her own. They were American girls with wealthy fathers and no background, who had gone to London to find titled husbands. They had found them, and they were miserable. Each had discovered that, beneath the aristocratic veneer, their dukes and their earls were cold, unfeeling, unfaithful, and usually in debt. Margaret would not make the same mistake.

She twisted her hair into a simple chignon and secured it with a pair of gold filigree combs. But her hands faltered as she began to fasten a diamond necklace around her throat. She ran the sparkling chain through her fingers without seeing its beauty. She would gladly trade all her diamonds and luxuries for a man who truly loved her, but she was afraid that no man would ever love her more than he would love her father's money.

Trevor followed the butler down a long hall, noting with appreciation the paintings of Italian and Dutch masters that lined the walls. He appraised their value with a knowledgeable eye. When Edward had wired instructions to Cairo, telling him to bring the necklace to the villa outside Rome where he was staying, Trevor hadn't expected the place to be quite so posh. If Edward could afford to let a house like this, he must have even more money than Trevor had realized. He cast an admiring look over his shoulder at the Rembrandt as he passed through a doorway and onto a portico of marble columns and malachite tile. If he'd known, he'd have upped his asking price for the necklace.

"Lord Kettering will be with you shortly," the butler informed him. With a bow, he departed, leaving Trevor to his contemplation of money, especially his lack of it.

Once he sold Edward the necklace, he'd have three thousand pounds. Unfortunately, he would need a great deal more money than that. Trevor thought of the letter he'd received at the dig in Luxor just over a month ago. It was the only letter he'd received from his mother since his departure from England ten years before. She had made no maternal inquiries about the health or happiness of her second son. She had informed him of his brother's death, inquired about his financial situation, talked woefully about the mess in which Geoffrey had left things when he died, and ended the letter with a demand that he come home and do his duty to the family. It was a duty that had been pounded into his brain since childhood, one she knew he would never ignore.

Knowing his mother had a flair for the dramatic and a tendency to exaggerate, Trevor had wired the family solicitor. Collier had been blunt and succinct in his reply. The debts of Trevor's late brother amounted to approximately two hundred thousand pounds, a staggering sum.

Trevor gazed between the marble columns at the Tiber River, staring at the last lights of sunset on the water. He wondered how he was going to repay a debt of that size. He thought of Ashton Park, of the tenants and their families whose livelihood came from Ashton lands, and of the village tradesmen who needed the patronage of the Ashton estates. The weight of his new responsibilities settled heavily on his shoulders. The fate of so many depended on him.

The sound of footsteps on the tile floor interrupted Trevor's musings. He turned and watched Edward approach.

"Trevor," the other man greeted him. "I'm glad you've finally arrived. I was worried." He frowned. "You look the very devil. Why in heaven's name don't you shave?"

Trevor rubbed a hand over his stubbled jaw. "My valet decided I don't pay him enough."

"You don't have a valet, and haven't had one since Cambridge days." He gave Trevor a long, hard stare, then said, "Damned malaria again, I suppose?"

"A touch. The journey from Cairo was pretty bad, I must admit. But I'm taking my quinine and I'm well enough now, all things considered. And yourself?"

"Fine, fine." Edward leaned closer, and his smile faded. "Did you bring it?" he asked in a low voice.

"Of course. Did you think I wouldn't?"

"As I said, I was worried. I know the chances you take, my friend."

"I had a bit of trouble," Trevor admitted. "But I handled it."

"Good. It's a lovely evening. Why don't we take a walk?"

Trevor straightened away from the column and followed the other man. They walked without speaking down a short path of lemon trees to a terrace at the edge of a pond. They continued on down a dock that jutted out over the water. It did not escape Trevor's notice that no one could overhear their conversation from here. He almost smiled. Edward was always so cautious.

He reached inside his jacket to pull a paper-wrapped box from the pocket. He unwrapped it, opened the box, and pulled back the protective layers of cotton to reveal the breathtaking collar of lapis and gold.

Edward gave a low whistle of appreciation. "You certainly didn't exaggerate the value of this piece," he said, taking the box to give the necklace closer examination.

"Eighth Dynasty, of course," Trevor told him.

"Wife of a priest. Unfortunately, there was little else of value in the tomb. It had already been robbed, but this was missed."

Edward slid the box into the inside pocket of his jacket. "I believe we had agreed on three thousand pounds if the necklace was as you described?"

Trevor gave a brief nod of agreement, and Edward handed him a wad of notes. "You did well," he said. "The museum will be very glad to get this piece for the Egyptian collection."

"Just don't tell them how you got it."

"I never do. So tell me. What delayed you?"

"Lucci. What else?"

Edward was vexed. "That man is proving to be a great inconvenience."

"That's one way of putting it. He stole the necklace from me before I even got out of Henet's tomb. He and his men must have followed me there."

"How did you get it back?"

Trevor gave the other man a wicked smile. "Let's just say that Lucci has an incredibly beautiful and very bored wife."

Edward laughed. "I see. Are you planning to return to Egypt?"

"No. I'm going home."

"I suspected as much. You're the best I've got, and I'm sorry to lose you. But at least I'll be able to see you more often." He paused and gave his friend a long, speculative look. "I heard about your brother, of course. How does it feel to be the earl?"

Trevor turned away and gazed at the swans gliding across the water. "Damned odd."

"Trevor, I have to tell you that I've heard rumors about some, *ahem*, financial difficulties. If I've heard the gossip, then—"

"Then so has everyone else," Trevor finished smoothly, betraying none of the dismay he felt. "Thank you for the information."

"I'm afraid the suicide of an earl does not go unnoticed."

"I suppose not. I'm going to Kent immediately to see for myself."

"When do you depart?" Edward asked.

"My ship leaves from Ostia tomorrow afternoon."

"Excellent. You'll stay the night here, of course. As you can see, there's plenty of room."

Trevor glanced from the luxurious villa in the distance to the lavish gardens that surrounded them. "It's quite a place," he said as the two men began retracing their steps along the path. "The Kettering estates must be doing well if you can afford to let a villa like this. Or does being a director of the British Museum pay that well?"

"Oh, I'm not leasing it. I'm a guest here. The house belongs to my wife's uncle, Henry Van Alden. He's American—millionaire, as you might guess. Made his money in chocolate, but now he's involved in all sorts of ventures."

Trevor wished he had rich relatives.

The two men halted at the steps leading up to the portico, and Edward turned to Trevor. "So, will you stay the night?"

"I wouldn't want to intrude."

"Oh, Henry won't mind. Archaeology is a hobby of his, and I know he'll want to talk with you about Egypt. Shall I have a room prepared for you?"

"I'd be glad to stay the night, if you're sure I wouldn't be imposing on your host. My things are at Signora Calvetti's *pensione* in the Piazza di Angelo."

"I'll send for them." He glanced down at Trevor's

rumpled traveling clothes. "Henry and his daughter are having a ball this evening. Formal dress will be required, I'm afraid."

Trevor shook his head. "I've been out of the ball-rooms too long. Besides, I'm a bit tired and I still have a long journey ahead of me. I'll give it a miss, if you don't mind."

"Of course. Malaria is a beastly thing, isn't it? Giuseppe will let you know when your room is ready. We have several other guests staying here for the next few days and breakfast is quite informal. Warming dishes on the sideboard any time until eleven o'clock. Now I must change or I'll be late. If you'll excuse me?"

Edward started to go inside, but paused and looked over his shoulder. "It's good to see you again, my friend."

He went inside, and Trevor took a seat on one of the wrought-iron benches in the portico. He sat there a long time, smoking a cigar, watching dusk turn to night. He thought about Edward's comment that rumors were flying all over London and wondered just how much was known. Damn it all, if everyone in society knew just how precarious the Ashton situation was, he'd never be able to raise capital. What the hell was he going to do?

2

Margaret hummed under her breath as she studied the couples waltzing across the parquet floor. She watched them from her hiding place behind the tall potted palms and ferns that screened a quiet alcove. From here, she hoped to watch the dancing and enjoy the music while avoiding all the men Cornelia insisted on introducing to her.

She took a sip from her fourth glass of champagne. A figure in black suddenly caught sight of her peeking between the palms. Margaret groaned in dismay and stepped back deeper into the alcove, but not before she saw Roger begin walking toward her. She gulped down two hasty swallows of champagne as he came around the palms.

"I thought I saw you hiding back here," he said. "Have I told you how lovely you look this evening?"

"Yes. At least twice."

She watched him struggle for something else to

say. He finally managed it. "I'm sorry if I keep repeating myself. But it's true. You look quite beautiful."

"You give me many compliments, Lord Hymes." She took another swallow from her glass. Lovely stuff, champagne. She decided to find out how far Roger was prepared to carry on this courtship charade. "Answer a question for me. Just what exactly is it that you find so beautiful about me?"

He stared at her, taken aback by the bluntness of her question. "Well . . ." He paused, studying her. Then he rallied and said, "You have a lovely face."

"Really? What about my hair? Does it look as dark and rich as mahogany?"

A genuine smile tugged at the corners of his mouth. He was beginning to perceive her point. "I'd say that's an apt description."

"And do my eyes sparkle like fabulous jewels?"

His smile widened. "No. Your eyes are brown."

She laughed, and so did he. She looked up into his face and realized that when his smile was genuine, when he wasn't saying the things he thought she wanted to hear, he wasn't irritating at all. If only he weren't so perfectly proper.

Still, she studied him for a moment. He did have a nice mouth. She wondered how it would be to kiss a man. Not the tentative pecks on the cheek she had received from the boldest of her suitors, but a real kiss.

A wild, reckless feeling swept over her, along with an overwhelming curiosity. Marrying Roger was something she had no intention of doing, but kissing him, well, that was something else entirely. She drained her glass, then tossed it carelessly into a nearby fern. "The gardens of the villa are lovely by moonlight. Perhaps you would care to see them?"

He stared at her in astonishment. "Now?"

Margaret saw the eager hope in his face and felt a glimmer of doubt, but she pushed it aside. "Meet me in the center of the maze at midnight," she whispered, then left the alcove to rejoin the ball, leaving Roger gaping after her.

The sounds of the party floated toward Trevor as a door opened behind him. Several men wandered out onto the portico to smoke cigars, and he did not want company. He wanted quiet and time to think. He rose and went down the steps toward a maze of high box-wood hedges, finding his way by moonlight. He entered the maze and took the first path, racking his brain for a way, any way, to raise two hundred thousand pounds.

Damn Geoffrey for getting the family into this mess. But then, his brother had always been a fool. Geoffrey, who couldn't be bothered to care about the estates he had inherited or do the work required to maintain them. Geoffrey, whose main concerns had been the most fashionable knot for his cravat and whether or not the Prince of Wales would invite them to the Royal Enclosure at Ascot again this year. Geoffrey, who wouldn't have known a sensible investment if it bit him, who had always had the arrogant assumption that money just came to peers of the realm by divine right. And now that the family coffers were empty, Geoffrey lay in the family plot with a bullet through his brain.

Trevor wondered if Elizabeth would wear black for the full year and pretend to grieve for her dear departed husband. Probably not, he concluded with cynical detachment. She hated black.

He took a turn in the maze and found himself staring at a solid wall of boxwood hedge. A dead end. He turned around and retraced his steps for a bit, then took another path.

Elizabeth. The vain and frivolous wife of a vain and stupid man, who cared even less about the estate than her husband did.

In her letter to him, Trevor's mother had bemoaned the dreadful condition of Ashton Park. The roof over the west wing leaked, the carpets were threadbare, and the drains had ceased to work properly more than three years before. Jewels handed down through generations had been sold, family portraits pawned for their gilt frames, and the gold-plated dining service for two hundred, a gift from Queen Elizabeth to the first Earl of Ashton, had long since gone on the auction block.

None of that mattered to Trevor. Jewels and portraits and tradition be hanged. Ashton Park mattered for only one reason: It was his. Leaky roof, worn carpets, bad drains, and all, it now belonged to him.

Trevor took another turn and found himself in a plaza. A fountain, its water gleaming silver in the moonlight, stood in the center. In the shadowy corners were stone benches partially screened by rose arbors and clearly designed for lovers' meetings. He took a seat on the nearest bench and stared between the rose canes at the fountain beyond, turning his thoughts from the past to the future. For the first time in his life, he had something that was truly his own, and, by God, he was not going to lose it because his brother had been an idiot.

The sound of rustling skirts broke into his thoughts, and Trevor leaned forward, watching as a girl strolled into the plaza. Dressed in a ball gown, she was clearly a guest at the party and had come out here for a stroll. She paused quite close to where he sat.

"Why don't you kiss me?"

Her whispered suggestion startled him. He thought for a moment she was speaking to him, but he was deep in the shadows of the arbor and doubted she could see him. Besides, he'd never met her before, and she would hardly make such a charming invitation to a perfect stranger.

Puzzled, he watched as she again whispered to thin air. "Roger, I want you to kiss me."

Tilting her head to one side, she considered that for a moment, then shook her head as if dissatisfied. "No. Too forward. That will never work."

She began to pace back and forth in agitation, preoccupied with her own thoughts and completely unaware of the man less than ten feet away. She stopped and lifted her head to look up at an imaginary partner. "Don't you want to kiss me?"

She sighed. "No, that's not right either."

Trevor realized what she was on about and smiled in amusement. The girl was planning a midnight tryst—obviously her first—and this was a rehearsal of some sort. He studied her with an appreciative eye. He could have told her there was no need to worry. With a woman like this, a man would have to be both blind and stupid to need encouragement.

The moonlight revealed a deliciously generous figure in a velvet gown of midnight blue. He noted the neckline of the dress and tempting expanse of creamy skin that made an inviting path to her cleavage. His gaze moved further down. Fiddle-waisted, her body was beautifully molded, every curve perfectly proportioned. When she turned her head slightly, he saw her wide, dark eyes, dumpling cheeks, and a mouth definitely worth kissing. He was intrigued, and silently applauded Roger's taste.

The sound of a discreet cough diverted his attention, and he glanced toward the plaza entrance, where a man stood, nervously shifting his weight from one foot to the other. This must be Roger.

"Lord Hymes." The girl beckoned him forward. "I see you found your way through the maze."

The man walked to her side. "Took me a few minutes," he said. "A rather tedious journey."

It seemed the romantic rendezvous was about to begin. Trevor glanced at the entrance again, and realized it was the only one. There was no way for him to escape without being seen. He could simply stand up, rustle the bushes to announce his presence, and make a quick retreat, but he really didn't want to spoil the girl's romantic moment. Besides, he was curious to see if she succeeded in her intention. He would leave if the situation became too intimate, of course. If that happened, they wouldn't notice his departure anyway.

The girl took a step closer to Roger. "I hope it was worth the trouble," she said softly.

Trevor grinned at the girl's hint for a compliment, recognizing it to be the first move in the game.

Roger, however, took no notice of the opportunity she'd given him. He glanced up at the sky. "Lovely night, what? A bit chilly for a stroll perhaps, but warm enough for February."

"Yes, it's a beautiful evening," she agreed, glancing at the moon overhead, then back at the man before her. She gave him a dazzling smile as she leaned closer to him. "Italy is so romantic, don't you think?"

"Er, yes, yes, I guess it is," he stammered, running

a finger inside his collar in a stiff and uncomfortable fashion. Trevor's grin widened. What a cold fish, he thought. Was the man frigid, queer, or simply stupid? He felt sorry for the girl, though. It was a shame that such a delectable woman should have to work so hard for a kiss.

Roger cleared his throat. "I must say, I was astonished by your invitation to go for a walk. Delighted, of course, but astonished. You have so many suitors."

"None of my suitors have ever kissed me," she said, abandoning any attempt to be subtle.

Trevor didn't hold that against her. Coy women had never held any charm for him. Besides, subtlety was not going to work with a man like this.

"I should hope not," Roger answered her pompously. "You are a lady of quality. No gentleman would presume to be so forward."

Trevor rolled his eyes. *To hell with the proprieties. Kiss her, you idiot. Can't you see that's what she's waiting for?*

"Of course not," the girl echoed with such consternation and disappointment in her voice that Trevor choked back a laugh.

"Unless he were engaged to you," the man went on. "Then it would be quite all right, of course." He took a deep breath, as if gathering his courage, then grasped her hands in his and suddenly dropped to one knee. "Margaret—may I call you Margaret?" Without waiting for an answer, he continued, "I have such sincere regard for you, that I feel compelled to express my feelings. I have a deep fondness for you, and I respect you utterly. You would be the perfect wife for me. Will you marry me?"

The sight of a fastidious Englishman down on one knee in damp grass proposing marriage with all the passion of a schoolboy reciting catechism was nearly too much for Trevor.

Despite how silly the man might look at the moment, Trevor knew that most women would have been delighted by such an offer and would have accepted it triumphantly. This woman, however, did not look delighted at all. Nor did she seem to find the situation amusing. Instead, she stared down at the man in astonished dismay. She opened her mouth to speak, then shut it again, as if she really didn't know what to say. This was clearly not what she had been hoping for.

A few passionate kisses, some romantic words, yes. But it seemed a marriage proposal had not figured into her plans. Trevor wondered what she would say.

She tried to pull her hands away, but Roger held them fast and went on, "I've been planning to ask you for your hand almost from the moment we met, but I confess that until tonight, I wasn't certain of your feelings for me. You can be so circumspect, my dear."

"Roger," she said, "I'm afraid that you have mis—"

"But your charming invitation to walk in the garden told me that you care for me a great deal more than I realized," he babbled on as if she hadn't spoken.

Once again, she tried to speak. "But I really—"

"Tell me you'll marry me," he urged. "We would be a splendid match, you and I. All of society will envy us."

"Yes, I'm sure they would," she murmured, "but I really don't think—"

"Mother is quite fond of you, you know, even though you're American. She already told me it was quite all right to ask for your hand."

Right-ho, Trevor thought, Mummy has given permission. How nice.

The girl was now trying desperately to free herself. "Oh, Roger, do get up!" she said, finally jerking her hands out of his grip. "I should have known this wasn't going to work. Let's just forget the whole thing."

The man stared up at her in bewilderment. "Forget the whole thing? I don't understand."

"I know you don't. You've made a charming offer. I'm flattered, really. But I can't possibly marry you."

"You are refusing me?" he asked in disbelief. "But you invited me out here! You led me to believe—"

"I'm sorry if I misled you, I truly am. That was not my intention. But we are ill-suited, I'm afraid, and if we were to marry, it would be a grievous mistake for both of us."

Trevor heartily agreed. This was a girl clearly out of the common run, a girl who desired passion even though she was obviously innocent of its ramifications. He doubted Roger was capable of giving her what she longed for, in the marriage bed or out of it.

There was a long, uncomfortable silence before Roger finally spoke. "I see," he said coldly, and stood up. "You're right, of course. It would be a mistake." His voice grew more contemptuous with every word he spoke. "I should have known better than to waste my affections on an ill-bred American. Good-bye."

He bowed stiffly and departed.

"Oh, hell!" she muttered after he had gone. "My first real kiss and he had to act like such a prig and spoil it all!"

Trevor couldn't help it. He burst out laughing.

Margaret whirled around with a gasp. She stared in shock as a man she had never seen before emerged from the shadows, a man of formidable height and wide shoulders, with rumpled clothes, rakish black hair, and an unshaven face. But the clothes were of excellent cut, and his voice, when he spoke, was deep, cultured, and very much amused.

"You can't blame me for laughing." He came so close to her that she had to lift her chin to look into his face. She caught a glimpse of angular features and deep-set eyes, then everything suddenly began to blur. She shook her head from side to side and hastily took a step back, then another, trying to clear her champagne-drugged senses.

"If you step back any further, you'll be in the fountain," he pointed out.

Her heel hit the tiled surround of the fountain, and she was forced to halt her retreat. "Who are you?" she demanded.

"I don't know when I've seen anything so amusing in my life," he said without answering her question. "He *is* a prig, and I'm glad you refused to marry him."

She realized that he must have seen and heard everything, and her shock turned to outrage. "How dare you lurk back there in the shadows, eavesdropping!"

"I was here first," he replied. "If you wanted privacy, you should have made certain there was no one else here."

That did not pacify her, but she had the feeling it wasn't intended to. "You should have made your presence known immediately."

"And interrupt one of the greatest moments of a girl's life? I couldn't possibly."

"It was a private conversation!" she shot back furiously.

He smiled at her, a slow, teasing smile, and began

to walk toward her. "Somehow, I got the impression it was kissing, not conversation, that you had in mind."

She was humiliated that this stranger had witnessed the embarrassing scene. But she refused to let it show. She tried to gather her dazed wits and muster some dignity. She lifted her chin and gave him her haughtiest stare. "I don't know what you mean."

"No?" He gently brushed her lips with the tip of his finger. The light touch paralyzed her, and she felt her heart pounding hard in her breast. Who was he?

"If you really want to experiment with kissing," he murmured, slowly stroking her lower lip, "you ought to choose a man who knows how to do it properly."

His words galvanized her into action. She grasped his wrist and violently pushed his hand away. "Like you, I suppose?"

"Is that an offer? Of course, I'd be happy to step in for poor old Roger." He leaned closer and added in a confidential whisper, "I promise not to ruin everything by dropping down on one knee and proposing."

His teasing smile widened, and she was certain that he was laughing at her. She opened her mouth to reply, but she could think of nothing sharp enough or scathing enough to shatter his arrogant self-assurance. Hot with embarrassment, dazed by too much champagne, and speechless with frustration and fury, she did the only thing she could think of. She ran away.

Still smiling, Trevor watched her hasty departure until something glittering in the moonlight caught his eye. He picked up the object and whistled. It was a woman's hair comb of gold filigree set with a multitude of diamonds. Toying with the jeweled comb that must be worth over a hundred pounds, he thought of the girl's enticing figure, trembling mouth, and innocently provocative attempts at seduction. It was an unusual and tempting mixture, and he felt a sudden rush of desire. A pity he hadn't been the one to take her for a moonlight walk. Perhaps she might have found her experiment a bit more gratifying. He certainly would have enjoyed it.

The following morning, Trevor was up early. He had noticed the stables during his walk with Edward the evening before, and it had been a long time since he'd gone riding. He bathed and dressed, then went down to the stables.

The head groom took him inside, and Trevor walked down the line of stalls, studying the horses with admiration. Whoever his host was, the man knew horseflesh. He paused thoughtfully beside a gorgeous black mare. The horse gave him a spirited neigh and shook back her mane as if daring Trevor to ride her.

Just then, a man entered the stables who was evidently of some importance. The groom hastened toward him, greeting him effusively.

"Good morning, Roberto," the man said in a booming voice that carried to where Trevor stood. "Bring Cheval, would you?"

The groom hastened away, and the man came up beside Trevor. He gave an approving nod to the mare. "Cinder's a fine horse," he said.

"Is she trained for riding?"

The other man laughed. "After a fashion. But she's very particular about who she allows to ride her. My daughter is one, but I suspect that's because they are kindred spirits. Both of them like to go fast, and neither of them are very good at obeying orders."

"A horse doesn't allow you to ride her," Trevor contradicted. "You allow her to carry you."

"Perhaps, but Cinder, like my daughter, has a mind of her own."

As if to prove it, the mare suddenly reared up, pawing the air with her forelegs. She landed hard, then gave the back of the stall a belligerent kick.

Trevor moved into the empty stall next to the mare's. He reached out and grasped the horse's mane, wrapping the long hair around his hand in a firm grip. With his other hand, he stroked the mare's neck in a slow, soothing motion. "Easy now," he said softly. "Easy."

At first, the horse fought against the hold Trevor had on her, shaking her head from side to side to free herself. But he waited patiently, without relinquishing his grip, and, after a few moments, Cinder gave in and quieted.

"Well now," the man said, "she seems to have taken a liking to you."

"She's just biding her time, waiting until I try to ride her. Then we'll see."

The man gave an amused chuckle. "True enough. I'm just about to go out myself. Care to ride along?"

"Certainly." Trevor let go of the mare, then stepped out of the stall. He extended a hand and introduced himself. "Lord Ashton."

"Figured as much," the older man answered, taking his hand in a vise-like grip for the customary handshake. "Edward's told me a bit about you. I'm Henry Van Alden."

Once the two horses were saddled, Henry waited in the stable yard astride Cheval, his roan gelding, watching with interest as the younger man mounted the mare. Trevor eased himself slowly into the saddle, careful to avoid any move that might startle the skittish horse, and gathered the reins. He took a deep breath and gave the groom a nod to step back. The moment Roberto was out of the way, Cinder gave an agitated snort, then tried to lower her head to buck, but Trevor kept a firm grip on the reins.

The mare danced about fretfully for a few moments, but once Trevor managed to quiet her, she graciously allowed her rider the privilege of leading her out into the stable yard.

"Excellent," Henry said as Trevor brought the mare to a halt beside Cheval. "You handle horses well."

Trevor sensed from this man that was a very high compliment indeed.

"Edward tells me that you're involved in archaeology?"

Trevor figured that was one way of putting it. "I have been, yes."

Henry pointed to the rolling green hills in the distance. "There's some excellent ruins that way. Care to see them?"

"Certainly." Trevor brushed Cinder's flank lightly with the crop, and the mare followed Henry's roan gelding out of the stable yard.

It was a fine spring morning, and the estate was beautiful. They rode for several miles before bringing their horses to a halt at the top of a ridge. Trevor looked down at the valley below. In a clearing stood the columns and stones of an ancient Roman palace, only partly excavated.

"My own little project," Henry explained. "I'm working on it myself. It's slow going, of course, since I'm only here three months a year."

"You could hire archaeologists to excavate it for you."

Henry laughed and shook his head. "I couldn't stand it if they found anything without me."

"It's quite an impressive dig," Trevor commented. "Roman architecture isn't my field of expertise, of course, but this looks to be in remarkably fine shape."

"Not bad, not bad. Some earthquake damage, but that's to be expected. Any of the valuable objects that may have been here are gone, of course. But several of the mosaics are perfectly intact." He began a dissertation on Roman archaeology, and explained some of the advanced technology he had discovered on this site, including indoor plumbing.

He looked over at Trevor. "But perhaps I'm boring you with all this talk about Roman ruins. Egyptology is your field, isn't it?"

"Yes. I've been living in Egypt for the past ten years."

"But you've just become the Earl of Ashton, I believe?"

"Yes."

Henry nodded and gave him a shrewd, appraising glance. "I understand you have inherited something of a financial crisis along with the title."

Trevor continued to gaze down at the valley below. "Edward talks too much. And I fail to see how that is any of your business, Mr. Van Alden."

"It isn't," Henry answered good-naturedly. "And Edward didn't tell me anything that hasn't been the talk of London for weeks. I already knew that the late Lord Ashton left his estate bankrupt and that you are without means or credit."

Trevor bit back the curse that rose to his lips. Good God, did everyone in England know about his financial situation? And were they all going to bring up the subject so tactlessly?

As if reading his thoughts, Henry held up one hand in a placating gesture. "I didn't mean to offend you, but as a businessman, I confess I am curious about something. If you had money, what would you do with it? Buy more land, I suppose?"

Trevor thought about refusing to answer, but Henry Van Alden was a very wealthy man, and he knew that wealthy men often made useful contacts. He reluctantly swallowed his pride and shook his head. "Normally, land is a safe and wise investment. But not in these times. With fixed rents and crop prices falling, tenant farming is simply not profitable, and I don't think that is going to change in the near future."

"So what would you do?"

"Industry," he answered. "Mills and factories are the way of the future, and that's where the money is."

Henry eyed him in surprise. "That's not a typical attitude for someone of your position. Most of your peers insist on living exclusively off their land rents, even though it is no longer a profitable source of income for many of them."

"Most of my peers don't seem to have a great deal of sense," Trevor answered dryly. "My brother certainly didn't."

Henry laughed. "Well, this is something I never thought I'd see—an aristocrat who doesn't think it beneath him to be involved in industry."

Trevor turned his horse around to head back to the house. "I am a practical man, Mr. Van Alden."

"Yes," Henry said thoughtfully. "I can see that."

3

Later that morning, when Margaret entered the dining room for breakfast, the smell of kidneys and bacon assaulted her. She'd never cared much for kidneys, and this morning the smell was particularly revolting. She paused in the doorway and pressed a hand to her rebellious stomach.

Cornelia was seated at the table beside her husband, Lord Kettering. He gave Margaret a smile that seemed understanding and rather sympathetic, and she managed a faint smile in return. She'd always liked Edward. He might be a viscount, but he wasn't stodgy.

Across the table sat the Duchess of Arbuthnot, who studied her with a displeased frown. "Margaret, my dear, you don't look at all well."

"I'm fine, Lady Arbuthnot," she whispered. "Just fine." She turned toward the sideboard, but not before she saw the duchess exchange a glance with

Lady Lytton, who shook her head with clear disapproval. Margaret realized she had just made another social blunder by addressing the duchess as Lady Arbuthnot, rather than the customary title of "your grace," or the more informal "Duchess." She didn't care. All these titles and mannerisms were enough to make one's head spin, and her head wasn't up to it this morning. She poured herself a cup of coffee and added a generous amount of sugar. Never again, she vowed, would she drink champagne. Once was enough.

She took her cup of coffee to the foot of the long dining table and sat down, careful to avoid looking at Edward's plate of kidneys. "Where's Papa?"

"Your father is giving some of our guests a tour of the gallery," Cornelia answered. "He said they would be in shortly."

Roger, she knew, was not with them. Cornelia had already told her of the viscount's dawn departure, news which had brought a feeling of profound relief. She took a scone from the basket on the table and nibbled it absently, her mind preoccupied with thoughts of the night before, thoughts which led inevitably to the stranger who had invaded her privacy.

Where had he come from? An image of him formed in her mind, an image of windswept dark hair and mocking eyes. Who was he?

A sound interrupted her thoughts, and Margaret glanced up. Her father entered the room with Lady Agnes on his arm. Behind the pair came Lady Sally, gazing rapturously at the tall man beside her, a man horrifyingly familiar.

It was *him*.

The man was incredibly handsome. Given the

darkness last night, the champagne, his disheveled appearance, and her justified outrage, she hadn't taken much notice of it. But she noticed it now. Masculine strength was carved in every line of his face, from the deep-set eyes and angular features to the determined line of his jaw and chin. He was smiling at the girl on his arm, a smile that, when it wasn't tinged with mockery, was devastatingly charming.

His gaze caught hers. Margaret felt heat flood her face as she heard her father introduce everyone.

"You know Lord Kettering, of course. This is the Duchess of Arbuthnot, whom you may know. Also, my niece, Lady Kettering. And this is my daughter, Margaret Van Alden. May I present the Earl of Ashton, Trevor St. James. He arrived last night from Egypt to conduct some business with Edward before he goes home to his estates in Kent."

"Trevor," Edward said, rising to his feet, "you look much better. You slept well?"

"Yes, I did. Thank you, my friend."

Margaret noted the familiarity with which the two men spoke and heartily wished her matchmaking family to perdition. This stranger was just another British lord, a friend of Edward's, recommended by Cornelia and invited here by Henry for the sole purpose of meeting her. She began crumbling her scone to pieces on her plate as she watched Henry play the hospitable host, showing the earl the breakfast dishes on the sideboard before taking his seat at the head of the table. Margaret shot her father a defiant glance which he did not seem to see, then she fixed her gaze on her plate.

A movement beside her caused her to glance up. She found that the man had taken the first seat to her left and was staring at her. She forced her hands to stop tearing her scone apart, but she could not look away.

His vivid blue gaze lingered on her as if she were the only thing in the room worth looking at. He had been looking at Sally in the exact same way scarcely two minutes before, and she was unimpressed. Still, she fought back the urge to squirm beneath the bold scrutiny. His jet-black hair fell over his brow in careless fashion as he leaned back and studied her through half-closed eyes.

His knowing smile told her he was thinking of the night before. She looked away, but she could feel him watching her. If he told anyone, her reputation would be ruined.

Margaret wanted to toss her scone in his face.

"So, Ashton, you're finally going home." The acerbic voice of the duchess caused the man to give her his attention, and Margaret nearly sighed with relief.

"I fear I must, Duchess," he answered.

"About time you did," she said tartly. "Gallivanting around Egypt digging in the dust is no occupation for a man of your background." She studied him thoughtfully. "You've changed."

He laughed. "I should hope so in ten years."

"It was May Week your final year at Cambridge that I last saw you."

"May Week? Did we dance, your grace? I think not, or I would definitely remember it."

"Hah! Perhaps you haven't changed as much as I thought. You are still very much your father's son." She frowned sternly at him, but he gave her a wicked smile in return, and, to Margaret's astonishment, the cantankerous old duchess actually blushed like a girl. "Don't waste your charm on me, young man. There are three beautiful young ladies here. Use it on them."

He returned his gaze to Margaret. "An excellent suggestion," he murmured.

Margaret opened her mouth to tell him not to waste his charm on her either, but Cornelia must have sensed her intention, for she quickly spoke. "Will you be able to attend Carnival with us before you return home, Lord Ashton?"

"I'm afraid I can't, Lady Kettering. I must return home, and my ship leaves this afternoon. But it's a tempting offer. This is a beautiful home." He turned to Margaret. "The gardens are quite lovely, wouldn't you say, Miss Van Alden?"

He was watching her like a cat watched a mouse hole, and she felt her scone disintegrating into crumbs in her nervous hands. "What? Oh, yes."

"Particularly the maze," he added.

Heavens! Was he going to tell everyone? Margaret reached for her coffee, but she was so jittery, she knocked over the cup. Coffee spilled across the white tablecloth and onto her dress. Everyone looked at her in surprise as she fumbled for her napkin.

"Margaret, what on earth is the matter with you this morning?" Henry asked, noting the flush in her cheeks and her agitated movements.

"I-I'm sorry," she stammered, feeling the amusement of the blue eyes watching her. "I do seem to be all thumbs this morning. I can't think what's come over me."

"Perhaps fresh air is what you need," Lord Ashton suggested. "A walk in the maze, perhaps?"

Margaret jumped to her feet. "Oh, no, I really don't think so," she managed to say and fled from the room without another word.

Henry watched her go, bewildered by her odd behavior. Margaret was normally so self-possessed.

He hadn't seen her blush and stammer like that since she was thirteen years old. He glanced at Ashton, who was staring at the empty doorway with an amused smile. Henry's bewilderment gave way to hopeful astonishment. Could it be? he wondered. Could it be that a man had finally struck her fancy?

The Duchess of Arbuthnot was better than *Burke's* when it came to information about English society. Margaret suspected Lord Ashton was nothing more than another suitor out to marry a fortune, and given what had happened last night, she wanted information very badly. Forewarned was forearmed.

She found the duchess alone on the south terrace. After a few desultory comments about the beauty of the blooming azaleas and the success of last night's ball, she slowly led the conversation to the subject she really wished to discuss.

But the duchess was an astute woman, and all Margaret's maneuvering was wasted. "Hah!" the older woman said, looking at her with undisguised amusement. "Think Ashton might be the man to finally suit your bill, young lady?"

Margaret abandoned her attempt to be subtle. She'd never been good at it anyway. "I think he might suit my father's, Duchess," she answered with complete candor. "He has a title, doesn't he?"

"Don't turn up your nose and talk of a title as if it's a disease. It won't do, Margaret."

Margaret bit her lip. "I'm sorry. I didn't mean it that way."

"Didn't you?" Her good humor restored by the apology, the duchess eyed Margaret with something akin to affection. "Poor child. You American girls are an astonishing lot. So brazenly forthright, and yet so naive." She shook her head. "But you came to ask me about Ashton."

The duchess settled back in her cane chair. "I can't tell you very much. I know a great deal about his family, his background, and his boyhood, but I haven't seen him in over ten years, so there's very little I can tell you about the man he is now."

"What do you know?"

"He isn't married, I can tell you that. Second son, of course. His older brother inherited the title first, but he died nigh on two months ago."

"I remember. His death caused quite a sensation. He shot himself, didn't he?" Margaret wondered if that fact might deter her father and Cornelia from the possibility of Ashton as a potential husband. "Could there be some insanity in the family?" she asked hopefully.

"Nonsense!" That emphatic answer dashed Margaret's hopes for an easy excuse. "The late earl shot himself because he couldn't pay his debts. Simple as that. A rather stupid man, a bit of a coward, but he was sane enough." She paused, then said, "I remember Geoffrey and Trevor as boys. As different as chalk and cheese, they were, even then."

"What do you mean?"

"Geoffrey was always the traditionalist, forever concerned with his image, vain as a peacock. Trevor was a rebel, always defying the rules, getting into scrapes. Even as a boy, Trevor was a law only unto himself."

Margaret could well believe that. "He doesn't seem a very honorable man to me."

"Nonsense," the duchess answered with unexpected vehemence. "He takes after his father, that's all. I ought to know. I—" She broke off, then cleared her throat and said, "I was well acquainted with the family. Their father was quite charming in his youth, rather a rake, and had a way with the ladies. But, as he grew older, Jonathan learned the importance of tradition and restraint. As I said, I haven't seen Trevor for many years, but he does take after his father. He's an honorable man, I think, although his reputation is not spotless by any means."

Margaret decided to get to the point. "Does he have any money?"

The duchess frowned with disapproval. "Really, Margaret, must you be so blunt?"

"I want to know."

"I won't lie to you, my dear. Trevor has always been rather a detrimental."

Margaret had been in England long enough to know what that meant, and it confirmed her suspicions about Trevor St. James. "A detrimental," she murmured with a satisfied nod. "A man all the ladies are mad for, but who has no money. I thought as much."

"You'll never get yourself a husband, Margaret, if you continue to reject every man who has less money than you do." The duchess sighed. "It isn't as it was in my young days," she mourned. "Not a gentleman in all of England today has the money his father had. With the economic conditions, you can't expect it of them."

Margaret did not want to debate the issue. She quickly asked another question. "If Ashton was so concerned about the estates, why did he leave England and stay away so long? I would think he'd want to stay close by after their father died, help his brother run things."

"You really don't understand English gentlemen at all, do you, my dear?" With that enigmatic reply, she leaned forward and patted Margaret's arm affectionately. "You will discover that they are fiercely proud. Geoffrey didn't want any help, and Trevor couldn't stand playing second fiddle, especially when it was no secret he thought his brother a prize fool. There was also a woman, of course."

"I see. An actress, perhaps, or an opera singer?"

"No, no, no. Lady Ashton, I'm talking about."

Margaret was shocked. "He had an affair with his brother's wife?"

"That is the story, although, I must confess, I rather doubt it myself. In my opinion, Lady Ashton is a vain and capricious flirt. But Geoffrey believed the affair to be genuine, and he cut off Trevor's income from the estate, which had been left in his care by their father. He also banished Trevor from the house and refused to recognize him in society. The whole matter caused quite a sensation, as you might expect, and Trevor left for Egypt."

Margaret opened her mouth to ask another question, but she saw Cornelia approaching and quickly rose to her feet. She didn't want to give her matchmaking cousin any ideas. "This has been very interesting," she murmured, "but I really must be going."

She remembered to give the duchess a curtsy before turning away. She rushed past Cornelia and crossed the terrace to enter the villa.

Cornelia watched her cousin depart, then she turned to the duchess. "I couldn't help overhearing some of your conversation. She's been asking about Ashton?"

"Of course. Doesn't she always ask about her potential suitors?"

"Only so she can find reason to dismiss them," Cornelia said. She sank into the chair vacated by her cousin. "I wonder, do you really think he could be the right man for Margaret?" she asked with a thoughtful frown.

"I'm beginning to think no man is the right man for Margaret," the duchess answered dryly. Cornelia was inclined to agree with her.

Henry signed his name to the contract with a flourish and set it aside. Across the desk, Edward shook his head. "Are you sure about this? Refrigeration is an awfully new idea."

"You're so conservative, Edward," Henry said with fondness. "Sometimes it's necessary to try new ideas."

"I know, but the idea of chilled beer appalls me."

Henry laughed, but before he could point out all the lucrative opportunities refrigeration could bring, a knock on the door interrupted him. It opened and Lord Ashton took a step into the study. "Forgive me for imposing," he said, "but I'm getting ready to leave, and I wanted to thank you, Mr. Van Alden, for your hospitality."

Henry beckoned the other man into the room. "Come in, Ashton. Your comments this morning about income from industry as opposed to land rents has intrigued me. I'm wondering if you might be able to postpone your journey home? I have a business proposition that I think might interest you. Something that may entail some risk, but very lucrative if it succeeds."

"Indeed? You've intrigued me, Mr. Van Alden," Trevor answered in surprise.

"That was my intention."

"I can't postpone my journey home for very long, I'm afraid, but I'd like to hear what you have in mind."

"Excellent. My daughter and my niece are going to a dinner party this evening with the other female guests, so we will be taking that opportunity for a poker game. You and I can talk business afterward. Dinner is at seven o'clock, then poker and brandy in the card room."

Trevor nodded and left, closing the door behind him.

Edward studied Henry in puzzlement. "You want to discuss business with Trevor?"

Instead of answering, Henry toyed with the quill in his hands for a moment. "Tell me a bit more about him, about his character. What sort of man is he?"

The other man considered the question. "I think highly of him. He's shrewd. He has determination and strength of will. He's the sort of man that other men like. The ladies," Edward added with a hint of envy, "also find him quite charming."

"What about his business acumen?"

"It's too bad about his finances, of course. Trevor has ingenuity, but I think that when it comes to his estate, he's fighting a losing battle."

"Would you have confidence in dealing with him, then?"

Edward hesitated, then said, "Yes, although I think he's sometimes a bit too cocky for his own good. He's a gambler, a risk-taker."

"*Tsk, tsk*," Henry said, laughing. "Sounds a bit like me in my youth."

"Perhaps. What are you planning, Henry? To go into business with him?"

"Possibly. But I'm really considering him as a possible son-in-law."

"What?" Edward stared at him in astonishment. "They only met this morning. Don't you think you're being a bit premature to consider him as a son-in-law?"

Henry shrugged. "For months, I've allowed Cornelia to take the discreet and proper approach, hoping Margaret would find a man who suited her, but that hasn't worked at all. I'm afraid my daughter may end up an old maid, or married to some dissolute fellow with no background or breeding. I think a more purposeful strategy is needed."

"What do you mean?"

"I'm going to suggest to Ashton straight out that he marry Margaret."

"You're joking!"

"Not at all. Ashton's in need of money. We both know that. He's got the background to give Margaret respectability, which you know I want for her and her children. I also think he'd make Margaret an excellent husband. Certainly, he's the best candidate I've seen so far. At least he's willing to earn his living."

"You don't even know him."

"But I do agree with your assessment of him. I also know Margaret won't be able to walk all over him. And she's not indifferent to him. You saw her at breakfast this morning. I think it's the perfect solution all the way around."

"Really, Henry!" Edward frowned. "You can't move people around like stocks on the Exchange!"

"You needn't look so shocked. Arranged marriages happen all the time. I think Ashton would appreciate the soundness of the idea. He seems a practical man."

"I dare say," Edward acknowledged doubtfully, "but he is not a *marrying* man. Besides, I wasn't talking about Trevor. I don't think Margaret would care a fig for the practicality of it. And she certainly won't like having her marriage arranged for her as if it's a business venture."

Henry grinned. "You're probably right. But my daughter is too stubborn for her own good, and always convinced she's right."

"Quite so. She reminds me of her father."

Henry laughed, not at all perturbed by that comment.

While Henry was making attempts to arrange Margaret's matrimonial future, the subject of his schemes was comfortably ensconced beneath her favorite tree, a picnic basket beside her and a book in her hand.

It was quite a scandalous novel, and banned almost everywhere. It had taken her months to get her hands on a copy. She took a chocolate from the box beside her and nibbled it as she turned the page, her eyes widening with each word she read. The man was actually undressing the woman.

She devoured chocolates and chapters until her sweet tooth was satisfied and the story was finished. She closed the book, but the erotic scenes she'd read were still vivid in her imagination. She had no idea people actually did things like that, and felt that way while they were doing it. She pressed her hands to her flushed cheeks. "Oh, my," she whispered. "Oh, my."

Flustered, she set the book aside. Impossible, she thought, leaning back against the tree. Nobody would really do those things. They'd die of embarrassment first. Or die laughing.

And yet, no one could make up things like that, could they? She considered the possibility for quite some time, listening to the drone of bees and the rustle of leaves in the warm breeze. If he were the right man, she thought dreamily, a man who loved you, then perhaps.

She slowly closed her eyes. If you were in love with the man, it would be all right. It might even be wonderful. She drifted off to sleep, an image of one man's dark blue eyes in her mind.

Something woke her. It was a fly, buzzing quite close to her ear, and she brushed it away. Then she opened her eyes and found the intensely blue ones she'd been dreaming of staring back at her over the top of a book. *Her book*.

Lord Ashton was sitting only a few feet away. She stiffened, instantly awake and on the defensive. For the second time in as many days, this man had invaded her privacy and spied on her. He knew things about her she wouldn't tell her closest friends. Margaret didn't like the power that gave him.

"Your taste in literature intrigues me, Miss Van Alden," he said, popping one of her chocolates into his mouth. After swallowing it, he added, "And your father makes fabulous truffles."

She leaned forward to snatch the book from him. But he held the novel above his head, out of her reach. He gave her a smile that dared her to climb across his lap to retrieve her property, and she didn't know whether to kill him or crawl under the nearest rock. She settled for a fierce scowl. "I thought you left."

"Your father has graciously invited me to stay a few more days."

She'd been right, then. He was just another suitor, titled and probably broke, who wanted a rich American heiress to save his precious estates. But when she looked into the amused blue eyes watching her, she felt a momentary doubt. If that was his intention, he wasn't playing his part very well. Suitors in search of a rich wife were gracious and scrupulously polite, and this man was not. But Margaret trusted her own instincts. Perhaps his approach was simply unique, his manner bolder than that of his predecessors. Still, she'd always found cool disdain to be the best defense against fortune hunters.

"I hope you enjoy your stay," she said with frigid politeness, then held out her hand imperiously. "Now, I'm sure it's nearly tea time and I really must be going. I would appreciate it if you would return my property."

"Certainly." But instead of handing the book to her, he reached inside his jacket and pulled her gold hair comb from the pocket. "I came looking for you in order to return this. You dropped it last night."

That reference to the embarrassing incident in the garden set her cheeks burning again, and she felt certain he enjoyed watching her squirm like a butterfly on a pin. She snatched the comb from him and dropped it into her basket. "I meant," she said through clenched teeth, "my book."

"Ah, yes. The book." He leaned forward and handed the book to her. "I found it interesting reading," he said, "but rather too fanciful."

She did not want to engage in a literary discussion with this man, particularly about this book. But she thought of the passages she had read and couldn't help being curious about his odd description. "Fanciful?" she asked, trying to sound completely uninterested in his opinion.

He shrugged. "Although it seems quite erotic when

you read it in a novel, the truth is that making love in a carriage is quite uncomfortable."

"Really?" she asked, her resolution to be coldly indifferent momentarily diverted by that interesting piece of information. "How would you—" She caught herself, noticing a teasing glimmer in his eyes. She dropped the book into her basket, then glared at him. "Do you enjoy embarrassing me?"

"Why are you embarrassed? Because I've caught you reading an erotic novel? I don't tell tales out of school, so it's our secret. And you don't really care what I think, do you?"

"No, I don't."

"Good. Then perhaps we can be friends."

Friends? So that was to be his technique, was it? She smiled, pleased that she had finally figured him out. She put the lid back on her box of candy, dropped the box into her basket, and rose to her feet. "That certainly is a unique approach, Lord Ashton, but I'm afraid you are wasting your time."

He stood up, giving her a puzzled look. "Wasting my time?"

He was good at dissembling. Very good, indeed. "I'm sure there are many heiresses who would fall for such a gambit," she said, "but I am not one of them. So if you are looking to marry a fortune, you will need to look farther afield. I have no interest in marrying you."

"Thank you for telling me," he said gravely, but the teasing gleam in his eyes remained. "When I am forced to chain myself to the married state, I'll bear that in mind. But all I suggested was friendship."

"After the discourteous way you have behaved toward me, you expect us to be friends?" She stared at him in disbelief. "Why?"

"I like you."

"Indeed? That is a pity." She looked him squarely in the eye. "I don't like you."

She stepped around him. His amused laughter followed her as she walked away, and Margaret had the uneasy feeling that she was not going to be rid of him so easily.

Edward handed Trevor a brandy and they settled into two of the comfortable leather chairs in the card room. They were awaiting Henry, who was in his study dictating correspondence to his secretary, Alistair Marston.

"So, my friend." Edward took a sip of brandy and eyed Trevor thoughtfully. "After all the excitement of Egypt, won't England seem a bit tame?"

"I'll find ways to amuse myself, I assure you."

"I should imagine. You've always liked adventure. I remember all the scrapes you managed to get me into when we were at school."

"I refuse to take the blame. You took as much pleasure in our escapades as I did."

"I must admit you are right." Edward laughed. "I remember one incident in particular. The night we snuck into your brother's room at Cambridge and pasted all the pages of his textbooks together. God, he was furious."

Trevor smiled at the memory. "Geoffrey never did have a sense of humor."

"Yes, well, it was a good thing old Walston didn't believe his accusation that we were responsible."

"He couldn't prove anything, so of course the headmaster didn't believe him."

"And you had already arranged a suitable alibi for

us, as I recall. You are too clever by half." He sighed pleasurably. "Those were halcyon days indeed."

Trevor lifted his glass. "Who says they are over? I'm sure we could think up some wild escapades to get into while I'm here."

But Edward shook his head. "No, no. Those days are over for me."

"You've been married less than a year. Has it changed you so much?"

"I doubt Cornelia would look favorably upon any escapades you and I would be likely to engage in. The Egyptian artifacts business is bad enough, but coming home drunk at four o'clock in the morning would displease Cornelia immensely." He took a swallow of brandy and added, "And I can tell you it is never wise to incur your wife's displeasure."

"True enough. You might be deprived of matrimony's only benefit."

The cynicism of that comment startled Edward. "That isn't it at all," he protested. "You know that if I wanted other feminine companionship I could easily find it. But I don't want it."

"And you never look at another woman," Trevor answered with gravity, but there was a hint of mockery in his voice.

Edward refused to be perturbed by it. "Of course I look," he said, laughing. "But that is all. My wife is the only woman I truly want."

"Really, Edward! You talk as if you're actually in love with your own wife."

"I am."

Trevor studied his friend's face and knew he was in earnest. He felt a stab of pity for him. "What a wretched state of affairs. It's a situation in which you can never win."

"Marriage is not a game to be won or lost, Trevor. There will always be vexation and grief, of course, but marriage can also make a man quite happy." He shook his head sadly. "You've always had the worst possible opinion of marriage. I cannot help but wonder why."

"Is there any reason why I should have a good opinion of it?" he countered in a hard voice. "Among our mutual acquaintance, I can think of no one who would recommend the married state as a way to make one happy."

"I can recommend it highly. It has given me much joy."

Trevor could have pointed out that Edward had been married so short a time that the novelty had not yet worn off. But he merely shrugged. "If you say so."

"God, Trevor, you needn't sound as if marriage is a fate worse than death. It isn't, you know. You must marry, and you may find it surprisingly pleasant. Believe me when I say it could make a different man of you."

"Why should I wish to be a different man? I am quite content being the man that I am, and I see no reason why I should want to change." He took a swallow of brandy and added, "It is true that duty will eventually force me to marry, but it will not change either my lifestyle or my temperament, I assure you. And it will certainly not make me any less of a realist."

Edward started to speak, obviously intending to debate the point, but Henry and his secretary entered the room at that moment, and he let the subject drop. Trevor was heartily glad of it, for he thought the idea of being transformed by love was unworthy of discussion between intelligent and rational men.

* * *

"You two have successfully divided the spoils of the evening between you," Alistair said with admiration as he looked from Trevor to Henry. It was quite late, and both men had been playing poker with Alistair and Edward most of the evening. Trevor had six hundred pounds more than he'd started with. It was unfortunate that poker could not be counted on as a means of earning a living.

"Too bad Hymes wasn't here," Henry said with a chuckle. "Trevor and I would have made even more. Nice enough fellow, excellent at whist, quite good at baccarat. But can't play poker worth a damn."

The mention of the name caught Trevor's attention. "Hymes?"

"Lord Hymes," Edward explained. "Viscount with estates in Durham. You may know him."

Trevor thought of the viscount on his knees the night before, making an utter ass of himself, and he smiled. In a manner of speaking, he supposed he did know Hymes. But he admitted nothing.

"What happened to the fellow anyway?" Edward asked. "I came down this morning and Giuseppe told me he'd ordered a carriage brought round and left at sunrise without a word to anyone. Not even a note."

"Really?" Trevor lit a cigar and blew three smoke rings toward the ceiling in rapid succession. His smile widened. "Awfully rude of him, I'd say."

Henry shrugged. "Well, I can't say I blame him. I understand from my niece that he proposed marriage to my daughter last night and she refused him. Only fitting he should leave, I suppose. Damned awkward if he didn't."

Trevor wondered if Margaret had told Lady

Kettering about his role in the events of last night. He rather doubted it.

Edward yawned, then shoved back his chair and stood up. "I think it's time to find my pillow."

"Are you sure?" Trevor asked. "The ladies have returned from their dinner party, remember. Cornelia's bound to be awake, waiting for you so that she can ask how you did and lecture you about how much you've lost."

Edward was a good loser. He grinned. "We haven't been married long enough for that yet," he answered. "If she's waiting up for me, it has nothing to do with poker."

The other men laughed as Edward picked up his glass and downed the last swallow of brandy. He turned to Trevor. "I'm glad you'll be staying a few more days. We still have much to catch up on."

Trevor glanced at Henry, then said, "I don't know how long I'll be staying, but we'll find time before I go."

"Excellent. Good night, gentlemen." Edward set his glass down on the table and left the room.

Henry's secretary also rose to his feet. "It's quite late. I think I'll turn in as well." He left, closing the door behind him and leaving the other two men in private.

Henry stood up and walked to the liquor cabinet, then uncorked a new bottle of brandy and brought it to the table. After refilling Trevor's glass and his own, he sat down, lit a cigar, and wondered how best to proceed. He'd learned long ago to trust his gut feelings, and from what he'd seen, he felt certain Ashton was the right man for Margaret. Charm would be needed to win her, as well as a persuasive tongue, audacity and quick wits. Ashton possessed all those qualities. He was also titled, and that counted for a great deal. In addition, Henry liked him. Yes. Ashton would do very well.

He leaned forward in his chair. "Lord Ashton, I'm an uncomplicated man. I've made my money by being willing to take risks, by seizing opportunities, and by being a good judge of men. I need a man to take on a rather unusual and very challenging task for me. The moment we met, I realized you might fit the bill."

Trevor swirled the brandy in his glass. "You've made me quite curious."

Henry glanced at the door to make certain it was closed and no one could overhear. "What I have in mind would be an ideal solution to your current situation. It would provide you with plenty of money to salvage your estates, and there would be enough left over for you to live in luxury for the rest of your life. Interested?"

"Who wouldn't be?" Trevor frowned thoughtfully. "Who do I have to kill?"

Henry threw back his head and laughed. "Think it's too good to be true, eh?"

"Let's just say I'm skeptical. Exactly what did you have in mind?"

"It's quite simple." Henry took a long pull on his cigar and blew the smoke out slowly. "I want you to marry my daughter."

4

"*What?*" *Trevor straightened* in his chair, uncertain he had heard correctly.

"I want you to marry my daughter."

"You must be joking."

"On the contrary," Henry replied, smiling. "I'm quite serious."

He was. Beneath that smile, the other man was very much in earnest. Trevor couldn't quite believe that a solution to his problem was being presented to him on a silver platter. Life wasn't that easy. Nonetheless, he stubbed out his cigar and leaned forward, deeming the idea worthy of his full attention, even if it was a colossal joke. "You hardly know me."

"True." Henry took a puff on his cigar. "But, as I said, I'm a good judge of men. And I think you might be the right man for my daughter."

No father had ever expressed that opinion about Trevor before, and he was astonished. "Why?"

"You're titled, for one thing. That's important."
Henry swirled the brandy in his glass and took a swallow. "My background isn't quite so illustrious. My parents emigrated to America from Holland. My father-in-law was a chocolate maker, and I built his little candy shop into a million-dollar business, which I have expanded to include many other ventures. It's made me a very wealthy man." His face hardened slightly. "But all the money in the world doesn't matter when you have no background. I want my daughter to have respectability. I want all the best life has to offer for her and her children. If you aren't born with a pedigree, you have to marry one."

"I see. That's where I come in."

"Exactly."

"But why me? I mean, there must be plenty of titled men who would be willing to marry Margaret." He thought of the ridiculous Lord Hymes. "She probably has them standing in line."

"Oh, yes. That is not the problem." Henry gave a sigh of long suffering. "But Margaret does not want to marry any of them. She's a stubborn young woman, and she has some very silly ideas about marriage. Many suitors have offered for her, but she has refused them all."

"And you think I'm the man who can change her mind?"

"Yes."

"Why?"

"I was at breakfast the morning after you arrived, Lord Ashton. I haven't seen my daughter blush since she was thirteen years old."

Trevor could have told the other man that it wasn't attraction to him that made her blush like that, but he refrained. This might be his golden opportunity, and he had no intention of ruining it. But he also wanted to know exactly what he was getting into. "Why has your daughter refused so many proposals? What exactly are her silly ideas about marriage?"

"She is determined to marry only for love. Practical considerations mean nothing to her."

"There are women like that," Trevor answered dryly, "although I must confess, I've met very few. It's inconvenient for their families, perhaps, but there it is."

"It's a ridiculous notion. She's turned down one suitor after another, and it won't be long before she'll be on the shelf. She's twenty-four already, well past marriageable age. She is waiting, she says, for a man who truly loves her. I've told her repeatedly that a woman in her position doesn't marry for love, but she won't listen to me. If she falls in love with someone inappropriate, it could be disastrous. She'd elope with a stableboy if she fell in love with him. I can't let that happen."

Trevor was beginning to see the whole picture. "You want me to make her fall in love with me, so that she'll marry me."

"I'm afraid it's the only way." When Trevor did not reply, he added in surprise, "I wouldn't have thought you the sort of man to be shocked by this."

Trevor wasn't shocked. The girl had to marry someone, after all, and he could appreciate Henry's position. It was probably every father's deepest fear. "What makes you think I can succeed where so many others have failed?"

"I don't know that you can. But it's worth a try." He downed the last swallow from his glass, then refilled it from the bottle between them.

"So," Trevor said, "your main concern is to see

your daughter settled in her own home with a titled husband who can give her respectability and security."

"Yes. If that doesn't happen, God only knows who she might take it into her head to marry. Or, she might not marry at all, and what kind of life is that for a woman? She's actually threatened to run off to a Greek island and live in sin with some starving artist who'll paint her in the moonlight. She'd do it, too, if she fell in love with the scoundrel."

Henry gave his mustache an irritable tug. "Besides, I want grandchildren. I didn't work this hard for the past thirty years to leave it all to charity. But most important, I want her to make a good match. As I said, I think you would be the right man for her."

Trevor did not answer, and the other man went on, "Of course, if you don't think you can do it . . ."

Trevor flashed Henry a wry glance and refused to be drawn in. He leaned back in his chair and stared into space, Margaret's image forming in his mind. The shape of her came first, the appealing violin shape, the generous curves. Wide brown eyes, a round chin, plump cheeks, and a small, straight nose. Creamy white skin and a becoming blush. It was an ordinary female face, an honest face. Too honest. "In order to secure her future, you'd allow her to be deceived?"

"I don't expect you to lie to her," Henry answered testily. "I'm hoping you might be able to persuade her. Besides, it's better to have a disillusioned heart and security than a disastrous marriage made for irrational reasons."

"Your daughter obviously does not agree with you."

Henry shook his head with impatience. "Margaret thinks marriage should be romantic, and life should be one exciting adventure after another. I love my daughter, but I have never claimed to understand her. The point is, she has no idea what marriage is really about. She's bound to be disillusioned, no matter who she marries."

That was true enough. Trevor had seen plenty of marriages and knew there was very little romance in them.

"This is in your best interests as well, Ashton. You have to marry to secure an heir." He paused, then played his last card. "And you need the money rather desperately."

Trevor shot him a sharp glance. "You seem to hone in on all the salient points, Mr. Van Alden."

"I told you, I've heard all the gossip. Your late brother's expensive tastes and talent for bad investments have never been a secret."

"You don't have to tell me about my brother's shortcomings. I know all about them."

"Well, are you going to do it?"

Instead of answering, Trevor took a swallow of brandy and asked another question. "What sort of dowry do you have in mind?"

Henry smiled. "I thought the financial arrangements would be important to you."

"You brought it up."

"True. Why don't you give me a starting point?"

Trevor ran his finger around the rim of his glass, and wondered just how much to ask for. He needed two hundred thousand pounds to pay off his brother's debt, but he had to add enough to ensure the future. Also, this was a negotiation.

"Five hundred thousand pounds."

Henry didn't even blink. He pursed his lips and leaned forward, ready to negotiate. "I'll give you a lump sum of two hundred thousand pounds as a marriage settlement—I do believe that is the sum of your late brother's debt? In addition, a monthly allowance of three thousand pounds for the care and support of your estate, and a monthly allowance for Margaret of five hundred pounds. The rest of her inheritance, however, will be held in trust for her children." He met Trevor's gaze across the table. "Do we have a deal?"

Trevor set down his glass and stared at it thoughtfully for a long moment. He thought of Margaret Van Alden's innocent curiosity about kissing and what that had led to. He thought of her face, which was as easy to read as a book. She was also very desirable, and had the promise of passion. He didn't have any doubt that he could persuade the girl to marry him, but he envisioned her innocent eyes and honest face, and something made him hesitate.

On the other hand, this was the perfect solution. He would have enough money to secure the estates, he would eventually gain an heir, and he wouldn't have to go through all the fuss of the marriage mart. He thought of the estate and all its responsibilities and shoved his momentary hesitation aside. "Yes," he finally said. "I'll do it. On two conditions."

Henry frowned, displeased. "You're hardly in a position to impose conditions."

"And it seems your chances of finding a suitable husband for your daughter are getting slimmer every day. I'll not be put on a monthly allowance like a schoolboy. If I marry your daughter, I will be the one to support her. To do that, I need capital."

"Very well. Three hundred thousand pounds up front then."

Trevor wondered if he could once again call

Henry's bluff. "Four hundred thousand," he said firmly. "Or find someone else."

Henry thought about it, then he said grudgingly, "Very well, but I still insist on giving my daughter an allowance of her own, and that my approval be given to any investments."

It was a concession, and Trevor suspected that the other man very seldom made concessions. "Agreed."

"You said you had two conditions. What's the other one?"

Trevor knew this was going to be an even more difficult point for Henry to concede than the other had been. "I want an absolutely free hand in this. No matter what happens, you will not question the means by which I obtain her hand in marriage."

"Don't think I haven't heard about your reputation, Ashton. Arthur has told me about your affair with your late brother's wife. He assures me it is untrue, although he also admits there has been talk of many others. I need a man who has a way with women, but if you are suggesting deliberately getting caught in a compromising situation, I will not condone—"

"I am suggesting no such thing. Her reputation will not suffer. And I will not take advantage of her innocence, if that is your fear. I give you my word of honor, and despite my rather black reputation, that is still worth something. Are we agreed?"

Henry considered the matter for some time. "Very well," he said, but his face darkened. "If you break your word, Ashton, if you dishonor my daughter in any way, I'll kill you with my own hands."

"I don't doubt it. But I do not break my word, sir. And I do not ruin innocent young ladies."

Henry was satisfied. "I believe you. In fact, you

remind me a great deal of myself when I was a young man. When I return to London, I'll have the terms of our marriage settlement drawn up. When you obtain Margaret's consent, we'll sign them. I feel it only fair to warn you that you don't have a great deal of time. It's only seven weeks until Easter. After that, Margaret will be in London for the Season, and if you have not obtained her consent by then, other suitors will be ready to court her, and I will not prevent them."

Trevor wasn't worried. Seven weeks was more than enough time, and competition from other suitors did not concern him. "What is her itinerary until then?"

"She will be in Rome for Carnival until Ash Wednesday, then she is planning to leave for Florence with Lord and Lady Kettering. She will return to London just before Easter."

"With Carnival going on, I doubt I'll be able to find rooms in Rome at this late date."

"I'll take care of that." Henry leaned forward in his chair. "Now, there are some things about Margaret that you need to know if you are to court her properly. You must become familiar with her likes and dislikes. She loves—"

"No," Trevor interrupted. "I'm not going to cater to her every whim. Besides, there is nothing you can tell me about her that would help me now."

"But—"

"I thought we had agreed this would be done my way. I assure you, your daughter's likes and dislikes are irrelevant. Good Lord, if I only did what she liked, she'd never fall in love with me. Women, I'm afraid, are like that."

"Margaret is not like most of the women you've known."

Despite her innocence, he doubted it. He'd known a lot of women. "It doesn't matter. Mystery is part of the game. Leave it to me, and don't question it."

Henry tugged at his mustache irritably. "I guess I have no choice."

"Neither do I," Trevor assured him and stood up. "And neither, it seems, does she."

He started for the door, but paused and turned to the other man once more. "It might also be advisable if you pretended to disapprove of me. Tell her you know best, assure her I'm a bad lot and quite disreputable, and forbid her to further our acquaintance. I have a feeling that might make me more appealing."

"That is ridiculous. I don't understand what difference that will make."

Trevor grinned. "All her other suitors probably didn't understand either, and look what happened to them." With that, he left the card room.

In his own bedroom, Trevor closed the door behind him and laughed aloud, a laugh of triumph and disbelief. The ideal solution to his problem had just fallen into his lap. How lucky could a man get?

He loosened his cravat and sank down into a chair, reminding himself that luck was a fickle mistress, enjoyable while it lasted, but not to be depended upon. He pushed aside the triumph of his momentary victory. If he was going to succeed in this courtship, he needed more than luck. He needed strategy.

He remembered her words of two days before. *If you are looking to marry a fortune, you will need to look farther afield.* Margaret might be innocent, but she was not a fool. She was also quite skittish about fortune hunters.

He had to come up with a plan, a campaign designed to pique her interest, spark her desire, and eventually earn her trust. The easiest way to do that would be to get her off alone somewhere, but even with her father gone, Cornelia would still be hovering at her elbow. Chaperones were a damned inconvenient thing.

He leaned back in the chair, picturing Margaret in his mind. Eyes the color of fine whiskey, too honest to conceal her feelings. Thick eyelashes that—thank God—did not flutter at him in the helpless, beguiling fashion so characteristic of society debutantes. A mouth too wide to be considered the fashionable rosebud shape. Not an outstanding beauty by society's standards, he supposed. But he thought of the full lips that had trembled beneath his touch and hinted at an underlying passion far more important than looks. She might not have the smallest waist in her circle of friends, but it was small enough to emphasize the lush curves of her body.

She was soft and desirable, but there was nothing coy or delicate about her. She was bold enough to look him in the eye and blunt enough to tell him what she thought of him.

Margaret was a woman who would never be able to deceive him. Nor would she be able to manipulate him, although he didn't doubt she would try. As a wife, she would suit him very well. Winning her would not be easy, but nothing worth having was ever easily attained. With a bit of ingenuity, he would succeed.

Tomorrow, he'd wire to England and inform Collier he was postponing his return home for another two months, instructing him to keep the creditors at bay. It would cause more gossip, but that could not be helped. He had to win over an heiress. Margaret Van Alden would be his wife. She just didn't know it yet.

*   *   *

By late afternoon the following day, Trevor concluded that if last night's thoughts were true, then his future wife would be a prize beyond price. But she was definitely not going to be easy to win. Especially if he could not even see her.

She'd had breakfast in her room, then she had taken a carriage to Lady Rathgate's villa to spend the day. Lady Kettering and the Duchess of Arbuthnot had accompanied her. Later, Margaret had sent a note saying they would be staying there for tea, as Lady Rathgate had insisted on it. He could have called on Lady Rathgate, of course, but he was not going to chase after Margaret, playing the lovesick schoolboy. For one thing, he wasn't lovesick, and for another, acting like it wasn't going to gain him anything.

It did not surprise Trevor that she was avoiding him. In fact, he'd expected this, and he chose to turn her absence to his advantage. He politely declined Henry and Edward's invitation to help them dig up Roman pottery, and four o'clock found him seated on a velvet settee in the drawing room with the ladies who had not gone to Lady Rathgate's. He was obtaining much needed information about Margaret, along with his tea and crumpets.

"Of course," Agnes Ellerby was saying, "Maggie is very modern, and has modern views. Very admirable, I think."

"Posh," Lady Lytton said, and gave her daughter a disapproving frown. "Agnes, dear, don't take any foolish notions into your head about these modern views. It won't do. Margaret is an American." She waved a hand in the air and added, "Suffragettes, the vote, and all that sort of thing. Not at all appropriate."

Trevor took a swallow of tea. "Miss Van Alden is a suffragette?"

Agnes giggled. "No, no. She doesn't hand out pamphlets and make speeches, if that is what you mean. But she is very outspoken and does have a taste for adventure. She comes very close to the edge of what is considered proper."

Trevor thought of Margaret's encounter with Roger in the garden, an image that always made him want to smile. "Really? In what way?"

Agnes brushed back a wisp of her dark hair and leaned forward, clearly willing to engage in gossip. "She went into the card room at Lady Longford's rout last autumn and played whist with Lord Neville, Lord Caverton, and Lord Edgeware. She even placed a few wagers. It caused quite a sensation."

"As well it should." Lady Lytton shook her head with such agitation that Trevor thought the stuffed partridge on her hat was going to take flight. "She was smoking cigars with the gentlemen in that card room, so they say. But what else can you expect from an American? Bold girls, all of them. They come over here with their fast ways and their gushing manners to marry our young gentlemen, stealing them away from our own English girls. It's frightful."

"Mama, that's not fair," Agnes protested. "Margaret doesn't gush, and she hasn't married one of our gentlemen. Quite the opposite. She says she'll never marry an Englishman."

"Well, of course she won't," the countess answered. "No gentleman would marry a girl who smokes cigars."

"Lord Hymes offered for her after the card room incident, Mama. I think you are being unfair."

Lady Lytton gave a rather unladylike snort of

displeasure. "That will be enough, Agnes. Margaret goes horseback riding alone, she makes the most outrageous comments, and she constantly addresses peers incorrectly because she can't be bothered to learn the rules of the peerage. Also, she defies her own father at every opportunity. No gentleman could possibly want a wife who would embarrass him and is so strongwilled that he could not control her. She's pretty enough, I suppose. Although she certainly doesn't have the figure to carry off those Worth gowns of hers," Lady Lytton added. "She's much too chubby."

Trevor felt a spark of irritation at the countess's spiteful words. He thought of Margaret's luscious shape and had to refrain from giving Lady Lytton a man's viewpoint on the subject.

"I still find her rather daring," Agnes added wistfully.

"But isn't daring rather inappropriate in a woman?" Sally turned to Trevor, her blue eyes wide. "Lord Ashton, what is your view?"

Sally was a slender, fair girl with a bland, chocolatebox sort of prettiness that left Trevor completely cold, but habit prompted him to lean a bit closer and give her a look that conveyed the opposite. "My view is quite a pleasant one at the moment, Lady Sally."

She smiled at him, preening slightly at that admiring remark. "Now that Lord Kettering has invited you to Rome, what are your plans for Carnival? We have reserved a splendid balcony for watching the celebrations Friday evening."

"A charming invitation. But Lord Kettering has already invited me to share his balcony on that night."

"Oh." Her lower lip nudged forward in a pout of disappointment. "We had so hoped to hear more of your adventures in Egypt. How wonderful it must have been."

He thought of the dust and the sweat, the cobras and the malaria, and he doubted Lady Sally would find it wonderful at all. "I'm sure that with all the excitement of Carnival at your feet, Lady Sally, talk of Egypt would seem rather tame."

"Sitting on the balcony is what seems tame to me," Agnes said. "I rather agree with Margaret that it would be much more exciting to abandon the idea of balconies and carriages and go out into the melee on foot."

Trevor straightened in his chair, his attention caught by Lady Agnes' words. This just might be the strategy he'd been searching for. He turned to the dark-haired girl. "Miss Van Alden wanted to participate in the celebrations rather than simply observe them, did she?"

"Yes. She thought it would make for a grand adventure."

"Adventure indeed!" Lady Lytton looked horrified. "Ladies of quality do not parade themselves in the streets like peasant girls. Only Margaret would have such an idea!"

"Miss Van Alden seems to be a woman who enjoys adventure," Trevor commented.

"Oh, yes." Agnes laughed. "She's always coming up with wild schemes like that. She would do it, too. But her father put his foot down and said absolutely not."

"I should hope so." Lady Lytton set down her cup and saucer and gave her daughter a stern look. "Her wild schemes are what get her into trouble, Agnes. Don't forget that."

The countess began another dissertation on the deplorable lack of good manners among American girls, a dissertation which she did not seem to find rude even though her host was American. Her diatribe was obviously meant for marriageable young English gentlemen such as himself. But Trevor wasn't listening.

An idea was forming in his mind, an idea of how to win Margaret Van Alden. It would make for a most unusual courtship, but he was courting an unusual young woman. It would require some assistance from Edward, but Edward owed him a favor or two from their school days. It was risky, but he'd never minded taking risks.

Trevor smiled and leaned back in his chair. If Margaret Van Alden wanted adventure, he would give it to her. Far be it from him to disappoint a woman.

Giovanni Lucci was a man who appreciated all the comforts of home. Perhaps it was because he spent so much time away that returning home was such a pleasure. Or perhaps it was because his lovely young wife would be waiting for him, ready and eager to satisfy his every need. Either way, Lucci was a happy man when he crossed the courtyard of palms and date trees that fronted his luxurious villa outside of Cairo.

But, to his surprise, his beautiful Isabella did not come running down the flagstone steps to greet him as she usually did when he returned from a business trip. When he entered the house, Yousef, his majordomo, was waiting to meet him.

The servant bowed. "Master, it is good that you have come home, for I have the most dreadful news. Madam is unwell, and took to her bed three days ago. We attempted to locate you, but, alas, we could not."

"Isabella is ill?" Lucci felt a slow, cold dread seep

into his bones. His beloved Isabella was never ill. "What is wrong with her?"

Yousef fell to his knees in wretched supplication. "Master, I have failed in my duties," he cried. "I am a worthless dog, and you should take my life. I am to blame for my lady's ailments!"

Lucci shook his head, too bewildered and worried about his bride to be concerned with the servant's distress. "Is she in her rooms?" he demanded.

Yousef nodded, his turban-wrapped head bent in sorrow. Lucci stepped around his kneeling servant and started for the stairs. He took them two at a time and quickly reached his wife's apartments.

She was lying in her bed, wrapped in silken sheets. Two young servant girls stood by, waving palm fans to keep the air cool. At his entrance, they fell to their knees.

"My wife, you are ill?" He pushed back the gauze draperies that surrounded her bed and sat down. He reached out to touch her cheek, and his heart twisted with pain at how pale she looked.

"My darling," she whispered and reached for his hand. "My dearest husband, you are home at last. How I prayed you would come." To his astonishment, she burst into tears, and he realized she was not simply ill. There was more to it than that.

"What is this?" he cried. "What has happened?"

Isabella brushed back the tears on her face and waved a hand to the two servant girls. "Send them away, husband. Please, send them away. We must speak privately."

He shouted an order, and the two girls fled, closing the door behind them.

"Oh, my dearest, I hardly know how to tell you!" she cried. "That man came here. He broke into the house in the middle of the night."

"Man? What man?"

"You know how awful I am about names." Her voice broke on a sob that tore at Lucci's heart, and she worked to regain control of herself. Finally, she looked at him with pain-glazed eyes. "That tall Englishman you introduced me to last autumn."

"St. James." Lucci's mouth tightened to a grim line.

Isabella nodded. "Yes, yes. That's the name. I remember now. He came in through my windows." With a trembling hand, she pointed to the French doors that led to her balcony. "The windows were locked, and he made no noise. I awakened to find him standing over me. He-he told me if I screamed, he would kill me. And then he—oh, blessed Saint Maria, I cannot speak of what he did to me!"

She didn't have to say it. Lucci knew.

"I tried to fight him off, but he was too strong. He hit me, and then"—she paused and swallowed hard, as if it was almost unbearable to go on—"when he had, had finished with me," she continued in a trembling voice, "he broke into my jewel case and took that beautiful lapis necklace you gave me. I was too frightened to scream for help. He— Oh, husband, I am defiled! I am ruined! I am so ashamed!" She burst into another flood of tears and began sobbing. Lucci stared down at his beautiful bride, watching her shudder with the revulsion and horror of her experience, and he felt a fury like nothing he had ever felt before. When she tried to speak again, he stopped her, unable to bear hearing anything more.

"Enough!" he roared, slamming his fist into the wall so hard the plaster cracked. "Say no more, my wife. St. James will die for this, I promise you, and it shall be a slow and painful death."

He turned to leave and did not see the flash of

spiteful triumph in his wife's gorgeous brown eyes, nor the satisfied smile that curved her full red lips.

There was no way she could get out of it. Margaret used every ounce of imagination she possessed, but she could think of no reasonable excuse to avoid dining with Trevor St. James. Illness would not suffice—she'd used that excuse too many times with other suitors, and her father would never believe it. Nor would a prior engagement be acceptable. Her father knew she had none.

She had no choice but to go down for dinner. Margaret smoothed the folds of her red silk gown and thought of Trevor's eyes, of the amusement that seemed to always lurk in their dark-blue depths, but it was not that which set off warning signals in her mind. It was the sense that, behind the teasing eyes and bold manner, he possessed an implacable will that she could not bend to her own. She felt that he knew her innermost secrets and would not hesitate to use them against her if it suited his purpose. She was certain his purpose was to get his hands on her money by marrying her, and yet, as she contemplated the possibility again, she felt a nagging doubt. He just didn't act like a suitor.

She shook her head, vowing not to waste her time trying to discern his motives. Tomorrow, they would be going into Rome for Carnival, and he had already told Cornelia that he was returning to England and would not be able to accompany them. So she had only this one evening to endure, then he would be gone.

Her mantel clock chimed quarter past eight, and Margaret knew she could delay no longer. She entered

the dining room, but paused just inside the doorway.
To the left of her empty chair sat the very man she was
trying so desperately to avoid. She wanted to turn
right around and depart, but that would be giving him
the cut direct in front of others. As tempting as that
idea might be, she could not do it. Besides, she'd been
running away from him long enough.

Feeling rather like a soldier heading into battle, she
walked to the end of the long dining table without a
glance at him and took her seat. "Sorry I'm late," she
murmured to the others, adding no explanation for
her tardiness.

The footmen began to serve the first course of clear
soup, and conversation centered on Carnival.

The duchess pronounced the festival to be quite an
exciting affair. Henry expressed regret that he would
be forced to miss it, as he was returning to London on
the morrow. Lady Lytton bragged about the superior-
ity of their balcony, which gave an excellent view of
the Piazza di Vittorio, and Lady Sally inquired about
Lady Kettering's choice of costume.

Cornelia laughed as Edward groaned. "I'm dressing as Pulcinella, and Edward—" she paused and gave
her clearly dismayed husband a teasing smile—
"Edward shall be Punchinello."

Amid the laughter that followed, Edward held up
his hands. "It was not my idea," he assured them. "I
do not want to attend the Ball as a hunchbacked
Italian clown," he added emphatically.

"Edward could not be bothered with something so
trivial as costumes, so he left me to choose them,"
Cornelia explained.

Ashton turned to Margaret. "What costume have
you chosen, Miss Van Alden?"

She reluctantly turned to him long enough to

answer. "Columbine," she said shortly and took a sip of wine.

"Indeed?" Ashton leaned closer to her and lowered his voice so that only she could hear him. "But if I remember correctly, Columbine's lover was Harlequin. Who will be your Harlequin, Margaret?"

Shocked as much by the intimate tone of his voice as by his bold words, she turned to give him the set down he so richly deserved. But when she looked into his eyes, her sharp retort was forgotten. The laughter and conversation that flowed around them faded into the background, and suddenly it was as if they were alone.

His gaze bored into hers with an intensity that left no doubt what he was thinking. He was looking at her as a lover might, she realized wildly. An inexplicable languorous warmth began to spread through her limbs, and she found herself leaning toward him, drawn by the irresistible magnetism of his look. She licked her dry lips and watched his gaze lower to her mouth. He wanted to kiss her, she was certain of it. Suddenly, she wished he would, and a small sigh escaped her lips. He responded to that feminine sound with a smile, an utterly male smile of satisfaction. She realized she had fallen into a trap.

Margaret sat back, gathering with an effort the defenses he had breached so easily. "You could play Harlequin to my Columbine, my lord," she said, striving to sound as if forbidden liaisons were offered to her all the time. "However, since you are returning to England and will not be attending Carnival, that isn't possible."

"On the contrary," he said smoothly, "I will be at Carnival after all. Hadn't you heard? Lord Kettering has graciously invited me to share his balcony, and I have already received several other invitations."

"What?" She glanced down the table at Edward, who was deep in conversation with the duchess. She suddenly felt like a condemned prisoner must feel when the cell doors clang shut. Was everyone in on this fortune hunter's scheme? she wondered.

She looked at Ashton again, who was watching her with an expression on his face that could only be described as gallingly smug. *Dear Lord*, she thought, dismay settling in the pit of her stomach like a stone, *I'm trapped.*

5

The following morning was a busy one. While servants made the preparations for their employers' stay in Rome, Edward escorted Lady Lytton and her daughters to their townhouse in the Piazza di Vittorio. Trevor did not accompany them. Instead, he rode into the city with the Duchess of Arbuthnot and her entourage.

In another carriage, Margaret and Cornelia accompanied Henry to the train station. While porters dealt with the luggage, the girls walked with him to the platform where trains departed for Calais.

Before going aboard, Henry turned to his niece. "Cornelia, my dear, I'm counting on you to watch over Margaret during the rest of your trip."

Cornelia took her responsibility as chaperone very seriously. "I will, Uncle Henry. Have a safe journey." She kissed his cheek, then moved some distance away, allowing Henry to say good-bye to his daughter in some privacy.

"Now, you do what Cornelia tells you, my girl," he said firmly. "And no back talk."

She mentally crossed her fingers and hoped she sounded like a dutiful daughter when she answered, "Yes, Papa."

"Good. It's necessary that I go back to London, but I'm quite concerned with leaving you to continue your travels without me. Especially just now."

"Just now?" she repeated, puzzled. "What do you mean?"

Henry tugged at his mustache and looked uncomfortable. "I know Edward and Ashton are old friends and business associates, and they will want to spend some time together. But with me gone to London, I can't say I like the idea of Ashton socializing with Edward and Cornelia while you are there. I can't say I like it at all."

Margaret couldn't believe what she was hearing. "You don't?"

"No, indeed. If I'd known earlier, I'd have tried to discourage it."

Still bewildered, she studied her father's concerned face. "I'm not sure I quite understand, Papa. What are you talking about?"

"I know he and Edward were at Eton and Cambridge together, but Ashton is a thoroughly bad hat."

"Really?" She was intrigued by that fascinating tidbit. "In what way?"

Henry made sure Cornelia was out of earshot, then he said, "Edward tells me he's been providing Egyptian antiquities to collectors and museums, but not always through reputable channels."

Margaret felt a delicious little thrill of excitement. "You mean he steals them?"

Henry frowned. "That's one way of putting it, I suppose, although it might be equally valid to say he simply excavates without getting the proper permits from the Egyptian government."

"And Edward is involved in this?" She could hardly believe it. Edward was so proper.

"He only has suspicions. No proof. Either way, I don't think Ashton qualifies as an appropriate suitor for your hand."

She turned away, studying a nearby kiosk and pretending vast interest in the many newspapers offered for sale. "Has Lord Ashton expressed such an interest?" She tried her best to make the question sound casual.

"He did ask me about you, and I'm sure he was thinking about courting you, but I made it clear that he would not be a suitable husband."

Margaret couldn't help feeling a flash of rebellion at that comment. Honestly, didn't she have any say in this courtship business at all? She could decide for herself which suitors were acceptable and which were not. Still studying the newspapers, which she could not read since she didn't know Italian, she asked, "Why wouldn't he be suitable? He's titled."

"Just because a man has a title doesn't mean he'd be right for you. I want you to gain respectability by marriage, not lose it."

This was getting more intriguing all the time. She turned back to her father. "He has such a black reputation, then?"

"Black enough, at least where women are concerned. There is talk that before he left England, he had an affair with his sister-in-law. Then, there was also some incident with the wife of the Greek ambassador while he lived in Cairo. I understand that the husband publicly called him out."

"An ambassador's wife?" she gasped, deliciously shocked. "How scandalous! What happened?"

"You don't need to know the details," Henry shot back. "The point is, Ashton isn't for you. Stay away from him, honey. I've made it clear to Edward and Cornelia that I don't consider him acceptable, and Cornelia has been given strict instructions to be by your side at all times."

"Really, Papa!" she exclaimed, irked by the stifling control others had over her life. With Cornelia watching her every second, all the fun of Carnival would pass her by. As much as she loved her cousin, Cornelia was really rather a stickler when it came to the proprieties. "I'm not a child."

He grasped her chin in his fingers and looked her sternly in the eye. "I know what I'm doing, Maggie. Now, for once, be a good girl and do what I say."

He gave her a kiss on the cheek and turned to board the train, missing the rebellious look Margaret sent him. But when Cornelia came up to stand beside her, she couldn't help but notice her cousin's expression. "Is something wrong?"

"Really," Margaret answered, "my father is sometimes the most frustrating man."

Trevor arrived at Edward's townhouse and waited for the other man in the library. He was helping himself to some very fine port when Edward entered the room. Trevor froze, his glass halfway to his lips, and eyed his friend askance.

Edward saw the expression on his face and scowled. "Don't you dare laugh," he said menacingly.

Trevor choked back his amusement, but he couldn't help making a comment or two. "Is purple hose really necessary?"

"I mean it, Trevor." Edward shifted the papier-mâché hunchback beneath his doublet of green and purple stripes to a more balanced position. "I feel like an idiot."

"Well, after all, Punchinello was a buffoon in the Italian comedies, wasn't he?"

"Enough." Edward reached behind and yanked out the offending lump of papier-mâché. "I hate this thing," he muttered and tossed the hunchback into a corner. "I refuse to wear it."

"Very sensible," Trevor said, lifting his glass with approval. "You'd never be able to sit comfortably on the balcony wearing that thing anyway."

Edward straightened his doublet and finally noticed Trevor's costume. "All black?" he said, eyeing the other man's velvet doublet, leggings and knee-high boots dubiously. "I thought you were dressing as Harlequin."

"So I am."

"Harlequin never wore black."

Trevor pointed to a tattered, multicolored velvet cape that lay across the back of a chair. "That is as close to accuracy as I get."

"I'm getting a different costume for the remainder of Carnival," Edward said as he poured himself a much-needed glass of port. He sank into a chair, shaking his head. "I don't care what it takes, I don't care how much it costs. Sitting on a balcony with a few friends when I'm dressed like this is one thing, but I refuse to go to the British Embassy ball this way."

Trevor decided to change the subject to what he really wanted to discuss. He closed the door to the library and sat down in the chair opposite the other man. "My friend, do you remember when we were about thirteen years old and the headmaster called us both in about that little explosion?"

"You mean Guy Fawkes Day, when we tried to make our own fireworks in the chemistry laboratory? Of course I remember."

Trevor swirled the port in his glass and went on, "And do you remember how I took all the blame so that you wouldn't get expelled?"

"Yes, of course. It was my third offense, and they certainly would have sent me home for good. With all the mischief you did, I don't know how you managed to graduate with only that one black mark on your record. You've always had the most confounded luck, Trevor. It's really quite galling."

"Yes, well, I'm hoping that luck holds out a bit longer. I need your help with something."

Edward was silent for a moment, then said, "If it's money, I'd be glad to loan you—"

"No, it isn't money. At least, not exactly."

His friend eyed him in puzzlement. "What is it, then?"

Trevor took a deep breath and said, "I need you to help me win the hand of a lady. I'm going to get married."

Carnival had begun. Margaret could hear it from her room as she dressed in her costume, a dim hum outside the house that grew louder with each passing moment until it became a roar of activity and confusion. But Margaret's room faced the back gardens of the house, and she had no idea what was happening outside.

"Oh, hurry, Molly," she urged her maid, shifting her weight impatiently as the girl fastened the buttons at her back. "I don't want to miss anything."

"Forgive me for saying so, miss, but if you'd stop moving about so, I'd be done quick as lightning."

She forced herself to stand still until her maid had finished. "There," the girl said, stepping back. "All done."

Margaret turned around. "How do I look?"

"Oh, miss, you look ever so lovely. The costume fits you perfectly."

"That's only because you've laced me so tight, Molly. I'm sure I'll faint well before dinner. Or worse, I'll belch, and Lady Lytton will be scandalized."

The maid laughed and Margaret turned away for a cursory but critical glance in the mirror. The gown was of striped velvet in many different colors and had slashed sleeves that puffed at her shoulders, then narrowed to a tight fit down her arms. Both the stripes and the sleeves had a rather slimming effect. Molly had piled her hair atop her head, which added height and also served to give an illusion of slenderness. The square neckline was a bit low, however. Ever conscious of her overly generous bosom, she gave a tug at the neckline, trying to pull it higher, but it would not budge. She gave up with an impatient sigh and turned away from the mirror. She grabbed her white gloves, pulling them on as she raced for the door.

"Wait, miss!" Molly called after her. "Your mask."

Margaret ran back into her room, grabbed the blue satin mask from her maid, and ran out again. She raced down one flight of stairs to the library, which had been chosen for viewing the festivities once the guests arrived. But Margaret had no intention of waiting that long to get her first look at Carnival. She ran through the library, making for the French doors at the far end that led onto the balcony, dropping her mask carelessly on a table as she passed it. She opened the doors, but came to an abrupt halt when she realized that she was not alone. Lord Ashton, dressed all in black and looking nothing like Harlequin, stood at one end of the balcony, leaning over the rail.

Gasping for breath, Margaret pressed a hand to her tightly laced ribs and paused, studying him. The velvet doublet he wore only enhanced his already wide shoulders, and the leggings fitted him perfectly, emphasizing his narrow hips and muscular thighs. Once again, it struck her just what a formidable man he was.

Not quite certain a glimpse of Carnival was worth an encounter with Ashton, she hesitated in the doorway. But before she could decide to make a hasty exit, he turned his head and noticed her standing there. "Hullo." He nodded to the raucous din below. "Sounds as if the entire world is down there, doesn't it?" He beckoned to her. "Come out and see."

Curiosity overcame her misgivings, and Margaret stepped out onto the balcony. She walked to Trevor's side, where she leaned over the rail to view the scene below. That afternoon, the streets of Rome had been quiet and deceptively sedate, but now that the sun was setting, it was as if the Eternal City had been magically transformed.

All the balconies of the mansions and townhouses that ringed the Piazza del Popolo were ablaze with light and adorned with bright-colored banners and tapestries. Carriages decorated with bouquets and ribbons tried to maneuver their way through the packed streets that spiraled out from the Piazza, taking their wealthy passengers to balls and routs at a snail's pace. The square below was packed with princesses and pages, knights and peasants, milkmaids and clowns, all of them boisterous and wild. Musicians played their flutes and accordions. Jugglers, acrobats, and magicians all performed their tricks.

"Oh, look!" she cried and pointed to three hot air balloons that floated high above the city. "I've always wanted to ride in a hot air balloon!"

"Why?" he asked and turned to look at her.

"Because it would be like a view of the world through God's eyes," she answered. "Don't you think so?"

"I've never thought much about it," he answered, still looking at her thoughtfully.

Margaret leaned over the rail, returning her gaze to the plaza below. "What a crowd! It won't be like this all week, surely!"

"During the day, no. Since the festivities continue until dawn, the days are rather quiet."

"Well, one has to sleep sometime, I suppose."

"Exactly. But you'll find this sort of revelry will go on every night until Tuesday evening at eight o'clock, when Lent begins."

She looked over at him. "You talk as if you've seen Carnival before."

"Several times, both in Rome and Venice. I'd have thought that since your father has a villa here, you would also have seen all this before."

She shook her head. "No. Papa only bought the villa a year ago. He came here on business, and when he found out there was a property for sale that had some excellent Roman ruins, he bought it, of course!" She glanced at the man beside her with a

wry smile. "My father is a passionate amateur archae-
ologist."

"Yes, I know. He showed me his project the first
morning I was there."

"Did he?" She laughed. "Bored you to death with
his pottery and mosaics, no doubt."

"Actually, no. He expounded some theories on
Roman technology I found quite interesting." Trevor
turned toward Margaret, studying her with a sudden
intensity that made her acutely aware of how close he
was. "What interests you, Miss Van Alden?"

He asked the question in a voice so low that she
barely heard it. She sensed a deeper meaning behind
his words than simple curiosity. "Oh, I doubt any of
my interests would appeal to you, my lord," she
answered lightly and escaped into the library.

He followed her, closing the balcony doors to muf-
fle the sounds of the tumultuous crowd outside. "No?
I've heard that you have quite a taste for adventure. Is
that so?"

Her steps faltered. The cats had been gossiping
about her again, and she wondered what information
Ashton had given them. Slowly, she turned to face
him. "A man of your rank and position should not
engage in gossip."

"Gossip is often quite useful to a man of my rank
and position." He walked over to the liquor cabinet
and poured himself a glass of port. "But I assure you,
I do not engage in gossip, I simply listen. So fear not,
Margaret," he added over one shoulder as if he could
read what was in her mind. "Your penchant for
romantic midnight rendezvous and your taste in literature are secrets I will take to my grave."

"Must you bring up those things?" she cried. "I
don't wish to discuss them."

"Perhaps not, but I find them interesting and very suggestive. In fact, they confirm what I have been told about you."

"Just what have you been told?" she demanded.

"That you are a very modern young woman who is fond of cigars, wagers, and daring escapades."

She knew the incident to which he referred. "Well, I'm sure it would please you to know that the cigars made me sick, I lost both of the wagers I placed, and my daring escapade into the gentlemen's card room ended with Lord Edgeware making sheep's eyes at me for weeks. It was a very disappointing experience altogether."

Trevor set down his glass and began to walk toward her. "Is it adventures you want, Margaret?" he asked softly. "If so, I can provide them, and I guarantee that you won't find them a disappointment."

She took several steps back as he approached, but the backs of her thighs hit the edge of a sofa table, bringing her to a halt. She froze, watching him warily, and felt as if she were being led into a trap. But she also felt an irresistible desire to know more. "What sort of adventures are you suggesting, my lord?"

"For a start, I was thinking that you might wish to explore the Carnival firsthand, instead of simply watching it from the balcony."

How could he know that was exactly what she wished? Wildly, she wondered if he could somehow read her mind. "Are you offering to be my guide?"

"Yes. Guide, bodyguard, and fellow adventurer. What do you say?"

Suspicious, she reminded herself again that he was probably just another fortune hunter. "What reason could you have for making me such an offer?"

"For the last ten years, I have lived a rather unorthodox life. I have spent my time in adventurous and often dangerous pursuits. Now that I have left that life behind and am back in what you might call civilized society, I find myself bored stiff. Balls and routs may be necessary social demands for an earl, but they can also be quite dull. You seem to share a similar view, and I think both of us would enjoy what I am proposing."

"I see." It sounded reasonable. Nonetheless, she was still wary. "If adventure and excitement are what you seek, wouldn't a man be a better companion for you?"

"Not at all. Men spend a great deal of time in the company of other men. We drink together, we play cards together, and we have all sorts of adventurous escapades. There would be nothing unique in that."

"What would we do?"

"Whatever you like," he promised. "I am at your service."

A quiver of excitement overpowered her suspicion for the moment. He could take her places she would never be able to go otherwise. He could show her things no one else ever could. Even if he were a fortune hunter stalking her, the bait he dangled to tempt her was irresistible. "What you're suggesting is highly improper," she said breathlessly.

"What of it? As long as we are careful, no one will know."

She licked her suddenly dry lips. "My father told me to stay away from you."

"Did he?"

An enigmatic smile curved Trevor's mouth, and he took another step toward her, closing the distance between them. He lifted his hands to cup her face, and the excitement within her grew stronger as his thumbs swept back and forth across her cheeks in a slow caress. She could feel his forearms brush against the sides of her breasts, and her heart began to hammer at the intimate contact. She knew she should reject his offer, push him away, and make a haughty exit, but she could not seem to find the will to move or speak. Instead, she could only stare into his dark blue eyes, mesmerized by the intensity of his gaze and the warmth of his body so close to hers.

"I'm not surprised your father told you to stay away from me." He bent his head until his mouth was an inch from her own. "But we both know you don't always do as you are told."

"That's true," she admitted in a whisper. "I don't."

"Nor do I," he murmured. "It seems we both find forbidden fruit to be the sweetest." His mouth came down on hers, capturing her lips in a kiss that was totally unlike the kiss of a dream lover. There was none of the sweet gentleness she had longed for, none of the chivalry and romance she had imagined. This man was real, and his kiss was something raw and powerful that heated her blood and made her ache.

She clung desperately to the table behind her even as her lips parted beneath the pressure of his. His tongue entered her mouth, tasting deeply of her, and his hands slid down to her waist, pulling her away from the table, forcing her to cling to him instead. Startled, she broke the kiss, managing a feeble protest as she grasped the folds of his heavy doublet and buried her face against his shoulder. But he was not deterred. He tilted his head and continued his explorations, trailing kisses along her throat, tasting her skin.

His teeth grazed her earlobe, and she shivered. She felt his arms wrap around her, crushing her breasts against his chest, imprisoning her body against the hard length of his. She bunched the fabric of his costume more tightly in her fists. "Oh, please," she gasped, her words muffled by the soft velvet. "My lord, you must stop."

"Must I?" he murmured against her ear, his warm breath sending shivers through her. "Why?"

"The door into the hall is wide open. Someone might see us."

"But doesn't that sort of risk make it all the more exciting?" he asked. "Consider this your first adventure with me, an adventure in kissing. Wasn't that what you wanted the first night we met?" His lips brushed the sensitive skin of her ear as he spoke. "Wasn't it?"

"Yes," she confessed in a ragged whisper, shaken by the maelstrom of feelings he was arousing in her. "But the guests will begin arriving at any moment. This has to stop." Even as she spoke, her arms slid up around his neck, and she clung to him.

"You haven't given me an answer." He pulled back and grasped her chin in his fingers, lifting her face to look into her eyes. "Before you decide, know this. I have every intention of using our time together to my advantage."

"What do you mean?"

He brushed his thumb slowly back and forth across her lower lip. "I mean that I intend to seduce you."

Margaret stiffened in his hold, coming out of the sensuous haze, once again cognizant of danger. She tried to pull away, but his arm tightened around her waist, holding her fast. "You presume a great deal, Ashton," she whispered.

"On the contrary, I presume nothing. I am simply telling you my intentions. I see no need to hide them."

He slid one hand to the nape of her neck, and once again she tried to pull away, but he tangled his fingers in the knot of her hair, imprisoning her. He tilted his head and kissed the base of her throat. "I have already told you," she said breathlessly, "I won't marry you."

He began nibbling on her earlobe. "Did I say anything about marriage?"

"No, but I can't think of any other reason why you would say such things."

"Can you not?" He laughed softly, nuzzling her ear. "I can."

Lost in the sensations he was evoking with his hands and his mouth, she could feel reason and control slipping away, and she fought to regain them. She wedged her arms between them. It wasn't much of a barrier, but it was all she could manage when she felt her knees buckling. "Stop," she gasped. "Oh, please, stop."

He immediately pulled back, but he kept one arm around her waist. "Your wish is my command."

She opened her eyes and stared at her hands, which were clenched into fists around the velvet folds of his doublet. She could hear her agitated breathing and the frantic thump of her heart, and she could not think of a single thing to say.

"Well, Maggie?" he asked, breaking the silence. "Will you come out with me for Carnival?"

Margaret looked up at him. Ashton was a rake, a gentleman only in name, and he could very well be a fortune hunter. What he proposed was dangerous and entailed serious risk to her reputation. Yet, even as she considered all the possible ramifications, she knew what her answer would be. Such a chance might never come her way again. Tempted beyond reason, she nodded quickly before she could change her mind. "Yes," she said. "I agree."

"Good. Tomorrow night at the Duchess of Arbuthnot's ball, we'll make our final plans. Reserve a waltz for me." He stepped back and let her go, smiling as he looked at her.

"What are you smiling about?"

"You are a bit mussed," he said, lifting one hand to smooth her hair. "You look like a woman who has been thoroughly and properly kissed."

"Do I?" She pressed her hands to her flushed cheeks and stepped hastily sideways to make her escape, reminding herself again that the door was wide open and anyone could have walked in and seen them.

"Yes, you do," he said as she walked away. "And I can't tell you how pleased I am to be the man responsible."

"Of all the men in the world," she said ruefully, "why did it have to be you?" She paused in the doorway and looked at him over one shoulder, an expression of confusion and desire on her face that made him want to pull her back into his arms and kiss her again. "I don't even *like* you."

"Not yet," he said beneath his breath as he watched her disappear from view. "But you will, sweet Maggie. You will."

Margaret didn't know how she managed to get through the evening and the following day without giving herself away. Every look or smile she received seemed fraught with significance, as if all her acquaintances knew what she planned to do, as if they knew she planned to mingle with the tumultuous crowd in the streets, as if they knew she'd been kissed.

When she thought of that kiss, of the extraordinary feel of Trevor's mouth on hers, all the feeling he had evoked came rushing back. Kissing was quite a heady experience. She hoped the other adventures he promised would prove equally exciting.

I intend to seduce you.

He certainly had the reputation for it, given what her father and the duchess had told her. He had seduced many other women. She knew she would have to be careful, but she wanted excitement, and if last night was any indication, Trevor St. James would be able to give her plenty of it. Control of the situation was in her hands. She would take only as much of what he offered as she desired, and she would give only as much as she wished in return.

Worried, Margaret glanced again around the luxuriant, glittering ballroom as her partner, a stout Italian ambassador, whirled her across the floor in a clumsy waltz. She did not see Trevor's tall, broad-shouldered frame anywhere. Where was he?

By ten o'clock, he had still not arrived. It was not until she had danced another waltz, a quadrille and two reels that he finally made his appearance, just as Edward was leading her out on to the floor.

"Sorry, Kettering," a deep and lazy voice interjected, "but I believe this waltz is mine."

Edward stepped aside, and Margaret breathed a sigh of relief. "Finally," she said as Trevor took her arm and led her to the ballroom floor. "I thought you'd never arrive."

"Miss me?" He pulled her as close as propriety would allow and began to lead her through the dance.

His question was ridiculous, and she shot him a look that told him so. "I was thinking you might have changed your mind."

"Not at all. Have you?"

"Of course not. What delayed you?"

"A charming opera singer named Lili Rossetti. Gorgeous woman, long black hair."

She couldn't suppress her sound of outrage, but the challenging, amused look he gave her was familiar enough now, and she realized that he was having her on. "You are truly a wretched man," she muttered. "Why must you do that?"

His expression changed, and he became as innocent as a schoolboy. "Do what?"

"Tease so."

"Ah, that." He laughed. "Perhaps because you fall for it so easily."

"Well, I won't again," she vowed. "I'm on to you now."

His hand tightened around hers. "I truly hope so, Maggie. Friends should understand each other well."

Before she could point out that they were not friends, he leaned a bit closer and said, "This ball will probably go on until dawn. Think up some excuse to go home early, by midnight at the latest. When you get home, change out of that ball gown and wait one hour to make certain everyone has gone to bed, then meet me in the back garden."

She nodded, tingling with excitement. "What should I wear? Men's clothes?"

He threw back his head and laughed again, loudly enough that several nearby couples glanced their way.

"Ssh," she warned with a nervous glance around. "What did I say that's so funny?"

"Men's clothes? Really, Maggie." He shook his

head, still smiling. His thick black lashes lowered, and his gaze swept downward, lingering on the low neckline of her gown. "I doubt you would fool anyone."

"Oh." She realized what he meant and felt hot color rush to her cheeks. "What should I wear then?" she asked as the waltz ended.

"Something sensible and comfortable. Can you fashion some sort of peasant costume? A shirtwaist, skirt and shawl ought to do it, with low-heeled boots."

"I think I can come up with something like that."

"Good." He took her back to Edward and Cornelia, who stood near the punch table with several of their friends. He released her arm and lifted her hand. "And for God's sake," he added in a whisper, "if you must wear a corset, don't lace it too tight. I'll not have you fainting if we have to climb walls or run through dark alleys."

He pressed a quick kiss to her fingertips and walked away, leaving the interested observers around them to speculate on what the Earl of Ashton had been saying to make Miss Van Alden blush twice during one waltz.

6

Trevor stood beside the garden wall, waiting. Though the night was dark, it was far from silent. The high stone walls that surrounded the back gardens of the townhouse did little to subdue the wild revelry of Carnival. Margaret would see many fascinating things during the next few nights, and Trevor was looking forward to seeing her reaction to the spectacle.

He thought of the evening before. He hadn't planned to kiss her so soon, but he'd seen the curiosity and awakening desire in her eyes, and the temptation had been irresistible.

He could still smell the tangy fragrance of lemon soap that clung to her skin and feel her body in his arms. He could still savor the sweetness of her mouth beneath his and feel the unexpected jolt of pure lust that had rocked him at that first taste of her. Desire flared inside him again at the memory of it.

He drew a deep breath and let it out slowly. Her passionate response to his kiss had been far more than he'd expected, and if he had chosen to take it further, he could have. But he knew that, for her, kissing was an experiment, and a few stolen kisses would not be enough to win her hand. Seducing Margaret into matrimony would require strategy, patience, and control. He could not afford to lose his heiress by moving too fast. He would make her wait for his kisses, anticipate them, long for them. That was part of the game.

A flash of white caught his attention, and he watched Margaret slip out the back door. She came toward him, her form only a dim outline in the moonlight. As she approached, he could see that she had taken his instructions to heart. She was wearing the plain white blouse, dull red skirt, and yellow straw bonnet of an Italian peasant girl. Her hair was caught back in a long braid and a coarse brown shawl was draped over her shoulders. Caught in the belt at her waist was a small, drawstring purse.

"Will I suit?" she asked as she adjusted her bonnet. "I had to borrow these clothes from one of the maids. She's the daughter of a farmer, I believe."

"I hope she doesn't know what you wanted them for," Trevor answered, opening the door of the back gate and leading her into the alley.

"Oh, no. She thinks I want to copy them for a costume." She glanced at the rough linsey-woolsey trousers and shirt he wore and gave a nod of approval. "We look quite like Neapolitan peasants, don't we?"

"Hiring a carriage is one thing, but if you want to walk the streets of Carnival, it's best to dress for comfort." Trevor closed the gate and took her arm, leading her down the alley toward one of the side streets that led into the Piazza del Popolo. "Did you have any trouble getting away from the ball?"

"Oh, no," she answered, falling in step beside him. "In fact, Edward developed a headache shortly after you left and saved me the trouble of an excuse to leave. A fortunate coincidence."

Trevor smiled to himself. Good old Edward. After this week, they'd be even on that episode from Eton. "Yes," he said. "Very fortunate."

"What are we going to do?"

"I told you I'm at your service. I thought tonight we'd just take a stroll around the plaza and stop for whatever piques your interest."

During the next two hours, Margaret found many things interesting, and Trevor found himself stopping every few minutes. The puppeteers and musicians charmed her, the rope dancers and fire eaters entranced her, and the organ grinder's tiny monkey in his red velvet suit amused her with his antics. Beneath the gas light of a street lamp, Trevor watched her place a soda wafer on the animal's nose. Margaret laughed with the uninhibited delight of a child when the monkey tossed his head, flipping the tidbit into the air then catching it in his mouth.

She had a nice laugh, merry and unrestrained, not like the twittering giggles women usually uttered, and he enjoyed the sound of it. Hearing her laughter made him want to pull her into his arms and kiss her again, turning that amusement into passion, but this was not the time or place.

Soon, he promised himself. Not tonight, but soon.

She accepted a carnation from the organ grinder, who placed a smacking kiss on each of her cheeks and lauded her beauty and charm with typical Italian hyperbole. But the man's admiring gaze lingered far too hungrily on the round neckline of her blouse and the voluptuous figure beneath it. Trevor scowled, and in a gesture of possessiveness that was totally uncharacteristic of him, stepped forward to take her arm. Once they were married, he decided, she was going to have a whole new wardrobe—with matronly dresses that buttoned up to her chin.

"Must you pull me along like a child's string toy?" she said as he led her away. "Are you in a hurry to get somewhere?"

Realizing he was practically hauling her across the plaza, Trevor took a deep breath and slowed his pace, astonished by the violent surge of feeling that had somehow caught hold of him. "The acrobats will be performing quite soon," he answered. "I don't want you to miss it."

"There's plenty of time," she pointed out, gesturing toward the stage they were approaching. "Look, they're just beginning to set up their equipment."

He led her to a place near the stage that gave an excellent view of the acrobats, but before the performance started loud and furious shouting began just behind Trevor and Margaret. Both of them turned around in time to see a tall, lean man dressed as Mephistopheles toss aside his grotesque mask, yank off his long black cloak, and let fly with a punch that knocked a man costumed as an Apache back into the crowd.

Margaret gave a cry of surprise. "A fist fight!" she exclaimed. "Oh, how exciting!"

Trevor, who knew the purpose of their outings was adventure, allowed her to watch the two men for a moment. But when he felt the crowd begin to change and saw other hot Italian tempers start flaring, he began pulling her back from the melee. "C'mon, let's get out of here."

"Oh, but I want to watch!" she cried, resisting his efforts to get her out of the way.

"Absolutely not," he said as he hauled her inexorably backward, knowing he had to get her out of here before things got out of hand.

Margaret, however, did not share his concern. "But I've never seen anything like this before," she shot back, struggling in earnest against his hold and slowing their departure. "I don't want to miss it."

The words were barely out of Margaret's mouth when the man in front of her slammed his fist into the face of his companion. At that moment, all hell suddenly broke loose around them. Curses and fists began flying.

Bloody hell, he thought, frustrated by her unexpected resistance, resistance which delayed his intention of a quick and safe departure. Visions of Margaret being hurt by the now-violent crowd flashed through his mind, and with that came the realization that he could kiss his four hundred thousand pounds good-bye, along with his life, if her father found out he had taken her out for midnight escapades.

"No time to argue!" he shouted at her. He turned her around to face him, then lifted her off the ground, throwing her over his shoulder like a sack of potatoes. "For God's sake, keep your head down!" he added as he began shoving his way through the crowd. He deftly sidestepped two punches aimed at his head and finally got her safely out of the fray.

Once they were on an empty side street, he set her down—none too gently. "Are you out of your mind, woman?" he shouted. "When á fight starts like that, the only sensible thing to do is get out of the way as quickly as possible!"

"I didn't expect the crowd to turn like that," she confessed in a slightly shaky voice. "It all happened so fast."

"If we're going to have any adventures in the future, I expect you to follow my orders. Damn it, Margaret, you could have been hurt."

"You're right, of course," she said mildly. Then she suddenly lifted her head to look at him, and the light of the street lamp over their heads revealed the wide smile on her face and the definite sparkle in her eyes. "But I must say, Trevor, it was the most exciting thing I've ever experienced."

"I suppose that was the goal this evening," he conceded. "Excitement and adventure."

"Yes, indeed. There are so many things I want to see, and I can't help but wonder what other adventures we shall have along the way."

Trevor did not want to think about that just now. "It's late. I think it's time to take you home."

He took her arm, and they began walking back toward Edward's townhouse. "So tell me," he said as they strolled through the crowd, "how does a young woman of good family develop such a thirst for adventure that she finds street brawls so interesting?"

"I read a lot," Margaret answered, laughing.

"So I've noticed."

That reference to the afternoon he'd caught her reading a forbidden novel caused her to give him an exasperated jab in the ribs with her elbow. "When I was a little girl, I spent a great deal of time alone. My mother died when I was three, and my father was often away on business while I was growing up. I was quite shy."

"Shy?" He gave her a doubtful glance. "I don't

believe that for a moment. Whenever I think of you, shy is definitely not the word that comes to mind."

"Nonetheless, it's true. I was—" She did not finish whatever she'd been about to say.

Curious, he prompted her. "Go on. You were . . ."

She took a deep breath. "I was chubby when I was little, and other girls teased me about it. It was very painful for me."

He recalled the malicious comments Lady Lytton had made that afternoon at tea, and he could see how comments like that could hurt a vulnerable little girl. He once again felt a surge of hot, protective anger. But he merely said, "I can understand how that might hurt."

"Anyway, the point is that I spent a great deal of time alone, reading. I loved books like *The Three Musketeers* and *The Last of the Mohicans*. I always thought d'Artagnan and Hawkeye had much more exciting lives than mine!"

"Most girls would have preferred Jane Austen and Charlotte Brontë."

"I read them, too. In fact, I read anything I could get my hands on. Classics, dime novels, serial papers, anything. It was my escape."

"Escape?" He glanced at her. "What a curious word to use. What do you mean?"

"I imagine it would be hard for a man to understand, but a girl's life is very restricted. We grow up with nothing more challenging to our minds than which bonnet to wear with which dress, and which color of thread to use when we embroider our handkerchiefs. Our exercise usually consists of walking back and forth with books balanced on our heads or cutting and arranging flowers. By the time I was sixteen, I knew that I could never be satisfied with such mundane activities, much to the dismay of my governesses."

"Governesses? How many did you have?"

She shot him a rueful glance. "Seven."

"Seven!"

"Well, six, actually. Mrs. Horton came when I was thirteen, but she only lasted a week. I don't think she counts. When I was seventeen, my father finally gave up on governesses altogether, thank goodness."

"You only say that because without a governess you were then free to do what you wanted," he guessed.

"Of course," she admitted, laughing. "But I really wouldn't have minded having a governess if any of them had taught me anything useful. Of what use is balancing books on your head? It all seemed very silly to me. But they all said young ladies did not learn things like biology and geometry."

"I know most English girls lead very sheltered lives, but I have heard that in America girls are given a much more liberal education, and are more free to express themselves."

"That is true, to a point. But the limits are still too strict for me. For example, after I read *The Three Musketeers*, I wanted to learn how to fence. I was fifteen. My governess at the time was English. She was very stuffy and very proper, and she was horrified by the idea. She absolutely forbid it."

He laughed, and Margaret joined him. "Why do I get the feeling that is not the end of the story?" Trevor asked.

"The next time my father came home, I convinced him there was nothing wrong with a girl learning to fence. I pointed out that it was a noble and graceful sport, steeped in fine tradition, and since I'd already paid for the lessons out of my allowance . . ." She gave him an amused glance. "My father hates to waste money."

"So you got your way and learned how to fence. Are you any good?"

"Not bad, I must admit. Although I've only fenced with other women, most of whom are less practiced at the sport than I, so it's hard to tell."

"We'll have to fence some time, and see how good you are."

She stopped walking and turned toward him, her face shining with pleasure, genuine pleasure, with none of the affected coyness another woman might have displayed. "Really?" she asked. "Do you mean it?"

Trevor was astonished by her reaction. He'd only made the offer because it was another opportunity to be with her, another step toward furthering his goal. Yet, she was looking at him as if he'd just offered her the Crown Jewels. He looked away, feeling uneasy. If he had a conscience, he might have called the feeling guilt. "I wouldn't have made the offer if I didn't mean it," he said in an offhand manner and pushed his momentary uneasiness aside. If she wanted to take such pleasure in something so trivial, that was all to the good.

He resumed walking. "This conversation is making me understand something that Lady Agnes told me about you."

"Agnes has been telling you about me?" she asked, falling in step beside him. "What did she say?"

"She said—with admiration, I might add—that you were a very modern young lady, and you have very modern views. I am beginning to understand just what she meant by that."

"Oh, I'm a quite a sensation among Cornelia's English friends, I know."

"Most American girls are. You do things no English girl would dream of doing."

"What is true of most American girls is doubly true for me, I'm afraid. I've always been rather a rebel. Tell me I can't do something, and I will always find a way to do it."

He knew he could not allow her to be that way with him. He said nothing more until they reached the back garden of the townhouse. Once inside the gates, he decided to make it clear who was in charge of their midnight outings. "Margaret, before I agree to any more escapades, I will have your word that from now on, when I give you an order, you'll follow it."

She started to speak, but he interrupted her. "You won't waste time arguing with me. You'll do what I say without question. Don't get the idea that I'm bluffing, or that you'll be able to get around me. I'm not your father to be cajoled or maneuvered."

She was clearly displeased with his choice of words, but she did not argue with him. She seemed to appreciate that he meant what he said. She bit her lip and did not answer for a long moment. He sensed the internal battle she was fighting, and he waited patiently, knowing he would win in the end. She was not a woman to easily surrender control or put her trust in another, but her desire to go out with him overcame this. She surrendered. "Very well. You have my word."

"Good. Tomorrow night, I think we should go back and see the acrobats, since we missed them this evening. They really are good."

"That would be nice, but Trevor, I doubt Chinese

acrobats could be as thrilling as what we experienced tonight."

"Don't be too sure of that. I'm sure many more exciting surprises lay ahead."

"I'm convinced you will be able to handle whatever happens." She gazed up at him in admiration, and he found that look quite a gratifying reward after what they had been through. "The way you spirited me out of that street brawl was quite heroic," she went on. "Really, I don't think I could have found a better companion for midnight adventuring had I planned it. How fortunate that we met."

She thought him heroic? An unexpected bonus, and one he was quick to take advantage of. "As to that, you have my complete agreement," he murmured, and took both her hands in his. "I, too, am glad we met. Especially at moments like this, when I have the chance to be alone with you."

Margaret wasn't certain she wanted to be alone with him, however. His disturbing words of the other night still echoed through her mind.

I intend to seduce you.

A dangerous game with a dangerous man, and now that the time had come to play it, she wasn't certain she wanted to do so. She'd thought control of the situation was in her hands, but Trevor was not a man to be managed or maneuvered to her wishes. She started to pull her hands away, but he only released one. He lifted the other to his lips. "Don't run away, Maggie," he murmured against her knuckles.

"I wasn't running away."

"No?" He turned her hand over and pressed a kiss to her palm, then looked up at her as he caressed the tender skin on the inside of her wrist. "Good. I was hoping we could tarry here a few moments," he murmured. He felt her hand tremble within his, and he pulled gently to bring her closer, expecting her to come into his arms.

But she did not react as he'd expected. She pulled her hand free, gave him a skeptical frown and folded her arms beneath her breasts, clearly unaware of how the gesture accentuated her generous curves. She was such an intriguing combination, with the romantic ideals of a schoolgirl and the cynicism of a jade. And the body of a goddess, he added to himself, his gaze lingering on the shadowy cleft of her cleavage.

"What exactly are your intentions, my lord?" she asked.

He leaned back against the wall of the garden. "I thought I had been perfectly clear on that point the other night in the library."

Even in the moonlight, he could see her blush. "You said you were going to seduce me."

"And you think that a vague statement?"

"I don't know what to think," she confessed with such clear bewilderment, he almost felt sorry for her. "I am not accustomed to such shocking proposals."

"No, you're used to much more honorable ones, I'm sure," he said, smiling at her. "From men who get down on bended knee and stammer out how fond they are of you before they offer you marriage."

"What I am used to," she said in a hard voice, "is men who look at me with dollar signs in their eyes."

He straightened away from the wall and reached out to grasp her chin in his fingers, lifting her face to study her beneath the light of the moon over their heads. "You underestimate yourself," he said, sliding his hand to the side of her face to caress her cheek. "A man would have to be an idiot if he didn't look at you with better eyes than that."

She quivered slightly beneath the light touch of his fingers. "And when you look at me, my lord, what do you see?" she asked.

He didn't answer for a moment, as if giving her question serious consideration. Finally, he said, "I see a woman who would make a man an excellent mistress, but a difficult wife."

She caught her breath. "Is that your goal then, Ashton?" she asked bluntly. "To make me your mistress?"

His hand curved around the back of her neck, and he drew her toward him. "You must know that I want you," he murmured. "I will do whatever it takes to have you."

Her hands flattened against his chest. "You don't mince words, do you?"

"Should I? You don't seem a delicate flower that would faint away at the idea of a man's desire for you."

"And your desire for me has nothing to do with my money, I suppose?"

His arms tightened around her, and he laughed low in his throat. "And you tell me I make shocking proposals? Maggie, I know there are women who pay men for their services, but no woman has ever offered to pay me before. I don't know whether to be flattered or insulted."

She stared up at him in shock. "That isn't what I meant at all!" she gasped. "You are outrageous!"

"Yes, well, that's probably a good thing. If I were just another humdrum English gentleman, you'd toss me aside without a second thought, and I'd never have the chance to do this." He captured her lips in a fierce, hard kiss, expecting a token resistance, but, again, she did not do what he expected. This time, she yielded immediately, opening her mouth beneath the pressure of his as she slid her arms around his neck.

Her sweet response started a fire inside him like a match to tinder. He ran his hand up her ribs to rest just beneath her breast. He slid his tongue along her lower lip, then between her teeth, tasting her.

She arched in his hold, an instinctive move that beckoned him and sent all thoughts of restraint spinning out of his mind. He pushed her back against the evergreen bougainvillea vines that covered the garden wall. He plundered her mouth with his tongue and leaned into her, but it was too much.

She turned her head aside with a startled gasp, breaking the kiss. He knew he had moved too fast. He had to stop.

Slowly, he pulled back, striving for control. Trevor looked down at her, his gaze roaming possessively over her face. He could see the trembling of her lip, hear her soft little gasps for breath, and feel the hammering of her heart against his hand. He was more pleased by her response than he had ever been by a woman's passion.

"Now do you understand my intentions?" he asked softly, running one finger down her soft, round cheek. He felt her shiver, and she looked up at him with an expression of vulnerability on her face.

"So," she whispered in an uncertain voice, "you are only interested in me, not my money?"

He lowered his head to press a kiss against her throat. "Maggie, right now, I'm only interested in one thing," he said with complete honesty, "and it isn't your money, I assure you."

He felt her relax in his hold with a little sigh and lean toward him as if inviting another kiss. But as much as he wanted her, as much as he wanted to linger here and sample more of what she would one day give him freely, he knew he could not. If he was to eventually win her, he always had to leave her slightly dissatisfied, wanting more. Patience, he reminded himself and reluctantly pulled away.

"It's nearly dawn," he said. "And I'd best take my leave. If we stay out here much longer, it's going to be light enough for someone to see us."

"You're right, of course," she answered stiffly, stepping back out of his arms.

"I'll see you tomorrow." Trevor grasped her hand and kissed it quickly, then left. He hoped he had left her aching with the same hot need he was feeling. If he was going to suffer the torture of unrequited lust, then by God, so was she.

7

The following night, Trevor was late. Margaret stood by the garden wall, fidgeting and trying not to be impatient. He was probably having some difficulty getting away from Lady Lytton's ball.

Lady Sally had spent most of the evening clinging possessively to his arm, and Margaret felt renewed irritation at the way he had tolerated the other woman's clearly desperate attentions. Really, the lengths to which some women would go to obtain a husband.

He had made no effort to avoid Lady Sally. In fact, he had danced with her three times. Margaret was not the only one who had noticed. Several other people had commented on it, some speculating that an engagement might be in the making. Others, more cynical, had disagreed, saying that Lord Lytton would never agree to such a match since he was quite short in the pocket himself and an alliance with Ashton would gain him nothing.

Margaret wondered again just what Trevor St. James was all about. Her first conclusion had been that he was another fortune hunter out to marry her for her money. But then he'd claimed he wanted to seduce her, not marry her. She thought again of the unswerving attention he'd given Lady Sally all evening, and she felt rather annoyed. If seducing her was his aim, he wasn't showing much enthusiasm about it. He hadn't given her more than a passing glance all evening.

Above the sounds of Carnival, she heard the church clock strike half past twelve and she shifted her weight restlessly from one foot to the other, wishing Trevor would give Lady Sally short shrift and be on his way. They were missing all the fun.

The squeaking of the gate drew her attention, and Margaret watched as Trevor slipped inside the garden. She gave a sigh of relief. "I was beginning to think you weren't coming tonight."

"I had a devil of a time getting away from Lady Lytton's."

"So I noticed."

"Did you now?" he drawled. "Margaret, I'm flattered you pay so much attention to my choice of feminine companionship."

"Don't you think you have enough to do this evening, without taking time for dalliance with Lady Sally?" The moment the words were out of her mouth, she saw that teasing expression in his eyes, and she wanted to bite off her tongue. She sounded jealous, and, of course, that was not how she felt at all. Carnival would only last a week, and she did not want to waste precious time.

Trevor, however, did not seem to notice the tartness of her question. "Lady Sally is a lovely and charming girl, but she has notions of a far more permanent liaison with me than mere dalliance."

His words paralleled her own suspicions about Sally. Nonetheless, Margaret could not help saying, "You presume a great deal, my lord. Not all women wish to obtain husbands. Suppose Lady Sally only wishes to engage in a bit of harmless flirtation with you and nothing more?"

"I doubt it. Where unmarried women are concerned, flirtation is never harmless. There is always a price attached, a price that usually includes a wedding band." Before she could point out that she was an unmarried woman who definitely had no such expectations, he added, "I'm inclined to think Lady Sally will find herself quite disappointed."

"Why is that?"

"I'm not certain I wish to sacrifice my freedom just yet. The pleasures of bachelorhood still hold a great deal of appeal for me."

She shook her head in disbelief. "Poor Sally. I think my father was right about you. Where women are concerned, you really are a callous devil."

"That doesn't seem to bother you."

"That's because I have no designs on marrying a title."

He paused in the act of opening the gate and smiled at her, placing a hand over his heart. "You wound me, Margaret. I assure you that I have more to offer a woman than simply my name and title. Although you made it clear to me shortly after we met that you have no desire to marry me, there are many women who would be delighted at the prospect."

"Ah," she said with a nod. "Not only callous, but arrogant and conceited as well." She slipped through the gate and waited while he closed it behind them.

"So, why have none succeeded in that aim?" she asked when he turned to her and took her arm to lead her out of the alley.

"I have never been the marrying kind."

"I thought an earl had to marry."

"It is definitely expected. But I've only been an earl a short time. Besides, why should I rush into matrimony, an obligation that is confining, difficult, and expensive?"

"For an heir, perhaps?"

"There is that," he said, nodding. "But is it worth giving up my freedom?"

"Is freedom so important to a man, then?"

"Of course. Is it not important to you? You said not all women wish to obtain husbands. Did it never occur to you that there are some men who do not wish to obtain wives?"

"Frankly, no," she confessed. "I don't know why, but I've never thought of it that way."

"Perhaps it's because you've never had the opportunity to talk to a man about the subject," he suggested.

"Perhaps." She smiled at him. "It really is quite fascinating to have a man's honest point of view on things. I'm glad we can talk like this."

"So am I, Margaret," he assured her solemnly. "So am I."

They strolled through the plaza, where they watched the fireworks, ate ice cream, and peered in the windows of the shops. Most of the stores were still open to take advantage of the tourist trade during the festival. When they passed a jeweler's, something in the window caught Trevor's attention, and when they had walked several feet past it, he suddenly stopped. "Wait here. I'll be right back."

He retraced his steps to the jeweler's and went inside, leaving Margaret standing on the sidewalk, staring after him in bewilderment. When he returned, he carried a small box in his hand, which he presented to her with a gallant bow.

"What's this?" she asked, taking the box.

"It's a present, a token of our midnight adventures. Not the most expensive or beautiful piece of jewelry you own, I'm sure, but it reminded me of you."

"Thank you." She opened the box and found the small silver charm in the shape of a violin that was nestled in a bed of blue velvet.

"I know you're rather unconventional, but I hope you have a charm bracelet."

"As a matter of fact, I do." She looked at him in bewilderment. "Why does a violin remind you of me?" she asked. "I don't play."

He smiled. "I'll tell you why—someday."

Margaret did not look at all satisfied by that answer, but that was fine with him. Keeping her intrigued was another part of the game. She asked him several more times why a violin reminded him of her, but when her repeated question elicited no response except a smile, she finally gave up and tucked the tiny box in her purse.

They walked to the center of the Plaza and watched the Chinese acrobats. "That was amazing," she said as they resumed their stroll after the show was over. "How on earth did he manage to stand on his head and juggle those balls with his feet?" she asked, stepping around a pair of men dressed like dominoes. "I've never seen anything like that before."

Before Trevor could comment, she noticed a tavern and came to a halt. "Oh, look. Can we go inside?"

"Absolutely not. Only one kind of woman goes into

a place like that, and you are not that kind of woman."

"Oh, for heaven's sake, Trevor! You sound like my father."

She started toward the front door, but Trevor caught her firmly by the arm. "No. I'm not taking you in there."

Margaret tried to pull free of his grasp, but she was no match for his superior strength. "This is my adventure, remember? You said you would take me wherever I wanted to go. Well, I want to go in there."

"You won't like it, Maggie. Trust me."

"I think I'm the best judge of what I like and don't like. I may never have another chance like this."

"You don't have the chance now. We're not going in there. I have no intention of getting into a knife fight with some drunken sod who thinks you might be fair game."

"These midnight outings were your suggestion," she pointed out. "You said you would be my guide and bodyguard, that you would stop for whatever I wanted to see."

When she attempted again to free herself from his hold, he only tightened his grip and pulled her hard against his chest, wrapping his other arm around her waist to keep her there. "I said no, and unless you want to create a public scene, I suggest you stop arguing with me."

He was holding her so close that the people passing by on the crowded street were giving them curious looks. Once again, Margaret got the uneasy feeling that beneath the surface charm, Trevor St. James was a man she could not bend to her will.

She shook her head at him in disapproval. "I never

would have thought you to be such a high-minded puritan, Trevor."

"That's one of the reasons I find you so fascinating," he answered smoothly. "Your unique point of view. No other woman of my acquaintance has ever described me as either high-minded or puritan."

She opened her mouth to add that he was also being unreasonable and tyrannical, but his words diverted her attention, and she forgot entirely what she'd been about to say. "Do you really think I'm fascinating?" she asked, unable to stop herself.

"Yes, I do." Before she could appreciate the warm little tingle of pleasure that confession evoked, he added, "I also think you are a woman whose father has indulged her far too freely."

The pleasurable feeling evaporated. "Are you saying I'm spoiled?"

"That sums it up pretty well."

"Well, of all the nerve! First of all, I don't care what you think. And second, you promised me—"

Her words were interrupted by the shuffling approach of a dirty, bearded man in a yellow cloak who pleadingly held out his hand and mumbled something in Italian.

Margaret looked into his watery eyes and felt an immediate stab of pity. "Of course," she said and reached for the purse tucked into her belt.

"Margaret, I don't think you should—" Trevor began, but his cautionary words were cut short when the man grabbed the purse and dashed down the street.

"Oh, no!" she cried, watching the thief run away. "He's got the charm you gave me."

"Stay here," Trevor ordered and went in pursuit of the thief. Margaret was in a quandary. She started to

follow, then stopped, remembering she was supposed
to obey his orders in situations like this.

But she might be missing out on an exciting adventure. Biting her lip in uncertainty, she watched Trevor
and the thief disappear around the corner.

What if Trevor got into trouble and needed help?
With that in mind, she sprinted after them.

She followed the pair through Rome's narrow,
twisting side streets, but soon lost track of the two
men. Worried about Trevor, hopelessly lost, and
uncertain about what to do, Margaret hesitated. But
before she could decide what action to take, she
heard footsteps, and Trevor reappeared out of a
side alley. He muttered a curse at the sight of her
and slowed down long enough to grab her hand in
his. Then he began running once again, dragging
her with him. "C'mon!" he shouted. "Let's get out
of here."

She heard more footsteps behind them and realized
they were being chased. Two men were following
them. Trevor led her down another street and into a
dark alley, but a brick wall blocked the opposite end,
cutting off any chance of escape. Their pursuers came
closer, and Trevor pulled her down behind an enormous pile of garbage to shield both of them from view.
The foul smell made her nauseous, and she pressed
one hand over her nose and mouth.

"What happened?" she whispered behind her
hand. "How—"

"Ssh," he interrupted. "Quiet."

Both of them waited, tense and silent, as the two
men halted just beyond the entrance to their hiding
place. They began speaking in furious Italian, obviously arguing.

"Englishman?" one of the thieves called out. "We

know you are here. You might as well come out and face us."

"Hell," Trevor muttered with a heavy sigh. "For God's sake, don't move," he added to her.

"Trevor, don't," she pleaded as he started to rise.

"At this point, I don't have a choice. They're drunk and looking for a fight." He stepped out of their hiding place to face the two men.

He took several cautious steps forward, disappearing from her view. Margaret heard a scuffle and stood up, unable to stand the suspense. She watched, her heart in her throat, as Trevor ducked the blow aimed at his head by the man in the yellow cloak. He then let fly with two hard punches, hitting the thief first in the solar plexus, then beneath the jaw. The second blow sent the thief sprawling backward, and the back of his head hit the brick wall with a sickening thud. He slid down to the ground, where he lay unmoving.

But Trevor had no chance to enjoy his victory. He turned just as the second man swung at him. There was no time to duck, and the thief's fist slammed into into his check. Trevor staggered back, stunned by the blow.

Margaret gave a cry of alarm. Hoping she could come to his aid, she looked frantically around for some kind of weapon. She spied a piece of wood sticking out of the garbage pile beside her. She grabbed it with her hands like a baseball bat and stepped out of her hiding place just as the thief pulled back his arm to hit Trevor again. Without thinking, she smashed the stick over the man's head.

The piece of wood snapped in half, but the damage was done. Trevor jumped out of the way as the thief fell forward onto the cobblestones, unconscious.

Still holding the broken stick in her hands, she

looked up at Trevor over the thief's inert body and gave a shaky half-laugh of disbelief. "Dear God," she gasped, stunned by what she had just done. "I hit him."

A feeling of triumph swept over her, a feeling so intense, so euphoric, that it made her dizzy. For the first time in her sheltered life, Margaret felt as if she'd done something important, something truly worthwhile. "Trevor, I did it."

If she expected praise, she was disappointed. "Let's get out of here," he said and stepped over the thief to take the stick from her grasp. Tossing it aside, he grabbed her hand and started out of the alley. It wasn't until they had once again merged into the tumultuous crowd in the plaza that he slowed his pace and finally came to a halt.

Breathing hard, Margaret stopped beside him. "Thank goodness," she gasped. "Are you hurt?" She looked up at him and saw the bruise already forming on his cheek. She reached up to touch his face, but he pushed her hand away. "You are hurt!"

"It's no more than I deserve for trying to play the hero. I should have known better." He touched his throbbing cheek. "And I thought I told you to stay by the tavern."

"I thought you might need some help."

"What if he'd seen you behind him in that alley? He could have grabbed you and used you as leverage to make an escape."

"I didn't stop to think about that," she admitted. "Anyway, he didn't get the chance." Trevor continued to glower at her, and she said, "I wouldn't change a thing. It was so exciting!"

He let out an exasperated breath and reached into his pocket. Pulling out her purse, he took her by the wrist with his free hand and slapped the small leather bag into her palm. "From now on, leave your money at home."

"I will," she vowed. "I swear."

"Don't make any promises unless you're going to keep them, Maggie," he muttered and turned away. He began walking back toward Edward's townhouse. Margaret fell in step beside him. During the short walk, he said nothing, and she found his silence unnerving.

When they reached Edward's garden, Trevor did not linger with her as he had the night before. "It's getting late," he said tersely. "You'd best go in."

He turned to leave, and she knew she couldn't let him go without giving him an apology.

"I'm sorry if you're angry with me," she burst out. "But I was only trying to help."

He paused with his hand on the gate. "I know."

"It's just that I've never come to anyone's rescue before. It may seem silly to you, but for the first time in my life, I feel as if I've done something truly worthwhile."

He looked over at her and studied her for a long moment. "I suppose that makes sense," he allowed, "in a crazy kind of way. But that isn't really the point, is it?"

She bit her lip and stared down at the grass beneath her feet. "No, I suppose not."

Trevor walked over to her and reached beneath her chin to lift her face. "If anything like this happens again, stay out of the way and let me handle it. I'm supposed to be *your* bodyguard, remember?" His hand slid to her cheek. "You could have been hurt."

He felt the change in her, a sudden expectancy. She moved closer, looking up at him in clear anticipation of a kiss.

Patience, he reminded himself, and did not give her the sort of kiss she was silently asking for. Instead, he pressed his lips to her forehead and said, "You must go in."

"It isn't that late," she pointed out, a note of consternation in her voice that made him want to smile.

"Late enough. I have a business matter to attend to."

"Business? At this hour?"

"Some of the business I do involves skulking about in the wee small hours."

"It sounds wickedly intriguing, and I suspect there are Egyptian artifacts involved. Can I come with you?"

"I'm afraid not. This sort of adventure is best done alone."

Her face fell. "Won't you tell me what you're up to?" When he shook his head again, she added hopefully, "Not even a hint?"

"No."

She placed her hands on her hips and sighed. "Do you realize that I find you the most exasperating man I've ever met?"

"I'm quite gratified to hear that." He disappeared amidst the dark shrubbery of the garden, leaving her to wonder exactly what he meant by that enigmatic comment.

The tavern was dark, lit only by a few small lamps and filled with the thick, blue haze of cigar smoke. It was also crowded, and it took Trevor several moments to find the man he sought. When their eyes met, the muscular Italian seated at a table in the corner gave a slight nod and gestured to the empty chair opposite his. Trevor approached the table and took the offered seat.

"You're late," the man said.

"I was unavoidably detained." Trevor reached for the bottle of wine on the table and poured himself a glass.

"Ah, yes. I saw the lady. I suppose I must forgive you. With such a bountiful figure, she could pass for an Italian woman at a distance. I admire your taste in women, my friend, but she is not what I would have expected of an Englishman. Most of your English ladies are far too thin."

"She's not English," Trevor answered, ignoring the other man's baiting smile. "Following me, Emilio? Sending notes demanding secret meetings? What is all this?"

"I heard you were in Rome and I decided to renew our acquaintance. I thought you might need some help."

"Help with what?"

"I heard from some of our friends in Cairo that Lucci is looking for you," Emilio answered.

"Is he?" Trevor was not surprised. "What else have you heard?"

"You stole a valuable Egyptian necklace from him, I believe."

"Lucci stole it from me first."

Emilio sighed and shook his head. "That was not wise, my friend. You know how ruthless Lucci can be. He'd kill you without a second thought."

Trevor shrugged and took a sip of wine. "He never has before. Besides, I fail to see your concern in this matter."

Emilio gave him an injured look. "After all we've been through over the years, you expect me to stand by and do nothing when I hear that your life is in danger?"

Trevor flashed the other man a sardonic grin.

"Spare me the pretended concern and tell me the truth."

"As I said, I heard you were in Rome. I also heard that you are retiring from the business."

"My, my, news does travel fast." He leaned back, studying the man across the table. "C'mon, Emilio. What are you after?"

"You have many contacts, my friend, contacts that would be very valuable to me. I was hoping—"

"You want the names of my buyers," Trevor finished for him.

"They are of little use to you now. An English earl does not smuggle antiquities. Besides, with your contacts added to mine, I would run Lucci out of business, and that would please you enormously, I'm sure."

"You expect that to be a good enough reason for me to give them to you?"

"Not give," Emilio corrected. "I am prepared to pay for them."

"Well, that's a first. How much?"

"That depends on what we decide they are worth. Why don't you give me a price?"

Trevor wasn't prepared to move that fast. He hadn't thought of selling his list, and he wanted time to decide how much it was worth. He drained the wine in his glass and shoved back his chair. "I'll think about it and let you know."

"When?"

"When I've made a decision."

With that, he rose to his feet and departed, leaving Emilio to finish the bottle of wine alone.

8

"*How noble, how chivalrous* of you!" Lady Sally declared, gazing with fervent admiration at the handsome man standing before her. "Coming to the rescue of a poor, defenseless woman. Facing down those two thieves in a dark alley all alone. Why, Lord Ashton, you are truly the bravest man I've ever met."

And the English say we Americans gush too much, Margaret thought. She glanced at Trevor, who was accepting the fulsome praise with a nonchalance that only served to increase her annoyance.

He was smiling at the petite and delicate blonde, who had no idea just how ridiculous she looked with that rapturous expression on her face. Her pale lashes were fluttering so rapidly, Margaret wanted to ask if she had something in her eye.

"It was nothing, really," Trevor said in an attempt at modesty that Margaret thought wouldn't fool anyone.

"Come now," Edward interjected, giving him an approving slap on the back. "Lady Sally is quite right. That was a very brave thing you did, saving a peasant woman's purse and getting a black eye for your trouble. It was probably all the money she had in the world."

Trevor shook his head in a dismissive way and, to Margaret's relief, changed the subject. "So, Lord Lytton, tell me, when you take up your seat in the House this June, what do you think will be the ramifications of last year's Land Act?"

The conversation switched to politics, and Margaret turned away, murmuring something about refilling her glass. Talk of the Land Act would lead to talk of cheap American wheat and how the Americans were to blame for British economic woes. She was in no mood to hear it.

As she made her way to the punch table, Sally followed her. "Excellent idea, Margaret," she said, falling into step beside her as they made their way across the crowded drawing room. "Politics are so dull, don't you think? Whenever the men start to discuss such things, I know I'm in over my head."

Not a difficult circumstance, Margaret thought. If the discussion did not involve fashion, gossip, or the weather, Sally was hopelessly lost. But she smiled politely for Cornelia's sake.

At the punch table, they found Agnes, and Margaret was grateful that she would not have to endure Sally's company on her own. "Agnes, how lovely to see you. Are you enjoying Carnival?"

"Yes, indeed. We've had so much fun, haven't we, Sally?"

But her sister wasn't paying attention. Instead, her gaze was fixed on the man across the room. "Lord

Ashton is quite a man, isn't he?" she said with a dreamy sigh. "So handsome. He's called on us twice since Carnival began, hasn't he, Agnes?"

Margaret was stunned. "He's called on you twice?" She glanced at Agnes for confirmation, and the dark-haired girl nodded.

Sally turned to them, her eyes sparkling. "I think he has formed an attachment to me," she confessed in a whisper. "He might even offer for me in London, once the Season begins."

Margaret took a sip of punch, trying to contain her growing outrage. Trevor had told her he wasn't interested in marriage, but Sally seemed to have the impression that he was. Either he was toying with Sally, or he was toying with Margaret. She was beginning to see how the man had won his reputation. She decided to remind Sally of that. "Given his reputation," she said in a calm voice that belied her inner feelings, "would Ashton make a good husband?"

"He is quite wicked, isn't he? But many a man changes his ways once he is married."

Margaret was doubtful. "Would your father agree to the match? Ashton is stone broke."

But it appeared nothing would dampen Sally's enthusiasm. She only laughed. "Why should that matter? Papa knows that most peers are financially strapped. If he were to offer for me, I'm sure Papa would agree." She sighed again, a sound that made Margaret want to grind her teeth. "He's so marvelous. So exciting."

Margaret wondered what Sally would think of him if she knew what he did in the wee small hours of the morning. But as much as she wanted to set Sally straight as to the facts, she couldn't. So, over the next several hours, she was forced to endure Sally's gushing comments and Trevor's indulgent tolerance of the English girl's attentions.

Later that evening, when they met in the garden for their next adventure, Margaret gave him a piece of her mind. Trevor failed—deliberately, she thought—to understand just why she was upset.

"Yes," he admitted. "I've called on her twice. I've danced with her. What of it?"

"She thinks you're going to marry her, as would any girl, given the circumstances. You are leading her on."

"Am I?"

She stared at him in astonishment. "You said you were not the marrying kind."

"True enough. I never have been. But, of late, I have found myself thinking more and more about the subject."

"You have?"

"Yes, indeed. You are partly to blame."

"Me? What are you talking about?"

"You reminded me that it is my duty to marry for an heir. And you were quite right."

Margaret felt as if her head were spinning. She hadn't said any such thing. Had she? "What are you saying? That Lady Sally would be your choice for a wife?"

"She would be quite a suitable wife for an earl."

"Really!" She stopped walking, and he paused beside her. Margaret felt insulted. "You talk of, of seducing me, but you talk of marrying Lady Sally?"

He seemed astonished. "Margaret, you have said quite clearly you don't wish to marry. I am an earl, and I have finally been forced to admit that marriage is something I will have to do. I have my duty to consider. Besides, it is only something I am thinking about for the future. I don't know why you're so upset about this."

She drew a deep breath, trying to contain her growing irritation. "I'm not upset! It's just that, that . . ." She spluttered, unable to articulate what she felt without giving him the false impression that she wanted him for herself. "I thought we had agreed not to discuss the topic of marriage at all!"

"You're quite right," he agreed mildly and tucked her arm within his. They resumed walking, and he said, "I won't bring it up if you won't. And as long as our . . . association continues, I will not be marrying anyone else, I assure you."

"How considerate of you," she answered dryly, but he did not seem to notice the sarcasm.

He said no more about the matter, and they spent the evening at the theater, where they watched several skits from the *Comedia dell'Arte*. Both of them had seen the old Italian comedies before, but watching from the penny seats in a bourgeois theater was a totally new experience for Margaret.

"I had no idea crowds could be so critical!" she said. "Throwing tomatoes at the stage. Heavens! I'd love to see the audience do that at the Academy of Music back in New York. Just so I could see the look on Mrs. Astor's face!"

"From what I've heard of your American Knickerbocker set," Trevor answered, "a tomato in the face is exactly what Mrs. Astor deserves."

Margaret laughed delightedly at the picture his words evoked. "It's not my Knickerbocker set," she assured him. "And a good thing, too! Stuffy old cats, all of them."

"Why? Because they don't approve of throwing tomatoes at hideously bad actors?"

"No, because they told my father he wasn't good enough to have a box at their precious Academy." She stuck her nose in the air and added haughtily, "Those Van Aldens are such upstarts, you know. We couldn't allow such rabble into our set, my dear. Their money may be green, but their blood simply isn't blue enough."

Trevor smiled at her parody of Caroline Astor. But behind the teasing and laughter, he sensed an underlying hint of hurt in her voice, and he realized that, though she might pretend not to care, the social ostracization was a wound that cut deep.

"It would be difficult, I imagine, to have the money your father has, but be unable to achieve the social position to go with it."

She sighed. "It's difficult for my father. He wants to move in the highest circles, and it hurts him a great deal when we are not invited to the right parties. It hurts him, not for his own sake, but for mine." She was silent for a moment, then she said, "I remember when I was sixteen and I made my debut. Papa was so happy about it, so excited. He made these lavish preparations. He had the best musicians, the best food, the best wine. He invited all the right people. But—"

"But?" he prompted when she fell silent.

"Nobody came."

He sucked in a sharp breath, hearing the pain in her voice. "That must have hurt," he said gently.

She stiffened. "Mrs. Astor and her friends are just a bunch of malicious old cats. I don't care two cents for their opinion."

"Whose opinion do you care about?" Trevor asked.

"There are few people of whom I think well enough to desire their good opinion. My father and

Cornelia. Edward. Some of my American girlfriends. That is all."

"And social acceptance in general means nothing to you?"

"Why should I want the acceptance of such hateful people?"

Her words struck a familiar chord. "In some ways, you and I are so much alike," he murmured. "I, too, am a rebel. But I have learned over the years that the price we pay for such an attitude is a high one. Especially you, since you are a woman."

"Why should it matter what other people think?"

"It shouldn't. But it does, Maggie. Don't fool yourself. It matters immensely. Unless you want to go live on a deserted island somewhere for the rest of your days, you must have a care for the opinion of others."

"I suppose you're right," she admitted. "I do try, for my father's sake. He has become quite obsessed with gaining respectability for me."

Trevor decided it was time to tackle the subject of marriage directly. "So, that's why your father is so determined to marry you off. Because he feels it would improve your social position."

"I knew it!" she cried and came to a halt. "He told you that he wants to marry me off."

"He mentioned it to me, yes," Trevor answered carefully. "He seems to feel you would gain a great deal by marrying a titled gentleman."

"Honestly!" she exclaimed in exasperation. "Why doesn't he just put me on the auction block at Sotheby's and be done with it!"

"He's right about one thing. You would gain respectability through marriage."

He glanced at her and saw her lift her chin stubbornly. "I'm not going to marry a man I do not love, a man who does not love me, just to be able to move in a higher social sphere."

"Is love so important then?"

She looked over at him, astonished. "It is everything."

"Perhaps," he murmured, but she scowled at him so fiercely, he decided to veer the conversation back to safer ground. At least now he knew for certain what he was up against. "So, tell me, what did your father do when the Academy, refused him a box?"

She relaxed slightly. "He went to Willie K. Vanderbilt and several others who had also been rejected by the Academy, and they all invested the money to build a new opera house. It's going to be called the Metropolitan, and they plan to open it next year."

Trevor laughed. "Your father is quite a man, isn't he? No wonder he's made so much money, as stubborn as he is."

"It runs in the family," she said.

"So I'm discovering."

When they reached the garden gate, he opened it for Margaret and followed her in. "So did you enjoy yourself tonight?" he asked.

"Oh, yes. It was great fun."

Trevor leaned back against the stone wall of the garden and studied her face in the moonlight. "And have you forgiven me for my attentions to Lady Sally?" he asked, smiling at her.

She turned away, pretending great interest in the blooming camellias. "Lady Sally can go hang," she said stiffly. "If she wants to be such a fool over you, why should I care?"

Why, indeed? he thought. It pleased him to know that she was beginning to care for him—a great deal more than she wanted to let on. He seemed to be making progress.

"What are we going to do tomorrow night?" she asked, changing the subject.

He shook his head. "We can't go out tomorrow night," he answered. "I have another engagement."

That got her full attention. "You do?"

"I'm afraid so, one I cannot refuse. I'm meeting a business associate at the Royale."

"That's a gaming club, isn't it? Well, that's perfect! I've always wanted to go to a gaming club."

"I'm not taking you with me."

"Why not?"

"God, Margaret. I may be slightly lax when it comes to observing the proprieties, but even I could not take a lady to a gaming club!"

She chewed her bottom lip thoughtfully for a moment. "Why? Women aren't allowed inside?"

"Only women of a certain type," he answered dryly.

"You mean mistresses and demi-reps."

"Exactly."

"Really!" she said, clearly aggrieved. "Life is so unfair to women. Unless we wish to sacrifice our reputations, we are barred from all that is fun and exciting."

"Step down off your suffragette soapbox, if you please. I can't change the world, and even if I could, I wouldn't. I like things the way they are."

"Of course you do," she countered. "You're a man."

"And you are most definitely a woman. So stop railing against things you can't change and give in gracefully. I'm sure you'll have a marvelous time at the Embassy Ball."

"Oh, yes, marvelous." She made a face. "Dancing

with fat ambassadors who are dressed in silly elephant costumes and who tread on my feet. A memory I'll cherish all my days."

His lips quirked in a smile. "I see your point."

She was quick to pounce on that concession. "Then can I go with you?"

"My God, give you an inch and you do take a mile, don't you? What if someone recognizes you?"

"That's unlikely. It's Carnival, and I imagine most people will be costumed. No one would recognize me if I wore something that covered my face."

"Perhaps, but it's still far too risky."

"I thought you were a man who enjoyed taking risks."

"Margaret, just because a man and a woman are friends does not mean she can throw his own words back in his face to serve her purposes. Forget it. I'm not taking you with me and that's final."

She opened her mouth to make her next argument, but he saw it coming and reached for her, pulling her into his arms with a suddenness that made her completely forget what she'd been about to say.

He bent his head and kissed her, a kiss totally unlike the first one in the library. That one had been raw and powerful, startling in its intensity. But this was something else, something slow and deliberate, blatantly sensual. His mouth grazed hers lightly, warm and persuasive, coaxing her lips to part for him. Margaret closed her eyes and obeyed his silent command, awash in the extraordinary feel of the feather-light contact.

His hands slid up between them to cup her face, and he pulled her lower lip between his teeth, sucking gently, as if she were a piece of sugar candy to be tasted and savored.

She could feel it happen, that strange, melting

sensation that seemed to rob her of all her strength. She wrapped her arms around his neck and clung to him, pressing closer, wanting more.

But he did not give her what she wanted. Instead, his hands slid away and he pulled back slowly.

Stunned, Margaret did not move for a long moment. When she finally opened her eyes, she saw him smiling at her. There was a strange, dark satisfaction in that smile, and she did not know why, until she realized that she was still clinging to him but he was not touching her at all. She released her hold and stepped back, feeling flustered and embarrassed.

"You did that on purpose," she accused, mortified that her words came out in a breathless hush. "To distract me."

"Yes, I did," he admitted, completely without remorse. "Did it work?"

"You are the most provoking man! I really don't know why I put up with you."

"You put up with me because I intrigue you. I'm the only man you've ever known that won't let you have the upper hand."

Before she could even form the words of an indignant denial, he closed the distance between them and pressed a quick, hard kiss to her lips. "I will see you Monday night. Enjoy yourself at the Embassy Ball."

"Oh, I'm sure it will be just too exciting for words," she said so dismally that he laughed as he walked back through the gate and disappeared into the alley.

Margaret remained in the garden after he had gone, wrapped in a confusing haze of emotions. Her lips still tingled from his goodnight kisses. The feelings he aroused within her with his mouth and his hands were intense, yes, but they were also rather

frightening. She felt as if her control were being
eroded away in tiny increments, and she wondered if
there would come a time when she would surrender
to him.

She shook off her uncertainties and told herself not
to be silly. Someday she would meet the right man, a
man who would not only desire her, but also love her.
Until then, she intended to have fun. And if Trevor
thought that his kisses, wonderful as they were,
would keep her from embarking on an exciting adventure like the Royale, he was mistaken.

"St. James did not board any ship bound for England.
I just learned of it an hour ago."

Lucci frowned at the man beside him, then glanced
around at the elegant crowd that filled the drawing
room. "Come with me," he commanded, and the head
of the Egyptian Port Authority followed him out into
the gardens and down a graveled path lined with
palms.

"When we are surrounded by British officials and
their wives, Signor Sallah, it would be wise to keep
your voice down. I don't want St. James to find out I'm
looking for him until he's on his knees in front of me."

"I understand." The Egyptian gentleman fell into
step beside him. "My men have checked all the mani-
fests of ships leaving Cairo the day after the burglary
at your villa. St. James did not go to England. He
went to Rome."

"Rome? Are you certain?"

Sallah stiffened at the question. "Of course I am
certain. He made no effort to hide his identity, either.
He did not seem to fear you would come after him."

"Then he is a fool." Lucci thought of his sweet wife

and how she had been so abused. Since he had learned of it, his rage, instead of dissipating, burned hotter with each day that passed. "I will go to Rome myself."

Sallah seemed surprised. "The two of you have battled over artifacts for years. Why all of this trouble to regain a necklace?"

"That is not your concern," Lucci answered sharply.

"Of course. I have given you the information you requested."

"You will be paid, Sallah," Lucci assured him. "Call on my secretary tomorrow, and you will find the money waiting for you."

"You are generous, as always," the other man murmured. "I am grateful."

"You have earned it. Now leave me."

Sallah bowed. "Give my regards to your wife. I heard she is ill. I hope it is not serious."

The Egyptian returned to the party, but Lucci did not. He sat down on a stone bench amid the palm trees and thought of his sweet young wife with anguish.

Isabella would not eat, she would not talk, and she would not come out of her rooms. She would wake in the night, screaming and sobbing. She would not let him touch her. "When he is dead," she would sob, pulling free of him, "then, only then, will I be healed."

Soon, my sweet, he promised her silently. *Soon.*

The following night, Trevor walked through the glittering game rooms of the Royale, feeling strangely out of place. Though his black evening suit was impeccable, he felt as if he were the one in costume as he moved through the crowd of knights, peasants, princes, and demons. Unlike Trevor, most of these men were on their way to or from some costume party or ball, and were dressed accordingly.

He spied a stout fellow in green velvet, with stuffed yellow spines all down his back and the head of his dragon costume tucked under one arm, who moved carefully through the crowd, trying to avoid hitting anyone with his immense tail. Trevor thought of Margaret's woeful words of the night before and grinned. If this dragon were representative of the men she was dancing with at the Embassy Ball, he almost felt sorry for her.

Almost, but not quite. He meant what he had told her last night. He could not let her gain the upper hand. If she ever felt she could control him or manipulate him, she'd toss him aside like yesterday's newspaper. He would not allow that to happen.

No, he would win his heiress by slow seduction, by giving her just enough of what she wanted to make her want more. With the right bait to tempt her, he would lead her just where he wanted her to go, without ever letting her realize that she was being led. And he planned to lead her straight to the altar.

Trevor paused beside the bar to get a glass of port, then moved toward the poker tables, knowing that was where he would find Emilio. A crowd had gathered around one of the tables, and Trevor caught sight of Emilio seated there, costumed as a Maltese sailor. His cards were in his hand and a worried frown was on his face.

Trevor realized why a crowd had gathered. Emilio was playing a woman.

Costumed as a Turkish slave girl, or, more accurately,

as the European idea of what a Turkish slave girl would be, she wore silks—a robe of shimmering gold belted with a blue sash over ivory trousers. A headdress of blue silk covered her head and shoulders, concealing her hair, and, since her back was to him, he could not see her face. But a woman who could give Emilio a run for his money at poker was worth watching. Intrigued, he maneuvered his way through the crowd until he was close enough to observe the play.

Emilio called her bluff, adding money to the pot, and laid down his hand. "Two pair," he announced, laying down his cards. "Aces and eights."

The woman said nothing, she merely fanned her cards out on the table, revealing a full house. She raked in her winnings as Emilio lifted his hands in a gesture of surrender. "I am finished," he announced, pushing back his chair. "After three losing hands, I would be a fool to play yet another with a woman who has beauty, luck, and skill on her side." He cast a glance over the crowd that surrounded him. "Would anyone care to take my place?"

Trevor decided to challenge her himself. "I will," he said, taking Emilio's chair.

The other man stood up and gave him a wide smile. "Trevor, you have finally arrived."

His smile faded as he looked into Trevor's face. "What happened to your eye?"

"Nothing important."

"A fight? Is that what delayed you? You are never late for an engagement."

"Traffic," he explained. "You know how crowded the streets are during Carnival."

"We were beginning to worry." Leaning closer, Emilio added in a low voice, "Your mistress plays the game well, my friend."

"My mistress?"

Startled, he glanced at the woman seated across the table. She lifted her head to meet his gaze, and, although a veil of ivory silk concealed the lower half of her face, the brown eyes above the veil that sparkled with mischievous laughter were all too familiar.

"Bloody hell!" he cried and almost dropped his glass of port. "What are you doing here?"

"Trevor, *mon cher*!" she exclaimed, her voice heavily laced with what he assumed was supposed to be a French accent. It wouldn't fool a child. "I have been waiting for you, of course," she went on. "And I'm having ze most glorious time. Zis poker—it eez quite exciting."

He was going to kill her, he decided. That ought to be exciting enough even for her. But before he could carry out his intention, Emilio pushed him into the vacant chair. "She said you did not expect her tonight and would be surprised to find her here. Since both of us were waiting for you, she suggested we play a few hands. Little did I know she would take all my money."

Margaret laughed up at him. "It eez only zee luck of a beginner."

"On the contrary, my dear Margaux," Emilio said, "you used your beautiful dark eyes to hypnotize me and distract me from the play. Deliberately, I think. Take care, Trevor, that she does not do the same to you."

"Not likely," he muttered through clenched teeth. His only wish was to get Margaret out of there before one of the many Englishmen present recognized her, but he could not do it now. He set down his glass on the green baize table with such force he was surprised it didn't shatter and glared at her, satisfied to see some of the laughter fade from her eyes. She hastily turned her head and began talking to one of the other men at the table.

Emilio leaned down to murmur, "Why didn't you tell me?"

"Tell you what?"

"That she was your new mistress."

"She isn't," Trevor said so sharply that Margaret stopped talking to the man at her left and turned her head in his direction, giving him an inquiring glance. But she saw the expression on his face and quickly looked away.

Emilio chuckled. "Is this not the woman you've been escorting about Carnival the past few nights? Despite her costume, I recognized her instantly, and when I engaged her in conversation, she immediately admitted knowing you."

"Did she?" he asked. If Emilio had recognized her, then others would, too. The scandal would ruin her, and him as well. His fury increased tenfold.

The deal passed to the man beside Margaret, and Emilio stepped back. "Five card draw," the man announced, and as he dealt the hand Trevor hoped to hell he'd have the cards to trounce her thoroughly and take every chip she had. It was no more than she deserved.

Determined to get her own way, she had openly defied him, putting her reputation at enormous risk. The possible consequences of her actions made his insides twist with dread, especially when he thought of what would happen if her father found out.

With an effort, he pushed aside that unpleasant possibility and returned his attention to the cards in his hand. He saw the possibility of a flush and, when his turn came, he tossed away his one useless card. "I'll take one."

It was another club, exactly what he needed, but Trevor was too furious to feel any elation. All he wanted was to get her out of there.

When he had begun the task of winning his heiress, he had never imagined just how trying to his nerves and his patience that task would be. She was spoiled, willful, and reckless, a combination that sliced through his self-control as easily as a knife through butter, and he realized he had underestimated her. It was a mistake he seldom made, and he vowed that it was a mistake he would not make again.

Margaret held with the hand she'd been dealt and raised the stakes by ten thousand lire. Two men folded, and when the play came to him, he matched her ten thousand and added ten thousand more.

Both men to his left bowed out of the game, leaving Margaret as his only opponent.

"Perhaps you should fold now," he suggested, deliberately baiting her. "It would be a shame for you to lose more money."

"I'll call," she said and matched his bet. She laid down her hand, revealing three queens.

Trevor smiled with grim satisfaction. "Very foolish of you." He fanned out his cards on the table to reveal his five clubs, sending a ripple of excited murmurs through the crowd. He raked in his winnings and stood up. "Gentlemen, I have other enjoyments to pursue this evening, so I must bid you goodnight." He gave Margaret a look that told her clearly she'd better get out of her chair and follow him.

She licked her lips nervously, but she didn't move. He came around the table, seized her wrist and hauled her out of her chair, much to the amusement of those around them.

"What are you doing?" she cried and made a frantic grab for her chips. She managed to seize only a handful before he dragged her away from the table. She tried to jerk free, but he tightened his grip and pulled her hard against him. "I would advise you to come along quietly, *Margaux*," he murmured in a low voice. "Even mistresses do not make scenes in the Royale."

"But I'm not finished yet!"

"Oh, yes, you are." He glanced across the table at Emilio, who was watching them in wholehearted amusement. "Emilio, we'll have to meet some other time."

"I understand," the other man said, laughing. "Call on me tomorrow afternoon."

Left without a choice, Margaret followed him out of the club. Trevor ordered a cab to be brought around, and, as the doorman departed to find one, she decided it might be best to try and explain.

"Trevor, I—"

"Don't say a word," he interrupted. "Not one word."

He said nothing more, and they waited in silence. As the moments passed and Trevor did not even glance in her direction, she realized just how angry he was.

She didn't know quite how to handle it. Her father was the only other man she'd ever known who dared express anger with her, and he was a man who bellowed when he was in a rage until his anger spent itself. Experience had taught her that if she held her ground and waited patiently, the storm would soon be over. But Trevor was different, and his silence was far more intimidating than her father's sound and fury had ever been. She knew that, with this man, she was out of her depth, and a tense, uneasy feeling gripped her.

When the cab arrived, the doorman of the Royale stepped forward to open the door for them. Trevor tossed her up into the cab, thrust a tip into the doorman's hand, and followed her inside, giving the driver an address on the side street closest to Edward's townhouse.

The cab jerked forward as it started away from the curb. Margaret pulled away her veil, which was beginning to feel suffocating, but the moment she did, she began to twist the swath of silk nervously in her fingers. Forcing herself to stop, she stuffed the veil into the pocket of the bloomers she wore and shot the man seated across from her an apprehensive glance, hoping to see some sign that his anger was fading. He was gazing out through the open window, but his hard profile told her that her apprehension was justified. He was still in a blazing fury.

The carriage crawled through the crowded streets at a snail's pace. All around them, the revelry of Carnival continued, but the silence inside the carriage was more deafening than the tumult outside, making Margaret more tense with each minute that passed. When the cab arrived at its destination, Trevor leaned his head out the open window. "Pull into the alley," he instructed the driver, "and stop halfway down."

"Very good, sir."

The cab rolled to a stop in the dark alley, but Margaret had no intention of giving Trevor the chance to unleash his anger. She grabbed for the door handle, intending to make a strategic getaway, but he was quicker than she, grasping her wrist before she could even open the door.

"Not so fast. We have something to discuss first, I think."

Margaret should have known she wasn't going to get out of this so easily. "Very well," she said, giving in to the inevitable. She knew she owed him an apology and decided the best course was to give it as quickly as possible and be on her way. "I'm sorry about tonight."

"You should be. Do you have any idea how many Englishmen have memberships at the Royale? Do you realize what will happen if any of them recognized you?" She didn't answer, and he went on, "Of course you didn't, since you never stop to think of the possible consequences of your actions."

She winced, fully aware that she deserved that. But he didn't give her the chance to admit it graciously.

"Disguise or no, someone might have recognized you. If our names are spread all over the society pages tomorrow, it would not surprise me."

"My disguise was very good. I'm sure no one—"

"You can't be sure of anything. Such a scandal would ruin you for all time. Putting the matter of your reputation aside for the moment, I don't suppose it occurred to you that you have also laid yourself open to blackmail?"

"Blackmail?"

"My God, Margaret, your father is one of the wealthiest men in the world. Blackmail is a definite possibility. You have been foolish and selfish, and what's more, you have broken the promise you made to me the other night. Is breaking promises such an easy thing for you?"

She lifted her chin, feeling the need to say something

in her own defense. "I don't think I can be completely blamed for that. You—"

"Not entirely, no," he interrupted before she could point out that he had also broken his word to her. "Your father definitely bears some of the blame as well."

She was astonished. "What on earth does my father have to do with this?"

"A great deal," he said grimly. "All your life, he has allowed you to wrap him around your little finger, and you've become so accustomed to having your own way that you are now a spoiled, willful child who acts without thinking, who doesn't consider the consequences on others, and who is badly in need of a good thrashing!"

No man had ever dared to say such things to her. Her temper rose, and she felt it was time to point out that she was not the only one who had broken her word. "I would like to remind you that when we began these adventures of ours, you promised to take me wherever I wanted to go. You broke your promise to me."

"Only to protect you," he shot back in frustration, his voice rising as fast as his temper. "It was for your own good that I ordered you not to go."

She was quick to contradict him. "You did no such thing. You never ordered me not to go to the Royale. All you said was that you wouldn't take me."

He was just about at the end of his tether. He drew a deep breath, striving to keep his anger in check. "That's splitting hairs," he said through clenched teeth. "You know damned well what I meant."

Her chin lifted in an imperious gesture that reminded him of her father. "Even if I did know," she flared defensively, "I'm not a meal in a restaurant! You cannot simply order me!"

Those words snapped the tenuous hold Trevor had on his temper. "By God, you try my patience!" he shouted back at her. "It wasn't only your own reputation you risked tonight. It was mine as well. If you think you'll be doing these insane things in the future, think again. Once we're married, I'll damn well put a stop to it!"

The moment the words were out of his mouth, he realized just what he had done. She froze to the pale, unearthly stillness of a marble statue, staring at him in shock. "What did you say?" she whispered.

The damage was done. All he could do was attempt to minimize it. "Maggie—"

"You snake." The carriage door flew open. "I'll never marry you!"

She was out of the cab before he could make a grab for her, then she slammed the door in his face so hard that it stuck when he tried to open it. Through the open window, he heard the iron gate of the garden clang shut, and he leaned back, cursing as he slammed the heel of his boot against the carriage door, forcing it open.

He was out of the carriage in an instant, but when he grasped the iron bars of the gate to pull it open, it did not budge, and he realized she had locked it behind her. He caught a glimpse of her between the trees and shrubs as she raced toward the townhouse, her silk robes shimmering in the moonlight.

He jerked on the bars of the gate again, but all he could do was watch in frustration as she entered the house and closed the door behind her.

"Damn," he muttered. She had soundly deserved

the lecture he'd given her, but knowing he was justified didn't do him much good now. With a few careless words said in the heat of the moment, he might
have ruined any chance to win her.

So much for being in control of the situation.

9

Margaret raced through the pitch-black corridors of the townhouse to her bedroom with all the panic of a startled deer. Trevor's words echoed through her mind like the gunshots of a hunter. *When we're married. When we're married.*

He had told her he wanted to seduce her because he desired her, but that was a lie. What he really desired was her money. Just like all the others.

Once inside her room, she stripped off her costume and stuffed the silks in the back of a drawer. She donned her nightgown, but she knew it would be futile to go to bed. Instead, she sank into the velvet chair beside her bedroom window and stared down at the moonlit gardens below. She recalled with humiliating clarity every touch, every kiss, and her initial panic gave way to a bitter sense of betrayal and disappointment.

Deep in her heart, she'd known it all along. Then

why was she so surprised to have her initial suspicions confirmed? Even as she asked herself that question, she knew the answer. Because she hadn't wanted to believe it.

She had ignored her own instincts, mesmerized by a charming smile and dark blue eyes. She had wanted to believe he was different from all the others, that his talk of passion was genuine, that his kisses came from his longing for her. She had been an utter fool.

He had called her a spoiled, willful child. Perhaps she was. Margaret was accustomed to getting her way and too stubborn to give up her romantic ideals.

By the time the sun rose, Margaret was once again in command of her emotions. Trevor St. James was nothing but a fortune hunter, and she knew how to deal with those.

"I'm terribly sorry, my lord, but Miss Van Alden is not receiving callers this afternoon."

Trevor studied the impassive face of the butler for a moment. "I see."

He wasn't surprised by Margaret's refusal to face him. In fact, given her reaction to his fatal words last night, he could hardly have expected anything else. He dropped his calling card into the silver tray on the table beside the door, then turned to the butler. "Would you tell Lord Kettering that I wish to see him?"

The servant departed and within moments Edward appeared. But as he started down the stairs, he caught sight of Trevor's grim expression and paused. "What is it? What's happened?"

"Is there somewhere we can talk privately?"

"Of course. Let's go in the library."

Trevor didn't speak until the library doors had closed behind them, and even then he told Edward of last night's events in a low voice.

"Damnation!" Edward muttered, sinking into a chair. "I arranged for us to leave the ball early because I assumed she was going out with you again. I had no idea. Did anyone recognize her?"

"I hope not." Trevor took the chair opposite Edward's. "Her disguise was quite good, but with all the people there, I can't be certain someone didn't realize who she was."

"Well, we'll know soon enough. Gossip travels fast. If I hear anything at all, I'll let you know." He leaned back in his chair and studied his friend for a moment. "You're certainly quite calm about all this, given the circumstances. But then, you've always been cool under fire."

"I wasn't last night," he answered wryly. "I can't believe she made me lose my temper."

"I can. Margaret has little regard for proper feminine decorum. Thank God Cornelia wasn't like that. I don't think I could have lived through it. Courtship plays enough havoc with a man's nerves as it is. I don't blame you at all."

"In any case, what's done is done. Now that she knows my intentions, it's going to be ten times more difficult to court her. She is refusing to see me."

"She might change her mind after she's had some time to think. She might relent and give you another chance."

"I doubt it."

Edward sighed. "Perhaps it's all for the best. I've seen her refuse countless suitors, all of whom were perfectly acceptable. She obviously doesn't want to marry. Besides, do you really want a wife who would openly defy you? I like Margaret, but God knows I shouldn't like to be married to her. Her independent streak would run any man into an early grave."

"Not this man," Trevor vowed.

"You are an earl," Edward reminded him. "You have your position in society to consider. I know you've already made arrangements with her father, but you're not bound by that. There are other heiresses."

Trevor didn't want another heiress. "If you think I'm giving up that easily, think again."

"But if she won't even see you, what can you do?"

Trevor stood up and started for the door. "Whatever it takes," he answered grimly.

As he walked to the carriage waiting in the street, Trevor knew he had very few options. The driver asked where he wished to go. An appropriate question, he thought wryly, and one for which he had no answer.

He knew she would be at the Vanetta Ball tonight, and he could easily get an invitation, but what would that accomplish? She would most likely refuse him a dance on some trumped up excuse. Even if she did dance with him, there was nothing he could say that would undo the damage of what had already been said.

It was time to take decisive action. The question was what action to take. With their adventures together obviously at an end, he would have no opportunity to get her alone. This meant he had little chance of seducing her into matrimony.

Suddenly, an idea came to him in a flash of inspiration, one so outrageous he nearly discarded it. But he thought of Margaret's thirst for adventure and romance and decided the outrageous might be exactly what he needed.

For such a plan to work, he would need the help of both Emilio and Edward. He'd have a hell of a time convincing Edward to go along with it, but desperate situations required desperate measures. He gave the driver Emilio's address and jumped into the carriage.

The following day, Edward took Cornelia and Margaret sightseeing. Baedeker guidebooks in hand, they set off in a carriage to see the church of San Sebastiano and the famous catacombs that lay beneath.

It was the last day of Carnival, and the carriage moved at a snail's pace down the Appian Way. Margaret was able to watch the festivities to her heart's content, but somehow, it didn't seem nearly as exciting now. She thought of those nights with Trevor and realized in horror that she actually missed him.

Margaret had refused to see him yesterday, and he hadn't appeared at the Vanetta Ball last night. She knew they would probably meet again at some point, perhaps in London, but there would be no more midnight adventures. She felt a pang of regret.

A rainbow shower of confetti suddenly came down over their heads, breaking Margaret out of her melancholy thoughts. Cornelia groaned in dismay, shaking her parasol in a vain attempt to dislodge the bits of paper from the netting and lace.

In the crowd that surrounded them, Margaret saw two boys, about ten years old, with a huge pail of confetti between them. She wasn't certain they had thrown it until she saw them readying to throw again. Another shower of the stuff rained down over the carriage, and she saw the boys make faces at her, daring her to respond. Unable to resist the challenge, she gathered two handfuls of the colorful confetti from the floor and stood up in the slow-moving carriage to return fire.

"Oh, Maggie, don't encourage them," her cousin pleaded. "They might do something ghastly, like throw one of those eggshells filled with flour, and then we shall be in no end of a mess!"

Margaret ignored her cousin's plea and continued throwing confetti at the boys until they gave up, melting back into the crowd.

"Really, Cornelia," she said as she fell back into her seat, "ever since you got married, you've become so matronly. Edward, you mustn't allow her to become one of those dull married ladies."

Edward gave a start and turned his head in their direction with a blank look. "What? I'm sorry, I wasn't paying attention."

His wife shot him a worried glance. "You seem quite preoccupied this morning, darling. Is anything wrong?"

"No, no, of course not," he assured her hastily. "What could be wrong?"

"I don't know, but you've been having headaches all week, and today you seem so nervous, like a cat on hot bricks. It's not at all like you, and I'm concerned."

"I'm fine, really. Perhaps it's just all the excitement this week."

Cornelia patted his arm and gave him an affectionate smile. "I know exactly what you mean. It will be nice to leave for Florence tomorrow. Perhaps there we can enjoy some peace and quiet. Carnival was quite exciting for the first few days, but these crowds are beginning to wear on me as well."

They soon reached the church of San Sebastiano. The group took a quick tour, then followed the gaunt

Franciscan friar who was their guide down a narrow set of stone stairs into the dark tunnels and caverns below. Wall torches provided the only light as the friar led them through the labyrinth of catacombs. The eerie glow seemed a perfect companion to the dead and heavy air.

As the friar guided them through the narrow, curving corridor, they passed the yawning black openings of many branching tunnels. There were also many shallow recesses roughly cut into the rocks which the friar explained in his broken English were the graves of the early Christian martyrs.

The friar paused and pointed to what had obviously been a cave, but which was now completely closed off with a stone wall. He told them Christians had hidden there in the time of Nero. They had lived for years in that dark and frightening place, sustained only by their faith.

The friar's eyes seemed to take on a fanatic glow as he recounted how their hiding had been in vain. Their Roman persecutors had found them by the thousands, trapping them in the caves and walling them inside. The Christians had been buried before death and left to die of starvation.

Margaret shivered. The friar looked like a man on the verge of madness, with his over-bright eyes, long beard, and unkempt hair. She turned, staring at the pitch-black opening of the tunnel across from her, and thought wildly of what it would be like to be forced to hide in that ghastly subterranean home for years and years. It would make anyone mad. She closed her eyes and shuddered.

Margaret did not realize she was alone until she opened her eyes. The friar, Cornelia, and Edward were now out of sight. Trying to banish frightening images from her mind, she started after her companions, opening her mouth to shout for them to wait for her. She had only taken a few steps before she was grabbed from behind, and a strong hand was clamped over her mouth.

She tried to scream, but the only sound she could make was a faint squeal. She struggled as her captor hauled her backward into the black tunnel from which he had come.

"Ssh, *mia cara*," a low, unfamiliar voice whispered in stilted English. "No one is going to hurt you."

His words did nothing to ease her fear. Her heart thumped wildly in her breast as she tried to escape, but her efforts were in vain. He dragged her through the dark corridor for quite a long distance, and Margaret finally stopped fighting, realizing she was only wearing herself out. They reached an area where several tunnels came together and torches illuminated the darkness.

Still keeping a firm grip on her, Margaret's captor turned her around to face half a dozen men dressed in the drab brown robes of Franciscan monks. One of the men stepped forward, pulling back the hood that shadowed his face, and she gasped in astonishment. "Emilio!"

The handsome Italian smiled at her and bowed. "My dear Margaux, we meet again."

Cornelia put her arm through her husband's as they began following the friar up the stone steps that led back into the church. "Really, Edward, what a macabre tour," she said. "Although I'm sure Margaret loved every minute of it. Didn't you, Maggie?"

Cornelia turned to glance behind her, but

Margaret wasn't there. She came to a halt, forcing her husband to stop as well. "Maggie?" she called, but her voice echoed through the caverns below with no reply.

"Edward, where is she?" Alarmed, she turned to her husband. "She was behind us only a moment ago."

"You know Maggie," Edward answered, "she probably found something fascinating down there that distracted her, then she probably got lost. You go on up into the church, and the friar and I will go find her."

He beckoned to the Franciscan who stood waiting at the top of the stairs, and the friar came back down. They started to retrace their steps, and Cornelia watched them. Edward was probably right, she told herself as she turned to ascend the stairs. Even on the most mundane shopping trip, Margaret was always wandering off. This time was no different.

She took a seat in one of the pews and waited, but as the minutes went by and Edward and the friar did not return, Cornelia began to worry. Half an hour passed before she saw her husband and the friar emerge from the catacombs below. A third person was with them, but that person wasn't Margaret. It was Trevor St. James.

"Lord Ashton?" Cornelia rose from her seat as the three men approached. "What are you doing here?"

Instead of answering, Trevor turned to the friar. "Leave us, please," he said in Italian.

The friar bowed his head and departed, leaving the three of them alone in the church.

"What is going on?" Cornelia demanded, glancing from Trevor to her husband and back again. "Did you find Margaret?"

"We don't need to find her, Lady Kettering,"

Trevor answered. "We already know exactly where she is."

Margaret had never felt more helpless in her life.

She was blindfolded and had no idea where she was being taken. She only knew that she was in a wagon traveling through the Italian countryside. They had long since left the main road, and the wagon bumped along the terrain in a most uncomfortable fashion. At least three men were in the wagon with her, including Emilio, that deceitful scoundrel. Another wagon, containing the other three bandits, followed close behind.

She knew that night had fallen. The warmth of the sun had faded to the cool of evening, cicadas chirped raucously all around her, and the night air was pungent with the scent of blossoming lemon trees.

Bound and gagged, she could see no way to escape. Despite her most determined efforts, the ropes around her wrists and ankles refused to loosen, and she only chafed her skin by trying.

Her initial fear had long since given way to frustration and outrage, but there was nothing she could do except wait for the wagon to stop and hope for the opportunity to escape. As time slowly crept by, she began to wonder if they were planning to cart her all the way across Europe.

Perhaps trying to escape was not a good idea. Emilio must have found out her true identity somehow and given a ransom demand to Edward and Cornelia. Her father would have to be notified, and would pay the money. Then perhaps these vagabonds would simply let her go.

The wagons finally halted. Margaret rolled and

wiggled herself into a sitting position, wincing at the pain that shot through her cramped muscles. One of the thieves untied her ankles, and she scooted to the edge of the wagon, intending to climb down. But the thief caught her by the arm and spoke sharply in Italian, obviously ordering her to stay put. Margaret could only hope they would eventually free her wrists and remove the blasted blindfold and gag. But it was not until she could hear the crackling of a fire and smell the delicious aroma of something cooking that she got her wish.

The bandits had made camp in a clearing. But beyond the light of the fire, she could see little else. Margaret knew with a sinking feeling of dread that even if she could escape from these thieves, there was nowhere to go.

A man led her to the fire, where Emilio and three of the others were seated. The sixth bandit was dishing up plates of food from a pot on the coals, and Margaret suddenly realized that bandit was a woman.

Bandits should have appeared evil and sinister, with twisted faces and murderous eyes, but these people were quite ordinary looking. The woman even smiled at her as she handed Margaret a plate of fragrant stew and a spoon. Margaret almost smiled back, then caught herself. These people were common thieves, people who could probably kill her without a thought.

Emilio gestured to the blanket on the ground at her feet. "Sit, Margaux."

The man who held her by the arm released her to sit down, but Margaret knew it would be foolish to make a run for it. They would certainly catch her before she could even reach the trees. Emilio watched her, smiling, and she realized he knew what she was thinking. Left with no choice, Margaret sank down cross-legged onto the blanket, vowing to wait for a better time. She balanced the plate of food in her lap. "Why have you brought me here?" she asked Emilio, her voice hoarse from hours of having a gag in her mouth.

Instead of answering, he spoke to the woman who stood nearby. The woman immediately reached for a goatskin bag and handed it to Margaret, then sat down.

"Water," Emilio explained. "Drink your fill."

Too thirsty to be proud, Margaret accepted the bag and took several hefty swallows of the cool liquid.

"Slowly," Emilio told her. "It is not good to drink so fast when you are so thirsty. You will make yourself sick."

She obeyed, taking the water in small sips until her thirst was sated. She then handed back the bag and turned again to Emilio. "You did not answer my question," she said. "Why have you kidnapped me?"

"Kidnapped?" He shook his head. "No, Margaux, you must not think such a thing of us. You are our guest."

"Guest? Is this how you treat guests?" She rubbed her sore wrists and glared at him across the fire. "And to think I actually believed you were a gentleman!"

Emilio threw back his head and laughed. He then translated her words to the others, and they found her comment equally amusing.

"Eat," he told her, nodding to the plate in her lap. "I know you are hungry, and my mama makes a fine stew."

"Your mother?" Startled, she glanced at the elderly woman beside her, who nodded, clearly understanding enough to confirm Emilio's words. "Your mother obviously does not know how despicable you are."

"She knows I have good reasons for everything I do."

"Reasons? What reasons?" she demanded. "If it's money you want—"

"No, no," he interrupted, shaking his head. "I am not so crude as that. I am no common street thief to do this merely for money."

Margaret was confused by that unexpected statement. "For what, then?"

"For something far more valuable to me than money." Emilio pointed to her untouched plate. "Eat, Margaux. We still have another two days of travel before we reach my camp, and you must keep up your strength."

Her heart sank. If not money, what was their reason for taking her? She realized there was more to this than simple kidnapping, and her fear returned. What did they really want?

10

That night Margaret slept on cold, hard ground for the first time in her life, snoring bandits all around her, the ropes that bound her cutting into her wrists and ankles, and an itchy wool blanket her only protection against the spiders, snakes, and other horrible creatures she was certain lurked in the darkness. She did not sleep well.

The following morning, Emilio's mother gave her some clothes. Margaret glanced down at the simple white blouse, homespun skirt, thick woolen coat, and sturdy leather boots in her hands. The clothes were so similar to the costume she had worn during her nights at Carnival with Trevor that she felt a sudden, absurd kindling of hope. Maybe he would come to her rescue.

But the feeling died as quickly as it came. Trevor was no hero. He would never risk his skin for her, especially since she'd made it clear he had no chance of marrying her and getting his hands on her money. That was all he was after.

Emilio's mother said something to her, and Margaret glanced up to find the woman watching her expectantly, waiting for her to change into the clothes. She knew the blouse and skirt would be much more comfortable than the delicate white lawn dress and heeled slippers she was wearing, but she glanced at the men all around her and shook her head, her face coloring.

The woman murmured something in Italian, patted Margaret's cheek as any mother might do, and unfolded the blanket in her hands to screen Margaret from view. Margaret didn't think one wool blanket offered much privacy, but it was better than nothing. She reluctantly changed into the clothes, but the men were busy packing up the gear and did not even seem to notice what she was doing.

The bandits left the wagon behind and continued their journey on horseback, taking her into the mountains of the Abruzzi. Margaret's spirits sank lower with each mile they traveled away from Rome.

She rode double with a big, hulking fellow who kept an arm firmly around her waist to ensure she did not try to escape. Though they kept her wrists bound, they had not forced her to wear the blindfold and gag. She was glad, but she knew their reason was not kindness. The countryside was mountainous and wooded. A blindfold and gag were simply not necessary.

By the third day, they had climbed high into the mountains, and the higher they climbed, the more desolate the landscape became. The lush winter greenery of the Roman landscape had changed to brown grass, snow-dusted mountain peaks, and gray granite rock.

By the time they made camp that night, Margaret still had no idea what they intended to do with her.

With her wrists and ankles bound, it was impossible to find a comfortable position for sleeping, and she lay on her side in the dark. Margaret shivered despite the thick wool blanket wrapped around her and stared into the glowing coals of the campfire, her imagination conjuring up all sorts of wild possibilities.

Maybe they weren't really bandits at all. Maybe they were freedom fighters who were going to ransom her for something useful to their cause—guns or ammunition or something.

Or maybe they were going to sell her to white slavers. She'd read a novel once where that had happened to the heroine. She huddled deeper into the blanket, telling herself over and over not to be silly.

The sharp snap of a twig caught her attention. Margaret sat up, listening intently, but all she heard was the uninterrupted snoring of the others. Suddenly a hand was clamped over her mouth, muffling her squeal of surprise as she was forced onto her back. In the dim firelight, she recognized the eyes of Trevor St. James.

Relief flooded through her, and she knew she would be safe. Trevor had come for her. He was rescuing her, just as she had hoped he would.

He lifted one hand, pressing his finger to his lips, and pulled something from the belt at his hip. Margaret caught the gleaming flash of a knife blade. He cut the stout ropes that bound her wrists and ankles, then straightened and began moving slowly backward. He beckoned her to follow him, and she rose to her feet, careful not to make a sound as she followed him out of the camp.

Trevor grabbed her hand and led her through the darkness. He said nothing, but the strong clasp of his hand was reassuring, and she followed him until they came to where his horse was tethered by a lone scrub pine. He halted and pulled her into his arms.

"Maggie, are you all right?" he asked in a whisper, pressing kisses to her forehead, her cheek, her lips.

She started to answer that she was fine, but the only sound she made was a choked sob. She threw her arms around his neck and buried her face against the solid, comfortable wall of his chest.

"I hope this means we're friends again," he murmured against her hair.

His words reminded her of what his true intentions were and brought all her anger flaring back. "Let go of me," she said through clenched teeth and pushed him away. "You liar. You cad. You snake."

He shook his head and sighed. "This is what I get for saving your life?"

"You only saved my life because you saw your future bank account slipping away," she whispered back.

"You could at least thank me."

"Thank you?" Her hands curled into fists. She wanted to slap him. "Thank you for what?" she asked, her voice rising. "For lying to me, for deceiving me, for being a greedy scoundrel? Thank you so very much!"

He grabbed her again, wrapping one arm around her waist and pressing his hand over her mouth. "For God's sake, do you want those thieving bastards to wake up? Be quiet until I've gotten you far enough away, then you can yell at me all you want."

The moment he took his hand away, she said in a low voice filled with loathing, "I don't want to go anywhere with you."

"Fine. Then you can go back to Emilio and his friends." He pointed the way they had come. "They're just over that ridge. Or"—he paused to glance at the barren terrain around them—"you can walk back alone with no food, no water, no blankets, and no map. Good luck."

She bit her lip, hating him, but she knew she didn't want to be left alone, and she certainly didn't want to die.

"It's me or them," he said shortly and untied the horse's lead rope. "Take your pick." He patted the horse's neck. "This is Hadrian, by the way."

She gave the beautiful black horse a doubtful glance. "A stallion? Is he trained?"

Trevor swung up into the saddle, and, as if in answer to Margaret's question, Hadrian shied, clearly resentful of the passenger on his back.

"After a fashion," Trevor answered with a hard yank on the reins. Once the horse was still, he held out his hand to her. "Your father told me you like a spirited horse. Where's your sense of adventure?"

"I think I've had enough adventure for awhile," she muttered, grasping his hand and swinging up behind him. "This is some rescue. Carrying me away on an untrained stallion."

"Do you know how hard it is to find a horse during Carnival? I can tell you it's next to impossible. Hadrian's the best I could get. At least he's a strong horse. We won't have to worry he'll drop dead along the way."

"Once we get back to civilization, both of you can drop dead," she told him.

"Talk like that will not get you very far. Keep it up, and you'll walk."

Knowing Trevor, she wisely closed her mouth and

said nothing more. Right now, she couldn't let herself think about what a bastard he was or what intentions he had for her future. Right now, the future didn't matter all that much anyway.

He'd never arranged a kidnapping before, but Trevor supposed that even with the best-laid plans, there was bound to be a snag or two along the way.

He guided the horse carefully through the canyon and wished he could see where he was going. Dawn was still several hours away, and the meager light provided by the thin sliver of moon overhead wasn't much help. They couldn't stop yet; he had to at least make a token show of getting away from Emilio.

"How did you know where to find me?"

Margaret's voice broke in on his thoughts, and he drew a deep breath. He'd known it wouldn't take her long to start asking questions. It was a good thing he had the answers ready. "Emilio sent me a ransom note, telling me exactly where to meet him, and from that, I knew which route he would take. Rather obliging of him, I thought."

"He sent a ransom note to you? Why?"

"Who else would he send it to? He thinks you're my mistress, remember?"

"I thought he found out who I really was."

"He didn't. If he did, he'd probably have wired your father demanding the money, and we'd both end up having a great deal of explaining to do."

"Emilio told me this wasn't about money."

"Of course it was about money." He turned his head to look over his shoulder at her. "Most things are, Maggie. Don't you know that by now?"

She glared back at him. "Yes, I know it." She was

silent for a moment, then added, "But, Trevor, you don't have any money."

"Thank you for reminding me," he said wryly. "I'd forgotten."

"What kind of ransom could Emilio hope to get from you?"

Trevor decided it would be best if he stuck as close to the truth as possible. He didn't want to tell her any outright lies. It wasn't so much that he had any kind of ethical problem with lying, but more because it was too damned difficult to remember what lies one told. It could get damned tricky and, right now, he was tired. "Emilio kidnapped you because he wants my list."

"I don't understand."

"We're in the same profession."

"Stealing antiquities for museums, you mean."

Trevor nudged her gently with his elbow. "We *acquire* antiquities for a variety of clients. Some are museums, yes, but most are private collectors, wealthy men to whom discretion is very important. I've been doing this for a long time, and my client list is excellent. That's what Emilio wants—that, and my recommendation. Since I'm retiring from the business, he offered to buy my client list, but I refused."

"You did? Why?"

"When you have something valuable, you don't take the first offer that comes along."

"I see," she murmured. "He must have feared that you would get a better offer, one he couldn't match, so he kidnapped me as an added incentive."

"Something like that."

Margaret was blessedly silent for a few minutes, then said, "Cornelia and Edward must be worried sick about me."

Trevor knew perfectly well what Cornelia was feeling, and it wasn't worry. It was rage. He could still picture her face when he'd told her what he had done. If Edward hadn't been there to help him convince her to go along with the plan, she just might have killed him right there in the church. In the end, she had agreed to help cover up Margaret's absence only because he had made her the same promise Henry had demanded of him—that he would not behave dishonorably, nor abuse her innocence. "They know I've gone after you," he said. "We'll be back with them in a week or so, and everything will be fine."

"A week or so?" she repeated in dismay. "Oh, no. What's going to happen when people find out about this? My reputation is going to be ruined. Papa will kill me!"

"Cornelia and I have already taken care of that. No one is going to find out about this, especially not your father. Cornelia and Edward have gone to Naples and are staying at a cottage in the country for the next two weeks. We'll rendezvous with them there. Everyone thinks you've gone to Naples, too. You will, of course, develop some kind of illness, and won't be able to see anyone, so any acquaintances who might look you up won't find out you're missing."

To avoid any more questions until he'd had some sleep, Trevor pulled on the horse's reins, bringing the stallion to a halt.

"Why are we stopping?"

He swung down from the horse, then grasped her around the waist to help her down. "Because I've been racing to catch up with you for almost three days and I haven't had any sleep. I'm tired."

"But Emilio will certainly come looking for us.

Shouldn't we keep going and get as far away from him as we can?"

Trevor shook his head. "It doesn't matter," he said, lifting the saddlebags from the horse's back. He slung them across one shoulder, then reached for the roll of blankets and pulled his rifle from its saddle holster. "Emilio will think we've gone back toward the main road for Rome. Come morning, he'll head in that direction. Since we're going to Naples, he'll never catch us. I hope you don't mind a scenic tour of the Italian countryside."

She bent down, peering at the thick wool blanket he spread across the ground. "I can't say I think much of the accommodations."

"Well, this is the cheap tour. You take what you get." He took the second blanket, a thick one of stuffed goose down, and laid it over the first. Tossing aside his hat, he placed his rifle within easy reach, then crawled between the blankets and folded back the edge in invitation. "Hop in."

She hesitated. "You didn't bring any more blankets?"

"I'm afraid not."

"You don't really expect us to share?" she said, sounding incredulous, scandalized, and rather outraged. That was a good sign, Trevor thought. Outrage was better than indifference.

"Why can't we each have our own blanket?" she persisted.

"Because it's damned cold up here, we can't make a fire without the risk of Emilio seeing it, and two of us under here means we'll both stay warmer. And if that's not a good enough reason for you, possession is nine-tenths of the law. Are you getting in or not?"

She didn't move, so he shrugged and rolled onto

his back, pulling the edge of the blanket up to his chin. "Fine. Have it your way. Knowing you, you probably steal the covers."

He shifted until he found a comfortable position, then closed his eyes and waited, knowing that, with the chill in the mountain air, it would probably be only a minute before she changed her mind.

It didn't take that long. After maybe fifteen seconds, she lifted the blanket and crawled in beside him, keeping as close to the edge of their makeshift bed as possible.

"Trevor?"

"Hmm?"

"Are there any, umm, snakes in this part of Italy?"

He smiled in the dark. "Of course," he answered. "Dozens of different kinds. Some are poisonous, I believe. There are bears, too."

"Oh, dear God."

The blanket stirred, and he felt her move closer to him. Another good sign. Damned if he wasn't making progress.

Margaret woke to the whistle of the wind through the rocky hills all around her. On her face, she felt the sharp sting of the cold air, but beneath the blanket she was warm. Still half-asleep, she snuggled more deeply into the blankets, and memories of the night before floated through her mind like the fragments of a dream. Memories of how Trevor had stepped right into the bandits' camp and rescued her just as the hero of a novel might have done.

But Trevor wasn't a hero. He was a snake.

That reminder banished foolish romantic fantasies

from her mind. She opened her eyes expecting to find him asleep beside her, but his place was empty.

She wondered where he could have gone. It was still quite early; the feeble gray light that penetrated the canyon told her it was barely dawn.

Footsteps crunched on the rocky ground, and she quickly closed her eyes, feigning sleep as she heard Trevor pass by. When the sound of his footsteps stopped, she risked a peek between her lashes and saw the heels of his dust-covered black boots scarcely a dozen feet away. The saddlebags lay on the ground beside him. She lifted her gaze higher, past his boots and the beige twill trousers tucked into them. Her breath caught in her throat. He wasn't wearing a shirt.

Never in her life had she seen a man's naked back. Marble statues were as close as she had ever been to such a sight. Her eyes opened wider and she studied him, fascinated by the hard, knotted muscles of his back and shoulders. They looked as if they were carved from stone, yet flexed beneath his golden brown skin when he moved.

David come to life. She suddenly wanted to touch him.

He bent down and reached into one of the saddlebags, pulled out a small mirror, then straightened and started to turn in her direction. She closed her eyes, hoping he hadn't caught her staring, but, after a few moments, curiosity got the better of her. She dared another look at him and made another startling discovery. He had hair on his chest. Astonished, Margaret stared at the triangle of thick black hair that tapered with his torso and disappeared beneath the waistband of his trousers. Something warm and aching began spreading through her limbs.

He was in profile to her, but he did not seem to notice her watching him. He hooked the mirror on a branch at eye level, then reached for the canteen and splashed water on his face. Then he pulled a small cup, a shaving brush, and a razor from one of the saddlebags.

Through the web of her lashes, Margaret watched as Trevor began to shave, fascinated by this male ritual she had never seen before. As he scraped away soap and stubble carefully with the razor, she remembered how he had kissed her face the night before, how his skin had grazed hers like rough sandpaper, the texture so different from the other times he had kissed her. How strange men are, she thought, strange and rather mysterious. Her gaze lowered, and she wondered how the hair on his chest would feel against her fingertips. The warm, aching feeling inside her intensified.

Trevor dabbed the last traces of soap from his face with a handkerchief, ran a hand through his wet hair, and pulled the mirror down from the tree. Margaret hastily closed her eyes again lest he should discover her watching, and listened to him approach.

"Maggie," he murmured close to her ear, "it's time to get up, love. We have to be moving."

She stirred with a sleepy sigh that sounded quite convincing. She made a great show of coming awake, yawning and rubbing her eyes as she rolled onto her back. But he hadn't put on a shirt, and the sight of his bare chest so close was even more unnerving than it had been from a distance. Her gaze lingered on brown skin and curling black hair. Her hands tightened around the edge of the blanket as she fought the almost irresistible urge to touch him, even as she reminded herself of what a deceitful scoundrel he was.

"Sleep well?"

His question sounded innocent enough, but when she raised her lashes, he was looking back at her with that knowing smile of his, and she realized that her pretense had been for naught. He'd known all along she had been watching him.

A hot blush of dismay and embarrassment crept up her cheeks. She looked away, shoved aside the blanket, and stood up.

He really was the most impossible man, she thought as she walked away. Around him, she couldn't seem to get away with anything.

For breakfast they ate apples and dried beef as they rode. Margaret chewed on a leathery piece of the meat and couldn't help thinking wistfully of strong, hot coffee, poached eggs, and scones dripping with butter. The tough and salty beef seemed very unsatisfying by comparison. Within an hour, she was hungry again. When they stopped for lunch, more jerky and apples did little to assuage her hunger.

Margaret tried to think of all this as a grand adventure, but she couldn't remember a single day of her life when there wasn't hot, luxuriously rich food to eat, and plenty of it. Adventures were one thing, but going hungry was something else.

Because the terrain was steep and rocky and they were riding double, their progress was slow. By late afternoon, it seemed to Margaret that they must have traveled twenty miles, but Trevor estimated that eight or nine was more accurate.

"How long will it take us to reach Naples?" she asked.

"With the route we're taking, ten or twelve days would be my guess."

Her stomach growled. "Trevor? I don't mean to criticize this tour, but are we to have apples and jerky for every meal?"

His laughter caught her by surprise. "Are you saying you don't like my cooking? Margaret, I'm devastated."

"Well, maybe it's a good thing," she said, trying to be optimistic. "My figure will slim down."

"God forbid!" His tone was so vehement, she was startled. "Don't you dare lose a single inch. I hate skinny women."

"You do?"

"Yes, I do. Your figure is utterly splendid."

He'd probably never told the truth in his life, but when he said things like that, it was hard to hate him.

Trevor reached into the pocket of his shirt and pulled out a fat peppermint stick. "Here," he said, handing it to her over one shoulder. "I'll not have you wasting away. That ought to hold you until I find a suitable place to stop for the night."

But it was another hour before he finally pulled the horse to a halt.

"Dinner?" she asked hopefully.

He pointed to the valley spread out below, where the rocky stream they'd been following widened into a leisurely flowing river. "How does baked trout strike you?"

She eyed the river with skepticism. "Unless you have a fishing pole tucked away in those saddlebags, I don't know how you'll manage to catch any trout."

"Really, Maggie, your lack of trust in my fishing ability hurts more than I can say." He nudged the horse forward, and they started down the rocky hillside.

It wasn't his fishing ability she didn't trust. It was his intentions.

"Once we're married." His words came back to haunt her once again, and Margaret reminded herself that Trevor St. James might have a smoother approach, but he was no different from every other suitor. But as she stared at his broad back, envisioning the hard, muscular strength that lay beneath the beige twill shirt, she suddenly wished he could have been different from all the others.

When they reached the river, he suggested she gather some wood.

"Just how are you going to catch these fish?" she asked, sliding off the stallion's back.

"I'll worry about that. You just get the wood."

Margaret watched him travel some distance downstream. When he rounded the bend in the river and disappeared behind the rocky hillside, she turned to find the wood for a fire.

Most of the wood she found was too green to burn, and by the time she returned, Trevor was making a fire pit out of the rocks and sand on the riverbank. Five plump trout were laid out on a handkerchief beside him, cleaned, skewered, and ready to cook.

Margaret dumped the pieces of beechwood she had gathered beside the fire pit. When she straightened, she spied the homemade fishing net that lay on the ground behind him.

"So that's how you did it. You brought a net with you. Very ingenious."

"I always try to be prepared. I wish I had brought a fishing pole, though. There's some nice spots for it around here." He reached for a few of the smaller pieces of wood to use as kindling and began laying them in the pit for a fire. "I'll need matches. Fetch me the saddlebags, would you?"

Margaret returned with the saddlebags, along with

the roll of blankets. She spread one of the blankets on the ground beside Trevor, then sat down, watching as he searched for the box of matches, finally dumping out the contents of the saddlebags to find them.

"You like to fish?" she asked.

"I love it. I used to fish all the time when I was a boy, but I haven't done it for years. My family home in Kent has some fine trout streams, but there aren't any in Egypt."

He turned away to light the fire, and she glanced down at the various articles strewn across the blanket. Among the packets of dried food, handkerchiefs, and shaving gear, she saw a dark-brown bottle filled with liquid.

"What's this?" She held up the bottle curiously.

Trevor glanced at her, then looked away. "Quinine."

He poked at the flaming kindling with his stick, sending sparks in all directions. "I have malaria. An inevitable consequence of spending ten years in Africa."

"Malaria never goes away, does it?"

"No. But the quinine helps."

"Is it very bad?"

"Sometimes," he answered, but he did not elaborate. He turned away, reaching for one of the larger pieces of wood, and she smiled to herself. Strong men hated to admit to weakness of any kind, even illness. Her father was the same way.

Margaret put the bottle of quinine back in one of the saddlebags and spied two bars of soap. "How long before we eat?" she asked.

"We'll need a good bed of coals to cook the fish," he answered. "Half an hour would be my guess."

She picked up one of the bars of soap and the comb, then she stood up. "I'm going to have a bath."

He glanced at her. "Don't use that soap. Use the other. That one's mine."

"What difference does it make?" she asked.

"Lemon verbena smells wonderful on you, but I don't think it would suit me."

"You brought lemon verbena soap for me?" she asked.

"That is what you use, isn't it?"

"Yes." She dropped the bar of soap in her hand and picked up the other. Lifting it to her nose, she instantly caught the tangy scent of her favorite fragrance. "Thank you."

"You're welcome. If you're going to have a bath before dinner, you'd better get going."

She glanced around, but the denuded beech trees provided no cover and it was growing dark. She didn't want to be far from the safety of the fire. And Trevor.

As if reading her mind, he said, "There's a shallow pool right there that ought to suit," and pointed to the bend in the river directly in front of their camp site.

"I couldn't possibly!" she said, shocked. "I'd be in plain view."

"Who's going to see you?"

She tilted her head, raising her eyebrows and giving him a pointed stare.

Trevor held up one hand. "Not even a peek," he said solemnly, but there was a mischievous twist to one corner of his mouth she found highly suspicious. "I swear."

"I don't believe you."

He shook his head as if disappointed in her. "You really should learn to trust me."

That did not impress her. She leaned to one side, trying to see behind him. With a sigh, he brought his other hand into view and uncrossed his fingers. "I promise I won't look," he said, moving so that his back faced the river. "I hope you realize how difficult this is going to be for a man of my wicked tendencies. If this gets out, it could ruin my reputation."

"What a sacrifice," she murmured and started toward the river.

"You have no idea," he said fervently, lowering his head to study her ankles appreciatively as she passed.

Trevor proved to be a man of his word. Over one shoulder, she kept her gaze fixed on him as she removed her outer clothing and waded into the river in her chemise and drawers. But even when she gasped at the icy coldness of the water, he did not glance in her direction. He kept his back to her the whole time she bathed and washed her hair. Margaret was relieved that he didn't look, but a tiny little part of her felt rather disappointed that he didn't even try.

Trevor knew he'd made a serious mistake. When this idea of getting Margaret off alone in the country had first occurred to him, his reasoning had seemed sound enough. He'd thought the intimacy of the situation would bring her closer to him, give her reason to trust him, and spark her passion. But he had completely underestimated the effect it would have on his own peace of mind.

He didn't have to turn around to know what he would see. He could imagine it well enough. Margaret was a proper woman, despite her adventurous spirit, and she'd probably left her undergarments on. When he thought of how she would appear, standing in the water with sheer white cotton clinging to every delectable curve of her body, his throat went dry, and it took everything he had not to turn his head and take a good look.

He was trying to be as honorable as possible about this courtship, he truly was. He'd promised her father that he would not take advantage of her innocence. He'd made the same promise to Edward and Cornelia. Like most promises, it had been easy to make at the time, but now, when he was forced to live up to it, he found that it was not easy at all. What a cocky bastard he'd become, to think that once he had her alone he could remember such promises, to think that he could arouse her passion without losing control of his own. By the end of this trip, he was either going to break his word or he was going to be insane.

Fortunately for Trevor, the water was too cold for her to linger over her bath. Within five minutes, he heard her get out of the water, and a few moments later, she sat down opposite him. She was fully dressed, but her blouse and skirt were damp from the wet underclothes beneath, and revealed enough to his imagination that she might just as well have left them off.

He occupied himself with cooking the trout while she combed the tangles out of her long hair. He watched her out of the corner of his eye, wondering what she'd do if he took the comb out of her hand and did it for her. It would give him the perfect opportunity to kiss her neck and inhale the delicious lemon scent of her skin.

But with the way he felt right now, kissing her would be pushing his luck. Being honorable was a damned difficult thing.

They ate without talking. Margaret was clearly too famished for conversation, and Trevor was in no mood for it anyway.

There was one trout left, and he caught her eyeing it with longing. But she glanced at him and did not reach for it.

Trevor sensed her hesitation. "Take it."

Reluctantly, she shook her head. "You need it more than I do, and I'm sure you must still be hungry."

"I've been hungry before. You haven't. You're not used to it." He leaned forward and lifted the skewer. He thrust the fish toward her. "Take it."

Margaret started to refuse again, but he forestalled her. "For once, don't argue with me. I told you before, I refuse to let you waste away to nothing." His lashes lowered, and he eyed the shadow of cleavage just above the round neckline of her blouse. "That would be a sin."

She almost covered herself with her hand, then didn't on the realization that such a move would be horribly gauche. His gaze seemed to burn her skin right through the thin cotton fabric. She stared at his face, lean and shadowed in the firelight with a hunger she sensed wasn't for food.

An owl hooted from one of the trees behind them and took flight, breaking the silence. She looked down at the trout he still held between them and pulled it from the skewer. Laying it on the handkerchief across her lap, she began to peel away the scaly skin.

"Why don't we share?" she suggested, feeling the need to say something. She pulled a piece of trout carefully from the bones and held it out to him.

He stared at her hand for a moment without moving, then took her wrist and pulled, bringing both her and the trout closer. He bent his head. His lips parted, then closed over the meat, and he began pulling it slowly from her fingers into his mouth. She stared at his dark head bent over her hand and felt the warmth of his mouth around her fingers. For an instant, she could not breathe.

She hated him, she reminded herself, she truly did.

Trevor lifted his head to look at her. He chewed the piece of fish and swallowed, but he did not release her wrist. "Excellent idea," he murmured, his thumb rubbing her palm in slow circles.

Pinned by the intensity of his gaze, she couldn't move. She ran her tongue over her upper lip, feeling painfully vulnerable. "Why would you want to marry me?" she whispered.

He let go of her hand abruptly and looked away. "I really don't see the point in talking about that. You made it very clear how you felt about the notion." He smiled at her, but the smile had a wry twist. "In fact, if memory serves, you called me a snake." He stood up. "I'd better get more wood. It's going to be cold tonight."

Margaret watched his back as he walked away in the moonlight, and she suddenly wondered if she had hurt his feelings that night in the carriage. He always seemed so sure of himself, but she felt a sudden prick of conscience, not liking the idea that she might have made him feel rejected.

Impatiently, she told herself she had nothing to feel guilty about. Until a man came along who proved his love and his devotion, she would never give hers. But as she watched Trevor walk away, a sudden yearning tugged at her heart, and she couldn't help wondering if she were wishing for the moon.

11

The following morning dawned clear and sunny, but as Trevor and Margaret made their way down through the rocky canyon, clouds began to move in, bringing with them a chilling mist. Margaret shivered and snuggled closer to the man in front of her, instinctively drawn to the warmth of his body.

Trevor glanced at her over one shoulder. "Getting cold, are you?"

"W-whatever g-gave you that idea?" she answered, her breath coming out in white puffs. She clenched her teeth to stop them from chattering.

He brought the horse to a halt beside a hawthorn tree that had been decimated by lightning and dismounted. With his knife, he began cutting away some of the dead branches.

"What are you doing?" she asked.

"I think it's going to snow, and before that happens, I want to have kindling dry enough to start a fire." He gathered the branches together, wrapped them in one of the blankets, and secured the bundle to his back. "Move up," he told her, "so I can sit behind you. You'll stay warmer that way."

"Why can't we j . . . just stop here for the night?"

Trevor pointed to small openings in the rock on one side of the canyon. "I'd like to find us some decent shelter first if it's going to snow. I'm hoping we'll find a cave big enough."

Margaret scooted forward, and Trevor wedged himself into the saddle behind her. He unbuttoned his greatcoat and wrapped its generous folds around them both.

Snuggled within the circle of his arms, she instantly began to feel warmer. She leaned back to rest her head against his shoulder with a contented sigh. Lulled by the comforting warmth of his arms, she fell asleep.

When the horse came to a halt, Margaret awoke, opening her eyes to a landscape of thick frost, gray mist, and falling snow. She straightened with a yawn and turned to give the man behind her an inquiring glance.

Trevor lifted one hand to brush snowflakes from her hat brim. "If you think you're going to fall asleep every time I let you sit in front, you can forget it. You missed my entire lecture on the breathtaking Italian scenery."

She yawned again. "That's why I fell asleep."

He laughed and chucked her lightly under the chin. "Sorry I bored you," he said, and his fingers tilted her face upward. Before she knew his intention, he pressed a quick kiss to her lips. "I can see I'll have to improve my skills as a guide," he said, pulling back slightly to look at her as his hand curved around the side of her neck.

The suede glove felt cold and rough against her throat, but the brush of his thumb along her jaw was a tender caress that heated her blood and started her pulse hammering. In his eyes she saw that look again, and she recognized it. Desire.

He bent his head, and she parted her lips, leaning closer to him in anticipation of another kiss. But he did not give her what she wanted. He paused, his lips an inch from hers.

"I'd love to," he murmured, smiling, "but not now."

She came to her senses in a rush of mortification, hating him for being so good at deceit, hating herself more for being such a fool. "Why did we stop?" she asked in a little voice. "Are we going to camp here?"

He pointed to a cave about ten yards away that had an entrance high enough to walk through. "Your accommodations, ma'am."

Her embarrassment was forgotten as she eyed the cave with some trepidation. "Don't bears hibernate in caves?"

"I believe so," he said cheerfully and dismounted. "But I'm more worried about bats."

She swallowed hard and tried not to shudder. "Bats?"

"My rifle can fell a bear. But bat caves are unpleasant for sleeping. Very messy."

She winced. "I can well believe it."

Trevor shrugged off the bundle of kindling on his back and dropped it to the snow-covered ground beside him. "Stay here," he ordered as he pulled the rifle out of its holster.

Margaret didn't need to be told that. This time, she had every intention of obeying orders. She watched as he moved toward the cave. Pausing about fifteen feet from the entrance, he lifted the rifle and fired. The rapport from the shot echoed through the canyon, then faded away into silence.

Trevor glanced over his shoulder at her. "No bats anyway."

He moved closer and unsheathed the knife at his belt with his free hand. Margaret watched as he peered through the opening, then slipped inside the cave and disappeared from view. She held her breath, waiting, but Trevor came out only a few seconds later. "All clear," he told her as he sheathed his knife and lowered his rifle. "It'll do."

She followed him inside. Dim gray light filtered in, revealing that the cave was a small one, only about ten feet deep and seven feet wide, with no tunnels or other caverns that could conceal a wild creature. The damp floor and walls were covered with moss and lichen.

"Home, sweet home," Trevor said. "At least for tonight."

"Next year I'm going to make my travel arrangements another way, if you don't mind." Deprived of the warmth of Trevor's arms around her, she began to feel the cold again. She shivered. "So I can be sure of hotels, with radiators and hot meals."

"C'mon, then. If you want a fire and food, we've got to find wood."

They didn't have to go far to find it. Just beyond their cave, the canyon ended, abruptly merging into a forest of beech and maple. The frosted branches of the bare trees rose into the gray mist above, and a carpet of snow-dusted leaves and debris covered the ground.

Back inside the cave, Trevor dumped the wood in a

heap. "Let's get a fire going, then I'll see if I can find something to cook on it."

While Trevor made a ring of rocks just inside the cave entrance and built a fire, Margaret began stacking the wood they had gathered. "Are you building the fire close to the entrance so that it's less smoky in here?" she asked, watching him as she worked.

"Yes, partly." He set a match to the kindling, then rose to his feet. "But mainly so that wolves don't decide to spend the night with us.

"Wolves?" she cried, staring at him as he picked up his rifle and walked around the crackling fire and out of the cave. She was dismayed that he was leaving her alone when there were wolves lurking about. She ran after him. "You didn't tell me about any wolves!"

"You'll be fine," he called back to her. "Wolves are quite shy of people, really, and in any case, the fire will keep them away. Just think of all this as another grand adventure."

"Wolves," she groaned. "Isn't that just dandy?" If she needed any further proof of the fact that Trevor was no hero, this was it.

Margaret went back inside the cave. Thinking of those wolves, she heaped several more logs onto the fire Trevor had made. Then she took off her bonnet, gloves, and coat, which were now soaking wet, and laid them out beside the fire. She unbraided her damp hair so that it would dry, then spread out the blankets to make their bed. She began going through the saddlebags to see what she could find among their supply of food.

There wasn't much to choose from. A few apples, dried apricots, a bit of cheese, and beef jerky, a food she was truly beginning to loathe. She set the food aside and returned the remaining gear to the saddlebags, then settled back to wait for Trevor.

When he returned, he carried with him a handkerchief-wrapped bundle that she prayed contained something better to eat than jerky. "Did you find something?" she asked hopefully.

Instead of answering, he paused at the cave entrance and glanced at the fire between them, which was now a roaring blaze. "Is it big enough?" he asked, as he edged around it.

She looked at the fire with doubt. "Do you think it ought to be bigger?"

He gave that serious consideration, then shook his head. "No, Maggie," he said as he set down his rifle and tossed the bundle in his hand toward her, where it landed in her lap. "If it were any bigger, people down in Naples would see it and think Vesuvius is erupting again."

"That's not funny."

"Yes, it is," he said as he pulled off his hat and gloves. "You just need a proper sense of humor."

"A proper sense of humor means I laugh at what you think is funny?"

"Of course."

That did make her laugh. He was watching her, still smiling, and something in his expression made her tingle. He always looked at her that way just before he kissed her, she realized, and her laughter faded into a hushed and self-conscious silence. She kept trying to hate him, but he made it impossible. How foolish she was, and how vulnerable. She sat up, then ducked her head and stared at the bundle in her lap, sensing his gaze still on her.

"You have a nice laugh, Maggie," he said quietly. "I can see I'll have to be as amusing as possible, so I can hear it more often."

Words, just words. She didn't want to hear him say

things like that. It was foolish to think there might be tenderness or love in him, foolish to think that a plain and chubby girl could inspire such feelings in a rake.

She fumbled with the knot of his handkerchief, untying it to find four small partridges wrapped inside. They were rather thin due to the hard mountain winter, but they were plucked, dressed, and ready to roast.

"You didn't shoot these birds with that rifle," she commented, feeling a desperate need to break the silence with trivial talk.

He removed his greatcoat, shook it free of snow, and spread it out to dry beside hers, then he sank down on the blanket beside her. "If I had, I doubt they'd be any good for roasting, since there'd probably be nothing left of them to fit on a skewer. Speaking of which, I'd better start them cooking, or we'll be having them for breakfast."

"I'll do it." She reached for two long twigs from the pile of firewood nearby. Using his knife, she began stripping the twigs of their side branches and asked, "So, if you didn't use the rifle, how did you catch them?"

"It's amazing what can be accomplished with a fishnet. When I came across a whole flock of them sitting in the snow with their heads under their wings, I just tossed the net over all of them and snared four at once."

Margaret put each of the partridges on a spit and rested them on the rocks that surrounded the fire. "There," she said. "We'll have to remember to turn them."

Trevor didn't answer, and she turned her head to look at him. He was staring at the mouth of the cave, but when she glanced in that direction, she saw nothing but the blazing fire and the falling snow beyond it. She asked, "What are you looking at?"

"It's been a long time since I've watched snow falling. We didn't get much of the stuff in Egypt."

"I've always wanted to go to Egypt. It seems like an exotic and exciting place. What is it really like?"

"Not very romantic," he said, laughing. "Hot as the devil. Dry. Full of cobras and scorpions. There was sand everywhere. In everything. In your food, in your clothes, in your eyes."

"Still, you must have liked it there. Ten years is a long time."

"Do you know what I liked?" He looked at her, his expression thoughtful. "I liked the freedom of it. I can remember that, as a little boy, I always felt caged, restricted. My nanny, Mrs. Mullen, was always saying, 'Don't play in the dirt, Trevor. You'll get dirty,' or, 'Don't go near the water. You'll fall in and spoil your new suit.' I think, by the time I was seven years old, I hated that woman. It was a relief to go to boarding school."

She smiled at him. "So, going to Egypt and digging up antiquities was nothing more than a way of playing in the dirt and getting revenge on your nanny?"

"In a way. Sometimes, when I was out on a dig with the men, we wouldn't bathe or shave for days, and I used to think, 'If only Mrs. Mullen could see me now, she'd die of shame because she failed to bring me up properly.' I always rather liked that idea."

"I know what you mean. When I was little, my nanny was Mrs. Stubbins. She had this thin, pinched face that always made her look as if she were eating persimmons. And she was always trying to make me learn to embroider, which I detested. I can remember sitting in the parlor on summer afternoons as a little girl, stitching these horrible samplers."

"A fate worse than death."

"It was. Satin stitches and French knots. Yuck." Margaret pushed aside thoughts of sour Mrs. Stubbins. "Tell me more about Egypt."

"What would you like to know? Did I find any mummies? Did I really steal gold and fabulous jewels out of the tombs of kings?"

"Well, yes," she admitted, laughing.

"Actually, gold and jewels are rare finds, mainly because over the centuries most of the tombs have already been raided, so unless you stumble across an undisturbed one, you aren't likely to find any valuables like that. And when you do find gold, it comes expensive. You have to pay the workman who finds it the weight of the object in gold."

"Good heavens, why?"

"It's a custom, for one thing, and if you didn't, you wouldn't find any workmen willing to dig for you. For another, it prevents the men from stealing. You see, if they did steal, it wouldn't be for the archeological value of the object, but for the intrinsic value of the gold itself, because they could melt it down. So you have to make it easy for them to be honest."

"What about mummies?"

"Oh, mummies are a dime a dozen. The trick is finding the entombed bodies of the important people. These days, no museum or collector wants to pay for the mummified body of Rameses the scribe or Nefertiti the maid."

"No, I suppose not," she said, laughing. "But isn't it illegal to do all this digging?"

"Technically, yes, although it depends." He grinned at her, and the firelight cast his face in amber glow and black shadow, making him seem more wicked than ever. "If you bribe the proper officials, you can get away with anything."

"Really, Trevor," she said, "it's all right to steal, if the bureaucrats are on your side?"

"If I didn't do it, someone else would." His grin faded, and he looked away, idly poking the fire. "I suspect your father would understand that. He grew up in poverty. But I don't suppose that sort of logic would cut any ice with someone like you."

"What do you mean, someone like me?"

"Have you ever been without money, Maggie? Have you ever known what it was like to live hand-to-mouth? To be completely on your own with no money and not many ways to earn it? Well, I have, and I can tell you it's no summer picnic on the Thames. It's no exciting adventure. It's just hell, pure and simple."

She frowned suspiciously. "How would an earl's son come to be in such circumstances?"

"Maybe because his father died and left his fate in his older brother's greedy hands," he suggested. "Or maybe because said brother hated his guts, refused to buy him a commission in the army, refused to use his influence to launch him in politics, and refused to loan him any capital to earn his own living. Then he cut off his brother's rightful allowance and forbid him to ever set foot in his own home again. And when he left England he was too bloody proud to go scrounging lodgings, meals, and loans off old schoolmates. Perhaps that is what happened."

She imagined him as a young man without means trying to make his way in the world on his own, and she felt her heart softening. But then she remembered he was a rake, a detrimental, and a better liar than anyone she'd ever met. "Or perhaps because he slept with his brother's wife," she shot back.

He stiffened. "So, that delightful rumor is still in circulation, is it? How reassuring to know some things never change."

"Rumor? Are you saying it isn't true?"

"Would you believe me if I said it isn't?"

"Probably not."

"Well, then, I won't bother to deny it. Denying rumors never makes them go away, in any case."

She frowned, finding such a reply highly unsatisfactory. "So you did sleep with her."

"It would be more accurate to say she slept with me."

The man could twist lies into truth like a Madison Avenue street vendor could twist dough into pretzels. "I don't understand."

"I came home one night after a long drinking bout with some of my wilder friends and I went straight to bed. I'm perfectly aware that, when I fell asleep, I was alone, but when I woke up, there she was, naked in my bed. She must have sneaked in without waking me, which isn't surprising since I was quite drunk that night. I refused, of course, but—"

"You did?"

"Believe it or not, Maggie, I do have some discernment about the women I bed. Elizabeth is a beautiful woman, but she's as cold and hard as a marble statue. Not at all my type."

"You expect me to believe Lady Ashton crawled into your bed and offered herself to you like, like some prostitute off the street?"

He shook his head. "You really are amazing. No other well-bred young lady would even know about prostitutes, much less refer to them in conversation."

"Don't try to get around me. I can't believe Lady Ashton capable of such a thing."

"Why not? Prostitution isn't a matter of geography, Maggie. Some of the world's best whores have been queens."

"Why would she do such a thing?"

He gave an abrupt shout of laughter. "I don't know what I'd do if I didn't have you around to keep me humble. Thank you."

"I didn't mean it that way. It's just that I, well, I . . ." Words failed her, and she could only stare at him.

He stared back at her. "I do believe I've finally shocked you."

"You have. I can hardly credit that a woman would do such a thing. She must have been very much in love with you."

"God! Maggie, I hate to shatter your romantic illusions, but love had nothing to do with it. She wasn't so enamored with me that she just couldn't help herself, I assure you. Elizabeth is far too cold-blooded and logical to let passion for any man dictate her actions. She wanted an heir, and Geoffrey certainly wasn't capable of giving it to her."

"He wasn't? Why not?"

"I can't believe we're having this conversation," he said, looking almost uncomfortable. "Why talk about the weather when there are such delightful topics as this?"

She said nothing, but simply waited. Finally, he sighed and said, "Geoffrey was virtually impotent. He couldn't, ah, perform his husbandly duties, if you take my meaning."

She did, and blushed to the roots of her hair.

"I'd known about his little problem for years, ever

since his friends at Cambridge took him to the local brothel. One of the girls there was a special friend of mine, and she told me all about it. At the time, I thought it quite amusing. Anyway, Geoffrey and Elizabeth had been married for nigh on five years, but she still had not produced the required heir, and she was getting rather desperate about it. An heir is everything to a woman in her position."

Margaret forced herself to look at him. "How did your brother find out?"

"He found us there, in my room. He must have gone to Elizabeth's room, discovered she wasn't in her own bed, and assumed the worst. I'd just woken up and found her there when he walked in. Both of us were naked."

"That must have been a horrible moment for him."

"He was rather put out about it, yes."

"Didn't you try to explain?" she asked.

"Of course. But, as much as it may surprise you, my explanations didn't cut any ice with him. I wasn't exactly a man of staunch morals, and my brother was inclined to believe me capable of any sort of debauchery. He stopped my income and banished me from the estate. I was cast out of the family. What he thought of Elizabeth's part in the whole thing, I have no idea. During the ten years I've been away, I received no correspondence from my brother at all, and only one letter from my mother—the letter informing me of Geoffrey's suicide. My mother never was a very compassionate or loving woman, and like Geoffrey, she was inclined to believe the worst about me. Probably because it was so often true." He leaned back, resting his weight on his hands. "So there you have it, the whole sordid story of how an earl's son found himself stone broke and desperate enough that he didn't really care if digging up antiquities is technically illegal."

Margaret frowned, uncertain about whether to believe him or not. "You don't look as if life has been so very hard for you."

"Only because it's been ten years, and I learned how to bend the rules. I've managed to make a life for myself and earn a decent living. No thanks to anyone else."

"And all this because your brother thought you had slept with his wife."

"Geoffrey's opinion of me was formed long before that, I assure you. He thought I was an impudent, rebellious libertine. And he was dead right about me. I can't really blame him for not believing my explanations. They sounded weak enough, in any case."

"And your opinion of him?"

"I thought he was a vain, strutting peacock who thought all the wrong things were important. And I was right, too. He was such a pompous little ass, even when we were boys. I just couldn't resist having a joke or two at his expense. Salt in his trifle and jam on his chair, that sort of thing. Not even when we were boys, now that I think of it. The Prince of Wales came to visit once, shortly before my father died, and I put pepper in Geoffrey's snuff box. He sneezed all over the Prince's coat."

"You are truly outrageous. Your poor brother. It's no wonder he was inclined to distrust you, tormenting him as you did."

"Only because he made himself such a tempting target. If he had only laughed, just once, and shrugged it off, I never would have done anything like that again. And he had a cruel streak a mile wide. When he realized the unmarried parlormaid was pregnant, he turned her out on the spot because of the impression she might give any guests who came to call. He didn't care that the fellow who'd done it refused to marry her, nor that she had no family to take her in. He even refused to pay her the wages she was owed. So don't go letting that soft, romantic heart of yours spare any compassion for Geoffrey. He wasn't worth it. In fact, the first night we met, Hymes reminded me of him. Hymes is another of the same type—one of those pretentious, stuffy, self-righteous blatherskites that Britain's upper crust manages to produce with such unerring consistency."

"And what did you think of me that night we met? You must have thought I was the greenest girl alive."

"Actually, I thought you were a sweet and tempting morsel, far too luscious for Roger's palate."

"You make me sound like a dessert!"

"So you are." He leaned toward her, then lifted her hand and kissed it. "Skin like cream," he murmured. "Lips like ripe berries. I've always had a sweet tooth."

"Don't," she said in desperation. She tried to pull her hand free, but he held it fast. "Don't say things like that to me."

"Why not?"

"Because you're a man who's sampled most of the desserts on the table. I'm just one more."

"Some desserts are more tempting than others."

"Some are also richer than others."

He stiffened and let go of her hand. "True enough," he agreed mildly and turned toward the fire. "A man would probably do better with roasted partridge. A steady diet of rich and resentful heiress might give a man indigestion."

*   *   *

Margaret turned over, the warmth of her body radiating toward his beneath the blanket. Patience, Trevor thought heroically. Patience, strategy, and a damned supply of fortitude.

He listened to the sound of her soft and steady breathing. He thought of burying his face in her hair, making her breathing quicken to gasps of desire. He didn't look at her, but he tortured himself with tantalizing images of her body, soft and lush. God, he wanted her.

He could do it. It would be easy.

She wanted him, too. He knew that well enough. He remembered her hand, trembling when he kissed it, and her eyes, wide and dark in the firelight when he'd caressed her palm. He'd never thought virgins to be all that desirable, but there was something fiercely seductive about Maggie's innocence, something erotic about the way she responded to his touch that inflamed his senses.

It wasn't too late. He could waken her now with his hands and his mouth, take what he wanted and give her what she wanted. What was he waiting for? But even as his body asked that question, his mind answered it. He curled his hands into fists and stared up at the dark ceiling of the cave.

He couldn't do it. He'd given his word of honor.

He'd promised both Henry and Edward that he would not compromise her that way in order to win her hand. It was laughable really, that he felt so compelled to keep his promise. But then, that wasn't the only thing stopping him.

He couldn't do it. It was too soon.

Margaret wasn't ready for that. She wanted him,

yes, but she had to want him badly enough that she'd go to the altar to have him. In order to make that happen, he had to build anticipation within her one kiss at a time, one touch at a time, until her desire for him was strong enough to overcome her fear.

Wait, he told himself, repeating it like a catechism. Wait.

He felt her move again in her sleep, drawing her leg upward, her knee brushing against his hip. He set his jaw and lay perfectly still, striving for logic when lust coursed through him.

He couldn't do it. It was too risky.

He began listing all the reasons why it made sense to hold back. If he took her now, she might—just might—feel compelled to marry him for honor's sake, or because of the possibility of a baby, or both. But she would always feel she'd been manipulated, and she'd come to resent him for it, even hate him. If he had to marry, he wanted no cold and dutiful wife in his bed.

Her leg slid sinuously along his body. *Oh, God.* He jerked away, her touch burning him, and sat up in desperation, thinking he might go for a walk. The air outside the cave was ice cold. It ought to do the trick.

"Trevor?"

Her voice startled him, and he glanced at her. Moonlight spilled through the cave entrance, gilding the long, dark hair that spilled across her shoulder with silver. "I thought you were asleep."

"I was," she said with a yawn. "I was dreaming." She stirred, rolling onto her back. She lifted her arms over her head and stretched, arching her back, her breasts thrusting upward against the wool blanket. Trevor's throat went dry, and he stared, envisioning the luscious shape of them beneath the blanket.

He tried to move away again and found that he could not. He felt his willpower fracturing into pieces, and he surrendered to the inevitable, laying back down beside her. "What were you dreaming about?"

"Mmm." She sighed, a sleepy, whispery sound so erotic it was nearly his undoing. "Have you ever wanted something so badly that it made you ache, something you know will someday be yours but that always seems to be just out of reach?"

Trevor gritted his teeth. "No," he lied. "Never."

"Well, I have."

He grasped for the thin threads of his control. "And what is that something?"

"True love."

Where did she get such ridiculous notions? "There's no such thing."

"Yes, there is, and someday I'll have it."

"Someday?" Flinging back the blanket, he sat up and turned toward her, bracing his weight on his hip and his forearm. "For God's sake, what does that mean?"

She turned her head to glance at him, her expression one of earnest sincerity. "When I meet the right man," she answered with such conviction she might have been a missionary quoting scripture. "A man who loves me just for myself, who wants me—just me—not my money. He'll be a true gentleman," she went on, "honorable and noble, who would go to the ends of the earth for me because I asked him to, a man who would die for me because he loves me."

That made him angry. The idea that while he was lying there making himself crazy with erotic images of her she was dreaming of some fictional white knight, some tragic, heroic figure that could never exist outside her imagination—in fact, some man that wasn't him. "That's the dream of a schoolgirl, not a grown woman," he said bluntly. "It's fantasy."

"No." She shook her head and looked away, gazing up at the roof of the cave. "It's real."

"No, it isn't. Do you want to know what's real?" He leaned over her, bracing his weight on his forearms, blocking out the moonlight streaming through the cave entrance, shutting out all the silly fantasies, forcing her to look only at him. He felt the curve of her hip against his and forgot all about strategy and patience and playing the game. "This," he said in a harsh whisper, bringing his mouth to within an inch of hers. "This is what's real."

He kissed her, not at all gently. He knew he was no noble gallant, and he wanted her to know it, too. She made a sound, a tiny squeak that might have been a protest, but he smothered it, opening his mouth wide over hers and tasting deeply. He tugged at the bulky wool blanket between them and pulled it away, then sank down against her, overwhelming her with his weight.

She was luscious, warm, and soft beneath him. He outlined her body with his hands, running his palms upward along the generous flare of her hips and the inward curve of her waist, then slid one arm behind her back. He opened his other hand over her breast, and made a low sound of appreciation at the full, round shape in his palm.

At the intimate touch, Margaret broke away from his kiss with a shocked gasp. She twisted beneath him, trying to evade his hand, but he would not let her. He cupped her breast in his palm, closing his thumb against his finger to tease her nipple through the fabric with a slow, coaxing motion.

She gave a sharp little cry and her back arched, an

instinctive reaction that pressed her breast against his hand and unknowingly asked for more. He knew he ought to call a halt, but he felt her hips move against his, sending exquisite shudders of pleasure through his body, and he could not find the will to do it.

"What are you doing?" She pushed at his hand, but it was a feeble gesture, uncertain and not at all an effective deterrent. "You can't mean to do this."

I'll stop, he promised her silently. *But not yet. God, not yet.*

Arousal was raging through him like wildfire, but he could feel her trembling, hear her tiny sounds of agitation and virginal confusion. He took a deep breath, reaching for control, but he could not seem to find it. He buried his face in the curve of her neck. "Maggie," he whispered. "God, Maggie, you are so sweet."

He tasted the delicate skin of her throat in gentle nibbles and murmured words designed to both soothe and arouse. He kissed and caressed her, drawing out her desire until she began to writhe beneath him, her breath coming in shuddering whimpers against his shoulder, her fingers convulsively pressing into his back.

He reached for the flap of his trousers, wanting to free himself of the aching pressure, but the first button caught, stubbornly refusing his fumbling, one-handed attempt to loosen it. In that brief, suspended moment, a vestige of unwelcome reality returned. If he didn't stop now, he wouldn't be able to stop at all. His hand stilled. "Oh, Christ," he muttered, "what am I doing?"

With a groan of agony, he wrenched himself away from her, his breathing harsh, his heart thudding in his chest, his body screaming for release.

"Trevor?" she whispered.

He heard the bewilderment in her voice, sensed the tentative question. He clenched his hands into fists and held his body rigid, knowing he could not look at her. If he did, if he saw her lying there all tousled and inviting, he'd come apart.

"I'm trying," he said in a strangled voice, "to be an honorable gentleman. For once in my life. Don't ruin it."

"But—"

"Go back to sleep, Maggie." He turned away and slid to the edge of the blanket as far from her as possible, his body still throbbing with frustration. "Just go to sleep."

12

Late the following day, they reached Sora, a picturesque village at the foot of the Abruzzi. A cluster of whitewashed stone cottages signified the village itself, which appeared to consist of only one street.

Margaret felt the curious stares of the few people they passed. It was understandable, she supposed, as Trevor dismounted to ask the man at the livery stable where they might find a room for the night. Sora was not on the tourist route, and strangers were bound to be noticed, especially at this time of year.

The man nodded in answer to Trevor's inquiry and beckoned Margaret to dismount. She slid down from the horse and approached the two men.

"There's no inn," Trevor told her, "but he says that the people just up the road would probably be willing to take us in for the night. They have an extra room."

He and Margaret walked up the empty street to a

somewhat larger cottage, where a rotund woman in a white apron was scattering feed to the chickens in the yard. She studied them with friendly curiosity as Trevor entered the yard.

Margaret hung back, waiting just inside the gate while Trevor spoke with the woman. Margaret listened as he explained something in a stream of fluent Italian, his voice vibrant in the languid, sleepy afternoon. Watching him, Margaret couldn't help thinking for the hundredth time about the intimate way he had touched her the night before. She'd known, only because of that forbidden novel she'd read, that men did such things. But nothing in the author's words had told her just how extraordinary it was, how intoxicating it felt to be touched in such a way.

His manner toward her since then had been scrupulously polite and very remote. Her attempts at conversation had been met with the briefest of replies, and not once had he touched her again. Margaret found herself wondering what she would do if he did.

Trevor stopped speaking, and Margaret came out of her reverie to find both of them looking at her. The woman approached her, smiling, and said something in Italian, taking her hands to give them an affectionate squeeze before she led her into the house, beckoning Trevor to follow.

She took them up a narrow flight of stairs to a small room with an iron bedstead, a washstand, and a window that looked out over the street below. She pointed to the pitcher and basin on the washstand and the chamber pot in the corner, then looked at them, her round face crinkling into an indulgent smile as she patted the bed in a decisive gesture.

Margaret understood the implication of that. She

felt color rush to her cheeks, but the woman's smile only widened. She said something to Trevor that made him laugh, and Margaret frowned suspiciously as the woman took the pitcher from the washstand and left the room.

"What did you tell her?" she demanded.

Trevor dropped the saddlebags and the roll of blankets onto the bed. "I explained that we are newly married and have been traveling through Italy on our honeymoon."

"What?"

"We were beset by bandits, but we escaped on one of their horses, which is why we have no coach and no luggage. Signora Bartoli was quite touched by the story."

She swallowed hard. Casting a furtive glance at the bed, she couldn't help envisioning both of them lying there. She could almost feel the touch of his hands and the weight of his body pressing her down into the soft feather mattress. "You told her we were married?" she repeated, warmth flooding through her body at the scandalous pictures in her mind.

"Italians are a very romantic, passionate people, but they are also good Catholics. We are a man and woman traveling without escort. What should I have told her?"

Margaret forced her gaze from the bed and turned toward him, but she could not quite meet his eyes. "You could have said I was your sister."

"Be sensible. You don't look at all like my sister. She'd never believe it for a moment. If I had told her that, we'd be spending another night sleeping outdoors, and since clouds are moving in and it looks like rain, I don't much care for that idea."

A knock sounded on the door, preventing any reply

she might have made. When Trevor opened the door, Signora Bartoli entered, carrying a stack of snowy white towels, a chunk of soap, and the pitcher, which was now filled with water. She handed the items to Trevor, talking all the while. She gave Margaret an affectionate kiss on each cheek, murmured what sounded like an endearment, and departed.

"I think she's adopted us," Trevor said, closing the door. "She feels terrible that a young bride should endure such a trial on her honeymoon."

Her chest tightened. "I'm not a bride."

"It's only for tonight, Maggie," he said. "You can pretend for one night, can't you?"

"I suppose so," she conceded with a sigh.

"Good. Then let's wash up and go downstairs. The signora offered us a hot meal, and I, for one, am looking forward to that."

After washing the travel grime from their faces and hands, they went downstairs and followed the delicious scent of spicy food and the noise of raucous conversation to the kitchen.

The room was a large one, but half the space was taken up by a long dining table, where an elderly but robust man sat at the head. He was flanked by two empty chairs obviously reserved for Margaret and Trevor. Beside those chairs sat two younger men. Two women, obviously their wives, sat beside them, one with a sleeping baby nestled against her shoulder. Six children, ranging in age from about five to fifteen, occupied the remaining space at the table.

Another place was set at the foot of the table, but Signora Bartoli was not seated there. Instead, she moved about the kitchen, stirring pots, filling wine glasses, and serving the first course of hot, spicy minestrone and bread to the others. The roar of conversation made Margaret wonder in amused amazement how anyone could hope to be heard above the din or how the baby could sleep so peacefully in his mother's arms.

Conversation ceased long enough for introductions to be made, but as Trevor began listing off names and translating relationships, the names all began to run together. Margaret ended up unable to remember who was who. All she knew was that her hostess was Sophia Bartoli, the older man was her husband, Gustavo, and the two young women were their daughters, who were married to the two young men. She wasn't quite certain which children belonged to which set of parents.

She gave a tentative smile to her host. His response was to give her a long, hard stare from head to toe. He must have approved of what he saw, for he smiled back at her, then waved her into the seat on his right. She accepted it, and Trevor took the empty chair opposite hers.

All around her, conversation resumed, and, with everyone talking at once, the noise level rose again, continuing unabated through the soup, the pasta, and the fish. For Margaret, who was accustomed to excruciatingly polite, very dull conversation, the meal was fascinating, even though she couldn't understand most of what was said.

The men were having a heated discussion, probably about politics, if their emphatic voices were anything to judge by. The children squabbled and played, returning their attention to food only when sternly reminded by their mothers to do so. Sophia spent most of her time bustling back and forth between the stove and the table, urging food on everyone else. The two young women sat together, obviously talking about the baby, who was still sleeping in his mother's arms, blissfully unaware of the havoc all around him.

Margaret watched her hosts and couldn't help feeling a hint of envy. These people were a family, the kind of family she'd never had. She thought of her own childhood, and images of the huge, luxurious dining room at the Newport house flashed through her mind. Her father's chair, empty, of course, as he was nearly always away on business. Mrs. Stubbins picking at her food and puckering up with disapproval every time Margaret had a second helping of anything. The footman, Hubble, stone-faced and properly silent as he served at table. Her mother, who had died when she was a toddler, existing only as a portrait in a gilt frame against the striped paper on the wall. And herself, a chubby little girl who had no brothers or sisters to squabble with as she ate, too intimidated by Mrs. Stubbins to play with her food and lost in the silence that was broken only by the tinkling of silver on china.

Sophia came up beside her, and Margaret realized that the older woman was about to refill her plate with a second serving of fish.

"No, no, please," she implored, holding her hands protectively above her plate to prevent it. "No more."

The older woman spoke to Trevor, and he said, "Sophia is worried that you don't like her cooking."

"Oh, no, it's delicious," Margaret replied, hoping she wasn't being rude by refusing. "It's just that I really shouldn't have any more."

She watched the older woman as Trevor translated her words. Sophia shook her head and spoke decisively. Trevor smiled, an unexpected response to the woman's stern tone of voice. Curious, Margaret leaned forward and whispered, "What did she say?"

"She says that since you are a married woman, you need to eat more."

"Why?"

He leaned back in his chair. His gaze moved to her mouth, down to her shoulders, and lower still in a lazy, leisurely appraisal before he looked up again and met her eyes. "Because there's always the possibility that you're eating for two."

She blushed again, a reaction that caused Sophia to laugh and beam at her with motherly approval before she gave her an affectionate pat on the cheek and turned away.

Trevor did not laugh. He simply looked at her, half-smiling, and she felt the impact of his gaze instantly—that powerful awareness of him, and only him, that cast a spell and blotted out everything else. It made her feel as if they were the only two people in the world. It was exactly the sort of look an adoring groom ought to give his bride—intimate, tender, and loving, a look of leashed passion and shared secrets.

They were only pretending, but he was good at it. So good that, for an instant, it seemed like the truth.

He looked away before she did, and the spell was broken. Margaret accepted a cup of coffee from Sophia and studied Trevor for a moment longer. She watched as he became involved in whatever the men were discussing, and she wondered what he really felt about her.

With ruthless honesty, he'd called her a spoiled child, but she could still hear the passion in his voice when he had called her "sweet Maggie." He'd teased her and embarrassed her and ordered her around, but he had rescued her from those men. He was only after her money, but he could look at her as if he wanted her love. With one word, he could provoke her to outrage, with one kiss he could unleash her desire. And every time she thought she had him figured out, he turned the tables on her.

Something he said made the men laugh, and Gustavo gave him an approving slap on the back. He hardly knew these people, yet it was almost as if he were one of the family, just another son visiting his mama and papa for Sunday dinner. But his own brother had turned him out. She didn't know for certain whether the story he had told her was true, but she was inclined to believe it was. Margaret wondered again if she was the biggest fool in the world.

I haven't figured you out yet, Trevor St. James, she thought, watching him. *But I will.*

When the meal was over, Sophia and Gustavo's children and grandchildren departed for home, and the house suddenly became quiet. Gustavo and Trevor went outside to smoke cigars, and Sophia began clearing the table. Margaret offered to help her, but Sophia refilled her coffee cup and sent her out of the kitchen.

She took her coffee into the parlor and immediately spied the homemade chess board and box of wooden game pieces that sat on a small table in one corner of the room. When Trevor and Gustavo came back into the house, Trevor saw her standing beside the chessboard and walked up beside her. "Do you play?" he asked.

"Oh, yes. My father taught me years ago."

"Are you any good?"

Her chin lifted at the challenge, and she turned to him. "Good enough that I eventually trounced him, and he hasn't played with me since. My father is not a man who likes to lose."

"I can believe that." He pulled out a chair for her. "Shall we?"

"Very well," she agreed, settling into her seat, "but I'll give you the same warning I always gave my father. I'll not let you win just because you are a man."

"God forbid!" He pushed in her chair, then sat down opposite her. "Why should you?"

"In playing games with gentlemen," she said primly as if quoting from an etiquette book, "a lady should take care not to allow a spirit of competition to over-come her. It is always best if she loses, so as not to hurt their feelings or wound their pride."

He shook his head. "And all this time, I've believed it was my superior skill at games that enabled me to win against the ladies. I feel quite disillusioned."

She laughed. "We'll see how you do this time," she said and reached for one of the white pieces from the box. But Trevor plucked it out of her hand before she could place it in front of her on the board.

"Since we are not allowing the sex of the players to influence the outcome, the lady does not automatically get the opening move." He pulled a black pawn from the box and hid his hands beneath the table. "All in the spirit of fair play, of course," he added, lifting his closed fists.

Margaret couldn't very well argue with that, even though she was accustomed to opening the game and preferred it that way. She hesitated a moment, then pointed to his left fist. He opened his hand to reveal the black pawn.

He handed the piece to her. "It seems luck is on my side."

She gave him a confident smile across the table. "You'll need it."

With that, they arranged their pieces on the board, and the play began in earnest. He opened with the queen's pawn, she countered with the bishop's. Both of them settled into intense concentration, scarcely noticing when Gustavo pulled his chair over to watch them.

She was good at the game. Trevor was surprised by that, not because of her sex, but because he wouldn't have thought Margaret patient enough for chess. He studied her face as she studied the board, the fierce little frown that knit her dark brows, and the stubborn set of her chin, and he realized what she lacked in patience she made up for in tenacity. Like him, Margaret liked to win.

The evening wore on. Sophia and Gustavo went to bed, leaving them alone in the parlor, absorbed in their chess game. Trevor knew Margaret's strategy was sound, and every move she made was calculated to further that strategy. But her singleminded tenacity eventually cost her the game. He allowed her to close in on him with her purposeful moves until she thought she had him trapped.

She slid her rook forward. "Check."

He moved his knight. "Checkmate."

Her shoulders slumped in disappointment. "I never saw that coming," she admitted with a sigh. "I should have."

He smiled at her across the table. "You're a good player, Maggie. You just need to be more flexible. Flexibility allows you to take advantage of opportunities and makes you less predictable."

She lifted her head. "What you're really saying is that you knew what I was going to do every step of the way."

"Not every step," Trevor said, laughing at her

glum expression. "There were times when you did surprise me."

"Beast. I feel quite humbled, since I couldn't fathom your moves half the time. I kept thinking perhaps you'd had too much wine with dinner."

"If I had, could you blame me? It was very good wine, and Sophia kept refilling my glass."

"I know. I've never met such hospitable people. We're strangers to them, but they treated us like part of the family."

"Well, when you have that many, what's two more?" He laughed. "Did you know that Sophia and Gustavo have nine children and twenty-six grandchildren?"

"Heavens! Can you imagine what a responsibility that would be?"

"Is that one of the reasons you are so opposed to marriage?" he asked, deliberately misinterpreting her words. "Because children would be a responsibility you don't want?"

Astonished by the question, she fell back in her chair, staring at him across the table. "I'm not opposed to marriage."

"Aren't you? It seems to me that you are."

"You just say that because I don't want to marry you," she countered with spirit.

"Well, I must confess, as a man who feels he has a great deal to offer a future wife, your violent opposition to the possibility did rather wound my pride." He gave a casual shrug. "But I've gotten over it."

"You have?"

"I'm not a fool, Maggie, and a man would have to be a fool to chase a woman who doesn't want him."

"I never said—" She stopped abruptly and bit her lip. "I never thought you were a fool," she amended.

"It's just that you're holding out for true love," he said lightly. "Isn't that right?"

"Don't laugh at me," she said.

"I'm not."

"Yes, you are. I don't think you even believe in love."

He heard the sudden hint of wistfulness in her voice and knew this was an opportunity of which he should take immediate advantage. He should take her hand in his and gaze into her eyes and say something sensitive and meaningful—tell her that of course he believed in love, and that he was thinking perhaps he'd found it with her.

But when he looked at her across the table, he found himself unable to say the words that just might win him the prize. He couldn't lie to her so blatantly about something she valued so highly.

"I'm not laughing at you, Maggie," he said gently. "It's just that I think people waste a lot of time, endure a lot of pain, and expend a lot of energy for something that doesn't really exist. I think that what most people call love is simply passion all dressed up."

"You're very cynical."

"Perhaps. But I've discovered that love is a rather unreliable emotion. Hardly sufficient motivation for a lifetime commitment."

"And what would you consider to be a sufficient motivation?" she asked, her eyes narrowing. "Money, perhaps?"

He knew that game, and he refused to play it her way. "You are very quick to accuse me of being cynical, when you seem to believe that every man who shows an interest in you wants nothing but your money."

"Like you, I draw conclusions based on my experience."

"Indeed?" He smiled at her. "I knew the first moment I saw you that you were a woman of the world."

"You *are* laughing at me." She lowered her gaze to the chessboard between them and said softly, "Perhaps it's foolish of me to believe that marriage should not be a business arrangement. Perhaps it's silly of me to think that people should marry because they are truly in love and for no other reason. But I do believe it. I've seen three of my closest friends marry because it was expected of them, because they were afraid to be labeled as spinsters, or because their families pressured them until they felt they had no choice, or because they believed the men who vowed to love and cherish them, without being certain of their character, or without waiting for proof of their devotion. And now they are trapped."

"What do you want, Maggie? What do you really want?"

She gazed down at the chess pieces. "I am determined that only the very deepest love will induce me into matrimony. I believe that there is a man out there, somewhere, who will love me for myself, even if I didn't have two nickels to rub together, even if I am headstrong and—I admit it—spoiled. A man who will love me all the days of my life. I will not marry until I find him." She lifted her head and saw his faint smile. "What's wrong with that?"

He could have told her what was wrong with it. He could have told her that she was setting herself up for bitter disillusionment, that nothing was more painful than innocence lost and expectations unfulfilled. Better to have no illusions and no expectations. But he could not tell her those things, and, even if he did, she would not believe him.

Trevor looked into her dark eyes and saw the defiance there, defiance that made him want to pull her into his arms, to kiss her and caress her until she stopped dreaming about some white knight who didn't exist and realized that the man she would marry was sitting right in front of her. But he also saw something else in her eyes, a sweet and painful vulnerability that made him suddenly wish he could spare her that disillusionment, that he could become what she wanted.

The moment he thought it, he realized what rubbish it was. If he listened to this much longer, he was going to start believing in white knights, too, and angels and miracles, as well. He set the chess piece back on the table and glanced at the clock on the mantel. "It's getting late, and we have to be on our way early in the morning."

"Of course." She rose to her feet, then picked up the lamp from the table and started for the stairs. But Trevor made no move to follow her.

When she reached the bedroom, she realized that Sophia had been there before going to bed. A nightgown had been laid out on the bed for her, and a tortoiseshell brush and mirror lay beside it. The gown was of plain white cotton, but the delicate embroidery and hand-knitted lace told her that it had been made with loving care. On the washstand rested a small jar. When she opened it, Margaret discovered homemade soap scented with lavender.

She placed the cork lid back on the jar and smiled at Sophia's thoughtfulness. The Italian woman had put the things there for her, certain that a bride would want to look pretty for her husband when he came to bed.

But Trevor was not her husband. Her smile faded, and she set down the jar with a thoughtful frown.

Trevor could never be her husband. He did not love her. He didn't even believe in love.

Margaret brushed out her hair with the tortoise-shell brush, washed with the lavender-scented soap, and put on the pretty nightgown anyway, reasoning that she wasn't doing it for him, but for herself.

She slid between the crisp cotton sheets and closed her eyes, knowing it would be best if she were asleep when Trevor came in. But sleep eluded her. Try as she might, she could not stop thinking of him and the passionate moments of the night before. She could not stop the bewildering rush of emotions that overcame her when she thought of the extraordinary touch of his hands and the brush of his lips on her skin. And she could not stop listening for his footsteps and wondering when he would come upstairs and lie down beside her.

But when Trevor finally came in, he did not share the bed with her. Instead, he took a pillow and stretched out on the floor near the window.

Margaret listened as his breathing deepened to the even cadence of sleep and told herself she should be glad that he was behaving honorably. She should be relieved that he had not touched her in that way again and that he'd abandoned his mercenary notions of marrying her. But she wasn't glad. She wasn't relieved. She was actually disappointed, and that was the most bewildering thing of all.

13

They left Sora early the following morning. In addition to his usual load, Hadrian was given another burden—a burlap sack stuffed with all manner of food from Sophia's kitchen. Trevor told Margaret the Italian woman had packed them so much they could probably get to Algiers before they ran out of food.

Sophia and Gustavo had tried to refuse payment for their hospitality, but Trevor somehow managed to convince them to accept five hundred lire.

"So, what tall tale did you give them this time?" Margaret asked as Trevor turned the stallion onto the road south, where the tumbled blocks and broken columns of an ancient Roman villa lay scattered amid the brown weeds and new spring grass.

"Why, Maggie, what do you mean?" he asked innocently.

She wasn't fooled. "If we were beset by bandits, how did we have the money to give them?"

"Oh, that. Well, we did manage to escape on one

of their horses, remember? The bandit just happened to have a bit of money in his saddlebags."

"How fortunate for us," she murmured dryly. "What a cool liar you are."

"It's a harmless lie," he told her as he stared at the road ahead. "They'll never know the truth of it, and they deserved the money. Are you saying I shouldn't have given them anything for their kindness?"

"Of course not. It's just that I'm continually amazed at how conniving you can be. I think you could convince anyone of anything if you set your mind to it."

"Not anyone," he countered wryly. "I didn't manage to convince you to marry me, did I?"

"You didn't even try. You just said it, as if it were a foregone conclusion."

"What should I have done? Knelt before you and asked for your hand, assuring you that my mummy approved of you, and waxing poetic about how much society would envy us?"

The vision of Trevor on bended knee prattling on like Roger was too much. She burst out laughing.

"I take it that wouldn't have worked," he said, laughing with her. "So, tell me, what would a man have to do in order to win you? What horrible ordeals would you put him through? Would you expect him to come charging in on his white steed, slay the dragon, and carry you off to his castle?"

She pretended to seriously consider that notion. "Well, yes, that might do the trick."

"No, it wouldn't. I've already done that, and I don't see you smothering me with affection as a result. But then, Hadrian isn't white, Emilio is a snake, not a dragon, and, as for your castle"—he gestured to the ruins around them—"it's not much, as castles go. The roof leaks."

Margaret's laughter faded into silence. She bit her lip and stared at his back, appreciating the truth of what he said. His motive might not have been a very chivalrous one, but he had rescued her. "I never thanked you for that, did I?" she asked, feeling contrite. "I'm sorry."

"Forget it. I don't want your gratitude."

She took a deep breath and asked the question uppermost in her mind. "What do you want?"

"I don't want you to see me as some lecherous fellow beneath your contempt, nor do I want you to see me as some gallant hero either. I'd like you to start seeing me for what I really am."

"And what is that?" she cried. "Every time I start thinking I have you figured out, you change. Getting to know you is like standing on quicksand."

"You might start trusting me. That would help."

"Trust you? You tell me we should be friends, then you tell me you're going to seduce me. Are you a villain or a hero?"

"Both. And neither. I'm just a man, Maggie, not as bad as you believe me to be, nor as good as you want me to be. Why does everything have to be black or white?"

"I don't know," she said, genuinely bewildered. "All I know is that if you want me to see you for the man you are, then tell me the truth. What manner of man are you?"

He didn't answer for a long moment, then he said quietly, "I think that's something you'll have to figure out for yourself."

*   *   *

She tried. She really did. During the five days that followed, she ran over all the events that had brought them to this point, but the more she tried to figure him out, the more muddled she became. It was like their chess game, where he seemed able to anticipate her moves, while his remained unfathomable.

Since that night in the cave a week ago, he had not touched her at all. She remembered his words about trying to be honorable, and she wondered why he bothered at this late date. She could still recall with scorching clarity every place he had touched her and kissed her. At night, she stared up at the stars while he slept and imagined him touching her again, wishing with fearful anticipation that he would, praying with hot shame that he wouldn't.

The countryside around them changed as they journeyed south toward Naples. Unlike the forbidding mountains of the Abruzzi, the landscape here was lush and green from the winter rains. The gray-green foliage of olive trees bespoke a warmer, milder climate, and meadows were already blooming with spring wildflowers. They stopped for lunch beside one such meadow, settling comfortably beneath an olive tree with a blanket and the sack of food Sophia had given them. After they'd eaten their fill, Trevor settled back on the blanket with an apple, and Margaret headed into the grove of trees for a walk.

When she returned, she found Trevor sitting cross-legged on the blanket writing letters.

"Who are you writing to?" she asked curiously.

"Among other things, I'm writing to Edward and Cornelia to let them know we are fine and should be arriving in a week or so," he answered. "I don't want them to worry, and if I post it from the next town, it should get there well before we do."

"Oh. Let them know that I'm quite well, would you?"

"I already have."

"Who else are you writing to?" she asked curiously, glancing at the completed letter tucked in the flap of his portfolio.

"I don't think that's any of your business. Don't be rude."

"I'm only trying to figure you out," she said with an artless smile. "You suggested I should. So tell me—what is it? A love letter to some long-suffering female acquaintance? Or correspondence about some smuggled Egyptian artifacts perhaps?"

"You'll never know."

"You think not?" She snatched it out of his portfolio and ran.

"Maggie, come back here!" he called, but she didn't come to a halt until she was some distance away. She held up the letter, waving it teasingly.

He rose to his feet. "Give it back."

Laughing, she shook her head and began walking backward. "This is your own fault for being so secretive. Tell me what it says, or I'll have to read it myself."

"I'll get it back before you have the chance."

"I don't think so." She unfolded the letter as if to read it, and he was after her in an instant. With a shriek, Margaret turned and fled. Her bonnet caught the breeze and flew off. Laughing, she made a grab for it, but it sailed through her fingertips and was gone. Her hair came down, whipping across her face as she glanced over her shoulder to find Trevor right behind her.

He caught her around the waist, pulling her hard against him, and the momentum sent him falling backward into the grass, taking her with him, his body cushioning her fall. She tried to rise, but his arm around her waist kept her there. Margaret was laughing too hard to struggle.

Trevor slid out from beneath her and rolled on top, pinning her to the ground. Seizing her wrists, he lifted her arms over her head. "I have you now," he said, grasping both her wrists with one hand as he took the paper from her fingers with the other. He stuffed the letter into his trouser pocket, vowing he'd destroy it at the first opportunity. The letter to his mother didn't contain anything she didn't already know, but he had no intention of letting her satisfy her curiosity by sneaking a peek at it later. He brought his hand up to caress her face. "You can't get away."

He was far stronger than she, and Margaret knew any attempt to escape would be futile. Her laughter faded away, and she looked into his eyes, as brilliantly blue as the sky, and glittering with intent. She realized that she'd been playing with fire. "I wouldn't have read your letter," she said in a shaky whisper. "Honestly."

"That won't save you. You challenged me, I won, you lost. Now I'm wondering what prize I should claim for my victory." He brushed the tip of his finger across her lip and gave her a wicked smile. "What should a man do when he has a beautiful woman at his mercy?"

She frowned. "Don't say things like that to me. Don't lie."

"What is the lie, Maggie? Telling you you're beautiful? But you are. So beautiful it makes me ache."

"Don't!" She turned her face aside. "I'm not beautiful, and it's cruel of you to say so."

"Cruel?" He stared at her in disbelief, shaking his head. "Sometimes I really think you're daft. What makes you think you're not beautiful?"

"I can look in a mirror."

She renewed her struggles in earnest, but he had all the advantage and he used it. She finally gave up and went completely still beneath him, panting from the exertion.

"You may be able to look in a mirror, but you obviously can't see a thing."

She opened her mouth to protest, but he interrupted her. "When I look at you, do you know what I see?" He took a deep breath, his gaze roaming over her face, not knowing quite how to begin. "I'll tell you what I see, Maggie."

The breeze caught a tendril of her hair, and it floated across her face, catching at the corner of her mouth. That gave him a place to start.

"I see your hair," he murmured, gently brushing the loose tendril aside, "which is as dark and rich as sable, and I imagine taking it down, seeing it fanned out around your face just as it is now. I think of tangling it in my hands, feeling it run like silk through my fingers. I see your eyes, and I always think of fine whiskey because they're brown and gold and make me burn inside when you watch me shave in the mornings. And I see these long, thick lashes that don't have that silly debutante curl and these dark brows that get a skeptical little crinkle between them whenever I say things you don't believe."

He touched her forehead as he spoke, then traced his finger along the bridge of her nose and down to her lips. "Then, there's your mouth. Wide and full and perfect for kissing." He moved his hand to the side of her face and touched her lips with his. "And your chin, stubborn as the devil, always testing me, doubting me, challenging me. But it's round as a cherub's, and that rather spoils the stubborn effect, I think."

He buried his face in the curve of her neck, tasting her in small nibbles. "You have the softest skin," he mumbled against her throat. "Warm and soft. So, so soft, like velvet." He drew his tongue along the column of her throat and felt her pulse hammering in the hollow just above her collarbone. He could hear her breath coming in little gasps between her parted lips.

He let go of her wrists and sat up, straddling her, feeling the exquisite shape of her hips between his thighs. "There," he said, not breathing all that evenly himself. "That's what I see, and so would any man alive with half a brain in his head and one eye open."

She opened her eyes and stared up at him in stunned amazement. "You really think I'm pretty? I'm not too fat?" she whispered, so painfully skeptical that he again felt that hard, hot anger surge inside him. The governess who'd made her think she was fat and plain was probably a sour old woman who had the shape of a scarecrow herself. And the malicious comments of Lady Lytton were no better. He knew *she* was a scrawny and sour old woman.

"You're perfect," he said. "Absolutely perfect."

He spread his palms across her ribs just beneath her breasts. "Do you remember that charm I gave you in Rome? I bought it for you because you remind me of a violin." He slid his hands reverently down her torso and back up again. "You have the same shape, with these lush curves that always make me want to touch you. You say you want a noble and chivalrous gentleman, and I've been trying, but Maggie, no man could look at you and feel noble or chivalrous. I know

I can't. I—" His voice cracked as his palms touched the sides of her full breasts, and he decided it was time to stop talking.

He kissed her. Her lips parted instantly beneath his. Her arms came up to hold him, pulling him closer, and the sweet way she yielded to him was almost his undoing.

Control, he reminded himself desperately, but even the idea of getting shot by her outraged father couldn't have stopped him now. Dying would be preferable to the agony he'd been going through for the past week.

He lifted his hips and shifted sideways to stop that particular torture, then began opening the buttons of her blouse. He slid his hand beneath the fabric and found the full shape of her breast. Above the lace edge of her corset, his fingertips caressed bare skin as soft and warm as the velvet he'd told her it was. He felt her nipple harden against his palm, and he closed his thumb and finger around the hard little button, teasing it through the fabric. She broke away from his kiss with a gasp.

He trailed kisses along her throat, her collarbone, and lower still, to the swell of her breasts above her corset. He kissed her there as he moved his hand down her ribs and across the seductive curve of her hip. He tugged at her skirt, pulling it upward, then slid his hand beneath.

She made a sound of protest as he slid his hand inside her drawers. Her thighs closed in instinctive denial against his hand, but he was not deterred. With infinite patience, he caressed her, murmuring coaxing words against her breasts as he worked his hand between her thighs. He finally reached his goal and touched the damp warmth of her, then slipped one finger gently inside her. He felt how ready she was when he stroked the tiny nub of her pleasure with his thumb and heard her little moans. His resolve fractured into pieces. God, he wanted her. Promises and intentions and honor be damned.

He started to withdraw his hand so that he could unbutton his trousers, but the sight of her face stopped him. Her eyes were closed and her lips were slightly parted. Her skin was flushed a delicate pink as she moved in an instinctive response to his touch. Fascinated, he caressed her and forgot all about his own pleasure as he watched her climax. Her body arched, and she threw back her head with a long, soft wail. When she finally fell back against the grass, panting, he smiled down at her, feeling pleased and, in a strange and alien way, satisfied.

He wanted to laugh at that notion. His body was throbbing with unrequited lust. And yet he was satisfied in a way that none of the bored wives or jaded mistresses he'd had in his life had ever satisfied him before. He withdrew his hand, pulled her skirt down over her legs, and quickly buttoned her blouse. Then he rolled onto his back and stared up at the sky.

"You're killing me," he muttered. "Inch by inch, you're killing me."

Margaret opened her eyes at the sound of his voice, but she could not look at him. The things he had done and the way it had felt when she, when she had . . . Oh, heavens, she couldn't even articulate it, that feeling, like an explosion, like fire and light, like nothing she'd ever felt before. At that moment, she wanted to laugh and weep and die of embarrassment.

"Believe it or not," he went on, "ruining an innocent woman is something I have never done, and I can't do it now. It was different when I thought we would soon be married, but you've made it clear you have no intention of marrying me, and I find myself reluctant to completely take away your innocence. As much as I want you, I can't do that to you. And I think it's going to kill me."

"I"—she drew a deep breath, trying to think—"I don't understand."

"Reflect on that erotic novel you were reading, specifically the part the man is supposed to play in the process, and I'm sure you'll figure it out."

"Oh." She blushed. Although she didn't realize exactly what he meant, she got the general idea that he had not finished and was in some discomfort as a result. "I'm sorry," she mumbled, still unable to look at him. "Are you, umm, are you all right?"

"I'll survive. Although—"

Hadrian let out a frustrated neigh, interrupting whatever Trevor had been about to say. The couple turned their heads to see the stallion rear back, tearing at the lead rope that kept him tethered to the tree.

"Hell!" Trevor jumped to his feet, but before he could even take a step toward the horse, Hadrian reared again, this time freeing himself from the branch by snapping the rope with a vicious yank. Free at last, he tore across the field at a run, his lead rope dragging on the ground. Trevor whistled for him, but the stallion was intent on his own course.

They looked at the olive tree, where the rope was still tied securely to the branch, its loose end dangling in the breeze.

"He broke the rope," Margaret commented. "What on earth could make him do that?"

Trevor pointed to the rise far in the distance, where several horses stood silhouetted against the sky. Hadrian was racing toward them at breakneck speed. As he approached, they turned and fled, disappearing from view on the other side of the hill. "Mares," he said with a sigh. "Wild ones, if I'm not mistaken. Probably live back in the canyons. Damn."

"Trevor, he had everything except the food Sophia gave us and one blanket. We have to go after him."

"We'll never catch up to him on foot. Those wild mares will lead him miles away."

"Perhaps we should wait here, then. Maybe he'll come back."

"I doubt it."

"Most horses will come back if they've run off. How do you know he won't?"

"Because he's a stallion, that's why," Trevor answered and began gathering up what meager supplies they had left. "He's got wind of a mare, and nothing else matters to him now."

As if to himself, he added, "I know just how he feels."

Left with no alternative, they resumed their journey on foot. In a way, Margaret was glad of it. Seated on horseback, pressed so close to him would have been unbearable just now. She was relieved that the absence of the horse made such intimacy unnecessary. That extraordinary thing he had done to her was still too fresh in her mind.

Was this passion? she wondered. This acute embarrassment that brought a hot flush to her cheeks and this tight knot in her stomach that made her feel quite ill? If so, it was an agonizing feeling indeed, nothing like what she would have expected. The tension inside her felt more like the symptoms of influenza than passion.

She should not have allowed it. She should have

said something to stop him, and her mortification increased as she realized that she had made no protests at all. Like the night in the cave, she had allowed him to do shocking things to her without ever thinking of gainsaying him.

Yet, Trevor was not a man to be easily denied. Any other man of her acquaintance would ask to call her Margaret, ask to take her hand, ask to kiss her. But Trevor never asked. He simply took what he wanted, and thereby never gave her the opportunity to refuse him anything.

I'm just a man, Maggie.

But he was not. He was more. More exciting, more dangerous, and infinitely more compelling than any man she had ever known. He was daring, bold, and handsome, an intoxicating combination.

Heavens, she sounded like Sally Ellerby, gushing and carrying on as if she were in love with him.

That absurd idea brought her to a halt. Margaret stood in the middle of the road, staring at his back as he walked on. Fear washed over her. She wasn't in love with him. She couldn't be. It was impossible.

Trevor stopped and turned to glance at her. "Are you tired? We can stop if you like."

"No!" she cried, alarmed by the suggestion. It wasn't even close to sundown, and the idea of sitting with him and making stilted attempts at trivial conversation was too much just now. She would rather walk and walk until she dropped from exhaustion.

Her violent reply caused him to give her a puzzled look, and she said in a quieter tone, "I'm fine, thank you. But it's quite early still, and I think we should continue."

"Very well, if you are certain."

They pressed on, and though Trevor twice inquired

if she would like to stop, she said no. But she was not used to walking such long distances over rough roads, and by dusk her feet ached so badly that when he insisted they stop for the night, she did not argue.

She followed him as he made for the shelter of forest that lined the road. He spread their one blanket on the grassy bank of a stream, and she sank down on it.

He sat down beside her with their bag of food. They ate in silence, a silence that became increasingly uncomfortable for Margaret with each passing moment. After they had finished, it was not yet dark enough to go to sleep, and she searched desperately for something neutral to say. "How far are we from Naples? Are we getting close?"

"If we were on horseback, I'd say we'd be there within three days. But traveling on foot, we're almost a week away, I imagine."

"I was afraid of that." She sighed and began unlacing her boots. She pulled them off, grimacing with pain.

Trevor, always acutely observant, noticed it. "Feet hurt?"

"That's one way of putting it."

"You might soak your feet in the water," he suggested as he stretched out on the blanket. "That would help."

She glanced at the stream only a few feet away and thought that an excellent suggestion. Turning away from him, she peeled off her stockings, then swung her legs over the steep bank and let her feet dangle in the cool water.

As she soaked her tired feet, she glanced over her shoulder at Trevor. His eyes were closed, and she thought he might have fallen asleep. Relieved at not having to make conversation, she soaked her feet in the stream, and the nervous tension she'd been feeling all afternoon slowly dissipated. The sun disappeared behind the hills, and twilight descended, bringing a distinct chill to the air. She pulled her feet out of the water and turned back around.

"Better?"

Startled, she glanced up to find he had opened his eyes and was watching her, smiling.

She looked away, reaching for one of the napkins in their food sack. "A bit, yes," she answered and began to dry her feet.

"Only a bit?" He sat up. "Perhaps I can be of some assistance."

He leaned forward and grasped her ankle. Before she could even guess what he intended, he pulled her foot onto his lap. She tried to pull free, but he would not let go.

"Trust me." He cradled her foot in his hands, his sun-browned skin a sharp contrast to the whiteness of her own. She watched as he massaged her foot. He began with her toes and worked his way down, until his thumbs were kneading her instep. All the tension she'd felt earlier was back in full force. Margaret twisted the napkin in her hands, insecure and afraid, and aching with a longing that no foot massage could soothe away.

"You have very pretty feet," he said casually. "Did you know that?"

Margaret could not have answered him if she'd wanted to. She felt as tense and taut as a bow string.

He must have sensed her feelings, for he paused and looked at her. "I'm not going to bite you, Maggie," he said gently and returned his attention to his task. "Lay back and relax."

She stretched out on the blanket and tried to do what he said, but his touch was so disturbing, that she could not. She was torn between the safety of good sense and the exhilarating wish for his love. She could feel her heart slipping out of her control and into his, and she was afraid. So very afraid.

He set her foot back on the blanket and reached for the other one to begin the process all over again. When he had finished, he wrapped the blanket around her and kissed her. "Go to sleep, Maggie," he said and laid down beside her in the dark.

Sleep? she wondered in disbelief. All her feelings were so mixed up, her thoughts so confused, her fears and wishes and hopes so muddled, sleep was an impossibility.

He had told her that she was beautiful, and had given her exact and specific reasons why he thought her so. Though she knew how empty compliments were, the words had been so sweet to hear. Sweet and somehow terrifying.

She wanted so badly to believe him. He was always asking her to trust him, but she was afraid to be made the fool. All her life she had wanted to let her heart rule her head, but her head always seemed to win that battle. She yearned to take risks, experience excitement, be daring and adventurous. Yet, try as she might, she could never seem to rid herself of her own deepest fears and insecurities.

Perhaps he meant what he said. He may have thought only of her money in the beginning, but time might have given him reason to form a more honorable and honest attachment to her. Perhaps he had truly come to care for her.

It was an astonishing notion. That this man, who seemed to have such a callous heart and whose reputation

proved he had no trouble making conquests, might be
falling in love with her.

If only it could be so. She hugged herself, wishing
with all her heart that it were true. If only she could
believe him. If only she could be certain.

During the next two days, Trevor did nothing to
relieve her uncertainties. He was moody and distracted. He did not offer to massage her feet again. He
did not kiss her or touch her. He hardly spoke a word
to her.

They walked and walked, and with every mile they
traveled, his mood seemed to worsen. On the afternoon of the third day, when Margaret casually asked
how much further he thought they had to go, he
nearly bit her head off with his reply.

"For God's sake, I told you three days ago we were
a week away. Do you have to keep asking me?"

"What on earth is the matter with you?" she countered in exasperation. "You're as grouchy as a bear."

He resumed walking without answering her. The
tension inside him was becoming unbearable. To be
so close to her without having her was the worst possible torture. His mood was not helped by the fact
that he did not feel well. By the time they made camp
that night, he had a splitting headache, and he knew
what that meant. It was the first sign of a malaria
attack, and he had no quinine.

They ate without talking, and afterward Trevor
laid down, hoping to ease the pain in his head.

"Going to sleep already?" Margaret asked in surprise. "It's quite early still."

"I'm tired."

"Don't you feel well?"

He opened his eyes to find her bent over him, frowning with concern. "I'm fine," he said. "I'm just tired, and I've got a bit of a headache."

"Are you certain that's all it is? You look quite ill." She reached out to touch his cheek. At the soft brush of her fingertips, something inside him snapped. He grabbed her wrist and pushed her hand away. "For God's sake, must you torture me?"

"What?"

"I'm just about at the end of my rope, so don't push me, Maggie."

She drew back with a hurt expression. "I don't know what you mean."

"Oh, yes, you do. You're trifling with me, and I don't like it. You know I want you, you know I want to marry you. I know you made it clear in Rome you didn't want to marry me, but I'd hoped I could change your mind. I am not a romantic man, and I will not fall to my knees and make myself a fool with stupid, gushing speeches of my affection. Nor can I tolerate this kind of suspense. When we arrive at Naples, I will leave you with Cornelia and Edward, and I will return to England alone. We will not be seeing each other again after that, because it would be agony to me to be so close to you and not be able to have you." He took a deep breath and said, "I want you for my wife, and anything less is unacceptable to me. When we get to Naples, you will have to make the choice, Maggie. It shall be marriage or nothing at all."

"Why must you make it so hard?" she cried.

"You are the one who makes it hard. For me, it is an easy choice and always was. If it is not the same for you, then I have my answer, don't I?" He moved to stand, but she grabbed his sleeve.

"And what, what of my money? Are you saying it does not matter to you?"

"How can I answer a question like that? If I say yes, it matters, you would put the worst possible slant on it, and I would be condemned. If I say no, it does not matter, I would be lying. I am not a rich man, and any marriage settlement your father wishes to bestow would be a most welcome benefit to me. But Maggie, I have met many wealthy women, and I can tell you quite honestly that I never asked any of them to marry me."

"You don't love me. You don't even believe in love," she countered.

"What am I supposed to say? I don't know what you mean when you talk about love. All I know is that until I met you, I never wanted any woman, rich or poor, passionately enough to spend the remainder of my life in her company. There, you have the truth as best I can say it. Make of it what you will."

Trevor rose to his feet and left their camp without another word. He knew he'd probably ruined any chance of winning her, but he refused to think about that. He went for a long walk in the forest, and he wished to hell he could just keep walking until he was as far away from her as he could get. Damn her, damn her money, damn her enticing body and her silly, romantic notions.

Love. Christ Almighty. Her idea of love was to have him on his knees.

By the time he returned, she was asleep. He looked down at her innocent face, and her earnest words about true love echoed through his mind.

She was so naive. To have her, all he had to do was say three simple words. All he had to do was give her the fantasy. All he had to do was lie. How simple. How easy.

He could not do it, and he knew everything was for naught. He banked the fire, pulled the blanket up around her shoulders, and laid down as close to her as he could get without touching her. Finally, he drifted off to sleep.

When Trevor awoke the following morning, his headache was even worse than it had been the day before. Though it was barely dawn, even the soft gray light seemed to pierce his skull like a needle. He turned his head to the side and saw that Margaret was still asleep. She lay facing him, her head resting on her folded arm. Her long hair had come loose from its knot during the night and fell over her shoulder and across her cheek in a soft, shimmering wave. At any other time, he might have taken a moment to appreciate the sight, but not this morning.

He rose to his feet and told himself that, perhaps if he bathed and shaved, he'd feel better, but, without his quinine, he could not stop what was to come.

He stripped off his shirt, removed his boots and socks, and waded into the stream. The bath soothed him, but did not stop his headache. He got out, and the sound of splashing water awakened Margaret.

She sat up, brushing the hair out of her face. "Good morning," she said, smiling at him.

He pulled on his shirt, tucked the ends into his wet trousers, and began to button his shirt, hoping she would not notice how wretched he felt. But her smile faded as she watched him, and he knew his hope was a futile one.

She frowned with concern as she studied his face. "You look quite ill."

"I'm fine," he answered, raking a hand through his wet hair. "Let's get moving."

They started off, and for awhile he was able to keep a steady pace, but as the morning wore on, he could feel himself getting worse. The pain in his head became acute, his body ached, and by the time the sun was high overhead, he could feel the chills of fever beginning.

When they came to a fork in the road, he hesitated, uncertain. The map he'd brought was gone, and he could not seem to think.

"Why are we stopping?" she asked. "Are we lost?"

He stared at the two paths ahead, and they blurred into one. Light began to flicker behind his eyes.

"Trevor, we're lost, aren't we?"

He tried to focus, but it was useless. "We've got a bigger problem than that."

His voice sounded strange in his own ears, fuzzy and distant. The sack of food slipped from his fingers, and the earth suddenly tilted sideways. He took deep breaths, trying to regain his equilibrium, but the ground beneath him would not stop shifting.

Margaret put her hand on his arm. "You *are* ill. I knew it."

"I"—he licked his dry lips—"I think it's—"

His knees buckled, and he could feel himself falling. He hit the ground with bone-jarring force, but that was nothing compared to the pain in his head. All he wanted to do was grab the nearest rock and smash in his own skull to stop it.

Margaret knelt down beside him and touched his face, her palm soft and cool on his forehead. When she spoke, her voice seemed miles away. "You're burning with fever."

"It's the malaria," he said hoarsely, striving to get the words out. "No . . . quinine."

"Malaria?" she repeated. "No, no. You can't. Not now."

"Sorry, Maggie," he mumbled. "Promised Cornelia . . . take care of you. Can't."

"Oh, God," she moaned. "Trevor? Oh, heavens. What do I do? What do you need?"

He heard the panic in her voice. He wanted to reassure her, tell her not to worry, but he couldn't seem to force his thoughts into words. The last thing he remembered was the soft touch of her hand on his cheek just before everything went black.

14

Margaret knelt beside Trevor in the middle of the road, feeling completely helpless. He was unconscious and burning with fever. She looked around, but saw no signs of civilization. She didn't know where they were, where she might get help, or what to do for him.

She knew almost nothing of medicine, but realized that the first thing she had to do was get water. She glanced at the stream which paralleled the road they'd been following.

After wrapping Trevor in a blanket, she pulled the bottle of wine out of their food sack. She poured out the chianti that remained, then went down to the stream and refilled the bottle with water.

She tried to force some water into him, but had little success. Using a napkin, she bathed his face and neck. Though she nursed him throughout the afternoon, his fever only worsened.

Trevor became delirious, muttering nonsense in several languages. She caught bits of Italian, French, and English, as well as a guttural language she concluded must be some sort of Egyptian dialect.

He mentioned names—some she knew, others she did not. He talked about Emilio, Edward, his brother Geoffrey, someone named Lucci, and a woman called Isabella. Margaret wondered jealously who Isabella might be, but nothing he said gave a hint of his relationship with her.

Trevor mentioned her name, too. Though Margaret strained to listen, his words were disjointed mumblings that made little sense. He awoke occasionally, his deep blue eyes over-bright and feverish as he stared at her without really seeing. He had moments of lucidity, when he seemed to recognize who she was and where they were, but those moments did not last long.

The sun went down, but still his fever did not break. Margaret continued to bathe his face, but it did little good. Her feeling of helpless frustration gave way to panic.

What if he died? She went cold at the thought, realizing how possible it was. People died from fevers. It happened all the time.

"No!" she cried, everything in her rebelling against that idea. "You're not going to die." Drenching the napkin in water, she dabbed his cheeks with it. "You're not going to die," she repeated with a choked sob. "You're not. I won't let you."

She could feel herself coming apart, and she knew she could not allow it. Giving in to tears and getting hysterical would do Trevor no good at all.

Think, she told herself, taking deep breaths to steady her nerves. When she was a little girl and she'd had a very high fever, they had put her in a cool vinegar bath to bring her temperature down. She might not have any vinegar, but she had plenty of water.

Margaret grabbed Trevor by his feet and dragged him toward the stream. She stumbled several times in the dark, but finally made it. After pulling off her boots and her stockings, she removed his shirt and his boots. Then she pulled Trevor into the shallow water at the edge.

In the cool water she felt his temperature begin to drop, and her panic began to subside. After a few minutes, she took him out of the stream and sank down into the soft grass on the riverbank. She arranged the blanket around them both and pressed her body close to his. There was nothing she could do now but wait and pray that his fever would break.

It did not, but he fell into a quieter sleep. Exhausted, she fell asleep beside him.

The clattering of wheels wakened her. She sat up, blinking her eyes against the bright morning sunlight, and saw a wagon coming along the road. She jumped to her feet and ran toward it, shouting and waving her arms to get the driver's attention.

The man, clearly a farmer, pulled the team of sturdy brown horses to a stop. He looked down at her for a moment, then frowned in puzzlement and asked a question.

Margaret beckoned to him to come down, but he seemed to have no inclination to do so. She wished that years ago she'd listened to the governess who had told her Italian would be important to her someday. She reached up and grabbed his arm, pulling him as she pointed toward the stream. "Oh, please," she said, "you've got to help me."

The man finally seemed to understand there was

some urgency involved and climbed down from the wagon. He followed her across the meadow to where Trevor lay unconscious and shivering in the blanket.

"Napoli," she said, gesturing to herself and the man at her feet, then pointing to the road. He gave her a blank stare in reply, and she wondered desperately how she could make him understand. Inspired, she reached into the sack at her feet and pulled out Trevor's portfolio. From it, she removed the letter he'd been writing to Edward and Cornelia. She pointed to the address. "We need to get to Napoli."

She felt like an idiot, speaking in English when the man did not seem to understand the language, and she realized the letter would do her no good, for the man obviously could not read.

She saw the farmer looking at Trevor with obvious apprehension, and she realized it wasn't that he didn't understand what she wanted, but he was reluctant to take a sick man anywhere. Perhaps he needed more of an incentive than Christian charity. "Lire," she said, rubbing her fingers together in a gesture she hoped he understood. "Much lire if you'll take us to Napoli."

Some gestures were universal, and he seemed to get the idea. Nodding, he picked up Trevor and carried him to the wagon. Margaret grabbed their things and followed.

With her help, the farmer lifted him into the back of the wagon, then resumed his seat. Margaret climbed in beside Trevor with a sigh of relief. The farmer snapped the reins, and the wagon lurched forward, heading down the road that branched to the left.

Trevor was still unconscious, and he was shivering violently with another attack of chills. She pulled the blanket up around his body to keep him as warm as possible. She cradled his head in her lap, raking her fingers gently through his hair.

"Everything's going to be all right," she told him. "You've been taking care of me long enough. Now it's my turn to take care of you."

Margaret did not realize until she felt the wagon jerk to a stop that she'd been sleeping. Coming awake with a start, she glanced up to find that the farmer had pulled off the road and into a grove of trees. The sun was directly overhead, and she knew she'd slept away most of the morning. Trevor was asleep, and he was still suffering from acute chills and fever. He lay on his side, his body curled against her and his head in her lap.

She glanced at the farmer inquiringly, and he seemed to understand, for he reached down beside him and lifted a metal lunch pail, then climbed down from the wagon. She nodded to show she understood and gently eased herself out from beneath Trevor, who did not awaken. The farmer held out his hand to help her down.

Margaret reached out to take his hand, but when she met his eyes, she hesitated for no definable reason and pulled her hand back.

He was staring at her in a very odd way, and what she saw in his expression caused prickles of fear along her spine. It was a look she had never seen in a man's face before, but instinctively she sensed danger.

He reached out to grab her hand and she jumped back, nearly stumbling over Trevor's feet. The farmer did not seem surprised by this, nor was he deterred. He climbed into the wagon after her. Margaret went cold with fear, realizing with a sick feeling of dread what his intentions were.

"No." She shook her head and took another step back. The back of her knees hit the wagon seat behind her, and she was trapped. He was breathing hard and smiling at her in a way that made her skin crawl. "No," she said more forcefully, but he paid no heed to her denials. When he reached for her, she turned to climb out of the wagon to get away, but he grabbed her arm.

"No!" she cried, clinging to the wagon seat. "Let go of me!"

The farmer wrapped his arms around her, yanking her backward with enough force to loosen her grip. She struggled, but he had her arms trapped beneath his own. She kicked him, her heels banging his shins, but his grip on her only tightened, and her struggles were futile.

She could feel him hauling her backward toward the edge of the wagon, but then she heard a shout of rage, followed by a yelp of pain. The man stumbled, and she was suddenly free. She turned around to see Trevor rise up on his knees, his knife in his hand.

"Mine!" The word was almost a snarl, and had all the savagery of a wild animal. His arm came up and he shoved her behind him, then leaned over the farmer, who lay flat on his back. Grabbing a handful of the farmer's shirt, he hauled the man upward with a strength Margaret wouldn't have thought possible given his weakened condition. He was shivering violently and seemed out of his senses, yet he was conscious of the man's intentions.

Trevor lifted the knife, and she could see how it shook in his hand as he pricked the other man's throat with the sharp point, drawing blood. He spoke in Italian, and she saw the man's face break out in a sweat. He began to shake.

Trevor hauled him toward the edge of the wagon and shouted at her to take the reins. Margaret scrambled up into the driver's seat and grabbed the reins just as Trevor pushed the man out of the wagon. "Ya!" she shouted, and the horses started forward.

Behind her, she could hear the farmer shouting at them in enraged Italian. She glanced back and saw that he was making no attempt to follow. Trevor, the knife in his hand, was still kneeling by the edge of the wagon to prevent such a possibility. But the moment they were a safe distance away, he collapsed, unconscious.

"They should have arrived three days ago." Cornelia lifted her teacup and glanced over its rim at her husband, whose face was concealed by the previous Monday's edition of the *London Times*. "Edward, are you listening to me?"

"Of course I am." He lowered the paper to look at her. "Trevor told me they might not be precisely on time. He said that if they were several days late, we should not worry."

Cornelia set her cup down and rose. She walked to the window, but her mind was too distracted to appreciate the beautiful view of Vesuvius. "I don't see how we can do anything but worry."

She began to pace the carpet of the drawing room. "I never should have agreed to this. I must have been out of my mind."

"I can see we are going to have to talk about this again," he said ruefully, setting aside his paper. "You agreed to it because Trevor and I left you no choice."

"A fact which still bothers me. Why on earth did

you agree to help him with such an outrageous plan? What were you thinking?"

Edward was silent for a moment, then he said, "When Trevor and I were at Cambridge together, I watched how the local girls fell all over themselves trying to get his attention. The funny thing was, he didn't really care. He's always treated women with a sort of affectionate indulgence, but nothing more. He's never gone out of his way to get a woman in his life, and if he took a fancy to a girl who didn't fancy him—which wasn't often, by the way—he just shrugged it off and said there were plenty of other women to choose from. I don't think he's ever been in love in his life."

"Well, that just proves my point."

Edward shook his head. "That afternoon in Rome when Margaret refused to see him, I suggested that he find himself another heiress, and he said no. He wanted Margaret, and he said he would do whatever it took to win her. I've never seen him react that way to a woman before. I think Trevor is actually falling in love with her, though hell would freeze over before he would admit it to anyone, even himself."

Cornelia was skeptical. "Perhaps he does care for her," she conceded, "but I cannot say that I approve of his methods of courtship."

Edward laughed, the indulgent reaction of one man to the wicked escapades of another, and the sound infuriated Cornelia. Her husband seemed to realize she was not amused. His laugh ended in a little cough, and he said, "Perhaps Trevor does not have the most orthodox way of winning a wife, but can you honestly tell me that more customary methods would work with Margaret? How many other men have tried that and failed?"

Many, but Cornelia was loathe to admit it just now. "That is not the point."

Her husband shrugged and reached for a crumpet from the tea tray. "Perhaps not, but everything will work out. Trevor's a clever chap, and he'll manage everything just fine. You know that as well as I do."

Cornelia, distressed, resumed her pacing. "I know nothing of the kind."

Ever since she had agreed to Lord Ashton's plans, she had regretted it, although at the time, he had made it sound the only possible course of action. Even now she did not know quite how he had persuaded her to go along with it, but he had a way of making even the most insane ideas seem reasonable.

It did not seem so reasonable now. For nearly two weeks, she had been living with the anxiety of her decision, and it was beginning to take a severe toll on her nerves. If anyone discovered the truth, Margaret would be ruined. Even if Ashton did succeed in marrying her, they would not be received by anyone in society, despite his title and position. And if Henry were ever to find out . . . Cornelia shuddered to think what her uncle would do. He may have wanted the match, but he could hardly approve of Ashton's methods.

"Edward, you and Ashton have been friends for a long time, but until he came to Rome, you hadn't seen him for ten years. Do you really know anything about the man he is now?"

Her husband swallowed a mouthful of crumpet and looked at her, puzzled. "What do you mean?"

Cornelia took a deep breath. "I mean, my darling, that there are men in the world who do not possess your good heart and honorable intentions. Men who, given the opportunity your friend has been given, would take advantage of a young, innocent woman."

Edward stared at her, clearly astonished. "Trevor would never do that."

"How do you know?"

"He gave us his word of honor."

Cornelia studied her husband's boyishly handsome face. She loved Edward, she really did, and his staunch loyalty to his friends was admirable, but he was so incredibly naive. "Do you really think he would make a good husband?"

"How can anyone answer a question like that with certainty? Trevor's always been a bit wild, I'll grant you, but he has never been a cruel man in any way. He doesn't gamble or drink to excess, and he loves his family estate much more than his brother ever did. He's got heaps of good sense, too."

"He's not the sort to be a faithful husband."

Edward smiled. "You could make the same accusation about most of the husbands we know, my dear." That caused her to give him a look of unhappy resignation, and he added, "And I think he might surprise you."

"I doubt it."

"Cornelia, I know this business defies your notions, and mine as well, of proper courtship, but what's done is done. I can tell you one other thing that might reassure you. When we were at school together, Trevor and I got into many scrapes, but when we got caught for one of our escapades, he took all the blame so that I wouldn't get expelled. I've never known him to break a promise to a friend or be cruel to any woman."

Cornelia sighed. "Even if you're right, there's no guarantee that Margaret will marry him, despite his confidence and yours. I certainly should not fall in love with a man simply because I spent two weeks alone with him in the country on some sort of adventure."

"I should hope not!" Edward stood up and walked across the room to her. He took her hand in his. "If you were that type of woman, I would never have won you, my dear. Sleeping on damp ground and trekking through the mountains are not for me."

"Nor for me," she said, softening as her husband lifted her hand and kissed it. "Well, I shall try to adopt your attitude and hope for the best. Perhaps—"

The door of the drawing room opened, interrupting Cornelia's lukewarm attempt at optimism. The maid, one of only half a dozen servants they had brought with them to Naples, bobbed a curtsy. "If you please, signora, there is a wagon coming up the road, and it seems in a mighty hurry."

"Thank you, Maria."

Cornelia pulled her hand out of her husband's and ran back to the window. Indeed, a wagon was approaching along the lane that led to the cottage, and its pace was rapid enough to give cause for alarm. At this distance, she could not make out who was driving, but she could see that it was a woman, and she seemed to be alone. As the wagon drew near, pulling into the graveled drive, Cornelia gave a cry of pure astonishment. "Good Lord!"

"Who is it?" Edward asked.

Cornelia whirled around and ran for the door. "It's Maggie, at last!"

Her husband followed her out of the house as the wagon came to a skidding halt by the door, sending gravel spewing in all directions. It was Margaret, but Cornelia hardly recognized her. Her peasant clothes were tattered and stained with mud, her face was smudged with dirt, and her hair, loose from its knot, was a snarled tangle that made her look almost wild.

"Heavens above!" Cornelia shouted. "Maggie! Oh, my dear! What has happened to you?"

Margaret gave her cousin only the briefest hug, too concerned for Trevor to bother with preliminaries. She gestured to the back of the wagon. "We must fetch a doctor at once."

Cornelia and Edward both looked into the wagon and saw Trevor lying there.

"My God!" Edward exclaimed. "What has happened?"

"Never mind that now. You must send for a doctor."

"Right," he muttered and started for the stables.

"And have him bring quinine!" she called after him. Turning to her cousin, she said, "We must get him into bed."

Servants were called, and Trevor was immediately taken into the house. He woke only briefly when two servants lifted him into a comfortable feather bed. Margaret ordered cool water to be brought up and, when it arrived, she pulled back the covers, opened Trevor's shirt, and began bathing his chest.

"Maggie, really," Cornelia said, turning her face away from the bare chest of the man in the bed. "I think you should allow a servant to do that. I hardly think it proper for you to be—"

"For heaven's sake, Cornelia, it's a little late for that," Margaret answered. She laughed, but the laughter had a edge of hysteria to it. "I've seen his bare chest at least a dozen times now. Please don't worry about my maidenly sensibilities."

Cornelia said nothing more about it, but she kept her face averted as she added, "What is wrong with him? Do you know?"

"Malaria. He takes quinine for it, of course, but the horse bolted three days ago, and we lost most of our supplies, including his medicine."

Edward entered the room. "I've sent a servant for the local doctor. How is he?"

Margaret shook her head. "I don't know. He's been like this for over two days. Cycles of violent chills, then a very high fever and delirium. During the last two days I don't think he's had more than half a dozen lucid moments."

She laid a hand gently against his cheek and felt its burn against her fingertips. "At first I was able to keep his fever down by bathing him in the stream, and I was able to get some water into him. But once we got the wagon, I had to drive, and I was no longer able to tend him. I knew by then we were but a day's ride from Naples, and my only thought was to get him here as quickly as possible. I only stopped twice— both times to ask directions. But now, I'm afraid I may have made the wrong decision. He's dehydrated and seems worse than ever." Her voice began to shake with all the exhaustion and worry she was feeling. "I hope I did the right thing. If he dies—"

She broke off with a sob and was silent for a moment, trying to regain her composure. "If he dies, I shall never forgive myself."

When the doctor arrived, he hastened to reassure her. "You've done everything you could," he said and pulled a large brown bottle out of his bag. "Without quinine, you could only make him a bit more comfortable."

"Will he be all right, sir?" she asked.

"These cases vary, but he seems a strong and vigorous man. We'll give him a good dose of quinine and see how he responds. I'll return tomorrow to check on his progress. If he worsens during the night, fetch me at once. In the meantime, continue your efforts to keep him cool, and try to get some tea or broth into him."

The doctor measured a dose of quinine into a cup, then held Trevor's nose closed to force his mouth open and poured the liquid down his throat. Trevor gave a choking cough, but swallowed the medicine.

"Give him another dose in about eight hours," the doctor told Margaret.

"Thank you, doctor," Edward said. "I'll show you out."

The two men left the room, but Margaret did not move from her chair. Cornelia walked over to her cousin's side and laid a hand on her arm. "Come, Maggie. You're exhausted. You need some supper, a bath, and sleep. There's nothing more you can do."

"No." She pulled her arm out of her cousin's grasp and took Trevor's hand in hers. "I'm staying right here."

To her surprise, Cornelia did not argue with her. "I'll bring you a supper tray," she said and departed from the room. But she left the door wide open.

Dear Cornelia and her proprieties, Margaret thought, gazing at the open doorway. After traveling alone with Trevor for almost a fortnight, after sharing such an intimate experience, she could not sit with him alone in a closed room? Margaret smiled faintly. As if Trevor were in any condition to take liberties with her just now.

She thought of the farmer who had tried to accost her and wondered how Trevor had found the strength to stop him. She recalled the savagery in his voice when he'd claimed her as his own and the way he'd held the knife, ready to slit the farmer's throat for daring to touch her. As ill as he was, Trevor had still been there to protect her from harm, to cherish her and keep her safe. Wasn't that what heroes were for?

She turned her head and looked at him. At the moment, he was sleeping peacefully, but, even in sleep, his face was drawn and weary, showing the ravages of the past two days.

He needed a shave, she realized. She gently touched his hot cheek, feeling the roughness of beard stubble graze her fingertips, and all the mornings she had watched him shave came back to her. She remembered every meal they had shared, every conversation, every laugh, and every argument. She remembered the way he had kissed her and the extraordinary way he had touched her. She knew all these intimacies were usually the exclusive privilege of husbands and wives.

His proposal—if one could call it that—echoed through her mind. *I want you for my wife, and anything less is unacceptable to me.*

Margaret closed her eyes, imagining what being married to Trevor would be like. The idea made her smile. She had always longed for excitement, and if the past few weeks were any indication, a lifetime with Trevor would never be dull. In fact, it would be quite wonderful. She realized how much she wanted to spend her life with him. How much she wanted him.

She loved him.

It was a stunning realization, and a humbling one. She thought of her own behavior, of how she had assumed the worst about Trevor from the very beginning. Cornelia's exasperated words of a month ago came back to her.

You dismiss every man who comes along without giving him a chance to win your affections.

At the time, she had blithely brushed aside her cousin's accusation, but it was true. She had dreamed of a prince, but she had fallen in love with a man. A man whose deeds proved him to be brave and honorable, a man who had made his desire for her clear from the very beginning. He had told her she was beautiful and fascinating, but didn't hesitate to tell her she was also spoiled and willful. Trevor had had many women, but he'd never asked any of them to marry him.

I never wanted any woman, rich or poor, passionately enough to spend the remainder of my life in her company.

By his own admission, he did not know what love was. Perhaps, when they were married, she could teach him.

She loved him. How ironic that she should discover it now, when it might be too late, when she might lose him forever.

The next few hours passed slowly. Cornelia brought her a hot meal, but Margaret left it untasted. Edward came in, urging her to go to bed and offering to sit with Trevor in her place, but she refused. A maid brought fresh water, and Margaret sponged Trevor's face and chest over and over as she listened to his incoherent mumblings and prayed for his fever to break.

It finally did, just before dawn. She straightened in her chair and pressed a hand to his forehead. His skin felt damp and cool to the touch. His delirious mumblings stopped, and he fell into a silent and peaceful sleep.

With a sob of gratitude and relief, she pressed a kiss to the back of his hand and said a prayer of thanks. Now that the danger was past, exhaustion washed over her, and she fell back in her chair. Still holding Trevor's hand in hers, she finally allowed herself to sleep.

15

Trevor awoke feeling weak, battered, and utterly wretched. He realized from the softness beneath him that he was in a bed, though he could not recall how he had gotten there. He knew he'd had an attack of malaria, but, as was usually the case with that affliction, everything seemed hazy in his mind. The last thing he remembered clearly was Margaret leaning over him, her dark eyes filled with worry and her fingertips touching his face.

He opened his eyes, blinking against the bright sunlight. The room was unknown to him, and he had no idea where he was. But when he turned his head, he saw that Margaret was still beside him.

She was asleep in an uncomfortable-looking chair, her head tilted at an angle that would give her quite an ache when she woke. There was a bucket of water at her feet, and a tray of untouched food on the bedside table. Her hair was loose and tangled, and there were purple shadows under her eyes that indicated a lack of sleep, as if she had been too busy looking after his needs to bother with her own. That notion stirred something deep inside him, an undefinable feeling that touched him like the warmth of spring after a long, cold winter. Of all the women he had ever known, he could recall none who would sit by his bedside and tend to him in such a way. Even his own mother wouldn't dream of doing such a thing.

Suddenly, she woke. Straightening in her chair, she saw that he was watching her. "You're awake," she murmured, smiling at him. "Thank God."

He looked into her dirt-smudged face and saw a tenderness in her expression he'd never seen before. Tenderness, relief, and something else he could not quite define. Suddenly, he felt uncomfortable and took refuge in teasing. "Worried about me, Maggie?"

But she did not respond as he expected. Her smile faded. "Yes," she said gravely. "Terribly worried. I was afraid you would die."

"If malaria hasn't killed me by now, it isn't going to."

"How do you feel?"

"Like I've been run down by a train." He took another look around. "Where are we?"

"Naples. We arrived last night. Do you remember anything about how we got here?"

He shook his head. "I know we lost the horse, and I remember we walked all that afternoon and the next morning. But after that, everything is rather a blur."

"That's not surprising. You've been ill for three days." She reached for a rag from the table beside her and dipped it in the bucket of water. Wringing it out, she began to dab his face with it. "I got us a ride in a wagon. Do you remember that?"

"No."

"Well, that's how we arrived here." She rose and dropped the rag into the basin. "I'll tell Edward and Cornelia that you're feeling better. Are you hungry? I'll have a breakfast tray brought in for you."

She walked to the door, but paused with her hand on the knob and turned to look at him. "Trevor, do you remember the night before you became ill? When you told me I would have to make a choice?"

His mouth tightened. He remembered it perfectly, as one of the stupidest things he'd ever done. "Yes," he answered. "I remember."

She ducked her head almost shyly. "Then perhaps you had best write to my father immediately for his consent. I should like to be married from London, and he can make the arrangements on our behalf. I don't wish for a long engagement, and I don't think you do either."

She lifted her head. "I love you," she said and opened the door. Giving him another smile, she departed, closing the door softly behind her.

Trevor stared at the closed door in utter astonishment. She loved him. When and how had this transformation taken place? If he'd known that being ill would do the trick, he'd have lost his quinine long before now.

A miracle. Elation washed over him, and he wanted to laugh aloud. She loved him. It was a bloody miracle.

"Engaged?" Cornelia sank down on the edge of the bed in Margaret's room and stared at her half-dressed cousin in astonishment. "To Ashton?"

"Who else?" Margaret stopped combing out her

wet hair and met Cornelia's eyes in the mirror over
her dressing table, laughing at her cousin's expression. "You seem surprised."

"I am stunned."

"I don't know why you should be." Margaret rose
and walked over to the closet. Cornelia had brought
all of Margaret's things to the cottage, and her maid
had placed a few of her favorite dresses in the closet.
Margaret pulled out a suit of pale yellow satin and a
Tuscan straw bonnet trimmed with ox-eye daisies and
yellow ribbon. "Weren't you determined that I should
find an Englishman who suited me?" she asked teasingly as she hung the suit on a hook and placed the
hat on a nearby chair.

But Cornelia was staring into space, seemingly lost
in her own thoughts. "It worked, then," she murmured absently.

"What worked?"

Cornelia recovered herself with an effort. "I mean
that, that we finally managed to acquaint you with a
man you actually like."

"Like is not the way I would describe it." Margaret
walked over to the bed and fell across it with a sigh
of pure contentment. "Cornelia, tell me something.
How did you know when you were in love with
Edward?"

"I-I don't know, really. It happened so gradually
that I can't point to a specific moment. Why?"

"When you realized it, how did you feel? Was it
this wonderful feeling that made you want to laugh
and sing and shout your love from the rooftops?"

"No, nothing so momentous as that. It was more
like a quiet sort of understanding. Why do you want
to know how I felt?"

Margaret rolled over to stare at the ceiling.

"Because I wanted to know if other people in love feel as I do."

"Are you in love with Ashton? Of course, you must be, or you would not be marrying him."

"You know me well enough to know that!" She sat up. "Oh, Cornelia, I've never felt like this before. It's, it's like this joy inside me that almost hurts, it's so wonderful."

"But you disliked him so. You wouldn't even receive him the last day of Carnival."

"I know, but everything is different now, and I've quite forgotten how I felt then."

Cornelia looked away. "I see."

Margaret was puzzled. "Aren't you pleased? Are you not happy for me?"

"Of course I am," Cornelia answered hastily and grasped her hands. "I am very happy for you. But are you certain, absolutely certain, that he is the right man for you?"

"I have no doubts at all." She jumped to her feet and spun around, laughing. "Once I realized how much I love him, every doubt in my mind disappeared. I am so happy I feel dizzy."

"You're making me dizzy, too. Will you stop spinning like a child's toy top?"

"Sorry," she said, not at all apologetic. She walked over to the window and pulled back the curtain. "While Trevor is sleeping, why don't we go for a walk? It's a gorgeous day."

"If you wish."

"This is a charming house," Margaret said, looking down into the garden below.

"Yes, it is. Edward was fortunate to be able to let it on such short notice."

"You must tell me everything that happened after I

was taken. Did you learn immediately what had happened?"

Cornelia sank back down on the bed beside her and looked toward the window without answering.

"Cornelia, what on earth is the matter? You seem very odd."

"Do I? Perhaps it is because I do not have your thirst for adventure. I find kidnappings rather a distressing business."

"It wasn't so bad, really. For thieves, they were rather amiable, in fact. And Trevor was wonderful. He crept right into their camp and rescued me. Of course, it seemed awful at the time, but now that I look back on it, it was truly the most exciting thing that's ever happened to me."

"I'm glad to hear it."

"Well?" Margaret prompted. "Aren't you going to tell me what happened?"

"We had just noticed your disappearance from the church when Lord Ashton arrived. Edward had already invited him to accompany us, but he felt that you were angry with him since you would not receive him the day before and he declined. Anyway, a note had arrived that morning informing him of your kidnapping and demanding a ransom. I didn't quite understand, but they didn't want money. It seems they were after some sort of list."

"Yes, yes, I know all about that. Go on."

"Lord Ashton arranged everything. He said he would go after you and that Edward and I should come here and wait. He wired to Naples and arranged for this cottage, so we left the servants to pack up everything and took the evening train here while Lord Ashton went after you."

"Poor Cornelia! You must have been worried sick."

"Yes, I was," her cousin replied, sounding so miserable that Margaret let go of her hand and put an arm around her shoulders.

"Well, I'm fine, truly. I'm all in one piece, and no real harm was done."

"Thank heaven. If anything had happened to you, I would never forgive myself."

"That's silly! It's hardly your fault that Trevor's enemies decided to kidnap me."

Her cousin seemed so distressed that Margaret spoke to cheer her. "How horrified Lady Lytton would be if she knew of this! I'm sure she'd look down her nose and say no British girl would ever let herself be abducted. How I wish I could tell the story just to see her face!"

Cornelia did not laugh. "You mustn't tell anyone. If word got out that you had spent a fortnight out in the wilds alone with Lord Ashton, there would be no end of a scandal, and your reputation would be ruined. Lord Ashton would also suffer for it, as would Edward and I, since we are acting as your chaperones."

"I know! I know! I promise I won't breathe a word. But people really are silly, aren't they? If they knew Trevor and I spent all that time alone together, they'd assume the worst possible things, and there's absolutely no reason for it."

Cornelia squeezed her hand. "I hope not," she said gently.

Margaret understood and blushed. "There isn't! Lord Ashton was— He didn't— I mean, nothing happened!" That wasn't the complete truth, but she certainly couldn't tell her cousin about those passionate moments in the cave and the meadow.

"I am glad to know he is a man of honor."

"Does Papa know about this?"

Cornelia was clearly horrified. "Heavens, no! He would never forgive me if he knew this had happened while you were in my care. Promise me you'll never tell Uncle Henry about this."

"Cornelia, you must not blame yourself, and I very much doubt that Papa would blame you either." She withdrew her hand and gave her cousin's back a comforting pat. "It angers me to think those men will never be brought to justice, but there's nothing we can do about that. I'm just glad Papa doesn't know. If he did, there'd be no end of a fuss. And since you and Trevor have been so cautious, no one else is going to find out what happened either."

"I hope not. Now, I'll send Molly to you and leave you to finish dressing."

Margaret watched her cousin's hasty departure, and again it struck her that her cousin's reaction to the whole affair was distinctly odd.

During the next few days, the subject of Margaret's kidnapping and rescue was scrupulously avoided. Cornelia was distracted and silent, Edward was too much the proper English gentleman to mention the subject, and Trevor spent most of his time resting. Now that he was taking his quinine again, by the third day after their arrival in Naples he was well enough that they began making plans for the journey home. Everyone was in agreement that they should leave as quickly as possible. All of them were eager to return to England, especially Margaret and Cornelia, who wanted to begin wedding preparations. Edward purchased tickets on the next available steamship, which would depart for Dover the following afternoon.

Trevor had already sent a wire to Henry, who had given them his consent and wholehearted blessing. He assured them that he would begin making the wedding arrangements. Margaret couldn't help being amused. She knew from her last conversation with her father that Trevor would not have been his first choice as a husband for her, but he wanted her married to a gentleman of quality so badly that even Trevor was deemed an acceptable choice.

As much as she wanted to be with Trevor during the journey home, Margaret was one of those unfortunate people who suffer from acute seasickness, and she was forced to spend the entire seven-day trip in her stateroom. Though Trevor wished to visit her, she could not bear the idea of him seeing her in such a wretched state.

When they disembarked at Dover, Henry was waiting on the quay to greet them, looking more ebullient than Margaret had ever seen him before. He shook Trevor's hand and congratulated him on winning the hand of the world's most beautiful girl, then he turned to her. "Maggie, my girl! You have made me a very happy man."

He enfolded her in one of his great bear hugs, and Margaret, very glad to see him and grateful to be on solid ground again, returned the hug and kissed his cheek. "I'm glad, Papa. I'm quite happy myself."

"Everything is arranged," he told her happily. "I obtained a special license, an announcement has been put in the papers, and the invitations have been sent out. The wedding shall be at St. Paul's at two o'clock in the afternoon on Saturday."

"Saturday!" Margaret cried. "But Papa, that's only three days from now! I don't even have a dress yet!"

*   *   *

Lucci had spent over a week in Rome before he learned the whereabouts of Trevor St. James. Immediately upon his arrival in the Eternal City, he had met with his brother, Antonio, and, between them, they had employed an army of detectives and engaged a network of contacts in all the major cities and seaports to search for his enemy. During the past week, their efforts had proved futile, and they had been unable to find any trace of Trevor. But on his eighth day in Rome, Lucci learned of Trevor's whereabouts by opening a newspaper.

The society pages of every paper in Europe, including the Roman ones, were suddenly filled with the news that British peer Trevor St. James, the present Earl of Ashton, had recently become engaged to Miss Margaret Van Alden, only daughter of American millionaire Henry Van Alden. The groom, it was reported, had only recently acceded to his title, and having been in Egypt for the past ten years, was eager to return to his estates in Kent. Therefore, the happy couple did not desire a long engagement and were to be married three days hence at St. Paul's in London.

Lucci tossed aside yet another newspaper. There was nothing more he could learn from perusing press reports. It was time for action. He rose from the sofa in his hotel suite and started to call for his brother so that they might make preparations to leave for London immediately. Suddenly, another thought struck him, and he paused with his hand on the bell pull.

Perhaps he was being hasty. Perhaps he should wait, postpone his vengeance a little bit longer. His hated enemy would soon have a wife, and that would provide the means for him to gain revenge for his beloved Isabella.

Yes, he decided, warming to the idea, that would be much better. Give him time to enjoy his wife, to take his happiness for granted. Then, and only then, take it all away from him.

Lucci smiled with quiet satisfaction. It was the perfect revenge.

16

It was amazing what could be accomplished with money. Margaret's fears about her wedding gown proved groundless. Worth was out of the question, of course, at this late date, but Henry dispatched a cable from Dover to Madame Valmont, the head of London's finest couturier. By the time they arrived in London, she was waiting to receive them at her showroom on Regent Street with some of her finest spring models ready to display, dozens of fabrics and trims from which to select her trousseau, and an army of seamstresses to get it all done in three days.

Trevor did not accompany them to London, choosing instead to take a separate carriage to Ashton Park, located only fifteen miles west of Dover. He planned to see his family and look over his estates. Margaret was a bit glum about that, wanting him with her to face the journalists who would surely be hounding her until Saturday. Nevertheless, she understood his reasons for going. He had told her that if the fuss of wedding preparations got to be too much for her, to send him an express cable at once and they'd simply elope, scandalizing everyone and giving the journalists something worthwhile to write about.

During the next three days, there were many times when Trevor's suggestion seemed quite appealing. The morning after their arrival in London, *Punch* ran a cartoon with a clear likeness of her purchasing the title of Lady Yankee-Doodle at Harrod's Department Store. It was most infuriating.

Edward was close by to keep her in good humor, reminding her of her own laughing words when similar jabs had been taken at Cornelia the previous year: *You should change the date to July fourth, play band music instead of the wedding march, have apple pie instead of fruit cake, and invite the rudest, most frightful people you can think of. That would serve them right.* Margaret had been joking when she'd said it last summer, but now it seemed like a fine idea.

The morning before the wedding, Trevor's mother, grandmother, and sister-in-law arrived in town and called at Henry's Mayfair mansion in the company of Lady Lytton to be introduced to the bride. Trevor, Margaret learned, would not return until the morning of the wedding. He had much to do at the estate.

The moment her future in-laws entered the drawing room, Margaret's eyes went straight to the tall, striking woman with touches of silver in her black hair. Her blue eyes and angular features were quite similar to Trevor's, and Margaret knew even before Lady Lytton introduced them that this was his mother.

"How do you do?" she murmured politely and gave the woman a tentative smile.

Her new mother-in-law did not return it. "A pleasure to meet you, my dear."

The greeting was so cold and formal that Margaret had no idea how to respond. Fortunately, Lady Lytton moved on with introductions and saved her the trouble.

She gestured toward a slender, incredibly beautiful blonde who was dressed in a manner far more luxurious than that of the other two ladies. "This is Elizabeth, Lady Ashton."

Margaret studied the woman, remembering Trevor's story about how Elizabeth had crawled into his bed one night for the sole purpose of producing an heir, and she could hardly credit it. This woman was as fragile and delicate looking as a Dresden doll, not at all like the evil vixen Margaret had imagined.

But the wide blue eyes of Geoffrey's widow looked back at her with such cold hostility that the sweet image was utterly spoiled. She made no attempt at civility, and Margaret reminded herself that appearances meant nothing.

Gesturing toward the plump, elderly lady at her left, whose attention seemed riveted on the nearby tea tray, Lady Lytton said loudly, "And this is the Dowager Countess."

The older woman continued to gaze at the pastries on the tray, and Lady Lytton jabbed her gently in the ribs. The dowager gave a start and looked up to give Margaret a beaming smile, clapping her hands together in the manner of a delighted child. "What a pretty thing you are!"

Margaret smiled in response to the elderly lady's friendliness, and the dowager turned to Edward. "These American girls have such lovely teeth," she told him. "No wonder our English gentlemen like them so much. And they do seem to have lots of boys,

don't they?" She patted Margaret's hand. "You look
like a fine, healthy girl, which is a good thing. You'll
get pregnant right away, I'm sure. Boys, my dear. Lots
of boys. May we have tea now?"

Cornelia smoothly ended the embarrassing silence.
"Yes, by all means, let's have tea."

Cornelia's efficiency and good sense proved
immensely valuable in helping Margaret through
those trying days, and Saturday afternoon found her
alighting from the wedding carriage in front of St.
Paul's with a calm serenity that surprised even her.
Taking her father's arm, she walked up the steps and
managed to smile pleasantly at the crowd of journalists and curious observers that were lined up on either
side.

Inside, the church was packed with people, and
among them she recognized several of her dearest
friends—Ann Croft, now the Marchioness of Glaston,
Josephine Farner, now the Viscountess Athersley, and
Eliza Whitmore, now the Countess of Seton.

She glanced at Viscount Athersley as she passed,
and remembered how Josephine had come to her just
before Christmas, begging for a loan to cover his latest
gambling debts because her father had just lost everything in a disastrous business venture. And as for the
Earl of Seton—he preferred his hunting lodge in
Scotland to the company of his American wife. Ann's
husband was absent, and Margaret was one of the few
people who knew why. The Marquess of Glaston had
syphilis, the inevitable result of his countless adulter-
ous liaisons.

Suddenly, Margaret's serenity shattered. She stumbled in her pearl-encrusted white satin gown and
would have fallen if her father had not supported her.
She recovered herself immediately, but had her father

not been clasping her arm within his so tightly, she would have run then and there.

She forced herself to lift her chin, and when she saw Trevor standing there waiting for her, she knew she could not run away in fear. She loved him, and she could never humiliate him in such a way. *He is not like those men,* she reminded herself. *He is not.*

Her father placed her hand in Trevor's, then stepped away. Margaret knew there was no turning back. Her bridegroom gave her a reassuring smile as she moved to stand beside him, but otherwise he remained grave, almost severe. Whenever she took a peek at him, he was staring straight ahead, more handsome and remote than she had ever seen him.

The ceremony lasted only fifteen minutes. Fifteen minutes, a few promises, and her whole life was changed. As Margaret took Trevor's arm and turned to walk out with him, the enormity of what she had just done nearly smothered her. She wondered with paralyzing panic if any bride, English or American, had ever thrown up in St. Paul's Cathedral. She was very much afraid she was going to be the first, and she knew the cartoonists at *Punch* would have a field day with that one.

Margaret did not throw up, although from the moment she had walked into the church, Trevor had steeled himself to the possibility that she might. Walking down the long aisle, she had looked as pale as her white satin gown. When she had placed her hand in his, he'd felt how she trembled, and her huge brown eyes had reminded him of a frightened deer. He was glad Henry had heeded his advice and arranged for such a quick wedding. A few more days and she probably would have called the whole thing off.

He had no such apprehensions himself, but then, he wasn't the romantic idealist Margaret was, and love had never been a factor in his decision. From the moment of his brother's death, his destiny had been set, and his visit to Ashton Park had only strengthened his resolve to marry Margaret as quickly as possible. Now, he was looking forward to enjoying some of the pleasures of matrimony. His bride, however, was clearly not in the same frame of mind.

In the drawing room of Henry's mansion in Mayfair, he studied her as she sat in one of the chintz wing chairs, talking quietly with three of her American friends. The late afternoon sun through the west windows fell on her, giving her upswept dark hair a gloss that reminded him of melting chocolate. The pearls of her gown gleamed like the iridescent drops of a waterfall. Trevor thought of all the weddings he had attended in his life, and he knew that no bride had ever looked more beautiful than his own. Or less radiant.

His mother moved to stand beside him. With her gaze also fixed on Margaret, she said in a low voice, "I think you have done well, Trevor."

"Thank you, Mother," he answered dryly. "I'm so glad you approve."

"I would have preferred an English girl, naturally."

"Naturally."

"But she's charming enough. For an American." She coughed delicately. "I understand from Lady Lytton that her father is one of the wealthiest men in America. That's excellent. Did you arrange a suitable settlement?"

His mouth tightened into a grim line, and he shot

his mother the cold, icy look he had long ago learned from her. She retired to the other end of the room in a huff, her curiosity unsatisfied, and Trevor returned his attention to his bride.

As if she sensed his scrutiny, Margaret turned to look at him. Her normally expressive face was grave and inscrutable, and Trevor had no idea what she was thinking.

She looked away without so much as a smile. A vague uneasiness stirred inside him, something that might have been guilt. He pushed it aside and turned his attention to Lord Seton, who was expressing great interest in Henry's extensive art collection and asking if he might see it.

"Of course, sir, of course," Henry answered, delighted. "Many of the best paintings are at my villa in Italy, of course, but I do have a fairly comprehensive collection here."

Trevor expressed a wish to accompany them, and the three men left the drawing room together. Henry and Seton walked down the long gallery ahead of him discussing art, which appeared to be a favorite topic for both. Trevor did not participate in their conversation. In fact, he barely heard what they said. He was thoughtful and silent until they reached the end of the gallery, where a set of double doors led into a ballroom. "Fencing equipment in the ballroom?" he inquired, noticing the foils and fencing masks that hung on the wall at the far end of the room.

"My daughter and several of her friends like to fence," Henry told him. "In this house, the ballroom is the only room large enough for them to practice. They've made a sort of club of it, in fact." He turned to Lord Seton. "I believe your wife participates, sir, whenever she is in town?"

The earl frowned slightly. "Yes. I confess, it bothers me not a little to know my wife is engaged in such a masculine sport. But it is beneficial exercise and harmless enough, I suppose."

Henry chuckled. "Anything to keep the ladies happy. I know my daughter enjoys the sport enormously. I've even fenced with her a few times myself. I must say, she's not bad at it, for a woman. Not bad at all."

They wandered back to the drawing room and rejoined the party. Throughout the afternoon and evening, Trevor continued to watch his wife out of the corner of his eye, but not once did he see her glance in his direction. He waited for her to smile or laugh or say something outrageous, but she did not. She spent most of the evening in an almost painful silence.

If he did not know her better, he might have thought she was frightened. Young ladies often were scared of their wedding night, but with Margaret, he could hardly credit such a notion. She was no wilting flower, thank God. He'd already given her a taste of lovemaking, and she had not been at all frightened by his passion or her own. But she looked more worried than he had ever seen her before, and, as the evening wore on, her apprehension only seemed to increase.

When the bridal dinner was over, she went upstairs with Cornelia. As if that were some sort of signal, the guests began to depart. His mother, his grandmother, and Elizabeth returned to their hotel, and he adjourned to the study with Edward and Henry for a congratulatory cigar. But though he managed to make casual conversation with the other two men, he could not stop thinking of Margaret's pale face. It was very disquieting to think she might be afraid of him.

With growing impatience, he waited for Cornelia

to join them. When she did, Trevor immediately rose to his feet. He paused beside her, and she whispered, "The third door on the right at the top of the stairs."

He nodded, bid them goodnight, and went up. He had no idea what reception he would be given by his bride. He hoped Cornelia had managed to ease her fears, but the moment he entered the bedroom, he knew such a hope was futile.

Dressed in an ivory silk robe and gown, she was seated at her dressing table, brushing her hair. Her hand stilled when he came in, and she turned to glance at him for only a moment before she looked away and resumed her task. Even from the doorway, he could feel the tension.

Trevor glanced around the room. On a table by the window, a bottle of champagne rested in a crystal bowl of ice. He closed the door behind him and walked over to it, thinking a drink would probably be good for both of them.

He took off his wedding jacket, then uncorked the bottle and poured two glasses of champagne. He carried them over to where she sat and placed her glass on the dressing table. Then he sat down behind her in an uncomfortable Queen Anne chair.

She began pulling the brush through her hair with quick, jerky movements, clearly unnerved that he was so close. "It was a, a nice wedding, I think."

"Very nice." Trevor took a sip of champagne, then set down his glass. Reaching over her shoulder, he took the brush out of her hand.

"What—"

"Ssh." He gathered the heavy, dark mass of her hair and let it fall down her back. "Drink your champagne," he said and began to brush her hair.

She reached for her glass and gulped half the

contents in one swallow, then set the glass back down. Her fingers skimmed restlessly over the edge of the vanity, straightened the perfume bottles, and fiddled with the silver comb while he continued to run the brush through her hair in long, rhythmic strokes. It was soft in his fingers, like threads of silk, and fragrant of the lemon soap she liked. He leaned closer, inhaling the tangy, sweet scent.

"When we were in Italy," he said softly, "I always wanted to do this."

She stopped fidgeting and went utterly still. "You did? Why?"

For an answer, he used the brush to push her hair aside, bent his head, and kissed the back of her neck.

She jumped at the contact as if she'd been burned.

He kissed her again, tasting her with his tongue. She made a tiny sound of agitation and started to stand up.

The brush fell from his hand, and he put his hands on her shoulders to keep her still as her hair fell against his cheek. "Maggie," he murmured against her skin, "don't be afraid of me."

"I'm not."

But he could feel her apprehension in the taut tendons of her neck and the rigid set of her shoulders, and he gave her a searching look in the mirror.

"Well, perhaps I am," she confessed and lowered her eyes. "A little."

A hint of a smile touched the corners of his mouth. "Always so honest," he murmured and drew a shaky breath, feeling rather ill at ease himself. His desire for her had been making him insane for weeks, but now, when he could have her without seductions or games, he found himself holding back again, waiting. Waiting for her to want him.

The realization made him want to laugh. God, he'd made love to more women than he could possibly remember, he thought, and he was getting himself all desperate about making love to his own wife. *His wife.*

He pushed her hair aside and kissed her ear, letting his hands glide up and down her arms.

The skin of her ear was velvety soft. He nibbled on her earlobe, listening to her breath quicken. Slowly, very slowly, he slipped his hands beneath her arms and touched the sides of her breasts with his fingertips.

"Do you think we did the right thing?"

Startled by the question, he stilled for a moment, then resumed stroking her with his fingertips as he brushed his lips along the column of her throat. "Absolutely."

"Are you sure?" she whispered. "You once said I'd make an excellent mistress, but a difficult wife. You don't think that anymore?"

"No, I still think you'll be a difficult wife. But I'm prepared to make the sacrifice."

His comment was so outrageous, she couldn't help smiling, but she also felt panic. "How noble of you."

Lifting one hand, he pulled back the collar of her robe and kissed her bare shoulder just beside the lace strap of her nightgown.

Her smile faded. "I-I'm afraid I will be a difficult wife, especially for an earl," she said, stirring restlessly on the seat. "I can never remember how I'm supposed to address people. I get them all mixed up."

"A serious failing indeed," he said, laughing against her shoulder, blowing warm breath on her skin. "But I think I can manage to live with it."

"I'll embarrass you."

"I'll survive." He slid his hands along her ribs to her waist and made a low sound of appreciation as he outlined the shape of her beneath the silk. No corsets or petticoats, just the soft reality of her in his hands. His desire for her was raging through his body, and his hands trembled as he reached for the silk ties of her robe.

"Must we have separate bedrooms?" she asked.

He let out a sharp sigh, his patience ebbing fast, and rested his forehead on her shoulder. Christ, couldn't they have conversations like this tomorrow? "We don't have to," he answered and gave the ties a tug. Her robe fell open, and he lifted his head to see her in the mirror.

With a gasp, she clutched at her robe and slid along the bench until she could stand. She belted her robe and turned to face him, crossing her arms protectively over her chest. She looked at him, her eyes wide and dark and vulnerable. "I should not like you to have affairs with other women!" she burst out. "I should not like it at all."

Was that what she was so worried about? Trevor looked at her, with her tumbled hair and silken robes and rigid stance, and thought that, right now, any other woman would be a more likely possibility than his own wife. Clearly, this wasn't going to work, and, short of just throwing her down and getting it over with, he was running out of options.

He thought of the gymnasium, and the masks, vests, and fencing foils he'd seen hanging on the wall. He grabbed her by the elbow and reached for the lamp. "Come with me."

"Where are we going?" she asked as he pulled her toward the door.

"You'll see."

He let go of her long enough to open the door, then seized her by the wrist and pulled her out into the hall. Around them, the house was dark and silent.

"Where on earth are you taking me?" she whispered as he led her down the stairs.

"Since I met you, I've developed a craving for midnight escapades."

They passed through the gallery and entered the ballroom. He set the lamp on a table beside the door and turned to her. "You once told me you fence very well, and I believe I should like to see it for myself."

"Now?" she asked incredulously, watching as he lit two of the gas jets set in wall sconces beside the door to give them more light. "You want to fence now?"

"Why not?" He tossed the matches back on the table, took a foil from the rack on the wall, put on one of the protective masks, and walked to the center of the large room, where he turned to her. She was still staring at him in disbelief.

He gave her a salute, then pointed the foil at her. *"En garde."*

Margaret, he knew quite well, could never resist a challenge, and he was pleased to see some of the tension leave her face. She donned a mask, took a foil from its hook and moved to face him in fencing stance. She returned his salute, and they began.

She was better than he would have guessed. Whoever had trained her had done it well, for, though she lacked his strength, she possessed quickness and cleverness. She used both to her advantage, but Trevor was not worried about the outcome of his challenge. He was far stronger than she, and he had many more years of practice behind him. He could have overpowered her in a few short minutes, but he chose not to do so. Instead, he was content to parry with her, to take a defensive stance and let her be the aggressor.

But his charming opponent had weapons far more dangerous than speed, and Trevor soon found his attention distracted by the enchanting way her ivory silk robe hugged her exquisite curves. He realized his mistake only when she managed to twist her foil over his in a lightning-quick move and touch his chest with the rubber tip of her weapon.

"A hit!" she declared triumphantly, stepping back with a wide smile, the first he had seen all day. "Acknowledge it, sir!"

Trevor was astonished. "How did you manage that?"

"By my superior skill, of course," she said, lifting her foil to continue.

"You think so?"

They circled each other warily, and he noticed how the erotic rhythm of her rapid breathing accentuated the full shape of her breasts. Beneath the thin silk, he could see her nipples, and the candlelight behind her plainly outlined her hips and thighs. He decided it was time to end this match and claim the reward of his victory. He immediately became the aggressor, using his superior strength for the first time in order to force her retreat.

With a cry of alarm, she scrambled back from his suddenly overpowering moves, but she was able to parry his thrusts well enough. She might even have managed to recover from his attack, but she stepped on the hem of her robe and stumbled. He disarmed her, and the foil went flying out of her hand as she fell inelegantly on her backside in a swirl of ivory silk and creamy lace that gave him an enticing glimpse of her long, bare legs.

"Not fair!" she said, laughing as she pulled off her

mask and accepted the hand he held out to assist her to her feet. "Not fair at all. You only managed that because I'm hampered by my gown."

He shook his head and removed his own mask. "That won't do. You are very quick to attribute the points you score to your skill. Yet, when I win the match, you immediately blame your long skirts."

"Of course," she admitted frankly. "Doesn't everyone?"

"I have never done so."

She smiled and walked over to where her foil lay. She picked it up and placed both it and her mask back in their proper places on the rack. "I claim that you have won only by default. Next time, I shall wear trousers, and we shall see how well you do."

He watched her reach up to extinguish the gas lights, and he suspected the sight of his wife's gorgeous hips in a pair of snug-fitting trousers would prove just as disturbing to his game as a silk negligee. But he refused to be diverted from the pleasures he was about to enjoy by contemplating those of the future. "Admit it, Maggie. I won, and it was not by default. And," he added when she did not reply, "for my victory, I expect to be rewarded."

She turned and met his eyes. Across the distance that separated them, he heard her sharp intake of breath at the desire she must have seen there, for he made no effort to hide it. But she looked at him without fear. "Assuming that I concede to you the victory—which I have not yet done—and grant you this reward you seek, what is it that you want?"

"I think"—he paused, as if giving the matter serious consideration, and cast a lingering glance over her from head to toe—"I think I want my wife to come over here and kiss me."

She hesitated, then slowly walked toward him. A mischievous smile curved the corners of her mouth. "You only think it, my lord?" She paused, still a few feet out of reach. "Are you not certain?"

His foil and mask clattered to the floor. "Quite certain."

"Then your victory is meaningless."

"Indeed? And why is that?" Trevor asked.

She blushed, but the look she slanted him from beneath her lashes was teasing. "Because a kiss on your wedding night is a prize you would have received anyway."

"Really?" He took a step forward and seized her before she could run. Ignoring her amused squeal of protest, he lifted her into his arms. "Enough, wife. No more stalling. I'll have my kiss, if you please."

She slid her arms around his neck. "I love you," she whispered.

He tightened his hold and kissed her, silencing her silly, romantic talk. The only kind of love that was real was the kind made in bed, and he intended to start loving her as soon as possible. They'd waited long enough.

Her mouth opened beneath his, soft and warm, tasting faintly of champagne. Her hand curled into his hair. She touched her tongue to his, and the tentative contact sent shudders of pleasure through his body. Christ, he had to get her upstairs or their first lovemaking was going to be on a ballroom floor.

He broke the kiss and turned toward the door. "Grab the lamp," he said tersely.

She obeyed, and they left the ballroom. He crossed the gallery with her in his arms, the tap of his boot heels on the parquet floor echoing in the silent house.

"Trevor, put me down," she whispered when they reached the stairs. "I'm too heavy to be carried up."

He stopped at the foot of the stairs and hefted her in his arms as if to test that. "I don't think so."

He mounted the stairs and took her to their room. Once inside, he set her on her feet beside the bed. He took the lamp out of her hand and set it on the bedside table, then turned toward her.

She was staring at him with wide eyes, as if suddenly recalling what this night entailed. One hand clutched the lace edges of her robe. Her hair fell all around her shoulders in lustrous dark waves, and he reached out, entangling a handful of the silken strands in his fist.

With his other hand, he reached for the tie of her robe and gave it a sharp tug. The bow came loose, and the silken ends fell away. Placing his hands on her shoulders, he slid the robe off her body in one fluid motion. The ivory silk pooled around her feet.

But when he lifted his hands to begin unbuttoning her nightgown, she turned abruptly, one hand reaching toward the beside table.

He realized what she intended, and he grasped her wrist to stop her.

"Leave it on. I want to see you, look at you."

She shook her head and pulled against his hold, trying to reach the lamp. He sensed her acute embarrassment and fear; he knew she didn't want him to see her body, but nothing on earth was going to stop him from enjoying the sight of her.

"Maggie, I have to see you. Don't deny me."

"I don't want you to see," she whispered painfully.

"I know."

He nibbled on her earlobe while his thumb stroked her wrist, and slowly, very slowly, she relaxed. He released her to reach for the top button of her night-gown and began slipping the pearl buttons free. She did not move, but by the time he unfastened the last one, she was trembling, her head turned away, her eyes squeezed shut.

He pulled the gown off her shoulders and caught his breath at the sight of her bare breasts, round and lush. "Oh, God," he whispered hoarsely as the gown slid down her arms and fell away, catching at the flare of her hips.

He slid his hands up her ribs to cup her breasts, and his thumbs brushed back and forth across her erect nipples.

"Beautiful," he murmured and lowered his head to kiss her breast. "So beautiful. I knew you would be. From the first moment I saw you, I knew."

Lost in the sensuous haze, she listened to his whis-pered words, felt his hands stroking her so gently, and, with an intuition born of this moment, she real-ized he had made love to her countless times in his imagination. That astonishing discovery disarmed her, took away every defense she had. All her fears and apprehensions vanished, leaving only her over-powering love for him. She knew that nothing had ever been so right.

He opened his mouth over her breast, suckling her, teasing and toying with her nipple, sending jolts of sensation through her entire body. She wrapped her arms around his neck, holding on tightly and shud-dering with mindless pleasure.

When he sank to his knees in front of her, she put her arms around his head, cradling him, exhilarated by the brush of his hair against her bare skin, the glide of his fingertips across her ribs, the warmth of his breath as he kissed her navel.

He slid his hands down over her hips and bunched silk in his fists. One tug, and her gown glided down her legs. Then he was touching her again, his hand sliding between her legs, caressing her in that secret place, just the way he had in the meadow. She grasped his shoulders to keep herself from falling and moved with his hand, unable to stop herself, unable to stop the moans that he was tearing from her throat with each stroke of his fingers. Exquisite pleasure washed over her in waves, higher and higher, until suddenly everything seemed to explode inside her and she cried out in ecstasy.

"Trevor! Oh, Trevor!" His breath was hot and quick against her tummy, and he held her hips in his hands, steadying her.

After a few moments, he rose to his feet and turned toward the bed. Grasping the top edge of the bed covers, he pulled back the counterpane and top sheet, then lifted her in his arms and placed her in the center of the bed. She fell back into the pillows and looked up at him. In his face, she saw the desire, the hunger for her, and she could not look away.

Slowly, his eyes never leaving hers, he began to undress. His white silk necktie and gray waistcoat landed on a chair. The pearl studs from his shirt landed in a crystal bowl on the bedside table with a clink.

He pulled the white braces from his shoulders and removed his shirt. The sight of his chest made her throat tighten. Without thinking, she said, "I think you're beautiful, too."

"That's a first," he said, chuckling. "I don't think any woman has ever said that to me before." He tossed the shirt aside and began to unbutton his black trousers, his gaze still locked with hers. But when he slid the trousers off his hips, she lost her nerve and looked away, staring at the ceiling. She wanted to look at him again, but her embarrassment was far stronger than her curiosity at this moment, and she kept her gaze fixed on the swirling pattern of the plastered ceiling.

The mattress dipped with his weight as he stretched out beside her on the bed. He touched her, a touch that seared her skin like fire, and she jumped, startled. His hand spread over her tummy, then moved lower, sliding again between her thighs. She stiffened as she felt his finger push against her, into her, a stretching sensation that was quite strange, but not unpleasant.

Against her hip, she felt something else, a vague outline of something hard that felt hot against her bare skin. She knew what that hardness was, what it meant, what would come next. *Mild discomfort,* Cornelia had told her.

His finger moved, stroking her inside as his thumb brushed her curls in a tiny circle that teased and toyed with her. "Trevor," she gasped, shivering as if she had a fever. "Oh, oh, heavens!"

He withdrew his hand and rolled on top of her, his weight pressing her into the mattress. He held himself above her, his weight on his arms, his hips moving slowly against hers. She could feel the hard and aroused part of him rubbing against her in that secret place where his fingers had touched her, and the pleasure washed over her again at the extraordinary caress. She gasped as the feeling rose within her, growing stronger, hotter, until she was arching against him, straining, feeling wild euphoria. She cried out at the peak, her hands convulsively kneading the powerful muscles of his back.

He slid his arms beneath her back, lowering himself onto her. He kissed her hair, her throat, her cheek, his breath quick and hot against her skin.

"It's time, Maggie," he said raggedly. "I've waited for you as long as I can. I can't wait any more."

She spread her legs, and the movement seemed to ignite something inside him. He made a rough sound deep in his throat as he turned his head to capture her mouth with his. He kissed her hard and, without warning, he thrust his hips powerfully against hers. The motion brought him fully inside her, inflicting pain like the slice of a knife.

She cried out against his mouth. This was far more than the mild discomfort Cornelia had warned her about. It was excruciating. All the pleasure evaporated, and she turned her face away. She could hear herself whimpering in pain and panic, but she could not stop. She pushed at his shoulders..

Trevor stilled on top of her. He nuzzled her neck, tasting her skin in delicate nibbles. He kissed her anywhere he could reach. "Maggie, Maggie," he murmured. "I've hurt you. I'm sorry."

The pain was already receding, and she heard the regret in his voice. She swallowed hard. Her arms slid back around him. "I'm all right," she whispered. "Is it, is it over?"

"No."

Margaret licked her dry lips. "That is . . . unfortunate."

Trevor groaned against her ear. "I'm sorry, darling."

She did not want him to be sorry. She did not want him to regret anything. She moved beneath him, trying to accustom herself to the feel of him inside her. The sharp pain was gone, and all she felt was a slight soreness deep inside. She moved again, tentatively.

"Don't," he ground out through clenched teeth. "For God's sake, Maggie, be still. I'm trying . . . to be easy."

He held himself so rigid above her that she could feel the tension within him. The realization that he was striving to hold back for her sake, to let her get used to this, made her love him all the more, but she did not want him to wait. They were married now. He didn't have to hold back. Guided by instinct and love, she moved beneath him again, rocking her hips in a way she hoped would push him over the edge.

"Oh, God," he moaned, pulling back slightly. "Oh, God. Maggie, wait."

She ignored him. She arched upward against Trevor, bringing him fully inside her again. He gave a harsh cry, and then suddenly he was thrusting into her with rough and frantic moves, his weight pressing her into the mattress.

She adapted to the rhythm of his body, moving with him. It hurt a bit still, but she knew he was holding back nothing with her now. He was losing himself in her with passionate abandon, and she was glad.

"I love you!" she cried, wrapping her legs around his hips and glorying in the feel of what was no longer pain, but pleasure, the pleasure of giving. "Oh, Trevor, I love you so!"

Suddenly, he clutched her tighter, she felt him shudder, and she knew she was giving him the same moment of intense, exquisite pleasure that he had given her moments before. He collapsed on top of her, breathing hard against her ear. "Maggie," he whispered, lifting one hand to touch her hair. "My wife."

At those words, a sweet and joyous tenderness unfolded inside her like a flower opening to the sun.

She turned her head to kiss his neck. "My husband," she answered, smiling against his throat. "My hero."

For a long time, she lay beneath him, content to simply savor the feel of his body, heavy and solid and reassuring. She caressed his back and felt his breath against her ear.

After a few moments, he stirred. "I must be getting heavy," he murmured. Before she could deny that, he pressed a kiss to her ear and rolled away from her. He reached for the counterpane, which had tangled around their feet, and pulled it over them both. After settling comfortably into the thick feather mattress, he slid one arm beneath her head to act as her pillow and wrapped the other around her waist. "No separate bedrooms," he mumbled.

Within moments, she knew from the even cadence of his breathing that he had fallen asleep.

But Margaret could not do the same. She felt so gloriously alive that sleep was an impossibility. Today, she had given him all that she had, and it had been no sacrifice because she loved him. Joy blossomed inside her, and she wanted to laugh aloud.

She lay awake for a long time within the circle of his arms, her cheek against his shoulder, happier and more content than she had ever been in her life. She knew that, in this man, she had found the true love she'd always dreamed about.

17

There was nothing better for a man to wake up to than the scent of a woman. Without opening his eyes, Trevor inhaled deeply of lemon soap, powder, and soft, feminine warmth, a combination that was uniquely Maggie. He'd woken many mornings to that luscious, tormenting fragrance, but it was different this time. More potent, more quixotic to his senses. A jolt of pure lust rocked him as he realized what it was. The scent of lovemaking.

He opened his eyes. The lamp had gone out, but soft gray light filtered in around the shuttered windows, telling him that it was morning. Margaret stirred beside him, and he turned his head to find her awake and watching him.

She was lying on her side, propped up on one elbow with her cheek resting on her palm, the sheet pulled up modestly over her breasts. Her long hair fell all around her face, spilling over her bare shoulders.

He rolled to his side and lifted his hand, his palm sliding over her round cheek, his fingers weaving through the silken tangle of her hair to curve behind her head. "Good morning," he murmured and pulled her toward him.

She lowered her lashes and blushed, but she came willingly, returning his kiss with a passion that inflamed his senses. He slid his free hand under the sheets, exploring her body as his tongue explored her mouth. He ran his fingers over her breasts, over the satin skin of her tummy, to slide between her thighs. He brushed his fingers lightly over her and felt how ready she was.

He withdrew his hand and broke the kiss. Ignoring her tiny, fluttering protest, he pulled aside the sheets that covered them. "Come here, wife," he murmured and pulled her on top of him so that she sat astride his hips. He reached between them, guiding himself to her opening, tormenting himself with the erotic feel of her damp warmth against the tip of his penis.

The sight of her, with her breasts bare to his gaze, excited him like nothing ever had before, and he realized it was what he wanted to see every morning of his life. "No separate bedrooms," he promised again and thrust upward, entering her.

Margaret closed her eyes, and she tilted her head back with a raw, startled cry. Remembering her pain of last night, he hesitated. "Did I hurt you?"

She shook her head. "No, no," she managed between tiny, panting breaths. She moved awkwardly above him, inexperienced, and he grasped her hips in his hands to guide her.

Just as he thought he could stand the sweet torture no longer, he felt her tighten convulsively around him. He surged upward, as deeply inside her as he could be, and climaxed in a rush that left him dizzy.

She snuggled against him, her cheek rubbing his shoulder, and he wrapped his arms around her. Trevor caressed the silky skin of her back and sank into a languorous aftermath, content to just lie here and hold her.

This was something he'd never experienced with a woman before, this sated peace.

He closed his eyes and breathed in rhythm with her, vulnerable and relaxed. Vague memories of other women passed through his mind, women he'd been perfectly glad to leave when it was over, women who could never keep him long enough to make demands on him, women who, no matter how skilled at love-making they might be, could never persuade him to stay long enough for this.

But Maggie was different. Maggie was his wife. Until this moment, he hadn't realized what that would mean. The intimacy of it should have alarmed him, but he found that it did not. Nor did it seem to alarm her, despite her apprehensions of last night. She seemed perfectly happy to lie here with him and laze the entire day away. She was so still, in fact, he wondered wryly if she had fallen asleep.

But then, to his surprise, she stirred and lifted her head. She did not meet his eyes, but instead kept her gaze lowered, staring down at his chest. He watched as a tiny, mysterious smile curved the corners of her lips.

That smile intrigued him. "What are you thinking?" he asked.

Without raising her eyes, she touched him, brushing her fingers across the hair of his chest in a tentative caress. "I think, my lord," she said shyly, "that I shall like being married."

Trevor laughed, a lusty laugh of utter contentment, and, to his own amazement, he realized that he was going to like it, too. He was going to like it very much indeed.

Henry signed his name to the bank draft with a flourish and handed it to Trevor across the desk. "That ought to enable you to begin refurbishing Ashton Park. Have you decided on what investments interest you?"

Trevor took the draft without looking at it, folded it, and put it in the pocket of his jacket. "I have several in mind. The first would be linen mills. There are none around Waverly. The closest is at Sittingbourne, about twenty miles distant. I have a great deal of land that is fallow at the moment, but which could easily be planted in flax. The climate is suitable. In addition to the fiber to make linen, flax would also provide linseed oil, thereby giving us two harvests out of one crop. I think we would gain a substantial return on such an investment."

Henry nodded and shot him a shrewd glance across the desk. "Not to mention the benefits it would provide for the village of Waverly."

"The prosperity of a village depends largely on the prosperity of its closest estates. As the earl, I cannot ignore my responsibility to the people of Waverly. Their livelihood depends on me, and their needs have been ignored for far too long. But I would not suggest it unless I felt we could make a reasonable profit."

"I agree with you. It is a sound idea. I know several excellent engineering firms in London who can design the mill for us. I take it you have a site on Ashton lands in mind."

"Of course. I also think it would be advisable for me to meet with your London accountants. They can draw up some preliminary estimates of cost and profit projections."

Henry nodded. "You said you had some other possibilities?"

"One in particular that I think would be highly lucrative, but it would also be very risky."

"The most lucrative possibilities always entail the greatest risk. What is your idea?"

"Electrical lighting."

"You don't think electricity is a passing fancy?"

"No, I don't. Do you?"

Henry shook his head. "No. In fact, electricity may very well prove to be the most important development of this century. But, assuming we are right, what is your idea?"

"There are many peers in our general acquaintance who have married American heiresses, and who, like myself, are trying to rebuild their estates. Their wives, of course, are accustomed to modern conveniences, and I'm sure they are finding that their homes on this side of the Atlantic provide little in the way of such amenities. Most English country houses are dark and dreary enough to depress anyone. I know a lot of peers would shudder at the thought of electrical lighting in their ancestral homes, but for domestic tranquillity, a man will make many sacrifices."

"Especially when he has the money to do so," Henry added dryly. He considered the possibilities, but, after a moment, he reluctantly shook his head. "Between us, I'm sure we have enough contacts to make such a venture quite profitable. But electricity is such a new industry, I know of very few men involved in it. How do you propose to gain the expertise you need?"

Instead of answering that question directly, Trevor asked, "Are you acquainted with Sir William Crandon?"

"If I'm not mistaken, he is a baronet. But more to your point, I think, he is a leading authority on electrical engineering."

"Precisely. His knowledge would be of great use to us."

"I'm sure it would. But I understand he's one of your more snobbish peers, and has been given offers of employment before. I doubt I could persuade him to engage in such a venture, especially since I have no connection whatsoever with the man."

Trevor smiled. "I do. He's an old friend of mine. We did some very profitable business in Thebes before he gained his title and returned to England. I think he could be persuaded to lend his expertise to this venture. For the right salary, of course. Although it has not yet been made public, I learned yesterday from Lord Seton—who is a cousin of his by marriage—that Crandon is about to be served by his creditors with a petition for bankruptcy."

Henry chuckled. "I knew I was right about you, Ashton. You have a talent for making the most of what you've got, and I think you were born to be an entrepreneur. Are you sure there isn't some Yankee blood in your background?"

Trevor smiled, thinking that there very well could be, given the notorious profligacy of his family tree. If there was, it was all on the wrong side of the blankets, and he refrained from saying so. Instead, he began enumerating other ideas for how they might make money off ventures in electricity, and Henry added a few ideas of his own. The two men were in the midst of working out how they might install electrical lighting systems

for entire cities when a knock on the study door interrupted their discussion. The door opened, and
Margaret peeped in.

Henry frowned in exasperation. "Thunderation,
Maggie, you know the rules. Unless the house is burning down, I will not be bothered when I'm talking
business!"

She gave him a smile as she entered the study.
"Since you are discussing business with my husband,
I didn't think the rule applied. Especially the morning
after the wedding."

His belligerence faded immediately at that gentle
reminder, and it amused Trevor a great deal to see
how such a tough and hardheaded man as Henry Van
Alden could be so easily manipulated by his own
daughter.

Henry coughed, looking apologetic. "Well, yes," he
said gruffly, "I guess you have a point. Sorry, honey."

"That's quite all right, Papa. I know how wrapped
up you get in business." She smiled at Trevor. "He'll
keep you in here all day," she warned.

"He can't," Trevor answered and rose to his feet. "I
have an appointment with my solicitors in"—he
pulled out his pocket watch—"half an hour. I'll be
back by mid-afternoon."

She sighed, looking up at him with regret. "Then
you shall not see me, I'm afraid. Since you and I are
leaving for Kent early tomorrow, Cornelia and I are
using this opportunity to do some shopping. After
that, we are going to Lady Longford's for tea."

"I'm sorry we won't have time for a honeymoon,
but I must get home."

"I understand," she answered. "We'll do it some
other time."

"As for today, perhaps we can find an hour or so to

fence before dinner." He took her hand in his and brought it to his lips. "Fencing with you is proving to be a most interesting exercise," he added in a whisper. "One I would like to repeat as often as possible."

"I, too," she whispered back, blushing at the reminder of the previous night.

Although he had not heard what they said, Henry could not help but perceive the blush in her cheeks, and he could make a pretty good guess as to the reason for it. He smiled at her as Trevor left the room, delighted by how well everything had turned out. "Tell me, how does married life suit you so far, Maggie, my girl?"

She walked to his chair and settled herself comfortably on one corner of his desk. "Very well, Papa," she admitted happily. "And I can see from the smug smile on your face that you are about to say I told you so."

He reached up to chuck her under the chin. "I wouldn't dream of it," he said mildly, but he was thinking it. The satisfaction he felt did not stem from being right about marriage, but from being right about Trevor. Margaret was truly in love with the man, it was as plain as day. And that notion made Henry Van Alden a very happy man.

Henry was not the only one who was happy. Margaret was quite content herself, a fact Cornelia commented on as they strolled through the textiles department at Harrod's.

"Maggie, you're positively glowing. This is quite a change from yesterday."

She laughed and shot her cousin a mischievous glance over the colorful bolts of chintz between them. "You're a married woman, Cornelia. Surely you know the cause."

But her cousin did not respond to the teasing with a smile. She looked back at Margaret with a serious face. "I'm glad you're happy, darling."

"I am happy, and you don't look glad about much of anything these days. You've been such a sobersides since Naples."

"I'm just tired. The trip home and all the rushing of the past few days have quite exhausted me."

Vague uneasiness stirred inside Margaret, but before she could pursue the subject further, her cousin gestured toward the fabrics all around them and gave an unexpected laugh. "My dear, unless you're planning to sew Lord Ashton a shirt—and knowing you, I doubt it—I don't think you'll find a wedding gift for him here."

"You're quite right," Margaret answered and pointed at the sporting equipment across the room. "I was headed in that direction."

She left the textiles department, and Cornelia followed her. She passed the golf clubs and cricket bats and made straight for the fishing gear, halting before a display of rods and tackle baskets. One rod took pride of place, and Margaret pointed to it with a cry of delight. "It's perfect! I knew it the moment I saw the advertisement in the *Times* this morning."

"A fishing rod?"

"Yes, indeed. Trevor is quite an experienced angler. He's going to love it!"

"It's a rather unusual wedding gift, isn't it?"

"Perhaps," she admitted. "What would you suggest?"

"I gave Edward a pair of gold cufflinks with his initials. He was quite pleased."

That idea left Margaret completely cold. She envisioned Trevor putting a present like that in a drawer and forgetting all about it. "No," she said. "Thank you for the suggestion, but for Trevor, this is exactly right."

A young man in gray flannel approached them. "Ladies, may I be of assistance?"

Margaret pointed to her intended gift. "That is the latest thing in fishing rods?"

"Oh, yes, quite."

"Do you think a man would appreciate it as a wedding present?"

The clerk recovered from his initial surprise and beamed at her. "Madam, any gentleman would be profoundly pleased. I must confess, I wish my wife had thought to give me such a gift."

"What did your wife give you, if I may ask?"

"Cufflinks," he said with a sigh.

Margaret choked back a laugh and wisely did not look at Cornelia. "I'll take it. Could you also outfit a tackle basket to go with it, please?"

"Certainly. Have you an account with us?"

"Yes, indeed. It's under my maiden name, Margaret Van Alden."

The clerk obviously read the papers. "Lady Ashton," he said in a new tone of hushed respect that contained none of the casual friendliness of a few moments before. He gave her a formal bow. "My apologies. I did not know— I'm new here— That is, I did not realize . . ." His stuttering words faded into a mortified silence.

Margaret looked back at him, surprised by his obvious and painful embarrassment. "That's quite all right," she said, hastening to soothe him. Leaning closer, she confessed in a whisper, "I've only been a countess since yesterday, and I'm not quite used to it myself yet."

The clerk, red-faced, gave her another bow and turned away to write up the order.

"Poor man," she murmured to Cornelia as they followed him to the counter. "He's quite upset. What difference does it make anyway?"

"A great deal of difference," her cousin answered. "A peeress should never be spoken to in such a familiar fashion."

"Well, I don't see how he was supposed to know."

"It is his job to know such things. And you probably should have reprimanded him."

"What? Heavens, the man feels badly enough as it is. Why should I do such a thing?"

"A countess would be expected to do exactly that. Put him in his place. Maggie, you are a countess, now. You must begin learning to behave like one."

"I certainly shall not," she answered with spirit. "Not if it means being rude to poor sales clerks and looking down my nose at people who are only being friendly. No, thank you."

Cornelia sighed. "When you begin managing Ashton Park, you will find a stern and aristocratic demeanor goes much further with English servants and shopkeepers than friendliness, particularly since you are an American. Believe me, I learned that lesson the hard way."

Margaret did not think she wanted to learn that lesson at all.

"But then," Cornelia added, "I didn't have a mother-in-law to help me. You'll be able to rely on Caroline to help you."

The idea of turning to Trevor's formidable mother did not appeal to Margaret. "Must I?"

"I know she seems a cold woman, Maggie, but you can learn a great deal from her. And you must.

English country houses are not easy to run, and you've no experience at the task."

"I've run Papa's households for a long time, Cornelia. I think I can manage."

"It's not the same. You're accustomed to all the modern conveniences, to servants who are friendly, and to leaving many of the details to housekeepers. Ashton Park will be different."

"Lady Ashton?" The clerk placed a charge slip before her and handed her a pen.

"Cornelia," she whispered, pen poised hesitantly above the paper. "How do I sign this? Margaret St. James? Lady Ashton?"

Her cousin gave a despairing sigh. "Margaret Ashton," she answered. "You never paid any attention to all the lessons I gave you on titles, and I knew you'd come to regret it one day."

Margaret shrugged and signed her new name with a flourish. "Well, now that I have use for such lessons, I'll pay attention. I promise."

"Would you like these delivered, my lady?" the clerk asked.

"No, thank you. Just have them wrapped, if you please, and I'll take them with me."

"To Lady Longford's?" Cornelia asked as the clerk departed to carry out her instructions.

"No. I'm going home. You can drop me at the house on your way. Make my apologies to Lady Longford, will you, darling? I'm so excited about this. I must give Trevor his present right away. He should be back from his appointment by now." She beamed at her cousin. "Oh, Cornelia, I know he's going to love it."

*　　　*　　　*

By the time Margaret returned to the house, she was tingling with anticipation. There was nothing more fun, she decided, than finding the perfect gift for someone you loved.

Her arms full with her packages, she fumbled awkwardly for the door pull, but before she could reach it, the front door opened. Sims had already heard the carriage approach and, like any proper butler, was there to open the door for her.

"Shall I take those for you, Lady Ashton?"

"Only for a moment, Sims. Thank you." Relieved of her packages, Margaret pulled off her gloves and tossed them onto the card tray. Her bonnet followed. "Where is everyone?" she asked, removing her cloak.

"Lord Ashton and Lord Kettering are in your father's library, my lady. They have just sat down to tea. Your father has gone out. Shall I take these to your room?"

"No. Give them to me." She draped her cloak on the coat tree and took back her packages, then started toward the long hallway that led to the library at the back of the house.

Trevor and Edward were indeed in the library. She could hear their voices as she approached that room along the carpeted hall.

"I must admit, it's been a rather stressful week," Edward was saying. "While you were in Kent, I thought sure Margaret was getting cold feet. But she seems to be very happy now. I think everything has turned out quite well."

"I think so, too," Trevor answered. "But I'm glad the whole thing is over and done."

"Courtship is a tedious business, is it not? Plays merry hell with a man's nerves. But, I must say, you've handled it all rather well."

Margaret halted outside the half-open door, curious to hear her husband's reply.

"You're wrong, Edward. There were moments when I thought I'd go out of my mind, I assure you. You just weren't there to see it. By yesterday, I was a wreck."

Margaret smiled, quite pleased to learn that her husband wasn't always as cool and collected as he appeared. She took another step forward to push open the door, but Edward's next words stopped her.

"I can't believe it actually worked. No other man of my acquaintance could pull off such an outrageous scheme. Really, you amaze me." Edward laughed. "Only you would think of arranging to have a woman kidnapped in order to woo her."

Everything in Margaret suddenly went ice cold. Trevor had arranged her kidnapping? No, she must have misunderstood. Numbly, unable to believe what she was hearing, she hovered outside the door, listening.

"Hiring your friend Emilio to snatch her away," Edward went on, still laughing, "and then coming to her rescue so that she'd think you the brave, strong hero. God, what an idea!"

Margaret suddenly felt sick. She swayed and leaned one shoulder against the door jamb to steady herself, straining to hear every word.

"I had to get her alone somehow," Trevor was saying. "Once she realized I intended to marry her, she wouldn't even speak to me. She left me little choice."

"Perhaps, but you must admit, it's a unique way of winning a wife."

"I suppose it is."

"But Trevor," Edward said in a suddenly serious voice, "if she ever finds out, she'll be devastated."

Too late, Margaret thought with bitterness.

"She's not going to find out," Trevor answered harshly. "There's no need for her to know. Ever. Do you understand?"

"I certainly won't tell her. The results speak for themselves anyway." Edward coughed and added, "She loves you, you know."

"Yes," he said. He did not sound happy. "I know."

"But you don't love her, do you?"

"I'm quite fond of her," Trevor answered. "But love her? No. Edward, you know how I feel about that emotion."

Margaret closed her eyes, raw pain ripping through her. She thought of all the times she had told him she loved him, but it wasn't until this moment that she realized he had never said those words to her. Not once. He was fond of her.

How stupid she had been.

"When I agreed to help you win her," Edward said, "I'd hoped—"

"Hoped what?" Trevor countered harshly. "That love would transform me? Make a new man of me? Lead me to mend my wicked ways?"

"Something like that."

"I don't believe in fairy tales!" Trevor said so savagely that Margaret took a step back from the door. "And Margaret has to stop believing in them, too. She has my name and position," he went on. "She has security and respectability. She'll soon have children to occupy her attention. She won't have to worry that I'll gamble away the money, or drink myself into a stupor every night, or shame her with blatant affairs. I'll be faithful to her as long as she is faithful to me. I'll be a good husband to her, and I'll try to make her happy. What more can a woman expect of marriage?"

Margaret choked back the hysterical laughter that rose in her throat. So he intended to be a good husband to her, did he? How noble of him.

The whole thing had been a farce, a string of lies from start to finish—the seduction, the kidnapping, the rescue, the wedding vows. She thought of last night, of how she had told him she loved him, over and over, while he touched her, while he made love to her.

Made love to her. Another lie.

What a fool she must have looked. A starry-eyed, gullible fool. How he must have been laughing at her romantic, school-girl notions, at how easily he had manipulated her. She wanted to run, she wanted to clamp her hands over her ears so she could hear no more, she wanted to die.

"Don't worry, Edward," Trevor said. "I'll take care of Maggie. Everything has worked out quite well. Margaret is happy, Henry is happy, Ashton Park is saved, and the creditors will be off my back."

Her pain dissolved into sparks of fury at those words. Her money. It always came back to that. She took a deep breath, then leaned her shoulder against the door and pushed it wide. "Another British peer saved from bankruptcy," she said in a shaking voice. "God bless America."

The two men glanced up to find her standing there. Simultaneously, they set down their teacups and rose. Edward stared at her for a moment, red-faced, then turned his face away. Trevor did not. He simply looked at her, his handsome face hard and unreadable.

"Maggie," he said and even had the gall to look her in the eye. "I thought you'd gone to tea at Lady Longford's."

"I changed my mind." Her grip tightened around the packages in her arms. "If the two of you are finished congratulating each other on your cleverness, I would like to speak to you privately, Ashton." She looked at Edward. "Leave us, please."

Edward glanced from one to the other and hastily started for the door. "Certainly," he murmured. He walked past Margaret and departed, closing the door behind him.

For several seconds, they stared at each other without speaking. As the silence lengthened, Margaret began to shake, the anger and pain inside her building until she thought she would explode.

Trevor began walking toward her, slowly, as if he were approaching a wounded animal. How appropriate, she thought wildly. That was exactly how she felt. She wanted to slash at him with claws and teeth, make him bleed as she was bleeding.

He halted in front of her. "Maggie—"

"You bastard." Her voice shook from the effort to remain in control. She dropped the packages at his feet. With her arms free, she could no longer contain her rage. Without thinking, she slapped him across the face.

He didn't move. He didn't react. He simply looked back at her with his calm, inscrutable expression and said nothing. That only infuriated her more.

"You manipulative, lying bastard." She lifted her hand to strike again, but he caught her wrist.

A glitter of danger flickered in his blue eyes, the only indication he felt anything at all. But his voice was surprisingly gentle. "I never lied to you."

Outraged that he had the gall to say that after everything she'd overheard, Margaret jerked free of his hold and took a step back. "You deliberately developed an acquaintance with me because you wanted my money. Do you deny it?"

"No. And you knew it perfectly well. You hurled that accusation in my face more than once. But you also wanted things from me, Maggie. You wanted excitement, you wanted adventure." He reached out, running one finger down her cheek and across her lips. "You wanted kisses, did you not?"

She turned her face away from his touch. "You said you desired me, when all along it was only my money you wanted."

"If I did not desire you, I would never have seduced you or married you, your money be damned."

Another lie. She could feel all the love she had for him changing to something black and cold, something akin to hatred. "You knew I did not want to marry a man who does not love me!" she cried, lifting her chin to look at him with all the pain and loathing she felt. "You don't love me, but you made me believe that you did so I would marry you."

His eyes shifted away from her. For the first time, he looked somewhat guilty. As if he realized it, he turned and walked away. Halting beside the fireplace, he turned on her. "What are you saying?" he demanded. "Are you saying that now I am condemned because I sought a more honorable relationship with you than simple seduction? Forgive me, madam, if I fail to see the crime in wanting you for a wife instead of a mistress."

"How dare you even mention honor in connection with what you've done! You arranged for friends of yours to kidnap me!" Even though she had overheard his conversation with Edward, even as she said the words now, she could still hardly believe he had done such a thing. "I was bound, blindfolded, and gagged, not to mention terrified! I was scared to death Emilio and his men were going to kill me or, or worse. And you put me through that just so you could rescue me and play the part of my knight in shining armor?"

"No. I did it because once you had discovered my intention to marry you, you wouldn't even speak to me, and I knew that if I didn't get you alone, force you to spend time with me, you would never give me a chance to win you."

"And you would never get your hands on my money."

"For God's sake, Maggie, stop throwing the money in my face!" he shouted. "What do you think I wanted it for? Do you think I wanted it for silk waistcoats and gambling funds and expensive mistresses? My worthless brother put our family estate in debt to the tune of two hundred thousand pounds, a sum I could never repay. His creditors were about to foreclose on Ashton Park, my mother and grandmother would have been without a home, and I would have lost the only thing I've ever cared about in my life, the only opportunity I've ever had to build a future for myself. When you are about to see your family turned out and your home taken away, then come and give me a lecture on morality."

She refused to listen to any excuses. "And you think that justifies what you did? Manipulating me? Lying to me?"

"As I said before, I never lied to you. I admit, there were certain things I did not tell you, but what I did tell you was the absolute truth."

"Lies of omission are still lies! You deliberately made me believe certain things."

"You believed what you wanted to believe."

She felt as if she'd been struck. Her hands curled

into fists. "And you conveniently failed to mention any fact that might lead me to believe anything other than what *you* wanted me to believe. You used me. You manipulated me every step of the way." She turned and gave the smaller package at her feet a hard kick that sent it skittering toward the wall. "I loved you! Can you understand that?"

She could feel the tears coming, and she squeezed her eyes shut. She clenched her fists so tightly her nails dug into her palms. "Of course you can't, since you don't believe in love, have never felt love, are in fact, incapable of love."

She opened her eyes and turned to look him in the face, but he was a blur by the fireplace. She blinked to keep the tears at bay and clung to her pride. She lifted her chin, and all the contempt that could come from love betrayed was in her voice when she said, "You once accused me of never considering the consequences of my actions. But it is you who does not consider consequences. You have only the most selfish disdain for my feelings. I loved you, which is exactly what you wanted. You deliberately set out to make me fall in love with you so that I would marry you, deliberately made me believe that you cared for me when you did not, and had no regard for how I might be hurt in the process. Well, Lord Ashton, your beloved estate is saved and you now have all the money you could wish for. I hope you choke on it."

She kicked the longer package and sent it sliding across the carpet until it hit his feet. "Your wedding present, darling. I bought it for you because I knew you would like it. I didn't realize at the time that it's the perfect gift for a fortune hunter—a fishing rod. Just the thing for hooking yourself an heiress. Perhaps you might mount it over the drawing room fireplace at Ashton Park as a trophy of your splendid conquest."

She turned and walked out. There was nothing more to say.

18

Trevor heard the door slam behind her with all the force of a rifle shot. He drew a deep breath and let it out slowly, then looked down at the long, tissue wrapped box that lay at his feet.

I bought it for you because I knew you would like it.

A vague feeling stirred inside him, something like the first chilly breeze of autumn, something that made him uncomfortable, something that might be remorse.

I loved you.

He picked up the package, staring at the froth of blue ribbons that adorned it, trying not to hear her voice, a voice that had cried out her passion for him only the night before, but which had just flayed him with scorn. He tried not to picture her eyes, eyes that had been warm and soft in this morning's light, but which had just stared him down with bitterness, regret, and contempt.

You don't believe in love, have never felt love, are incapable of love.

With a curse a sailor might have been proud of, he dropped the gift and walked over to the liquor cabinet. He poured himself a glass of Henry's much-loved Kentucky bourbon. Foolish, romantic girl, when would she grow up? When would she stop believing in fairy tales?

Trevor lifted his glass, staring at the golden brown liquid within, the color an exact match for Maggie's eyes. He pushed away that fanciful imagining and swallowed the liquor in one draught, then grabbed the bottle and sank into one of the leather chairs that faced the fireplace.

He stared into the flames and thought that getting drunk was a fine idea. He poured himself another drink. But not a second glass of bourbon, nor even a third, could blot out the image of Maggie.

He'd hurt her. Badly. He knew it, and he regretted it. But it could not be helped, and if he had it to do over again, there was only one thing he would change. He'd be damn sure not to talk about it afterward.

The door opened, and he saw Edward standing in the doorway. "Henry's home and he's demanding to know why Margaret won't come out of her room and why Cornelia is in tears. Both of them are saying it's all your fault. He's wondering what happened between ten o'clock this morning and now, and he wants to know where the hell you are. What do you want me to tell him?"

Trevor sighed and turned back to stare into the fire. "Nothing. I'll talk to him myself."

"I'll tell him you're in here." Edward started to close the door, but paused and asked, "Are you all right?"

"I'm fine. Bloody damned fine."

Edward again started to close the door, but Trevor's voice stopped him. "How's Maggie?"

"She's locked her door and refuses to come out. How do you think she is?"

Trevor took a swallow of bourbon, felt it burn his throat. "That doesn't sound too serious. She's just upset, and her pride is hurt. She'll get over it."

Edward crossed the room and sank down in the chair beside his. "Will she?"

He shifted uneasily and kept his gaze on the fire. "Of course. She's not a child. How hard can it be for her to abandon these romantic notions of hers?"

"Is that all they are?" Edward settled into the opposite chair. "Romantic notions?"

Trevor didn't answer, and Edward went on, "You still don't understand it, do you? I told you before, you've taken on a great responsibility."

"Indeed I have. I got married."

"That's not what I meant. You persuaded Margaret to fall in love with you, and she has, with all her heart and soul. Have you no inkling of what that means?"

His words were so similar to Maggie's that Trevor's tight control snapped. He stood up and turned away. "For God's sake, Edward, stop prattling on about love!" he shouted. "You sound like a lady novelist."

"Getting a bit defensive, aren't you?"

That was so close to the truth he slammed his glass down on the table hard enough to rattle the lamp that rested there. "Damn it, Edward, I did what I had to do, and you know it."

"I know. But that's no longer the issue. What are you planning to do now?"

"I'm going talk to Henry, then get drunk," he

answered and refilled his glass. "Not the most responsible thing to do, perhaps, but quite understandable, given the circumstances."

"And after that?"

"Tomorrow, I am taking my wife to my estate exactly as I planned."

"You can't be serious." Edward stared at him. "God, Trevor, do you think Maggie would go anywhere with you just now?"

He smiled grimly, staring into his glass. "Edward, you seem to be laboring under the misapprehension that she has a choice. Let me enlighten you. She doesn't."

To his surprise, Edward began to laugh. "You know, this is really becoming quite a comedy. A contemporary version of Kate and Petruchio. He wanted her money, too, as I recall."

Trevor turned to give his friend an icy stare. "Do you have a point?"

"I do. To my knowledge, no one has ever been able to make Maggie do anything she didn't want to do. Once she gets an idea into her head, no one can stop her, not even her father."

"But I am not her father. I am her husband. We are leaving in the morning, and at Ashton Park, Margaret will take her place as my countess and learn to be a dutiful wife."

"Right." Edward stood up and started for the door. "Margaret, a dutiful wife," he repeated as he walked out. "God help you."

Margaret sat curled up in the chair by the window, staring out at the darkness beyond. She did not cry. She had already done that. She had cried for her stupidity, her gullibility, and, most of all, for wasting her love on a man who loved nothing and no one. Now, she had no tears left.

She closed her eyes, remembering how she had let him touch her, kiss her, do those intimate things to her. She remembered how she had told him over and over that she loved him, how she had touched him and called him beautiful. How she had thought he was her true love.

How blind she had been.

No, she realized with bitter irony, she could not even give herself that excuse. She'd known from the start that Trevor St. James was a fortune hunter, a liar, and a rake. She'd known about his financial troubles and his questionable activities in Egypt and his notorious reputation with women. She'd known all that, but she had fallen in love with him anyway.

You believed what you wanted to believe.

Trevor had lied to her, yes. But worse than that, she had lied to herself. She had convinced herself that he loved her but just didn't know how to show it, that his love for her had changed him, transformed him into an honorable and noble gentleman when he was nothing but a deceiving, manipulating scoundrel who was incapable of loving anyone.

A knock on her door made her jump. The knob rattled, and she heard Cornelia's voice. "Maggie, let me in. Please."

She had to face the world eventually, she supposed. She might as well start with her cousin. Margaret rose slowly from the chair and walked across the room. She pulled back the bolt and opened the door.

Cornelia let out a sigh of relief at the sight of her. "Maggie, everyone is worried about you, especially your father. You wouldn't come down to dinner, you refused to let the maid in with a tray, and you won't talk to anyone. How pale you look." She gestured to the tray in her hands. "Good thing I've brought some strong, hot tea. I think you need it."

Tea, Margaret thought idly. The English cure for everything. How English Cornelia had become. "You look as if you need it as much as I do," she commented, noticing the puffiness beneath Cornelia's eyes that clearly showed she had been crying. She pulled the door open, and her cousin entered the room.

Cornelia set the tray on the dressing table, pushing aside the perfume bottles. Then she poured out two cups, added a generous amount of sugar to each, and handed one cup to Margaret. Taking the other over to the chair by the window, Cornelia sat down.

"Well," she said, and took a sip of tea. "Well."

"This is like a nightmare." Margaret leaned back against the dressing table and looked at her cousin. "He manipulated me from the start. He arranged that kidnapping, Cornelia. He hired those men, and then he pretended to rescue me, all for the sole purpose of getting me alone so that he could seduce me, persuade me to marry him. And Edward knew about it."

Cornelia turned her face away. "Do we have to talk about this?"

Margaret studied her cousin, remembering that this wasn't the first time Cornelia didn't want to talk about the kidnapping.

And suddenly she realized why.

"You knew about it, too," she whispered. "My God, you knew all along the kidnapping was a sham. Didn't you?"

Cornelia kept her face averted and didn't answer.

Her voice rose to a shout. "Didn't you?"

"Oh, Maggie!" Her cousin looked up at her in hopeless misery, tears glistening in her eyes. That was answer enough.

"You knew, and you participated in it. You lied to me, too."

"I'm so sorry," Cornelia said with a sob. "I didn't know beforehand, truly I didn't. But once Ashton told me what he had done, once I learned Edward was in on it, I had to go along. There was no other choice."

"No choice?" Margaret's hand's curled tightly around the teacup, and she suddenly wanted to hurl it through the window. "How about just saying no? Or didn't that occur to you?"

"Of course it did!" Cornelia sniffed and brushed tears from her cheeks. "But Ashton had already arranged matters, and Edward thought it would work, and I-I agreed to it because, well, I knew Henry approved of Ashton and they had already made the arrangements for a marital settlement, and, you must admit yourself that Ashton has rather a way of persuasion with him, and he assured me his intentions were honorable and that he was quite fond of you."

"Fond of me?" Margaret repeated furiously. "Fond of me?"

"You're angry. Oh, dear, this is all my fault. I'm so sorry."

Unable to bear Cornelia's genuine regret and tearful apologies, she turned her back. "I don't suppose you could have at least told me about it in Naples?" she asked tightly, staring down at her reflection on the silver tea tray.

"I've felt beastly about it ever since, Maggie, honestly! And I wanted to tell you. But you looked so happy, you looked so much in love with Ashton, I just couldn't do it."

Margaret hardly heard what Cornelia was saying. Her mind was focused on something her cousin had said a moment before, something that was just beginning to penetrate her consciousness. "What do you mean, the marital settlements had already been made?"

Margaret set down her tea cup with great care, feeling as if the earth were shifting beneath her feet. Slowly she turned around. "My father and Trevor arranged this marriage between them in Rome?" she said, thinking it out as she spoke. "They bargained over me as if this were a, a business deal? Papa paid him to court me, didn't he? Paid him to marry me. Oh, my God."

Never had she felt more humiliated.

"Oh, Maggie, no!" Cornelia cried and jumped to her feet. "You're putting the worst possible connotation on it. Wealthy families always discuss marriage settlements. They have to, for the protection of everyone's interests."

Margaret hardly heard. "Trevor, Edward, you. Even my father. God in heaven," she choked, "is there anyone who was not in on this conspiracy?"

"It wasn't a conspiracy!" Cornelia denied, and grabbed Margaret's hand. "Oh, darling, please believe me. We did not plot this as if it were a battle campaign. I'm sorry, I truly am."

Apologies did not make things any better, but she did not point that out. Her cousin obviously felt bad enough as it was. "I'd like to be alone, if you don't mind."

"Of course." Cornelia practically ran for the door. But, with her hand on the knob, she paused and glanced back at her cousin. "We were only doing what we thought was best for you."

Margaret had no answer for that. She knew guilt weighed heavy on Cornelia's shoulders and that she desperately wanted to be absolved. But, just now, Margaret could not oblige her. She felt as Caesar must have felt when he looked into the faces of those who had stabbed him.

What she felt must have shown in her face. Cornelia burst into tears and fled.

Betrayal. Margaret walked over to the bed and pulled back the covers, feeling as if she were a puppet and everyone else had been pulling her strings. She had been manipulated and betrayed by everyone she loved.

She turned off the lamp beside the bed, then crawled beneath the covers. She lay in the dark, trying to sleep, but she could not help remembering the night before, when she had not slept in this bed alone. A sob of renewed heartache and pain broke from her throat, and she realized she'd been wrong. She thought she'd cried all the tears she could, but it seemed there were plenty more left. Grabbing her pillow, she hugged it tight, burying her tear-stained face against the cool linen pillowcase.

She could feel herself fracturing into pieces. She curled into a ball around her pillow and did something she had not done since she was a chubby sixteen-year-old debutante whose party no one wanted to attend. She cried herself to sleep.

Margaret woke the following morning feeling quite different from when she had fallen asleep. The discovery of Trevor's deceit had destroyed her illusions and broken her heart, but all her anger and pain had somehow fused during sleep into cool and calm resolve. Her family's participation in her husband's schemes, she knew, stemmed from their love for her. But Trevor's motives could not be dismissed or forgiven so easily. He did not love her and never had. Because of that, she knew exactly how to proceed.

She asked for a full breakfast to accompany the tea a maid had already brought to her room, and she ate every bite. When Molly, her own maid, came in a few minutes later to help her dress, Margaret was sorting through the stacks of mail that had come during the hectic days before the wedding and for which she'd spared only a cursory glance. But now she went through them slowly, searching for one letter in particular—the one from Pelham & Smythe, the family's London attorneys.

"Oh, ma'am!" Molly cried, seeing her sorting through the mail as if she hadn't a care in the world. "You've no time for that this morning!"

Margaret serenely continued her task. "There's no rush, Molly, I assure you."

"Beggin' your pardon, my lady, but I'm to get you dressed as quick as possible so's the upstairs maids can start packing your things for the journey to Kent. We've no time to dawdle."

"Ah, here it is," Margaret exclaimed, pulling out the letter she'd been searching for. She opened it and scanned the contents. It gave the customary congratulations on her approaching wedding, but there'd been one line she distinctly remembered. Yes, there it was.

The marital agreements have been handled, of course, but if there is anything further we can do to assist you in the matter of your marriage, please call upon us.

She tapped the letter thoughtfully against her

palm, then gave a decisive nod. "Yes, Mr. Pelham, I think I will need some further assistance," she murmured to herself.

A movement out of the corner of her eye caught Margaret's attention, and she glanced up to find Molly still standing by the bed, wringing her hands and looking quite distressed. "Molly, I'm not going to Kent today. So you see, there's no rush to be off."

"Not going? But I heard Lord Ashton say he wants to be on his way by nine thirty so you don't miss the train, and it's almost eight now."

She dismissed Trevor's wishes with an airy wave of the letter in her hand. "Lord Ashton is perfectly free to leave any time he wants to, Molly. But I am not going anywhere." She jumped off the bed, unmindful of the stacks of letters that went scattering in all directions. She ran to her secretaire and pulled out a sheet of her stationery. After opening the inkwell, she grabbed a pen and scribbled a note. She blotted it, folded it, and placed it in an envelope, which she addressed directly to Mr. Pelham. "I want you to take this down to the second footman—Albert, isn't it?— and have him deliver it immediately." She handed the letter to the maid. "It's very important."

Molly took the letter with a resigned sigh. "But what am I to tell his lordship?"

"Tell him just what I said. He can leave when he pleases, but I'm remaining in London."

"Oh, no, ma'am, I couldn't!" Molly stared at her in horror. "He's my new master. If I tell him that, he'll give me the sack, sure and he will."

"He will not. You have my word on that. Now, go on."

Molly swallowed hard and turned toward the door. "He's not going to like it, my lady," she warned as she departed. "Lords are used to having things their own way, ma'am, and that's a fact. He's not going to be happy."

Trevor definitely was not happy. He stopped eating his breakfast and stared at the maid in disbelief and anger as she told him what her mistress had said. His expression must have conveyed something of what he felt, for when he rose slowly to his feet, the girl took a step back and said, "If you please, sir, I'm only telling you what she said."

Trevor realized that he was alarming the girl, who was very young and obviously afraid of getting fired. It had been a long time since he'd dealt with servants, and he'd forgotten how easily they could be intimidated. He spoke gently to the maid. "It's quite all right, Molly. I will handle this."

She relaxed with relief. "Yes, sir. Thank you, sir." Bobbing a curtsy, she left the dining room.

Edward chuckled and shot Trevor a grin across the table. "Dutiful wife, eh?"

Trevor ignored him. He took a step toward the door intending to go upstairs and make the situation clear to his wife, but Henry spoke.

"Let me talk to her. I might be able to persuade her, reason with her."

Trevor wanted to say that persuasion was irrelevant and reason futile, but he refrained. He nodded and sat back down. "Try, by all means."

Henry departed, but by the time he finished his breakfast, Trevor knew that he'd been right. So much for persuasion and reason. It was time for more effective measures.

He set down his fork and rose. He turned to Cornelia.

"Would you please make certain that the carriage will be ready to leave as planned? We must not miss our train. And instruct the maids to be ready to pack Lady Ashton's things. We will be leaving at nine-thirty."

She hesitated a moment, then gave him a reluctant nod. "Of course."

"Thank you." Trevor strode out of the dining room and went upstairs. He could hear Henry's booming voice before he reached the top of the stairs.

"Damn it, Maggie! It wasn't like that! I've never heard anything so ridiculous."

When Trevor reached her room, he paused in the doorway and glanced from Henry, who was red-faced and pacing, to Margaret, who stood in her nightgown, arms folded across her breasts and her jaw set in that stubborn way he knew so well. Neither of them noticed him.

"Ridiculous? He hired men to abduct me, and you say it's ridiculous?"

"Ashton already explained all that to me. He had his reasons."

"And you can condone it?"

"Of course not. But it serves no purpose to dwell on it now. No harm was done."

She stared at her father as if unable to believe what she was hearing. "No harm?" she repeated. "You arranged this marriage like a business deal, then after he abducts me and carts me around the Italian country-side for a fortnight, you say no harm was done?"

"There was no damage done to your reputation. Ashton saw to that."

"There's more at stake here than my reputation!" she cried. "We're talking about how the two of you have arranged the rest of my life. How could you do this to me?"

Henry stopped pacing and looked at her. "I only did what I thought was best for you."

"Next time you want to do what is best for me, you might consult with me first, Papa."

Father and daughter stared at each other for a moment without speaking, and Trevor took advantage of the moment. "Enough," he said, his voice cutting like a whiplash through the silence. "Mr. Van Alden, I'd like to speak with my wife privately now."

"Ashton," Henry began, but Trevor sensed what was coming and cut him off.

"With all due respect, sir, I will handle this. It is a matter between husband and wife, and does not require your intervention. Besides, if you do interfere, she'll be turning to you for sympathy every time she and I disagree about something."

Henry pressed his lips together, and the eyes of the two men met in mutual understanding. He gave Trevor a curt nod and walked out of the room without another word.

"Papa!" she cried, but he closed the door behind him without a backward glance. She turned on Trevor. "I hate you."

It was a childish thing to say, and Trevor ignored it. "We are leaving for Kent shortly. I suggest you put on something more suitable for travel."

"I'm not going to Ashton Park, today or any other day. This morning, I will be meeting with my family solicitor. To discuss filing a petition for an annulment."

"It's a little late for that. Or have you forgotten about the other night?"

"Don't you dare be glib about that!" she cried. "I'm sure it was only another conquest for you, but it was very important to me!" Catching back a sob, she turned away.

He watched her for a moment, noting the way she was shaking and how she wrapped her arms around her ribs as if making the effort to contain it. He could appreciate that she was still angry and hurt, but he would not allow himself to be influenced by tears or manipulated by guilt.

"It was important to me, too, Maggie," he said quietly. "I wish you could believe that and have a bit of trust in me."

"Trust you? After all the things you've done? I'd just as soon trust a snake."

"You trusted me enough to marry me."

"Well, it was a foolish thing for me to do, and I fully intend to rectify my mistake." She turned toward him and lifted her chin. "If I cannot gain an annulment, I will file for divorce."

"You must be joking. On what grounds?"

She glanced over her shoulder and smiled at him, but the smile was a bitter one. "Kidnapping your future wife is not sufficient? Well, given your reputation, I'm sure I can accuse you of something legitimate."

"Not since we got married, which is all that would be relevant. Besides, I would have to agree to a divorce, and I assure you, I will not. A divorce is impossible."

"That's an odd thing to say, especially for you." Her smile turned mocking. "My darling husband, don't you know money can buy anything?"

"Not a divorce in England, my dear. Things may have changed in the ten years I've been away, but they haven't changed that much. To the best of my recollection, I have not committed adultery since Saturday. I am not insane, neither of us are already married, nor are we related."

He mirrored her mocking smile with one of his own. "And we both know I'm not impotent or homosexual. There are no other possible grounds. Besides, you would have to get the money to sue for divorce from your father. Given his concern for respectability, his support of this marriage, and the scandal such a proceeding would bring, I doubt you'll have much success."

"I have money of my own!"

"Which passes into my control as your husband." He saw her stricken face and realized she'd had no idea that would be the case. But he would not back down. "Feel free to try for a divorce, by all means. You can write as many letters to your solicitors as you wish, but you will do it from Ashton Park." He looked at his pocket watch and said, "It is now three minutes after nine o'clock, and we are leaving at half past. Therefore, you have exactly twenty-seven minutes to put on a dress and be downstairs in the foyer. I suggest you use less time than that if you want to take any clothes with you, since the maids will have to pack them. If you are not in the foyer and ready to leave by half-past nine, I will come up here, throw you over my shoulder, and carry you down to the carriage myself. As you well know, I am quite capable of doing such a thing, and I won't give a damn what you happen to be wearing at the time. Do I make myself perfectly clear?"

"Perfectly," she shot back. "When reason fails, use brute force."

"Exactly so."

He stalked to the door and opened it to find a cluster of maids hovering in the hall. They parted to let him pass, and Trevor strode down the hall toward the stairs, thinking, not for the first time, that he was going to earn every shilling of his marriage settlement.

19

The journey to Kent was the longest two hours of Margaret's life. Trevor's mother and sister-in-law made no attempts at conversation, and the dowager spent the journey in the dining car. Trevor did not share the train compartment with them either, preferring to spend the brief trip in the smoking car.

Her spirits sank lower with each mile they traveled away from London. Cornelia and Edward were returning to the Kettering estate in Hertfordshire in a few days, and her father planned to leave for New York the following week. She had already learned that Trevor had no plans for them to return to London for the Season, so she would not have that to look forward to. Even though her family promised to visit her in May, that seemed like little consolation to her on a cold and rainy day in March. Her new relations clearly disliked her and would be no substitute for her own family. She had never felt so alone or so abandoned in her life.

Her mood lightened a bit when they reached the village of Waverly. The mayor and a welcoming committee of other local dignitaries greeted the new earl and his bride at the train platform. With much pomp and ceremony, the mayor made a speech, specifically mentioning the beauty and sweetness of the earl's American bride and how glad they were to meet her. The vicar's wife presented her with a bouquet, and local children sang "Yankee Doodle." The high street was decorated as if for a holiday and crowded with people who waved flags and handkerchiefs and cheered as the two Ashton carriages passed by.

Another stop was made at a platform especially erected for the occasion in the center of town. There were more speeches, more curious stares, and more bouquets.

These people had obviously gone to a great deal of trouble to welcome her, and Margaret was quite touched by their efforts. But as they prepared to leave the village and continue the few remaining miles to Ashton Park, she found that it was possible for their enthusiasm to go too far. She watched in astonishment as the horses were unhitched from the carriage and a group of a dozen men prepared to take their place.

"What on earth are they doing?" she asked as Trevor climbed into the lead carriage beside her. The carriage lurched forward, and she gasped, "They aren't going to pull us to your house themselves, are they?"

"Yes, I'm afraid they are," he answered. "It's a tradition."

Margaret's staunchly democratic American heart

recoiled from the sight of men pulling a carriage as if they were animals, but the men were laughing and seemed genuinely happy to do it. As they left the village, church bells rang out to send them on their way. She smiled and waved at people as they passed, and she admired the rolling hills and greenery of the countryside. But as they traveled onto Ashton lands, she couldn't help seeing that their condition did not speak of happy prosperity.

She knew nothing about agriculture or the management of country estates, but she did not need that sort of expertise to see that the Ashton lands had been shamefully neglected. About half the fields had obviously lain fallow for several years and were in no condition for spring planting. The fences surrounding the pastures were falling down, and the animals within their confines looked gaunt and listless.

The tenant cottages were in no better condition. Many of them were unoccupied, and those that were lived in looked just as ramshackle as the empty ones. The tenants waved and cheered and followed the carriages as they traveled toward the house, but their joy was a thin veneer over years of neglect. She wondered if the fervent greetings of the townspeople and tenants stemmed as much from hope that things would improve as from tradition.

For the first time, Margaret began to appreciate the enormity of Trevor's responsibilities. She knew how depressed the English economy had been, and how dependent tenants were on the prosperity of their landlords. By all accounts, his brother had been a spendthrift and a fool, and when he had died, Trevor had inherited an incredible burden. She slanted a sideways glance at him from beneath the brim of her bonnet, and she found his handsome profile grimly resigned. It was evident that he fully appreciated the difficulties that lay ahead of him.

Margaret looked down at her hands, hardening her heart. She refused to feel sorry for him. Trevor might have needed an heiress to save his estates, but that did not justify how he had tricked her. There were plenty of American heiresses who would have jumped at the chance to buy the title of Lady Ashton. Why couldn't he have just chosen one of them?

The men pulled the carriage off the main road and down a lane that curved through a forest of chestnut and maple trees. She was beginning to wonder how far these poor men were going to have to haul them when she caught her first glimpse of the house between the trees.

She leaned forward, hoping to see more, but it was not until they had topped a short rise where the forest ended and a valley spread out before them that she got a good look at Ashton Park. Situated on the opposite side of the valley, it was an imposing structure, and Margaret could not help catching her breath at the sight of it.

Centuries had mellowed the limestone walls to the color of honey, and the house was beautifully situated, with fine views in every direction. A stream curved in perfect parallel with the sweeping arc of the graveled drive. Four stories high, with beautifully laid out gardens, terraces and fountains, Ashton Park was the equal in size and architectural beauty to any of the opulent mansions of Newport.

But any similarities to the luxurious houses she was accustomed to ended there, and the closer they got to the building, the more dismayed she became. As they crossed a charming stone bridge and pulled into the drive, where a group of servants were waiting to greet them, she noticed that the stream and ponds were clogged with algae, the gardens hopelessly overgrown, and the magnificent fountains were silent. Everything showed the potential for beauty, but she knew that restoring Ashton Park to its former grandeur would require a great deal of money. Her money, she reminded herself.

The carriage stopped in front of the wide stone steps that led into the house. Trevor jumped down from the carriage and offered his hand to her. She took it and stepped down, glancing around her at the shabby gardens. Something of her dismay must have shown in her face, for his lips tightened into a thin line, but he said nothing.

They walked past the servants and up the front steps, where they paused for more speeches. Trevor spoke to the tenants, saying that although many changes had taken place during the years he had been away, he was glad to see that the tradition of bringing home the bride had not changed one bit. He spoke of continuity, of the land, and of his hopes for a prosperous future.

He held out his hand to Margaret and presented her to the tenants, who cheered more fervently than ever. Trevor released her hand and stepped back, and she realized that she was expected to speak. Totally unprepared, she looked over her shoulder at her husband, shaking her head frantically, but Trevor looked back at her with a resolute expression, and, unless she wanted to make a fool of herself in front of all these people, she knew she had to say something.

"Thank you," she said haltingly, staring down at the sea of faces. Since she fully intended to petition for a divorce, she would be an utter hypocrite to talk of the future or her happiness in her marriage. She simply said, "I am overwhelmed by your kindness. You have truly made me feel welcome."

If they were disappointed by this, they did not show it. There was more cheering and more speeches.

The butler, Chivers, spoke next. He presented the bride with a gift from the household, a massive tea tray of solid silver. She accepted it graciously, posed for photographs, and was introduced to the household staff, which consisted of only a dozen servants. They went inside the house, and her first view of the interior did nothing to improve her spirits. It was hideously dark, incredibly ugly, and overly ornate. It was also freezing cold.

They took afternoon tea in the library, a room which, in Margaret's opinion, had only one positive attribute—a blazing fire in the grate. If it was this cold in the house in March, she thought, what must it be like in January?

Trevor did not have tea with them. His steward, Blakeney, called him away to discuss business, and she watched him walk out of the library with a sickening lurch in her stomach. Although he had seemed like a remote stranger ever since their confrontation the day before and was completely different from the exciting, adventurous man she thought she had married, he was still the closest thing to an ally that she had. That was a depressing thought, indeed.

She took tea with the rest of her new family, who made no attempt to include her in their conversation. She sat in an uncomfortable chair of worn velvet that stood in one corner of the room, while the dowager devoured seed cake and cups of tea. Caroline and Elizabeth discussed local gossip involving people of whom she knew nothing.

She knew the two women were shutting her out

deliberately, but she was too tired and heartsick to care. She remained silent, wondering wearily just how long it was going to be before she could go to her own room and collapse.

Just when she thought she wouldn't be able to stand it another moment, Trevor reappeared. He took one look at her huddled in the corner and crossed the room to her side. "You look tired, my dear. You must want to rest before dinner."

He held out his hand to her, and she was so grateful for the acknowledgment of her existence that she didn't care about his lies. She put her hand in his and stood up. "I am tired."

He took her upstairs, and they wound their way though a maze of dark corridors, lit only by windows half-obscured by heavy velvet draperies. But the dim light could not hide the threadbare carpets and moth-eaten upholstery. It could not disguise the tarnish and dust that spoke of an inadequate staff, nor the oppressive atmosphere that spoke of long hardship.

Trevor seemed to read her thoughts. As they turned down yet another corridor, he said, "As you can see, it's going to take a great deal of work to make this house a comfortable home."

And a great deal of money, she thought again. *My money*.

"Maggie," he went on, "the house is your province, and I hope you will take on the task of refurbishing it. Feel free to make any improvements you feel are necessary."

"I can spend my own money," she said tartly. "How generous of you, my lord."

He ignored her attempt to start a fight. "All I ask is that you consult with me regarding any major renovations. We are man and wife, and I want us to work together in this. I want us to mutually decide what things should be done."

This might be his home, but she did not intend to be here long enough to make any improvements to it.

"I do have a word of advice for you," he said. "When it comes to the house, don't let my mother walk all over you. She will, you know, if she thinks she can. To my mother, tradition is all, and she will not like it if you start changing things. Always remember, you are the countess, and you have final say over whatever is done within the house."

"Except, of course, for you," she answered, in no mood to be conciliatory.

He acknowledged the truth of that with a nod. "Except for me. However, as long as I know ahead of time what you intend to do, I will support your decisions as often as possible."

To Margaret, that was not much consolation. It still seemed that he was only giving her permission—and conditional permission at that—to spend her own inheritance.

They finally came to the bedrooms of the west wing, which Trevor explained were their private quarters. "This is your bedroom," he said, opening a door into a room of red velvet, gold damask and gilded cornices. It was as ornate and dark and oppressive as the rest of the house, and she hated it on sight.

Margaret walked through the sitting room and looked at the elaborate shell-shaped bed of dark walnut. She couldn't help remembering his vow on their wedding night. *No separate bedrooms.*

He had obviously forgotten that promise, or it had simply been another lie.

Trevor opened a door that led into another

bedroom, larger and even more elaborate than her own. "And this is mine."

Their eyes met, and the austerity of his expression softened slightly, reminding her of the man she thought she had married. "An English house gets quite cold at night, Maggie," he said quietly. "I want more than a coal fire and quilts to keep me warm."

He sounded as if he meant it. But that could be a lie, too. He needed an heir, after all.

She stiffened and watched the tenderness vanish from his expression. "I'll send your maid to you now and leave you to rest. Dinner is at eight o'clock." He bowed to her and departed.

She watched him go, and she had the sudden desire to call him back, to ask him to hold her, to tell him she loved him. It was absurd, because she did not love him, not anymore. She had thought he was noble, brave, and trustworthy. But what she had thought to be real was a mirage, a fantasy she had created.

You believed what you wanted to believe.

With a sudden stab of fear, she realized that she no longer knew what was imagined and what was not. It was as if her entire world had been turned topsy-turvy. Truths were lies, and love was a joke. Everyone was a stranger, including her own husband, the man whom she'd thought only two days ago was her one and only. Maybe all of this was just a dream from which she would awaken. But she had the sickening feeling that her life here was not so simple as that. Nor so easy to escape.

Trevor toyed with his glass of wine, studying his wife down the long length of the dining table. She looked utterly miserable. The spirited, strong-willed woman he knew—the one who liked going on midnight adventures and who could never resist a challenge—was gone, and in her place was a stranger. He didn't like it. He didn't like it at all.

Part of the reason for her unhappy mood must be the house. It was a depressing sight indeed, especially since he could recall the days when it was a place of grace and beauty, the pride of the county. But he loved this house as much now as he had when he was a boy. It had not taken him long to rediscover everything that had enchanted him in childhood, the priest's hole hidden in the library, the dark corners of the wine cellar, the huge chestnut tree where he'd spent many an afternoon with a book.

Though he loved this house, he could not expect Maggie to instantly share that feeling, and without memories of better times to encourage her, it must seem a dreary and inconvenient place, especially given the amenities and luxuries she was accustomed to.

He watched her pick at her food, and he couldn't blame her. Mutton and boiled potatoes could hardly compare with the cuisine prepared by French chefs that had been served at her father's home. Yet she'd eaten beef jerky and dried apricots without complaint and with a much healthier appetite than she had tonight.

His mother and Elizabeth occasionally tried to draw him into the conversation, but speculation about the state of the vicar's health did not interest him overmuch. Margaret they completely ignored, and he grimly vowed to have a talk with his mother about that. His grandmother, bless her, had talked with Maggie in a friendly way just after they sat down, but soon after the soup, she had fallen asleep in her chair.

He realized he was looking for excuses to explain Margaret's unhappiness, and he knew there were none.

Although the food was not of excellent quality, it wasn't the reason she sat twirling her fork and staring into space. The dark and dreary house was not the reason all the light had gone out of her pretty face. His family's unfriendliness wasn't the reason she hadn't said two words during the past hour.

The reason was him. He could not lay the blame anywhere else. Ever since yesterday, he'd tried to tell himself that it was just hurt pride and disillusionment, but he found himself unable to dismiss her feelings so easily. Edward's words came back to him.

She loves you, you know.

He reminded himself that her unrealistic notions about love had been fated to shatter eventually, but somehow that sort of reasoning was not much consolation tonight. He found her idea of love overly sentimental and unrealistic; she thought his was cynical and callous. But there had to be a way for them to find some common ground in this marriage. Divorce was out of the question, and the idea of separate lives after the nursery was full did not seem to have the appeal for him that it once had.

After dinner, Maggie went upstairs to bed. Trevor was tempted to follow her, but he remembered how she'd reacted to his earlier inference that he wanted her to keep him warm at night. He didn't think it likely she would receive him with any willingness. But he vividly remembered the details of their wedding night.

He could not believe that those sweet, hot memories

did not torture her as well. He would not believe that, because of the way he had been forced to play the courtship game, he had lost his passionate and responsive wife. He refused to believe it.

Rising from the table, he excused himself from the others, took a bottle from the case of bourbon Henry had given him as a wedding gift and went into his study. Without bothering to call for a servant, he built a fire in the grate and poured himself a drink, then sank into one of the shabby leather chairs and stared into the flames, trying to concentrate on the estate and all the things he needed to do during the coming months.

But staring into the fire reminded him of campfires in Italy, the bourbon reminded him of Maggie's eyes, and thoughts of the estate only made him wonder how he could make her think of it as her home.

That seemed an impossible wish at this point, but he could not accept the alternative. He hadn't married a cold and passionless woman, damn it, and he didn't want to live with one. He certainly didn't want to make love to one.

He wanted his Maggie back, the one who provoked him and challenged him, and who was passionate in his arms. To regain the woman he had married, he knew he was going to need some of the things that had won her in the first place.

He lifted his glass and took a deep breath. "Here's to patience, strategy, and fortitude."

Despite his resolution, Trevor had little opportunity to seduce his wife during the month that followed. He had other matters to attend to, matters which, though not more important, were more immediate.

His first priority was the drains. In their present condition, the only thing the drains seemed capable of doing was giving the estate and its environs a typhoid epidemic. He put Blakeney in charge of repairing them.

His second task was the fields. He offered cash settlements to any man willing to tenant on his lands and work his fields for the planting season. The response was immediate. Word spread throughout the county and, within a week, he had renewed previous leases and drafted new ones for all the empty cottages. Once the drains were repaired, he put Blakeney to the matter of fixing and whitewashing the cottages.

Trevor went to London for a week and bought enough horses to fill his stables and cows to fill his pastures. He also bought some things for Maggie, inspiring the giggles of more than one shop girl during his venture into the utterly feminine environs of Harrod's toiletries department. His foray into some less respectable shops in Soho caused much less comment. He returned to Ashton Park with the engineers Henry had hired to discuss the building of the linen mill. Plans were drawn, and construction began.

But, as busy as he was, thoughts of Maggie intruded on everything he did. He saw her at meals, and those brief moments were enough to keep her in his thoughts day and night.

His mother kept him informed of her activities, which were limited. She wrote letters, walked in the grounds, and generally stayed out of everyone's way. Her manner worried Trevor greatly because he knew such behavior was so unlike Maggie. Yet, sometimes, when he studied her across the dining table, he wondered if he really knew her as well as he'd always thought he did. She continually wore an expression of quiet inscrutability, and he realized he no longer found her easy to read. But he knew she was not happy.

He tried to encourage her to take an active role in the running of the household, but she showed no interest in that. She left everything in the hands of his mother, a situation which contented Caroline quite well. He told his mother to include her in the management of the household and teach her how it was run, but he knew that, without Maggie's cooperation or his constant presence to enforce his wishes, Caroline would never do so.

He did discuss the situation of servants with Chivers, knowing the house was not adequately staffed. The butler recommended that half a dozen gardeners, four housemaids, two footmen, six stable grooms, and an additional kitchenmaid be added to the staff immediately. Trevor agreed and dismissed the butler, returning his attention to other matters. But Chivers did not depart.

"Speaking of kitchenmaids, sir," the butler said, "we may have a problem with Annie."

"Whatever the problem is, Chivers, I'm sure you'll handle it."

The butler gave a discreet cough. "Well, sir, this may be an issue for her ladyship, rather than myself."

Trevor looked up from the ledger he was studying. "What do you mean?"

"Annie has been walking out with a foreigner on her afternoons off, sir."

"So, what of it?"

Chivers frowned with the air of one who smelled something unpleasant. "He's an Italian sailor. He's staying in Dover, but he's been to see her every Sunday. Not a nice young man, in my opinion, sir.

Annie has no family to look after her, and someone should speak with her about it. I was thinking her ladyship might have a talk with her. Lady Caroline has already tried, but Annie won't listen. Since her ladyship is closer in age to Annie, the girl might listen to her."

Trevor suppressed a smile. "I think that who Annie spends her time with on Sunday afternoons is her own business. I don't think we need to worry about it."

The butler bowed in deference to his decision, but clearly didn't like it. He left the study, and Trevor dismissed the matter from his mind.

He worked from sunrise to midnight and fell into bed exhausted each evening. But sleep often eluded him. His mind was tortured by how close Margaret was to him, and yet how far. Only a few dozen feet away, yet the distance seemed like a thousand miles. Time and again, he reminded himself of his rights as a husband, but he did not claim them. Patience, strategy, and fortitude became his catechism.

A month after their arrival in Kent, the crops had been planted, the major repairs made, and construction had begun on the linen mill. Trevor's horses arrived from London, and he knew it was time to turn his attentions to the most important project of all: seducing his wife.

Margaret wandered through the gardens of Ashton Park. It was a fine April morning, and she enjoyed the fact that for once it was not raining. She walked along the herbaceous border, thinking idly that ox-eye daisies would go far better with the delphiniums than the Michaelmas daisies planted here. They would bloom at the same time and make a nice show in June.

But this was Caroline's own garden, and she suspected her mother-in-law would not appreciate any advice from her. Besides, what difference would it make? She did not intend to be here long enough to see it bloom.

She came to the arbor, where she liked to read her letters when the weather was fine. Sitting down on a stone bench beneath a tangle of climbing roses, she pulled out the latest missive she had received from her London solicitors, hoping for a more decisive response to her inquiries about dissolving her marriage than she had received a fortnight ago. That letter from them had been tactful and cautious. They had urged her not to be precipitate, to think things over.

But she had written them again, stating that she had thought things over and wished to proceed. She scanned the typewritten lines hopefully, but she did not find the answer she wanted. Mr. Pelham was blunt and succinct, stating quite plainly what Trevor had told her a month ago. Her chances of obtaining an annulment were nil, and her chances of obtaining a divorce were slim at best.

She folded the letter, put it in her pocket, and stared ahead of her at the overgrown boxwood hedges of a maze. She no longer berated herself for being a fool. There was no point. Her anger at how she had been tricked was gone. Anger was a difficult emotion to maintain with nothing new to feed it, and Trevor gave her no excuse. She hardly ever saw him, and when she did, he hardly spoke to her.

She tried very hard to hate him, but hate, like anger, was very difficult to cling to. She knew he was busy spending her money, but even in that, she could not condemn him, for he was not throwing it away on gambling and women and lavish parties. She knew he was improving his estates. Though she resented the means by which he had obtained her money, she could not fault the way in which he spent it.

Perhaps she had simply grown up. A sad smile curved her lips at the thought. Her father had told her once that love wasn't everything. Cornelia had said that no man would ever live up to her expectations. Trevor had said that her idea of true love was only a school girl fantasy. Perhaps they had all been right, and she should just make the best of things. She should just resign herself to living in an empty marriage, do her duty by having the Ashton heirs, and accept the fact that Trevor did not love her and never would.

But she knew she could not do that. She could not live without love. Without that, everything else was meaningless.

A sound caused her to look up, and she found Trevor standing beside her.

"I thought I might find you here. My mother says you often sit here in the mornings."

She looked away. "Was there something you wanted?"

"Yes. I want to show you something. Come with me."

She stared at the hand he held out to her without moving to take it. She did not want to go with him, but she could not sit here forever. She stood up, careful to avoid touching him. "Where are we going?"

"You'll see."

He led her out of the garden and down to the stables, where a groom had two horses ready. He'd mentioned at dinner the night before that he had purchased horses when he was in London, and Margaret figured the chesnut mare must be one of them.

"Her name is Truffles," Trevor said. "I thought it was appropriate." He put the reins in her hand. "Try her out. I know you like a fast horse, and she's fast enough, I think, even for you."

Margaret stared at the mare for a moment, then turned her head to look at the sprawling green meadow outside the paddock. It had been so long since she'd gone riding. She bit her lip and glanced at her husband. Instead of the challenging, teasing expression she expected to see, his face was grave.

"Are you ordering me to come with you?" she asked.

"No. I'm asking you to come because I think you might enjoy yourself."

She wanted to ask why it mattered. Her hand tightened around the reins and she lifted one foot to the stirrup. "I'll race you to the oak tree," she told him and vaulted into the side saddle, curling one leg around the pommel. Before he could move, she was off.

She urged Truffles into a gallop, and the crisp morning air whipped her face as she raced across the meadow. She wasn't dressed for riding, and within moments, her fashionably tiny bonnet of yellow straw and purple roses fell back, caught only by the lavender silk ribbons at her throat. Her skirt of lavender silk went flying up in the wind, but she didn't care. It felt exhilarating to go riding again.

She reached the oak tree at the other end of the meadow before he did. Reining in the mare, she turned, smoothing her skirts and adjusting her hat as she watched him ride toward her.

"Not fair," he said, halting Avedon, his big, black gelding, beside her. "You only won because you got such a good head start."

"True," she agreed. "But you were right. She's a fast horse."

"She's your wedding present." He looked away. "No matter what happens, I hope you'll keep her."

He knew she was still hoping to get a divorce. Margaret held her breath, waiting, but he did not ask her about it. Instead, he gestured to the lodge gates that led out to the fields and pastures beyond. "Shall we ride on? I'd like to show you what Blakeney and I have been up to."

He wanted her to see it, perhaps to justify to her what he was spending her money on. She wondered why it should matter to him. She nodded, and they rode past the lodge and down the road. "I heard," she said, noting the freshly planted fields on either side of them, "that you've put in flax, and you're building a linen mill."

"Yes. This way, we have our own flax supply to make fabric."

She hated to give him credit for anything, but it was a sound idea. He took her past the tenant cottages, and she could not help noticing how different they looked from that bleak day when she had first seen them. He showed her the mill under construction, and it was far larger than she'd expected. He told her they would eventually employ about three hundred people. What he didn't say was how helpful that would be to the local economy. She knew how hard he had been working, and she could not help being impressed by all that he had accomplished in one short month.

"Are you hungry?" he asked. "You must be. It's after noon. Let's have lunch."

But instead of turning his horse in the direction of the house, he started for the woods.

"Where are we going?" she asked, following him.

He gave her the same maddening reply he had given her the last time she asked that question. "You'll see."

He led her through the woods of oak and chestnut to a clearing where a blanket was spread out on the grass. Beside it was a picnic basket and a bottle of wine. "I thought a picnic would be nice."

After dismounting, he tied their horses to a tree branch. Then he helped her down. They sat down on the blankets, and he opened the basket, pulling out a paper wrapped package. "Smoked trout," he said and laid it on the blanket. Reaching again into the basket, he pulled out a small burlap bag. "Dried apricots."

She smiled, remembering Italy. "Is there beef jerky in there, too?"

"Of course. I know how fond you are of the stuff."

Her smile faded, and she felt a sudden, absurd desire to cry. *Damn him,* she thought. *He knows just which strings to pull.* She looked away, feeling all her carefully welded indifference cracking. She grabbed the loaf of bread he laid beside the trout and tore off a piece. "Now what?" she asked in defense. "Now are you going to tell me how beautiful I am?"

He did not react to her scornful question as she expected. He merely shrugged. "I might, but why should I? You wouldn't believe me, would you?"

"No, I wouldn't."

"Well, then, I won't say it. If I did, you'd call me a liar, and I refuse to get into a fight with you today." He shoved the ball of butter toward her and handed her a knife, then reached for the wine. "Let's eat."

They ate without talking, and it wasn't long before she found the silence stifling. She wanted to fight, and he would not cooperate. To goad him, she said, "So, now that you've spent a sizable chunk of my money planting your crops and putting your lands in order, what's next? The house, I suppose?"

"Yes," he said calmly. "I want to completely modernize it. It's so dark, I want to put in electric lighting. And, God knows, it could use some bathrooms, don't you think?"

She thought of the chamber pot in her room and heartily agreed. Until she came here, she'd thought chamber pots had gone out of use ages ago. It was barbaric. And taking a simple bath was just as bad. She thought of the poor maids who hauled jugs of hot water every day for her bath from kitchens that seemed miles away. It was downright primitive.

"It's your home, Maggie," he said gently, "and I want you to be comfortable there."

Everything in her rebelled at that. She shoved aside the remains of her meal and began angrily brushing crumbs from her skirt. "Comfortable? It wouldn't matter what renovations were made, I still wouldn't feel comfortable. A home requires a warm and loving family." She gave him a tight smile. "We both know how you feel about such sentimental nonsense, and your family has hardly welcomed me with open arms. They turn up their noses every time they look at me, and I know they're thinking I'm just some uncivilized little American. But," she added bitterly, "I don't see either of them turning up their noses at my American money."

"I know, and I'm sorry about that." He looked over at her. "But, unfortunately, we can't choose our relations. I can't change the fact that Elizabeth is a vain and empty-headed nitwit who is jealous of any pretty woman between fifteen and thirty-five, nor can I change the fact that my mother is a snob. However, I intend to do what I can. Elizabeth doesn't know it yet, but she will be moving to London shortly. As for my mother, she resents anyone she feels is a threat to her position. I will talk with her, but I can only do so much. As I told you before, she will walk all over you, if you let her." He paused, studying her face. "I wouldn't have thought you would allow anyone to walk all over you, Maggie."

She opened her mouth to remind him that she was getting a divorce and she didn't care two cents what his mother thought of her or did to her. She was leaving, and it was time to make that plain.

But he did not let her say it. He jumped to his feet. "You know, you sound angry, and as I said, I refuse to fight with you today. I think what you need is vigorous exercise."

He stood up and walked to a fallen tree nearby. He snapped off two of the dead limbs and began pulling away their side branches.

"What are you doing?" she asked, watching him. "And if you say 'You'll see' to me again, I'll throw something at you."

Instead of answering, he tossed one stick at her feet and pointed the other one at her. "*En garde.*"

She stared at him doubtfully. "With sticks?"

"Why not? My brother and I used to practice with sticks when we were boys."

"I suppose you usually won, and your brother hated you even more because of it."

He grinned. "You suppose right. But then, I hated him for being such a bad loser."

She rose to her feet and picked up her makeshift saber. "All right, I'll fence with you, but I think you should spot me points at the outset because of my clothes."

"You do use that excuse often, don't you?"

"You try fencing in a skirt, with a corset and bustle, and see how you do." She brandished her stick. "Five points."

"Highway robbery," he said, shaking his head. "I'll give you three."

"Done."

They sparred, neither of them willing to lose nor playing to win. But when she backed him against a tree and said, laughing, "I've got you, now," he twisted his stick out from beneath hers and brought it down hard in a move that snapped hers in half. Panting, she straightened, pressing a hand to her corseted ribs and staring ruefully at her broken saber. "I suppose," she said, glancing at him, "you're going to say you've disarmed me and claim victory because of it."

His eyes gleamed teasingly. "No, that might be dangerous just now. I know the damage you can do with a stick in your hands."

Laughing, she tossed aside her weapon and sank down into the grass. He stretched out beside her, and they both stared up at the blue sky overhead for several minutes. She was thinking of that night in Rome, and she wondered if he was, too. She turned her head to look at him and found he was looking at her. His hand reached out to touch her face, and she tensed. "Are you trying to seduce me again?"

He moved closer, and his fingertips brushed her cheek. "I'm trying to be romantic. Is it working?"

"No," she whispered. But it was a lie. Already, she could feel his seductive pull, the magic tingle when he brushed his hand down her cheek and along the side of her throat, working his way slowly down to her breast. She looked into his eyes, and she could feel herself falling under his spell all over again. So easy, so easy. What a fool she was. She squeezed her eyes shut. "Don't," she whispered. "Don't."

She tried to pull away, but he wrapped his arm around her waist and slowly rolled on top of her. His weight pinned her to the grass, his body hard and heavy on top of hers. She held her breath, waiting for the inevitable as she felt his hands slide along her hips.

"Maggie," he whispered against her ear. "Look at me."

She shook her head desperately and kept her eyes closed. She didn't want to look at him, she didn't want to see him looking at her as if he loved her.

He gripped her chin to hold her head still. "Look at me."

She could not fight him. She opened her eyes and looked into his, and there she saw the awful truth. She still loved him, despite what he had done, how he had used her and manipulated her and lied to her. She still loved him, despite a month of struggles to fight it, to deny it. She still loved him, and he did not love her. Because of that, all the power was his, and like always, he would not hesitate to use it to get what he wanted.

"Why are you doing this?" she whispered. "You have my money, your debts are paid, your estates are secure. You have everything you wanted."

"Not everything," he murmured and bent his head to kiss her.

With a sob, she turned her face away, and she knew the answer to her question. She knew why he had arranged all this. She knew the reason for the mare, and the picnic, and the fencing. "True," she said in a hard voice as his lips caressed her cheek. "There is still the matter of an heir, isn't there?"

He sighed and pulled back. Rolling away from her, he stood up. "It looks like rain. We'd best start back."

They rode to the house in silence.

20

The morning after their picnic, Trevor entered her sitting room and found her writing a letter to her solicitors. He leaned over her shoulder, but she made no attempt to hide what she was doing.

"So," he said, straightening, "you're still planning to divorce me."

"Did you think a picnic would change my mind?"

He grinned, seeming not at all perturbed by her correspondence. "No," he answered. "I told you that you could write your solicitors as many letters as you wish about a divorce."

Margaret had the infuriating impression she was being indulged. She set down her pen and turned in her chair to look at him. "But you seem confident that my efforts will prove futile."

"Yes, but stranger things have happened. There's nothing I can do to stop you anyway." He shook his head. "I didn't come up here to talk about our marriage anyway."

"Then why did you come?"

He started for the door, beckoning her to follow him. "Come with me."

She didn't move. "Why?"

"I want your opinion about something. It's important."

She followed him downstairs and across the long length of the house to a room she'd never seen before. One glance told her it was a music room. There was a grand piano and a harp, and various sofas and chairs arranged around small tables. It was decorated in ochre yellow, dark brown, and white. A thick layer of dust told her this room was little used.

"What an ugly room!" she exclaimed.

"Is it?" he asked innocently. "Why?"

He was looking at her with that boyishly innocent expression of his, and she was instantly suspicious. "Because it is," she answered guardedly.

"What would you do to improve it?"

Margaret gave her surroundings a cursory glance. "That's a pointless question. I told you, I'm not staying."

"I understand, but what would you do if you were?"

She looked around more carefully. "Well, I suppose the first thing I would do is get rid of those heavy draperies around the picture window," she said, pointing to the swathes of ochre yellow velvet.

"Why?"

"For one thing, they must be ages old, and they're a hideous color. They're dusty and worn, and with the way they've been hung, they cover up half the window." She crossed the room and pulled one of the drapes back to look out. "There's a fine view of the lake and the woods from here. Why should such a view be hidden?"

"Would you have no drapes at all, then?"

"No." She stepped back a few feet to study the window. "I think I'd put drapes on either side, but they'd be a neutral color. Ivory damask. I'd hang them straight down without touching the glass, and I'd put a plain valance over the top. That way the drapes would frame the window like a picture, enhancing the view rather than detracting from it."

He leaned one shoulder against the door jamb. "What else would you do?"

Margaret pointed to the hideous baroque sofa table. "I'd get rid of that thing," she said decidedly. "I hate gilt paint. And I'd replaster the ceiling," she added, glancing overhead. "It looks like there's been water damage."

She began to walk slowly around the room. "The Queen Anne fire screen is lovely. I'd keep that. But I'd move the Ming vase. It's cracked on one side, so I'd put it over in a corner, where you could hide the crack." She pointed to the heavy brass figurines on the mantel and shuddered. "What are those things?"

"Statues of the goddess Kali. My great grand uncle Monty brought them back with him from India in 1848."

"Well, I mean no offense to Uncle Monty, but they're awful, and I can't think of a single room in which to put them. I'd toss them out."

"So much for old Monty's brass goddesses. Anything else?"

She nodded. "I'd change the color scheme. A music room is a place to relax, and it ought to be a serene and restful place. Yellow is the wrong color—too busy. I'd decorate in ivory and green, which would be soothing. When I came into this room after a long, hard day, this would be my haven, a place where I could feel at home—"

She broke off, suddenly realizing what Trevor was doing. He was trying to involve her in the renovations of his house so she would develop an emotional attachment to it. He wanted her to redecorate it so that she would begin to think of it as her home. A clever and devious tactic, and just like him, too.

He was a devil.

"That's what I'd do," she said, meeting his eyes, "if this were my home. But it isn't. I am going to get a divorce."

But he did not seem perturbed by her comment. "A divorce takes time. In the interim, you might as well give yourself something to do. I'd like you to redecorate our house."

"I don't want to."

"Would you rather spend your time wandering aimlessly around the house and grounds, bored stiff? That's not like you, Maggie. Redoing the house would be an adventure of sorts, and a challenge as well. I know how you love a challenge."

The idea did have a certain appeal. Because she had nothing else to occupy her time, she spent most of it thinking about him, and that was dangerous. She sought excuses to refuse. "Your mother won't like it."

"Hard luck for her, then. She'll have to get used to it."

Margaret drew a deep breath. "This little ploy of yours won't work, you know. Just because I agree to redecorate your house, that doesn't mean I'll change my mind about the divorce."

"Fine."

"I'm just warning you."

"Fair enough. I consider myself warned."

She licked her lips nervously. "I don't want to do this."

"Why?" He straightened in the doorway, watching her as a cat might watch a mouse. "What are you afraid of?"

"I'm not afraid of anything," she answered.

"I think you are," he said softly and began walking toward her. "I think you're afraid my 'little ploy' might succeed, that you might change your mind about leaving."

"That is ridiculous."

"Is it?" He halted in front of her. "Then why not do as I ask?"

She'd been neatly trapped. No wonder she couldn't beat him at chess. Still, it would be immensely satisfying to prove him wrong, to show him that all his schemes were not going to work this time. "All right," she said recklessly. "I'll do it."

She walked past him, but not before she caught his satisfied smile. "I hate that man," she muttered as she went upstairs to seek refuge in the safety of her bedroom. "He's too clever by half."

But even in the privacy of her room she could not escape him. On her bed were a box of chocolate truffles, a silk-lined basket of lemon soaps and colognes from Harrod's tied with a jaunty yellow ribbon, and three novels—quite erotic novels, she realized when she opened one of them.

He really was a devil.

The following morning, Trevor took the next two necessary steps toward developing domestic bliss. The first was to pack Elizabeth off to London, just as he had told Maggie he would.

As he expected, she was delighted by the prospect of living in town, but she was not delighted by the allowance he stipulated for her.

"God, Trevor, you can't expect me to live on two hundred pounds per month!" Her china-blue eyes widened with dismay. "I couldn't possibly."

"You've been living on a lot less than that, according to Blakeney. Ten pounds a month."

"You know perfectly well that's only here in the country. I can't maintain a household on two hundred a month."

"I thought you might say that." Trevor pulled a sheet of paper from the top drawer of his desk and handed it to her.

"What's this?" she asked, frowning at the list of items and their corresponding amounts.

"A budget, my sweet. I know you find such things hard to grasp, but you'll have to live on it."

"This is ridiculous! I could never lease a house in Mayfair for a rent of twenty pounds. And only ten pounds a month for clothes? Why should I have to live with such tightfisted economy? You're rich now. You could afford to give me a lot more."

"Possibly, but I won't. If I did, you would gamble it away." She started to speak, but he interrupted her. "Are you forgetting who you're talking to, Lizzie?" He watched her scowl at the hated nickname. "I watched you lose eighteen hundred pounds on a whist game the day you celebrated your fifth anniversary, money that Geoffrey couldn't afford to lose. Geoffrey didn't seem to care about the family coffers overmuch, but I do."

"I've changed, Trevor. Honestly. I haven't gambled in years."

"Only because there was no money to do it with. I've talked to Collier. I know where your money went. Yours, and Geoffrey's too. The pair of you spent every shilling you got your hands on, and when that was gone, you borrowed more. So, you're on a budget now, and I warn you—if you exceed it, don't come whining to me, for I won't pay up. I think you know I'm not the fool my brother was. If you get into debt, I'll end the allowance altogether, and you'll languish out here in the country for the rest of your life."

Tears began to glisten in her eyes. "How could you do this? Don't you know how hard things have been for us this past year? Mutton every night, and a fire only in the library even in the winter. No parties at all." She sniffed, and a tear fell with perfect timing down her porcelain cheek. "How can you be so cruel?"

He laughed. "Oh, Lizzie, you should have been an actress. You would have done so well with melodrama."

She crumpled the sheet of paper in her hand, and her tears dried as easily as they had begun. "This is insufferable!" she said and paced back and forth across the floor. "You're such an arrogant bastard. You always were."

He grinned at her. "You're only saying that because I didn't succumb to your charms ten years ago."

She turned around and faced him. A mocking smile curved her lips. "What conceit you have! You always did. And I didn't want you because you were so irresistible, you know."

"Yes, I know. But that hardly mattered, since I didn't want you at all."

The smile disappeared, and she looked at him with loathing. "God, how I despise you."

"A thought that breaks my heart." He watched her storm out, and he sighed. He really was losing his touch with women.

His next meeting was with his mother, and he suspected she would not be as easy to deal with as Elizabeth had been.

He was proven right. The moment she swept into the room, she began to speak. "Ashton, really, I'm glad you wanted to meet with me this morning. We must discuss what is to be done with your wife."

"Yes, Mother. That's exactly—"

"I realize that she's an American and cannot be expected to know how an earl's house is to be run, but really! She came down this morning wanting to know if we could breakfast at nine instead of eight so that she could go riding beforehand. I explained about the servants' schedule, and she actually said we could change that. And she asked about taking out the Michaelmas daisies in the south gardens and putting in ox-eye daisies instead. You know how I have continued to keep up the south gardens myself and how I detest ox-eye daisies. They get so shabby, you know. And she says she is going to redecorate the entire house. Redecorate! Can you imagine? I said, of course, that wouldn't be possible, but—" She broke off and frowned at him. "What are you smiling about?"

He didn't say it was because his mother's obstinacy would spur Maggie on with her decorating efforts, a consequence that suited his plans very well. "You," he answered. "How you hate anyone usurping your power. Now I finally understand why you and that frivolous chit Elizabeth get along so well. She never tried to take over."

"I don't know what you mean. I certainly have no wish for power. That belongs to men. We women have a different role, and that role includes the smooth running of the household. Now, I'm sure she's a sweet and charming girl—for an American— and I can fully understand why you married her. But she simply must understand how things are done. Until this morning, she expressed very little interest in the household, and I must say, that was a blessing, for she knows nothing! She is greener than Elizabeth ever was."

"Mother—"

"I cannot understand why these American girls insist on marrying into our great families, then try to make everything here the way it is in New York. Why on earth don't they just stay home, then? That reminds me of another thing. Bathrooms, Ashton! She wants to put in bathrooms! And electric lights! What would your father say?"

"Mother, I told her we would—"

"I know that Americans have no sense of tradition themselves, but can they not at least respect ours? You mustn't misunderstand me. I appreciate the financial assistance she brings to this marriage, indeed, I doubt we should have managed much longer without it, but . . ."

She continued to ramble on about Margaret's money, and Trevor decided to employ his father's technique. "That will be enough, madam!" he roared, slamming his fist down on the desk. "Sit down."

It worked like a charm. She immediately fell silent. Staring at him in shock, she sank into the chair across from his desk.

"Really, Trevor, you sound just like your father," she said with injured dignity.

"Since my father was the only person in this family besides myself who seemed to have any sense, I will take that as a compliment."

"There is no need to insult me."

"I wanted to meet with you because I wanted to clarify a few things for you. I have asked Margaret to redecorate the house, and although she is to consult with me about major renovations, the decorating is to be totally left to her." He could see his mother becoming incensed, and he added, "I have advised her to consider any advice you may choose to give, because I know it will be sound advice, if rather conservative."

She frowned at the backhanded compliment. "How gracious of you, Ashton. And you are going to allow her to put in these bathrooms and electric lights, I suppose?"

"I am."

"This is impossible!" she cried. "I cannot allow Ashton Park to be polluted in such a way!"

"You seem to forget that I am the earl, madam," he said coldly. "You answer to me, and you have no choice but to allow it."

She went pale, appreciating for the first time that her power was indeed being taken away. "And what on earth shall I do while she is turning Ashton Park upside down?"

"You can help her."

"Help her? You must be joking. Help her turn Ashton Park into one of those vulgar New Plymouth mansions?"

"It's Newport, Mother, and I suspect you only find them vulgar because you've never lived in them. If Mr. Van Alden's mansion in London is any indication, they are the most gracious and comfortable houses imaginable."

"There are things more important than comfort, Ashton," she said with haughty scorn. "There are traditions, time-honored ways of doing things."

"Fine. Then you can go to London and help Elizabeth get settled. I suspect she'll need more help with domestic management than Maggie will anyway. After that, you can return here and teach Margaret how to manage an English household."

"I see. And after I have done that and trained her to be a countess and she no longer needs my help, what will I do with my time then?"

"Travel," he said promptly, and winked at her. "I recommend Italy, myself. It's quite romantic, you know. Maybe you'll meet some wealthy gentleman who'll sweep you off your feet, and you'll fall madly in love with him. You might even marry him."

"Really, Trevor, I've never heard anything so ridiculous in my life. Where on earth have you been getting such romantic notions?"

Margaret was still awake. Trevor dismissed his valet and began to undress, staring at the crack of light beneath the closed door that connected his room to Maggie's. He could imagine her sitting up in bed reading a book, clad in one of those flimsy silk nightgowns from her wedding trousseau. Or perhaps she was sitting at her dressing table, brushing her hair.

Those thoughts brought an instant physical response from his starved body, and he pushed aside erotic imaginings with a curse. He didn't want to imagine her. He wanted to see her. He wanted to touch her. He just plain wanted her.

He jerked off his tie, removed his waistcoat, and began unbuttoning his shirt. Maybe he should just go right in there and tell her that from now on, they'd be sleeping together. Hell, she was the one who hadn't wanted separate bedrooms to begin with, and if he could get her in bed, seducing her into lovemaking would be much easier.

He yanked off his shirt and tossed it aside, thinking about that notion, but reluctantly abandoned it. She wasn't ready yet. He knew that, as hard as she tried to pretend, she was not indifferent to him. Their picnic had proven that. He knew that if he had pressed her, he could probably have taken more than just a kiss. But if he had, she would have resented him all the more for it afterward.

He could at least talk to her. He walked over to the door and hesitated a moment, wondering if he should knock. But this was his house, and his wife, and he had every right to walk into her bed chamber any time he chose. He grabbed the handle and opened the door.

She was reading a book, but not in bed. Instead, she was curled up in one of the overstuffed chintz chairs by the window, her hair flowing loose. She looked up as he entered the room, and quickly shut her book. She shoved it into the drawer of the table beside her chair almost furtively, as if she didn't want him to know what she'd been reading.

"I'm glad you're awake," he said. "I wanted to talk with you."

He sat on the edge of her bed. Her robe was open, and he could not help noticing how the pale pink silk of her nightgown could not disguise her generous breasts. In the lamplight, he could clearly see their swelling shape, the darker pink skin of her aureoles, the taut nipples. He didn't want to talk.

She flushed and drew her robe closed.

He looked away and drew a deep breath, trying to remember what he'd intended to say, what vague pretense he'd come up with to be in here, to be with her.

"I wanted you to know that I've arranged for Elizabeth to live in London. She'll be leaving within the week. My mother will accompany her, and help her get settled. My grandmother also wishes to go, since she wants to do some shopping."

"I see."

"And I've spoken with my mother about you. She now understands her role quite clearly. And yours."

"My role is only a temporary one. I still want a divorce."

"I don't."

"Let me go."

"No."

"You can keep the marriage settlement you already received. I won't fight you for it."

"No."

"Why not?" she said in frustration and genuine bewilderment. "If we divorce, you can remarry and still gain an heir for your precious title."

"That's not the point."

"What is the point?" she cried, her frustration dissolving into despair.

"You are my wife, you belong to me, and I won't let you go. I will not relinquish what is mine."

She drew herself up proudly, pulling her delicate robes around her like a shield as she rose to her feet. "I don't *belong* to you, and I will not stay here as your wife. You don't love me, our marriage is a farce, and I will not live as a hypocrite in a loveless union. As soon as my father returns from New York, I will go to London and live with him."

Trevor suddenly rose to his feet, wrapped his arm around her waist, and brought her close, all in one fluid motion that gave her no time to react. He brought his mouth down on hers and kissed her, a hard kiss intended to demonstrate possession.

She was stiff in his hold, but she was not pushing him away. He gentled the kiss, pulling her lower lip into his mouth, tasting her as he slid his hands up and down her rigid spine, using persuasion instead of force. He kissed her and stroked her until she yielded with a tiny sound against his mouth, relaxing in his hold to mold herself against him, a reaction that made him want to explode in response.

In that moment, he would have done anything to have her, promised anything she asked for just to lie down with her and relieve the aching tension. He wondered who had just demonstrated the greater power. With an abrupt move, he let her go and walked away.

"I will not consent to a divorce," he said quietly, turning to look at her from the doorway between their rooms, "so if you want one, you'll have a fight on your hands. Furthermore, you made a promise to me that you would stay long enough to renovate the house, and I expect you to keep your word."

"As faithfully as you have kept yours?" she countered bitterly. "Or have you forgotten that promise in church about love, honor and cherish?"

She was still fighting him. Stubborn, proud, skeptical, and absurdly sentimental. Shades of the Maggie he knew. "If you obey, I will cherish," he said quietly. "If you honor, I will honor.

And as for love . . ." He paused and cast a long, lingering glance over her body. "I'd be happy to stay the night and love you as much as you want."

Hot color flooded her cheeks, but he suspected it was more from anger than embarrassment. "You don't understand anything," she murmured. "You're not talking about love, you're talking about, about mating."

"They are both the same, and it is only romantic women and foolish men who think differently."

"You really believe that, don't you?" She slowly shook her head. "That only proves how ill-suited we are."

"Ill-suited or not, we are married."

"Not forever. I will not stay married to a man who does not love me. I don't care how long it takes, I will divorce you."

"I know you're determined to try, but I give you fair warning, I will do everything I can to change your mind. And I won't play fair."

"You never do," she shot back as he shut the door.

Inside his own room, Trevor thought about their conversation. He had no doubt she meant what she said, but so did he. He would do everything in his power to change her mind.

Two things gave him hope that he could. She'd responded to his kiss like the passionate woman he remembered. And she'd been reading a book, not one of the novels he'd given her, but something even more promising than that. It was a copy of *Debrett's Correct Form*. She was reading up on titles and proper forms of address.

A slow, satisfied grin spread over his face.

During the two weeks that followed, Trevor waged the seduction of his wife with all the strategy and planning of a military campaign. He stalked her—keeping her in plain sight as he followed her on her morning rides. He forced her into conversation at meals and endured her defensive barbs with unruffled calm. He left her gifts—bribes, she called them—in special places where he knew she would find them. He went to her room every night to talk, using the renovation of the house as his excuse. He did everything he could think of to breach her defenses and force her surrender.

The frightening thing for Margaret was that his campaign was beginning to take its toll. Her resistance was eroding, and she sometimes caught herself actually beginning to believe in him again and imagining that he really did love her. And every time she did, she berated herself for being a fool. She tried to avoid him, but that was impossible. She tried to ignore him, but he would not be ignored. She tried to harden her heart and hate him, but that was futile.

By the time Cornelia and Edward arrived for their visit in May, she was at the end of her rope.

"Honestly, Cornelia, he's making me insane," she said, pacing back and forth across her sitting room. "He won't leave me alone."

Cornelia settled into a chair and removed her traveling gloves and bonnet. "What do you mean?"

"He follows me when I go riding. He leaves these little gifts—lemon verbena cologne and chocolate truffles and romantic novels—all over the house for me to find. Last night, there was an emerald bracelet in my soup plate. He's driving me crazy!"

Cornelia was smiling long before Margaret reached the end of her list of grievances. "Poor Maggie. What an awful husband you've got."

"It's not funny!" she cried. "I know why he's doing

this, and it isn't out of any love for me. He wants an heir, for one thing."

"Well, of course he does. Children are the primary purpose of marriage, you know."

"And," Margaret went on as if her cousin hadn't spoken, "he's trying to charm me into stopping divorce proceedings because he's afraid that when I succeed in getting a divorce, I'll take my money with me."

"A divorce!" Cornelia sat up straight in her chair. "You can't be serious."

"I am completely serious."

"Do you realize what you're saying? A divorce is impossible. The scandal alone would ruin you."

"I don't care."

"Why on earth should you want a divorce? From what you've said, Ashton is turning out to be quite an adoring husband." She paused, then added, "I must admit, I'm relieved. Surprised, too. I never would have thought him the romantic type."

"He's not. He's just trying to manipulate me again for his own purposes. Trevor will do anything to save his estates. Once he has his heirs and his investments are profitable, he'll grant me a divorce quick enough."

"Forgive me for saying so, but you're not making sense. The gifts, the attentions—"

"It's all for show. He's not doing these things to demonstrate affection for me. He's only trying to keep me around long enough to get what he wants. I cannot live like this, in an empty and meaningless marriage. He doesn't love me."

"Are you certain?"

"Oh, yes. I heard him say so."

Cornelia looked up as the maid entered with a tea tray, then glanced at Margaret. She waved it away. "I hope you don't mind, Maggie, but I think both of us would do better with some Madeira." Margaret dismissed the maid and into a chair.

"I don't need a drink," she said with a sigh. "What I need is a divorce."

"Oh, Maggie, think about what you're doing. If you divorce, it's highly unlikely you'll be able to remarry a respectable man."

"Why should I want to remarry at all?" she asked bitterly.

"A divorce in England is almost impossible to obtain."

"So I've been told."

"Wouldn't it be simpler to try to make your marriage work? Even if he doesn't love you, he's fond of you, and you have a lot in common. You both like adventure and excitement. Not all good marriages are based on love. Many couples are quite content with shared interests and some degree of affection."

"I would not be content," she said. She looked at her cousin with hopeless resignation. "I could not bear it. I love him too much to be content with his fondness and affection. Don't you see?"

Cornelia sighed. "Oh, Maggie, I'm sorry you're so unhappy. I feel as if I am to blame."

"No, you're not. I know you and Edward were persuaded to cooperate in Trevor's plans and felt you were doing what was best for me. Trevor never told me he loved me, and no one forced me to marry him. That was my choice. I convinced myself he loved me when he did not."

"Maggie—"

"But that's all changed now," Margaret said with a rueful smile. "I guess you could say I've done what everyone wanted me to do. I've grown up. I've given up all my romantic ideals, and I'm starting to see the world for what it is, not what I want it to be. Trevor married me for my money, I was a fool, and I'm beginning to think there's no such thing as true love."

"How can you say that? You still love him."

"And what good does it do me?"

"He's obviously fond enough of you to give gifts he knows you like. Most men aren't so thoughtful. Maybe in time he'll come to love you and your marriage will still work out."

Margaret thought about that for a moment, and she couldn't summon up even the smallest hope that it would happen. Of course Trevor gave her things she would like, but that proved nothing except that he knew her weaknesses and could exploit them. No matter what gifts he gave her, no matter what he said or did, her trust in him was shattered, and she could never regain it. Nor could she bear to spend her life with him, loving him as she did, knowing he did not love her. "No, Cornelia," she said, shaking her head. "For me at least, happily-ever-after is a fairy tale." She smiled sadly. "And only schoolgirls believe in fairy tales."

21

Since they had traveled most of the day, Edward and Cornelia retired to bed early. Margaret followed suit, hoping that Trevor wouldn't want to have another talk about the house. She didn't want to discuss where to put the bathrooms or which paintings ought to be consigned to the dustbin. She didn't want to see him at all. To guard against it, she bolted both the door into the hall and the one into the master chamber. She assumed he had a key, but hoped he would take the hint.

He didn't. Trevor came to her room, but not for the reasons she expected and not by the usual means.

She was seated at her dressing table brushing her hair when a squeaking noise caught her attention. In the mirror, she could see the reflection of the tall armoire, and she watched in horror as its doors slowly opened. Transfixed by the eerie sight, she wondered if Ashton Park had a ghost.

"Good Lord!" she exclaimed as Trevor stepped through the doors of the armoire, pushing through her clothes. Her brush clattered to the floor, and she jumped to her feet. Turning to face him, she said, "Heavens, you frightened me! What on earth were you doing hiding in there? Were you spying on me?"

"If I were, it's no more than you deserve for locking your door against me," he answered, brushing dust and cobwebs from his clothes. "I thought about kicking it open in the old-fashioned heroic tradition, but these doors are made of solid English oak. I thought this a better option than breaking my leg."

She was unimpressed. "Wouldn't your key have been easier?"

"Definitely," he said and grinned. "But where's the adventure in that?"

"How did you get in there?"

"There's an iron ladder behind this armoire that leads down through an old laundry chute to an underground passageway."

Margaret was too curious to remain upset. "A secret passage? How exciting! But what on earth is it for?"

"Family legend has it that the countess of the tenth Earl of Ashton had it installed while her husband was fighting the French on the Peninsula so that she or her lover could enter and exit without being seen by servants or guests. The passageway leads to the gamekeeper's cottage. Convenient, don't you think?"

"She had an affair with the gamekeeper?"

"Shocking, I know, but the story goes that they were actually in love." He caught her skeptical expression and said, "There it is again. That little crinkle between your eyebrows that says you don't believe me."

She folded her arms across her breasts. "You're making this up. The gamekeeper's cottage is a quarter mile away. Why would anyone go to all that trouble?"

"In romantic liaisons, discretion is all."

"Let me see," she said, walking over to the armoire. Pushing back her gowns, she peered inside and realized he was telling the truth. The back of the armoire had been removed, and by the light of a lamp on the wooden floor beyond she could see a hole leading down into darkness. "Unbelievable!" She turned to him. "Show me the rest of it."

"Ask me nicely and maybe I will," he said.

"If you don't show me, I'll simply go by myself."

"With your fear of spiders?" He slowly shook his head, his eyes full of laughter. "I don't think so."

"Spiders?" She swallowed hard and cast a doubtful glance at the secret passage. But even the possibility of spiders wasn't enough to deter her from this adventure. "You wouldn't have shown it to me at all if you didn't intend to show me the rest."

"You'll have to change first," he said, gesturing at her silk nightgown and bare feet.

"Oh. Of course." She grabbed a striped muslin skirt and shirtwaist from the armoire and a pair of slippers. "Turn around."

"You must be joking. I'm your husband, remember?"

"Don't remind me," she shot back. "Just turn around. And no peeking."

"It seems we've had this conversation before," he said, but he did as she wanted, saying, "One of the reasons I got married was so I wouldn't have to do this."

She ignored that comment and quickly slipped into

her clothes. "All right," she said, tying her hair back with a ribbon. "Let's go."

Trevor led her through the armoire and into the small space beyond. Picking up the lamp, he began to descend the ladder. Margaret followed him down through the dark shaft until its walls of brick and timber changed to dirt and she knew they were underground. They started down the tunnel, and she glanced around, noting the sturdy oak beams that supported planking over their heads and kept the dirt tunnel from caving in. "A bit like a mining shaft, isn't it?"

"The man who built it was a miner, I believe. But how would you know what a mining shaft looks like?"

She grinned at him. "When I was a girl, I always spent August at my Uncle Johann's summer house in the Catskills. That's Cornelia's father, by the way. Anyhow, there were some abandoned coal mines there, and Cornelia's brother Andrew and I went down in them once to explore."

"You must have been out of your minds. Abandoned mines are dangerous."

"I know, but we were just kids. We were foolish, I suppose, but we wanted to meet Abraham."

"Who?"

"Abraham's a ghost and quite the local legend thereabouts. He died in the mine, and was said to haunt the place. We wanted to see him."

"And did you?"

She laughed. "No, I'm afraid not. We did get lost, though, and had to spend the night down there. There were ten search parties out combing the county for us, and one of them finally found us. Uncle Johann told Papa about it, of course, and there was no end of a fuss."

"I can imagine. Your poor father."

"You're a fine one to talk, what with all the scrapes you got into as a boy. Edward told me about some of the trouble you got him into at school. Something about blowing up the chemistry laboratory when you tried to make your own fireworks?"

"Oh, that. Well, like you, I've always been rather fond of adventure. Without it, life can seem very tame. That's why I thought you might like to see this. We haven't had an adventure in quite a while. What do you think of this one so far?"

"It's quite exciting. I'd always heard that these old country houses had secret passages, but this is the first time I've ever seen one." She laughed. "I'm afraid these things have rather gone out of fashion in America. None of the mansions on Madison Avenue have them."

"I suppose not. A shame, if you ask me."

"I agree." She looked over at him. "I must admit, Trevor, you do come up with some exciting adventures."

Coming from Maggie, that was high praise indeed, and it pleased him. "There are several more hidden passages and rooms in the house."

"Really? Where?"

He had no intention of telling her. He would save those secrets for future expeditions. He pointed ahead of him. "We're almost there."

She could see nothing but blackness outside the circle of lamplight. "How can you tell?"

"I've been through this passage many times. As a boy, it was one of my favorite places." Struck by a memory, he laughed. "I met old Lord Kettering, Edward's father, down here one night when I was about eleven. He was coming down the ladder from my mother's room."

"What?" she gasped. "Edward's father had an affair with your mother?"

"For several years." He noticed her astonished expression. "Maggie, in our social circle affairs are quite common."

"I know, but it never ceases to shock me." She shook her head. "And your mother seems so, so fastidious. I can't imagine her carrying on a clandestine affair."

"She did, though. More than one, I assure you. I can recall at least seven different lovers." He paused, then added, "Once a woman has provided the heir and the spare, she is usually free to do as she pleases, provided she is discreet."

"I see. And your father did not mind this?"

"I don't think he ever really noticed. Besides, what could he say? He spent half his time in Cumberland with the Duchess of Arbuthnot anyway. He was hardly in a position to criticize."

"The duchess? You're having me on."

"I'm not. They were lovers for nigh on eight years."

"Doesn't it bother you?" she asked, "to know that your parents were unfaithful to each other?"

"It did when I was a boy, but I got over it. I came to the realization that it's quite common among the peerage. Even expected."

"It's no wonder, then," she murmured as if to herself.

"What?"

"It's no wonder you have such a low opinion of love. How could you not when it is so cheaply demonstrated?" She came to a halt. "Is that how it would be for us? Once the heir and the spare, as you put it, have been provided, will you go your own way and have your lovers and think nothing of it?"

He stopped walking and turned toward her. There was a heavy tightness in his chest. "Will you?"

Margaret looked down at the dirt floor of the tunnel. "It would be wrong. I would not do it. Indeed, I could not."

The hard tightness in his chest suddenly relaxed. "Then I won't either," he said quietly, but he knew she did not believe him.

The tunnel ended abruptly, and she looked up to see the square hole of a trap door in the planking above their heads.

Trevor reached up, setting the lamp on the edge, then grasped her waist and lifted her through the hole. She pulled herself up and over, giving him a brief, enticing glimpse of her bare legs just before she disappeared through the opening. He followed her inside the cottage.

Margaret glanced around the interior of the small stone cottage. A fire was laid in the grate, cheese, fruit and wine were laid out on the table, and the bed had been made.

"The first morning after our arrival, I went for a walk and found this place," she said. "I looked in the windows and thought it was deserted. But it looks quite cozy now."

Trevor didn't answer. Instead, he set the lamp on the table and walked to the fireplace. He lit a fire, and when he turned toward her, he found her frowning at him. "A fire, wine, a bed," she murmured. "All the necessities of a seduction."

"Yes," he agreed frankly.

She bristled at that, all her defenses coming to the fore. "You presume too much."

"Is it presumption for me to arrange a romantic rendezvous with my wife?" he countered and walked to the table. He pulled out a chair for her. "Or to want to make love to her?"

She glanced down at the chair, but did not move to sit. "In light of my intention not to remain your wife, it *is* presumptuous."

He walked around the table and took the chair directly opposite her. "I'd prefer to call it hopeful. Why don't you sit down so we can discuss this while we eat?"

She sat down stiffly. "You take me for granted, Ashton, and I don't like it."

He poured wine for both of them. "Maggie, I've learned never to take you for granted," he answered and held out a glass to her. "I find that the moment I do, you take it into your head to do something completely unexpected."

Margaret took the glass and swallowed a sip of wine. "You shouldn't have told me that. Now you've shown me that you have a vulnerability. Aren't you afraid I'll use it against you?"

"No," he said. "This isn't a war between us, Maggie. At least, I don't want it to be."

"And what about what I want? You know my feelings about our marriage and my intentions. Yet you continue to ignore them." She gestured to their surroundings. "This, this seduction is all for the purpose of obtaining your heir, and has nothing to do with me. You don't love me." She stood up. "And I don't love you."

He'd intended to wait, to soften her resistance, but the opening she'd just given him was too good to pass up. He rose and walked around the table, watching her as she backed away from him. "You don't love me?" he asked softly. "You have accused me of lying to you, but apparently it is you who have lied to me, madam. For I remember our wedding night very clearly, and all the times you told me you did love me."

"That was before!" she cried, backing away as he came toward her. "Before I learned what a deceiving scoundrel you really are. I don't love you anymore."

"No?" He continued to walk toward her, watching as she unknowingly backed herself into a corner of the room. "Forgive me if I need to find out for myself just what your true feelings are."

He took one more step forward. Her shoulders hit the walls of the corner behind her. She was trapped. He slowly bent his head to kiss her.

"You are despicable," she said, turning her face away to evade the move. "You'll do anything to get your own way."

"True." He pressed tiny kisses along her cheek to one corner of her lips. "But I already warned you I wouldn't play fair," he murmured and slid one hand into her hair to turn her face toward him. He brushed his lips over hers. "I want to make love, you want to make war, and all's fair in both."

She made a sound of agitation against his mouth. "Stop it. Don't do this to me."

"Kiss me back."

"I won't" she said, resisting him.

Undeterred, he continued to kiss her, coaxing her to respond. But she brought her hands up protectively between them and remained unyielding. "Kiss me back," he urged. He began to brush his tongue back and forth across the plump curve of her lower lip as he slid one arm around her waist. He caressed the small of her back and nibbled on her lip until slowly, very slowly, some of the rigidity left her, and her lips parted beneath his persuasion.

"C'mon, Maggie," he coaxed against her mouth. "Kiss me back. Kiss me."

With a moan, she slid her arms around his neck and pressed closer to him instead of pulling away, her body molding instinctively to his as she surrendered. His hungry body responded instantly to the move, and he deepened the kiss, slanting his mouth over hers and sliding his tongue between her teeth to taste her.

She met him halfway, her tongue touched his, and lust surged through his bloodstream like wildfire. He began unfastening the buttons of her blouse.

She broke free of his kiss and reached down to grab his wrist. "Stop. I don't want this."

Her hold was no deterrent, and he continued undoing buttons, his knuckles brushing against her breast as he unfastened each one. He bent his head to kiss her exposed throat, tasting her sweet, lemon-scented skin. "Do you really want me to stop?"

"Yes!" she cried desperately, pushing against his chest. "I don't want you to touch me. I hate you."

He tightened his embrace and nuzzled her blouse open to trail kisses along her collarbone. "No, you don't. You love me."

"I don't." She pushed at him halfheartedly, and he ignored it.

"You do," he answered. "It's only pride that makes you fight it." He grasped a handful of her blouse and pulled it out of the waistband of her skirt.

She began to quiver in his hold, and he knew her resistance was slipping. He undressed her, pausing with each garment that was removed to kiss and caress her. But still she fought him with words. "Don't do this," she whispered, squeezing her eyes shut. "You can't mean to do this."

"I mean it, Maggie." After undressing, he slid his hands up her torso to caress her breasts. "You love me," he murmured.

"I never loved you!" she cried again.

"Liar." He nibbled her earlobe and caressed the taut tips of her breasts until she began to make small sighs in her throat and tilted her head back in a yielding arch. He pressed his advantage, lowering his head to her breast, licking her. The soft skin of her aureole was like velvet against his tongue as he circled her nipple, teasing.

She kept her eyes closed, and her arms came up to cradle his head and pull him closer. He wanted to show her how luscious she felt, how beautiful she was to him. He wanted to please her and ravish her and cherish her. Most of all, he wanted to hear her say that she loved him.

Slowly, he kissed his way up her body, his hands trailing down to the lovely swell of her hips as he captured her mouth with his.

"You love me," he murmured against her lips. "Say it." He knew how proud she was and what it would cost her pride to tell him what he wanted to hear, but he didn't care. Nothing had ever impelled him like this, and he wouldn't be denied. Like an addict craving opium, he wanted to hear her tell him that she still loved him. He wanted to hear it again and again. "Admit it."

She tore her mouth from his. "I won't," she gasped, shaking her head. "I won't."

Stubborn, stubborn Maggie. "Stop fighting this," he murmured and slid his hand between her thighs. He brushed his fingers back and forth over her soft curls, coaxing, tempting, then caressing deeper as she began to writhe against his hand, gasping with pleasure. He needed to hear her admit the truth, wanted to hear it more than he'd ever wanted anything in his life. "You love me. I know you do. Say it. Say it."

He moved his hand so that only one finger touched her, caressing the nub at the center of her desire, over and over, until he finally forced from her the words he wanted so desperately to hear. They tumbled out between her soft cries as she climaxed. "Yes, yes!" she cried with a sob, her arms encircling his neck to hold onto him. "I love you, Trevor. I love you. I love you!"

With a shout of joy and triumph, he slid his hands beneath her buttocks and lifted her. He entered her and felt her legs wrap around his waist as she buried her face against his shoulder. He thrust into her again and again, savoring the feel of her body closing around him. He came in a rush, his senses exploding in a white-hot flash of almost unbearable pleasure. It was like nothing he'd ever felt before.

She was crying. He could feel her tears on his shoulder, feel the silent sobs shaking her as he held her. He moved toward the bed, cradling her with one arm as he pulled back the counterpane. She did not open her eyes as he laid her down on the bed and crawled in beside her, but kept them shut tight as if she could not bear to look at him. He watched the tears slide from beneath her closed lids, and for the first time, he truly understood how badly he'd hurt her. He felt all the pain he'd caused her like a knife through his own heart.

A fierce, protective tenderness surged inside him, and he caught her tears with kisses, vowing to himself never to make her cry again. As he held her and stroked her, he made a startling realization. All this time, he'd thought he was seducing her, but that wasn't so. Somehow, with her romantic notions of love and her stubborn belief in its power, she'd made him believe in it, too. Somehow, the seducer had become the seduced.

For the first time in his life, Trevor knew what it was to be truly in love.

When he awoke, the bright morning sunlight hit him full in the face, and he shut his eyes again. Still half-asleep, Trevor turned on his side, reaching for Maggie. But all he touched was a heap of tangled bed covers.

Instantly awake, he sat up, staring at the empty place beside him. She was gone. He shoved aside the counterpane and rose, memories of last night and her tears making him suddenly uneasy. He dressed quickly and left the gamekeeper's cottage. He tried to tell himself that she'd probably wanted some breakfast or a bath and didn't want to wake him.

He marched up to her room, but found it empty. Turning around, he retraced his steps down the stairs to the dining room. But the only one there was Edward.

His friend looked up from his kidneys and bacon. "Good morning."

"Where's Maggie?"

"She and Cornelia took a carriage out a short while ago." He gestured to the mantel of the fireplace with his fork. "She left you a note."

He crossed the room, snatching the folded piece of paper that was tucked behind the clock. He noted that it was barely eight o'clock, too early to take a carriage anywhere. If Maggie wanted a morning ride, she'd have taken Truffles out, as she usually did. He opened the note and scanned the few lines written there, lines which confirmed his fear.

"What does it say?" Edward asked.

Trevor looked up, staring past his friend, as his vision seemed to go dim. "She's left me," he said numbly.

Edward did not seem surprised. "Well, of course. What did you expect?"

His friend's complacency turned his numbness to anger. "You knew about this," he said through clenched teeth. "Didn't you?"

Edward didn't bother to deny it. "Yes, I did. She came to our room quite early this morning and told my wife she was leaving you. She begged Cornelia to go with her. They packed her trunks and left about half an hour ago."

"And you didn't try to stop her?"

Edward met his eyes with a level stare. "No."

He strode over to the table, facing his friend. "Bloody hell, Edward! Where did she go? Kettering Manor? London?"

"If you must know, she went to London. Henry's back from New York, and she's gone to stay with him. She and Cornelia are taking the nine o'clock train."

"Damn! I won't let her do it, Edward."

His friend was silent for a long moment, studying him. "Why should you care?"

"I care," he said tightly.

That didn't satisfy Edward. He rose to his feet, staring at Trevor across the table. "What are you saying? That you love Margaret after all?"

"Of course I love her!" he shouted and slapped the note down on the dining table hard enough to rattle Edward's tea cup. "She's my wife, damn it!"

"My, my," Edward murmured, and a sudden grin lit his face. "How the mighty are fallen."

"What's that supposed to mean?" Trevor demanded, grabbing the silver pot on the table to pour himself a cup of badly needed coffee. "And what's so damned funny?" he added as his friend began to laugh.

"You are." Edward shook his head and gave him a pitying glance. "What a wretched state of affairs to find yourself in," he said, quoting Trevor's own words of three months before. "To be in love with your own wife."

Trevor gave his friend a fierce scowl. "Not funny, Edward."

"Not meant to be," Edward said cheerfully and sat down to finish his breakfast.

"Maggie, are you sure you want to do this?" Cornelia asked as the open carriage traveled along the wooded stretch of road halfway between Ashton Park and the village. "Maybe you should reconsider, think things over."

"There's nothing to think over," Margaret answered, turning to stare at the dense forest that lined the road. "I can't stay with him, Cornelia. I can't." Her voice broke. "Let's not talk about it."

"All right. But I wish—"

Whatever Cornelia wished was interrupted by the neigh of horses and the jerking motion of the carriage as the driver pulled back hard on the reins and brought them to a stop.

"What is it, Howell?" Margaret asked.

He didn't answer, and she stood up, gazing past the driver's box to the four men on horseback who

stood in the road, blocking their way. They wore ker-
chiefs over their faces, and each one had a pistol
pointed at the carriage.

"Don't move!" the man in front shouted to them,
nudging his horse forward. The others followed suit. One
grabbed the reins of the lead horse, and two of the others
surrounded the carriage, pistols lifted with ominous
intent. The leader pulled his horse to Margaret's side.

"We are kidnapping you, Lady Ashton," he said in
a thick, unmistakably Italian accent.

"I don't believe this!" Margaret stared at him in
disbelief, then, suddenly, she began to laugh. "I simply don't believe it!"

The man's brows drew together in a puzzled
frown. Clearly, he had expected her to shrink back in
terror, not burst out laughing. "It is true, signora."

Howell turned in his seat, also staring at her as if
she'd lost her mind. "They's highwaymen, milady," he
said. "Best not be laughing at 'em."

"Highwaymen, my foot!" Margaret sank back in
her seat, her whole body shaking with mirth. "He's
unbelievable," she told Cornelia, gasping for breath
between uncontrollable bursts of laughter. "My husband is simply unbelievable! Italian bandits kidnapping me again! He can't think I'm that big a fool, so
this must be a prank."

She looked up at the man, wiping tears from her
eyes. "Tell me, signor, how did Trevor manage it? We
left Ashton Park scarcely half an hour ago. He must
have known this might happen and had you staying
nearby just in case. That must be it."

All of them stared at her in silence, as if dumb-
founded.

"Oh, come now," she coaxed, "you don't have to
pretend with me. You can tell me the truth."

The leader of the group lifted his pistol and pointed it directly at her. "You will come with us."

She lifted her hands in surrender and stood up. "Of course," she said, chuckling. "I wouldn't want to spoil the joke."

"Joke?" the man roared at her. "You think this is a joke, signora? Let me assure you, it is not! It's vendetta." He turned in his saddle, slamming the butt of his pistol into the back of Howell's head. The driver slumped forward, and Margaret's amusement vanished. She stared at the blood that smeared the back of Howell's head, and she realized with dawning horror that this was not a joke at all. This time, she was being kidnapped for real.

22

Ten minutes after his conversation with Edward, Trevor sent for his steward, shaved, and changed his clothes. He left Davis, his valet, to pack a bag for him and returned downstairs to meet with Blakeney, giving the steward instructions about what to do while he was away. He didn't intend to be gone long—just long enough to grab Maggie and drag her back here—but in case circumstances forced him to go to London with her, he wanted to be sure construction of the linen mill proceeded smoothly.

Edward was waiting for Trevor, his own traveling bag beside him. "I'm going, too."

"Why didn't you go with them in the first place?"

His friend shrugged. "Call me a hopeless romantic, but I wanted to see for myself what your reaction to Margaret's departure would be. Maggie said you wouldn't care, but I rather suspected you would be a bit displeased about it."

Trevor was more than a bit displeased. He was furious. He was also trying to deal with the glimmer of fear that nagged at him—the fear that, no matter what he did or said, it would not be enough. That it would be too little, too late. That Maggie would never come back.

Impatiently, he checked his pocket watch. Twenty past eight. There was still plenty of time to get to the train station. But he paced back and forth across the foyer like a caged tiger as he waited with Edward for Jenkins to bring his carriage around.

The grinding sound of gravel on the drive had Trevor flinging open the front door without bothering to wait for Chivers to open it for him. But the person pulling a carriage into the drive was not Jenkins. Instead, Cornelia sat on the driver's box, and Trevor knew something was terribly wrong.

He ran down the front steps to meet the carriage as it pulled in front of the house, Edward on his heels. The vehicle came to a sudden halt, and Cornelia jumped down into her husband's waiting arms. "They've taken Maggie," she choked, forcing the words out between sobs. "We w-were on our way to the sta-station when they jumped us. Oh, Edward, it w-was awful!"

Trevor glanced at the unconscious Howell, who was sprawled on his stomach across the carriage floor. "Who, Cornelia?" he asked sharply. "Who were they?"

She shook her head, burying her face against her husband's chest. "I d-don't know," she answered, her voice muffled by her husband's shirt. "But there were four of them. Italians."

"Oh, God." Trevor felt as if he'd been kicked in the stomach. He recalled Emilio's warning, and he knew who had taken Maggie.

Lucci is looking for you. You know how ruthless he can be.

"Margaret laughed at them," Cornelia went on, her shaking voice breaking into his thoughts. "She laughed. She thought you were behind it, that you'd sent Italian bandits to kidnap her again. She thought it was a joke. Oh, God!"

"Darling," Edward said, pulling back to give her a hard shake, "try to get hold of yourself. Where did they go?"

"I don't know. They hit Howell over the head and took Maggie away on horseback. They t-told me t-to come back here and t-tell you that they'll be sending you instructions later," she said to Trevor. "And, and . . ." She paused, shuddering, then went on, "They said this is a vendetta against you. If you contact the police or anyone else, they'll kill her."

Trevor turned to the white-faced servants who had gathered by the front steps. "Chivers," he said to the butler, "Have a footman send for Doctor Travers to see to Howell. He's hurt."

"Very good, sir. Shall I send for the magistrate?"

"No, not yet. Alice?" He turned to the parlormaid. "Fetch some brandy for Lady Kettering and bring it into the drawing room. Edward, let's get her inside."

Edward nodded and escorted his sobbing wife into the house. They took her into the drawing room, where a shot of brandy helped her compose herself.

"Why?" she asked helplessly. "Why would they do this?"

"For money?" Edward guessed. "Maybe we'll get a ransom note."

Trevor shook his head. "No, it wouldn't be for money." He considered for a moment. "Over the necklace?" he murmured, raking a hand through his hair. "Why would he take Margaret because of the necklace? That doesn't make sense."

"What necklace?" Cornelia asked. "Do you know who these men are?"

"I've a pretty good idea, yes."

She sniffed into a handkerchief and snuggled closer to her husband. "They didn't say anything about a necklace."

Trevor sat motionless for a few minutes, thinking back on every encounter he'd had with Lucci during the past ten years. Every time Lucci had appropriated one of his finds, he'd either been able to get it back or steal something of equal value in return. It had always been something of a game between them, and Lucci had never done anything like this before.

Another possibility struck him, one that made far more sense. Isabella.

All of this had to be because of Isabella, because he'd slept with Isabella on his last night in Cairo. He'd slept with Lucci's wife, and now Lucci was going to—

"Oh, Christ! I'll kill him!" He jumped to his feet and ran for the door, oblivious to Edward and Cornelia, who were staring at him as if he'd suddenly gone mad. Perhaps he had. Thoughts and memories and bits of conversation were tumbling through his mind like the shifting colors of a kaleidoscope. "Chivers!" he shouted. "Chivers, get in here!"

The butler appeared within moments, as unruffled and calm as only an English butler could be under such circumstances. "Yes, sir?"

"Chivers, what was it you were telling me a month ago about the kitchenmaid? She was walking out with an Italian, wasn't she?"

"Yes, sir. An Italian sailor, staying at a rooming

house in Dover." The butler's long nose quivered with disapproval. "You said at the time, sir, that who Annie walked out with on her afternoon off was no one else's business."

"It is now," Trevor answered grimly. "Send her in here, would you?"

"Very good, sir." The butler bowed and departed.

"What are you thinking?" Edward asked. "Could there be a connection?"

"I don't know, but they must have been spying on the house, waiting for an opportunity to take Maggie. How would four Italian men go unnoticed in a quiet English village?"

"They wouldn't. Staying in Dover, claiming to be sailors on leave would be a perfect disguise, if they could get information about the house and its routine."

"Who better to give them that information than a kitchenmaid?"

Edward shook his head. "But again, why? Lucci's never done anything like this out of spite. You don't think it's money. What other reason could there be?"

"A very good one, I think. The leader mentioned a vendetta." He glanced at Cornelia. Wanting her out of the room, he said, "You're still distraught. Perhaps you should lie down."

She frowned at him. "I'm not going anywhere. Why would these men want revenge on Maggie?"

"Not Maggie. Me." Trevor briefly related the history of his contact with Lucci, ending with circumstances of Henet's necklace and his brief tryst with Isabella. Cornelia's reaction was exactly what he expected.

"You slept with that man's wife? How could you?" She rose to her feet, her distressed expression giving way to outrage. She twisted the handkerchief in her hands as if she wanted to wring his neck with it. "No wonder he's after you. If Maggie gets hurt because of you—"

"I never claimed to lead a blameless life, madam," he snapped, angrier with himself than he was with her. He knew that at this moment Maggie could be suffering the worst possible consequences of his actions. "It happened before I ever met Maggie. And if it's any consolation to you," he added grimly, "you may flay me with a buggywhip when this is all over. It's nothing less than I'd do to myself, I assure you."

"Don't tempt me," she shot back.

"Stop this, both of you. Recrimination and guilt are hardly useful now. The question is, what do we do next?" Edward asked.

At that moment, Annie arrived. The red-haired maid bobbed a curtsy and gazed at Trevor with wide green eyes. "You sent for me, sir?"

"Yes, Annie. Sit down."

She plopped down in the nearest chair as if afraid to come any further into the room.

Trevor leaned against the fireplace and folded his arms. "I understand from Chivers that you've been walking out with an Italian sailor from Dover?"

"Yes, sir. Mr. Chivers told me I shouldn't, that it don't look respectable, him being a foreigner, sir, and a sailor." She swallowed hard. "Am I in trouble, sir?"

"No, Annie, but your mistress might be."

Astonished, she stared at him. "It's true, then? Alice came runnin' in ter the kitchen and told us her ladyship been kidnapped by bandits, but Alice is always makin' up stories, and Cook and me thought she was havin' us on, sir."

"Well, we don't know what's happened yet, Annie,

but we think the Italian fellow you've been walking out with might be involved in her disappearance."

Annie burst into a flood of tearful explanations. "Oh, sir, I wasn't meanin' anything by it. Indeed, I wasn't. But he was ever so handsome, and had the nicest manners. Mr. Chivers, he said I shouldn't be walkin' out with no foreigner, but I don't see why that's so. I usually walks out with Davy—he's the fishmonger's son, sir. But Davy was starting to take me for granted." She tossed her head. "Fit to be tied, I was, and—"

"Yes, I'm sure," Trevor cut in tersely, uninterested in his kitchenmaid's love life. "Annie, tell me about this Italian fellow."

She sniffed into her sleeve. "His name's Antonio, sir. Tony, we all call him."

The name confirmed Trevor's suspicions. Antonio was Lucci's brother.

"Well, sir," Annie went on, "I met him at the bakery about a month ago. Sunday, it was, just after service. He was goin' to pay three pence for a current bun and dish of tea, and I told him that was highway robbery—" She broke off, and flushed a deep red at her poor choice of words. "Anyway, sir, that's how we met."

"And so, you started walking out with him? Did he ask you questions about the house?"

"Yes, sir, ever so curious he was. He wanted to know the routine, sir, and when her ladyship went riding, and was she going to town for the Season. Things like that."

"Annie, if Tony were involved in the disappearance of my wife, do you know where he and his friends might have taken her?"

She blushed again, lowering her head. "Well, sir,

sometimes I'd meet him in the grove just past Purvis Lodge," she mumbled. "The house is locked up since old Purvis died last summer and they're still tryin' to find his son who's off in Australia or someplace like that, so it's deserted there. But I'm sure Tony wouldn't kidnap her ladyship. He has the nicest manners."

Trevor turned to Edward. "Purvis Lodge. That's it."

Annie stood up. "Will that be all, sir?"

He waved at her to go, and the maid scurried out like a frightened mouse. Cornelia shook her head, watching Annie depart. "Silly girl, walking out with a man she doesn't even know." She glanced at Trevor. "Do you really think they're at Purvis Lodge?"

"Why not?" he countered. "It's the perfect place. It's deserted, it's surrounded by woods, it's boarded up like a fortress, and it's only a mile from here. What better place to take her?"

Edward rose to his feet. "What are you going to do?"

"Lucci wants to see me. I'll just pay him a visit before he makes the invitation."

"You're not going alone," Edward said stoutly. "I'm coming with you."

"No." Trevor shook his head. "I'm sending you for the magistrate."

Margaret strained against the ropes that bound her wrists behind the back of her chair, but her struggles were futile. The ropes simply would not loosen, and she was rubbing her wrists raw by trying. The bonds around her ankles were no more cooperative. They hadn't gagged her, but Margaret didn't see how that was going to help her. They were deep in the woods—if she screamed, no one would hear her.

She glanced across the dusty drawing room at the two men playing cards. The windows were boarded up, and the room was lit only by a lamp on the table between the two men. She knew the other two were outside, but that was all she knew. Their conversation was always in Italian.

And they were villains. She thought of the other time she'd been kidnapped and how she had thought Emilio an evil, horrible man. But he had been kindness itself in comparison with these blackguards. She shivered, remembering the groping fingers of the animal who had tied her up, who now sat playing cards as if he hadn't a care in the world. Lucci, the others called him.

What were they going to do with her? A vendetta, Lucci had said. Vengeance. She shuddered, and fear began seeping into her soul. Her imagination, overactive at the best of times, was already picturing many possible fates, none of them pleasant. She closed her eyes and said a prayer that Trevor would rescue her.

Trevor knew every inch of the countryside around Ashton Park, including Purvis Lodge. It was surrounded by a dense stand of chestnut and maple trees and covered by tangled ivy vines and the canes of climbing roses gone wild. With its boarded windows and thorny roses, it seemed impenetrable.

Crouching low in the dense shrubbery, he moved silently around the perimeter of the house until he could see the front, where two men stood on the steps, pistols in hand, smoking cigars and speaking Italian in low voices. Lucci was not one of them.

As he hunkered down in the thick undergrowth and studied the two men standing guard, he began considering his options. He could wait for Edward to arrive with the magistrate and his men, but the idea of relying on a country magistrate to save Maggie worried him. In all likelihood, Mr. Shelton would just go barging in, and Maggie would get hurt. He wanted reinforcements who would haul Lucci off to jail, but he didn't want them to do anything stupid.

He fumbled on the ground and grabbed a pair of fist-sized stones. He tossed them into the forest at his right and watched the men lift their heads sharply at the sound. They looked at each other and nodded, then one of them put out his cigar and came around the side of the house with his pistol raised, passing about twenty feet in front of Trevor as he circled the house. Another well-thrown rock led the man into the forest at the back of the lodge, and Trevor followed silently behind him. The man paused amid the trees, looking around with some uncertainty, and Trevor jumped him, the gun falling from his hand and knocking him unconscious with a blow to the head.

One man out of the way, he thought with relief. Three more to go. He took the man's gun, dumped out the bullets, and tossed the weapon into the underbrush. Then he crept back around to the front to wait and watch. It didn't take long for the second guard to become impatient. He paced restlessly in front of the door for several moments, then looked down each side of the house.

A prudent man would have alerted Lucci at this point, but Trevor was counting on past experience in dealing with Lucci's men. Instead of facing his employer, who would be outraged, the guard would attempt to investigate the situation on his own. As expected, the man came around the side of the house exactly as the other had done. Trevor jumped him, and within seconds, another unconscious Italian lay on the ground. Trevor disarmed him, then circled back to the front of the house and slipped noiselessly inside. *That's two.*

He could hear Margaret's voice coming from the room on his right, which, if he remembered correctly, was the drawing room. Relief flooded through him at the sound of her voice. She seemed to be all right for the moment.

"What are you going to do with me?" she asked.

"Signora," Lucci answered her, "if you don't shut your mouth, I will gag you. Do you understand?"

"Yes," she murmured and fell silent.

Lucci spoke again, this time in Italian. "I find myself growing bored with this game, Antonio. Do you think St. James has sweated enough over his wife's abduction? Perhaps we should send for him and end his suspense."

"Whatever you think, Lucci," the other man replied. "Do you want me to go?"

"No. Send Stephano. I don't want Trevor using you as a hostage to trade for his wife."

Trevor was back outside before Lucci finished speaking, knowing he had the perfect opportunity to get rid of Lucci's third man. He waited beside the door, his back against the wall, listening as Antonio's footsteps approached. The moment he stepped outside, Trevor seized him, clamping one hand over his mouth and jamming the point of his pistol against the other man's temple. "Don't make a sound, Antonio," he murmured, "not one sound, or I'll blow your brains out. We're going to take a little walk."

He pushed Antonio down the front steps and guided him into the cover of the trees. In a lightning-quick move, Trevor slammed the butt of his gun against the other man's neck. Antonio's body slumped to the ground. *That's three.*

"All right, Lucci," he muttered as he started back toward the house, "now it's just us."

When he reentered the house, it was silent. He slipped over to the drawing room, but he didn't dare look inside and risk being seen. He waited.

If he were lucky, Margaret and Lucci would start talking again, enabling him to determine their positions inside the room. If he were very lucky, Lucci would start wondering why Antonio did not reappear and would come to investigate.

A long, tense silence passed, then Lucci spoke, and Trevor knew today was not his lucky day. "It seems my brother has met with some sort of mishap," he said loudly. "I think, St. James, it would be best if you joined us."

Damn. Trevor didn't move, hoping Lucci was only guessing, but the other man's next words dashed that hope.

"I can see you quite clearly in the glass doors, my friend."

Trevor looked to his left, saw his reflection in the closed French doors that led into a library, and cursed himself for not noticing them the moment he entered the house.

He let out his breath in a slow hiss between his teeth and stepped inside the drawing room, holding his hands up with his gun pointed toward the ceiling. He glanced past Margaret, who was bound hand and foot to the chair in which she sat, and saw Lucci standing behind her. He also saw the gun Lucci had pressed beneath her jaw.

Lucci smiled. "You should have noticed the doors, Trevor. Very sloppy."

"I'm getting too old for skulking about, it seems."

"Drop the gun on the floor and kick it away."

Trevor did so. Keeping his eyes on Lucci, he asked, "Are you all right, Maggie?"

"Yes."

Lucci stepped back, relaxing slightly now that Trevor's gun was safely across the room. "As you can see, she is well enough. For the moment." He studied Trevor for a few seconds, then he said, "You are here sooner than I had intended."

"You underestimated me," Trevor answered and smiled back at the other man. "But then, you always did."

Lucci's face hardened. "It doesn't matter. But I confess, I am curious. How did you know where to find me?"

"You must be accustomed to stoic Arabic servants. English kitchenmaids are a much more talkative lot. They can't help bragging to other servants about their handsome suitors."

"My brother is a handsome man, isn't he?"

"He's also lying in a heap in the woods, unconscious. He'll have a hell of a headache when he wakes up. The other two are back behind the house, and I doubt they'll be able to help you either. When are you going to learn to hire thugs with some intelligence?"

Lucci shook his head. "You shouldn't have done that. Ah, well, it doesn't matter now. You are here, which is exactly what I wanted."

"Now that I'm here, why don't you let her go? She's of no use to you now."

"Oh, but she is," Lucci replied, placing his free hand on Margaret's left shoulder. "She is going to prove very useful to me. In fact, when you are dead, I think I'll keep her. I've become quite fond of her." He slid his hand upward, his fingertips fanning across her cheek. Margaret made a sound of agitation, and Trevor took an involuntary step forward.

Lucci tightened his grip on the pistol. "Don't move."

Trevor froze, watching in silent agony as Lucci twined his fist in Margaret's hair and jerked her head back. With his pistol still poised beneath her jaw, he pressed a wet kiss to her cheek, his eyes gleaming with expectation as he studied Trevor's face.

He wanted a reaction. This was to be his vengeance—Margaret's degradation as he watched, helpless to stop it. He refused to play up. Folding his arms across his chest, he forced a look of bored amusement to his face. "All this for a woman? If you wanted her, you should have just said so."

Margaret, thankfully, did not react to his indifferent attitude. She sat motionless and silent, and Trevor hoped she understood what he was doing. Lucci's reaction was not so circumspect. He straightened and moved his hand to her breast, cupping it in his hand. "She is very lovely."

Margaret turned her face away, her expression one of repugnance and fear. Trevor's guts tightened at the sight, but he merely shrugged. "I suppose so."

"She is your wife. How can you be so callous?"

Trevor pretended to suddenly understand. "Ah, now I see what this is all about. You found out about my little tryst with your wife, and now you are thinking to gain some kind of revenge by having mine." He shook his head. "Lucci, really, after all this time, don't you know me better than that?"

Lucci straightened and let go of Margaret. "What do you mean?"

Trevor knew that if he and Maggie ever got out of this alive, he was going to have a lot of explaining to do. "Well, you know how I feel about women. They're pleasant enough, but hardly worth getting all desperate about."

"But she is your wife!" Lucci shouted, clearly becoming frustrated by Trevor's refusal to play the game.

"So? She's also a wealthy American, and now I have control of her money."

"You married her for money?"

"Of course I did! Why else would a man get married?"

Lucci took a step toward him, enraged. "I married for love!" he cried.

Trevor looked at him with pity. "You mean you went to all this trouble because I slept with Isabella and you were jealous?"

"You didn't just sleep with her!" Lucci stared at him, his face twisted with pain and loathing. "You defiled her, you raped her. You bastard! She tried to fight you off, but—"

"What?" Trevor stared at him for a moment, then he started to laugh. "You must be mad."

"I knew you would deny it."

"Of course I deny it." He made a sound of contempt. "No woman is worth that kind of trouble. What other lies did she tell you?"

"You are the one who lies, Trevor. Isabella would never lie to me!"

"Lucci, Isabella would lie to God if she thought she could get away with it. I know you don't want to hear this, but Isabella invited me into her bed. I didn't rape her." As he spoke, Trevor cast his mind back to that night in Cairo, desperately searching for anything that might help him now. "I can prove it. You were away in Alexandria on business when I was with her, and I know you returned three days after I left. How was she when you arrived home? Was she injured? If she tried to fight me off as she claims, were there bruises on her?"

"I will not hear this!" Lucci shouted, shaking his head in denial. "She was hysterical when she told me what you had done. She was crying. Her clothes were torn. She showed them to me."

Trevor took a small step forward. "It's easy enough to rip your own clothes, fake a few tears, act out a few hysterics. Did she have any bruises?"

"They were gone by the time I got home."

"In three days?" Trevor watched a glimmer of doubt cross the other man's face, and he pressed his advantage. "Bruises may fade, but they don't disappear in that short a period of time. She must not have fought me very hard."

"Of course not. She's a woman. How could she? She was afraid."

"For God's sake, Lucci! Open your eyes. Your wife has had dozens of lovers, and none of us have ever had to use force. What are you going to do—kill us all?"

"Silence!" The pistol trembled in Lucci's hand, and he lowered it slightly, pointing it directly at Trevor's groin. "My wife is a virtuous woman, and I'll not believe your lies. You've defiled her body, but you'll not slander her name."

He knew he was pushing Lucci over the edge and the other man might just shoot them all, but he had no other options. "Virtuous? How virtuous can a woman be when she's slept with half your business associates? Her exploits are legendary. Even you must have heard the rumors about her long before I ever met her."

"Lies!" he cried. "It's all lies."

"The only one who has lied is Isabella. She told me herself how you would believe anything she told you. She bragged about it." He took another step forward. "She probably discovered the necklace gone after I left. Yes, I stole it, I confess that—you knew I would try. Can you imagine what she must have felt? I left a paste copy, but it clearly didn't fool her, and she must have known it wouldn't fool you. How else could she explain the disappearance of the necklace? How else could she revenge herself on me for making such a fool of her? She probably sobbed out the story to you, and begged you to avenge the wrong I had done her."

All the color drained from Lucci's face, and Trevor knew he was on the right track. "Lucci, she's your wife. You love her, and you would do anything she asked you to do. But she's not worth it. She's spiteful, she's a liar, and she's slept with half the men we know."

The Italian shook his head. "No, no, I won't hear this."

"Everyone knows what she is, Lucci," he said quietly. "Everyone but you."

"I won't listen to your lies! I'll kill you!"

Lucci lifted the gun as if to carry out his threat. "No!" Margaret cried and jerked violently in the chair to which she was tied. The chair toppled over, careening into Lucci and knocking both of them to the floor.

Margaret landed heavily on top of Lucci, and Shelton's men burst into the room as a gun went off.

Trevor dove for his gun and came up, pistol in hand, as Shelton's men surrounded the two bodies on the floor. Lucci pushed at the woman on top of him, rolling her body away from his, but before he could get to his feet, the magistrate's men seized him.

Trevor shoved his way through the men crowding the room as Lucci was dragged away, his only thought to reach Maggie. Suddenly, he noticed the dark trickle that was seeping from beneath her body and staining the dusty wood floor.

"Christ, no!" he shouted and fell to his knees beside her. "Edward, help me!"

She was lying on her side, still tied to the chair, unmoving and silent. He pulled out the knife he'd concealed in his boot and cut the ropes at her wrists. Then he handed the knife to Edward. Trevor pressed his fingers to Margaret's neck, feeling for a pulse as Edward finished freeing her.

She was alive, but her pulse was weak. "Maggie!" he cried, rolling her onto her back, "Christ, Almighty! Maggie, say some—" He broke off at the red smear across her ribs, right breast, and shoulder. The blood had soaked completely through her wool traveling dress. Her eyes were closed and her face was ashen gray. No, he thought frantically. No, no, no.

"Oh, my God," Edward whispered. "She's been shot."

Trevor yanked at his shirt, tearing it off. "Take my horse and get Dr. Travers," he told Edward, pressing the shirt to the wound beneath her breast. "Ashton Park is halfway between here and his surgery. I'll take Maggie and meet you there."

"Right." Edward ran out of the room.

Trevor slid his arms beneath his wife and lifted her gently. The magistrate stepped forward. "We'll take her ladyship in my carriage," he said, and Trevor followed him. The men parted to let them pass, men who only six weeks before had hailed the arrival of their American countess with songs and cheers and smiles. Now their faces were grim, their voices silent.

Trevor carried her out of the house and into the woods, where the magistrate's carriage was tucked away in a clearing. He laid her gently across the seat, then climbed in to kneel beside her. As the carriage jerked forward and started for the road, Trevor held his shirt pressed against his wife's body, feeling the blood seep through his fingers. With his free hand, he touched her face, her round, cherub's face, and could only think of one thing. It pounded through his brain in time with his heart. *Don't die, my love. Don't die.*

Margaret felt as if she'd been trampled by a runaway horse. Her whole body hurt. She tried to open her eyes, but her lids felt so heavy. Her chest burned with a searing pain that made it hard to breathe. She could feel softness beneath her, and she knew that she wasn't lying on the floor of that deserted house any longer. She was in a bed.

All around her, she could hear sounds. Cornelia snapping out orders about boiling water and rags. Maids sniffling and sobbing and carrying on. Doors slamming and footsteps pounding. And sudden silence.

She wondered where Trevor was. The horrible thought that she'd been too late and the Italian had shot him flashed through her mind. But then he spoke, his voice low and soft and very close beside her. She focused on it, listening intently.

"Maggie, Maggie, you're going to be all right. Cornelia and I have stopped the bleeding, and the doctor will be here any minute. You'll be fine. You'll be fine."

His voice was so low. Margaret strained to listen, astonished to realize she had been wounded. She vaguely remembered a gun going off, but then she'd blacked out. She must have been shot.

"Oh, God," he groaned. "I wish you'd open your eyes, your bourbon whiskey eyes, and look at me. I didn't mean all those things I told Lucci. You know I didn't. I just said them as a way to stall for time."

His fingers touched her face. She could feel them gently touch her cheek, her chin, her lips. She wanted to tell him that she'd known what he was doing with Lucci, but she couldn't seem to find the strength to open her mouth. She felt so weak, she couldn't find the strength to move.

"I want to tell you so many things," he said hoarsely. "It was the money at first. I wanted you from the minute I met you, but it was the money that made me decide to marry you. I didn't think love mattered, you see. I'd never been in love, never in my life, and I didn't even think it existed. I told you that, remember?"

She remembered. It was the night they played chess.

"I've known lots of women. You know that. But none of them ever really meant anything to me. I enjoyed their company, but it was never anything but a fleeting desire, fine while it lasted, but soon over. With you, it was different. I know you won't believe me, I know I've shattered your trust. But I swear I'll make it up to you. I will."

Margaret knew he was holding her hand. She felt his fingers tighten suddenly in a hard grip around hers. And she waited for him to speak again, hoping this was not a dream.

"Maggie, you can't leave me. You're my wife, and I won't let you die." His voice rose to an angry shout. "Do you hear me?"

She wanted to tell him that yes, she could hear him, and so could the rest of the house.

"I know you can't hear me," he went on urgently, "but if you could, I'd tell you I love you. And I wouldn't say it just because it's what I think you want to hear. I'd say it because it's true. I love you."

Margaret could feel him brush the hair back from her forehead. He kissed her cheek.

"I never knew what love was until I met you," he whispered into her ear. "I never felt it for any woman, and I never thought it was real or that it could ever last. You kept talking about true love, and I didn't believe you. I thought you were just naive. But I was wrong. Now I know what true love is, and I'm afraid Maggie. For the first time in my life, I'm afraid. I'm thinking maybe it's too late. I'm thinking that you'll die and I'll have to go on without you. And if that happens, my life is going to be so dull and colorless. Empty. And I wouldn't even be able to kill myself to be with you in the classic romantic tradition, because you'll be in heaven, and, well, we both know that's not where I'll go when I die."

Hid voice rose again in desperation and he pulled back. "Dammit, Maggie! If you die, who's going to go on adventures with me?" he choked. "Who's going to fence with me and make me laugh and challenge me the way you do? Who's going to call me a hero?"

Margaret struggled to open her eyes. When she did, she saw him kneeling beside her bed, not looking at her, his head hung low.

"If you die," he said in an agonized voice that touched her heart, "I'll never be able to show you

Egypt. I'll never be able to take you up in a hot air balloon. I'll never be able to tell our daughters they don't have to learn to sew, and I'll never be able to tell our sons they can play in the dirt any time they want. I'll never be able to take you to that Greek island and paint you in the moonlight. I was going to take you to Capri in the autumn for a honeymoon. Maggie—" His voice broke, and he let go of her hand. His powerful shoulders slumped as if there was no strength left in them, and he laid his forehead against the bed beside her. "I love you, and if you die, I'll never have the chance to prove it to you."

Margaret felt a joy so powerful, so overwhelming, she wanted to shout it to the heavens. Straining for all her strength, she lifted her hand to touch his hair. "I'm not . . ."

He straightened, turning his head to look at her. Her hand fell away and he caught it in both of his. "Maggie?" He leaned closer to her, looking at her as if hardly able to believe she had spoken.

"I'm not . . . going to die," she whispered. "I hate it when the . . . heroine dies at . . . the end."

"So do I," he answered tenderly and moved closer to kiss her.

She swallowed and closed her eyes for a moment. "Do something for me," she said, opening them to look at him again.

"Anything."

"Tell me you love me again," she whispered. "I love a love scene."

Trevor threw back his head and laughed with joy and relief. Then he told her over and over and over again, until even Margaret's romantic heart was satisfied.

*   *   *

Dr. Travers arrived at Ashton Park for the second time that day and was immediately taken to Margaret's room. He cleaned and dressed the wound, then stepped out into the hall to talk with her waiting family. "She's lost some blood and she's weak, but it's only a flesh wound. It looks worse that it is. There's always a chance of infection, of course, but I think she's going to be fine. I'll leave instructions with you, Lady Kettering, on what to do next, but the most important thing is bed rest. I'll be back to check on her tomorrow."

Henry arrived a few hours later, looking at Trevor as if he wanted to strangle him with his bare hands. But when he came back downstairs after seeing his daughter, his expression was much more benign. Whatever Maggie had said to him during their brief visit must have reassured him. Trevor knew he deserved all the other man's wrath, but he was relieved just the same. Henry's wrath was never pleasant.

By the following evening, Margaret was strong enough to sit up in bed, and the whole family gathered in her room for after-dinner drinks and a visit. She sipped a cup of tea and held Trevor's hand as they told her the latest news.

"Lucci, his brother, and the other two men are safely behind bars," Edward was glad to report. "They've been charged with kidnapping and attempted murder. Shelton says the trial will be in about two weeks."

"I'll see that they all hang," Henry muttered. "That woman, Isabella would hang, too, if I had my way. Unfortunately, lying to your husband isn't against the law."

"She'll pay for what she's done," Edward assured

him. "In response to my inquiries this morning, the British Embassy wired back that the Egyptian authorities are doing a full investigation of Lucci's antiquities business. It appears that there are many illegal transactions, and my contact at the embassy says they are preparing to confiscate all his assets. Isabella will have nothing."

Trevor turned to his wife. Low enough that only she could hear, he murmured, "I'm sorry you had to find out about my tryst with Isabella. It was a brief and rather sordid experience. I never wanted you to know about it."

She whispered back, "It doesn't matter. That was before we met, and I would never hold anything in your past against you, Trevor."

"Thank God for that," he muttered.

Conversation went on all around them, but Margaret and Trevor said nothing, too wrapped up in each other to participate. Cornelia looked at them and rose to her feet. "Everyone, I would like to propose a toast," she said, as she lifted her glass of Madeira. "Here's to true love."

"Hear, hear," Edward and Henry said simultaneously and raised their glasses. Trevor raised his glass, as well. Touching it to his wife's cup of tea, he smiled at her. "I'll drink to that," he said softly. "Without true love, what else is there?"

Margaret smiled radiantly back at him, completely in agreement with that sentiment.

Epilogue

Capri was beautiful, especially at night, when the moon glistened on the ocean and illuminated the ancient Roman ruins. Margaret shifted restlessly against the hard marble column where she was posing and earned a rebuke from her husband.

"Don't move." Trevor looked at her over the top of his easel. "I'm almost finished."

"Good thing," she answered cheerfully. "I'm getting a crick in my neck."

"You wanted to be painted in the moonlight," he reminded her. "Don't complain because it takes such a long time. It's dark out here."

"I'm not complaining," she answered. "Actually, I think this honeymoon is one of the best adventures you've thought of yet."

He groaned. "I can tell I've set a dangerous precedent. Adventures, adventures, all the time." He took another dab at the canvas. "There," he said. "I'm done."

Margaret jumped down from her perch. She reached for the robe of gold silk that matched the wickedly skimpy nightgown she was wearing and shook the sand out of it. Pulling it around her, she walked to his side to have a look at the canvas.

She peered doubtfully at it and didn't know what to say.

"Well," he prompted when she made no comment, "what do you think?"

She took a deep breath. "It's awful."

He dabbed blue paint on her nose. "Impudent. Do you always have to be so honest? Don't you know you're supposed to say it's wonderful? I'm your husband, and you're supposed to flatter me."

"I am?" She frowned. "Let me see, flatter, hmm, I can't remember. Was that part of the vow, to love, honor, and flatter?"

"Yes, it was." Dropping palette and brush, he seized her, and both of them tumbled into the sand, laughing.

Trevor pulled the edges of her robe aside and rolled on top of her. She recognized the expression in his face and wrapped her arms around him. "I'm afraid we're very scandalous. The servants at this villa think we're a pair of decadent adventurers."

"So we are."

"I know." She smiled up at him, joyously happy. "Isn't it wonderful?"

"Yes," he answered gravely. "I love you."

She touched his cheek tenderly with her fingertips. "You only fell in love with me after you seduced me," she teased.

He shook his head. "It was the other way around. I think you seduced me."

"Does it matter?"

He laughed low in his throat, the wicked laugh she loved. "Hell, no. Madam, you can seduce me any time you like."

"I will, sir, I will," she assured him. "Every single day."

He bent his head. "God, I love being married," he muttered, then kissed her.

Let HarperMonogram
Sweep You Away

TALLCHIEF by Dinah McCall
Bestselling and Award-winning Author
Ever since the night Morgan Tallchief lost the only woman he would ever love, he has struggled to seal away the past. But now Kathleen Ryder is back in his life, and Morgan is helpless against his own rekindled desire.

THE SEDUCTION by Laura Lee Guhrke
Desperate to restore the family's fortune, Trevor St. James seduces heiress Margaret Van Alden. He realizes, too late, that the attractive American has awakened dreams of love he has long denied—until now.

ALWAYS IN MY HEART by Donna Valentino
Time Travel Romance
When a diary transports Matt Kincaid back to the Old West, he becomes the reluctant groom in a shotgun wedding. His bride can handle a gun, but is Katie Monroe prepared for Matt's soul-searing passion?

CHANCE McCALL by Sharon Sala
A HarperMonogram Classic
Jenny Tyler has been in love with Chance McCall for years, but the hired hand wants nothing to do with the boss's daughter. When Chance leaves the ranch to discover his forgotten past, Jenny is determined to find the man who has stolen her heart.

And in case you missed last month's selections...
A CHILD'S PROMISE by Deborah Bedford
A HarperMonogram Classic
Desperate for a better life, Lisa Jo Jensen agrees to marry ex-marine Johnny Owen. She never expects her modern-day marriage of convenience to lead to old-fashioned romance.

HOMECOMING by Janet Dailey, Fern Michaels, Dinah McCall, and Deborah Bedford

Four bestselling authors bring together a collection of romances that celebrate homecomings and the joy of love.

UNFORGOTTEN by Tamara Leigh
Bestselling Author

Twentieth-century businessman Collier Morrow is cast back to medieval England, where he meets Catherine Algernon — a dead ringer for his lost love. Is he somehow being offered an opportunity to regain his heart's desire?

DESERT STORM by Nan Ryan
National Bestselling Author

Angie Webster's arranged marriage to a man twice her age is unbearable, until she meets her spouse's grown son, Pecos McClain. Under the hot Texas sun, Pecos and Angie will find passion beyond their wildest dreams.